Dear Reader,

Welcome to another month of Harlequin Duets, the series designed to double your reading pleasure!

This new and exciting series is written by authors you love, and published in a great new format. Have you ever finished reading a romance and wished you had another one you could start right away? Well, we have the answer for you. Each and every month there will be two Harlequin Duets books on sale, and each book will contain two complete, brand-new novels. (You'll always have your backup read with you!)

Harlequin Duets features the best of romantic comedy. In *The Cowboy Next Door* by Laurie Paige, the heroine is determined to resist any and all sexy cowboys, until she meets her next-door neighbor. And if you think that's too close for comfort, try *Meant for You* by Patricia Knoll. Here, the hero and heroine, two complete opposites, end up sharing the same house!

Ruth Jean Dale spins a delightful tale of mayhem created by a little girl when she "appropriates" a very special penny in *One in a Million*. Then Kimberly Raye takes readers to the wild, wild West in *Love, Texas Style,* when a New York lawyer goes looking for her own real-life cowboy hero...but doesn't get *quite* what she was expecting.

Enjoy all our stories this month from Harlequin Duets!

Sincerely,

Malle Vallik

Malle Vallik
Senior Editor

P.S. We'd love to hear what you think about Harlequin Duets! Drop us a line at:

Harlequin Duets
Harlequin Books
225 Duncan Mill
Don Mills, Ontari
M3B 3K9 Canad

D0959289

# One in a Million

## *Amber knew there would be trouble.*

"Mama!"

"Sophie, please give Mr. Sterling the pennies. All of them," Amber said.

She leaned over, slipped her hands beneath Sophie's arms and lifted. Another seven or eight pennies fell from the folds of her clothing.

Quintin Sterling looked astonished. "Thanks. She's kinda tricky for such a little kid."

"I'm *ten*," Sophie yelled. "How old are you?"

"Thirty-three." Quintin blinked as if he couldn't believe he'd responded so readily to the command in the little girl's voice.

Sophie nodded approvingly. "That's almost grown-up."

Amber sighed. "You're not ten, Sophie, you're four."

Sophie gave a so-what shrug.

Amber smiled politely. "Goodbye, Mr. Sterling." She stepped on the escalator with Sophie.

"That's Quintin," he called after them, hoping his suspicions were correct and Sophie still had *the* penny. Because then he'd have an excuse to track down her gorgeous mother....

# *"You're attracted to me."*

"I was attracted to the man I thought you were," Suzanne said, inching backward.

"But you're not attracted to me now?" Brett took a step forward.

"Why would I be?" She took another step back. "I mean, you're good-looking and you've got a great smile and that little scar near your right eye is sort of sexy, but..." She seemed to shake away the admission. "But you're still not the kind of man I'm looking for." Her back came up flat against the wooden divider separating Daisy's stall from the next.

"Really?" He stopped inches shy of actually touching her.

She licked her lips and cleared her throat, her gaze hooked on his. "Really."

"I think you want me."

"In your dreams."

"There, too." That was part of the problem. She'd haunted him all night long. A particular vision of her stretched out on the riverbank wearing nothing but a smile and her red cowboy boots....

HARLEQUIN DUETS

ISBN 0-373-44070-7

ONE IN A MILLION
Copyright © 1999 by Betty Duran

LOVE, TEXAS STYLE
Copyright © 1999 by Kimberly Raye Rangel

This edition published by arrangement with Harlequin Books S.A.

® and TM are trademarks of the publisher. Trademarks indicated with ® are registered in the United States Patent and Trademark Office, the Canadian Trade Marks Office and in other countries.

Printed in U.S.A.

# RUTH JEAN
# DALE

# One in a
# Million

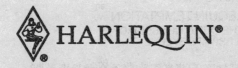

## HARLEQUIN®

TORONTO • NEW YORK • LONDON
AMSTERDAM • PARIS • SYDNEY • HAMBURG
STOCKHOLM • ATHENS • TOKYO • MILAN • MADRID
PRAGUE • WARSAW • BUDAPEST • AUCKLAND

Dear Reader,

I always wanted to write a book with foot chases through the San Diego Zoo and the Wild Animal Park. It seemed like such a natural—all those canyons and trees and structures, animals and people and sunshine. But the books I wrote never seemed to have a place for those scenes—until *One in a Million*.

This book was one of those "magical" experiences for a writer; everything just fell into place. This book needed those chase scenes; it needed the eccentric characters I'd been saving up for just such a special project; it needed fisticuffs and skullduggery; and it definitely needed a man, a woman and a child who would find everlasting—

Oops! Almost gave away the ending.

I do hope you enjoy *One in a Million*—and the next time you visit the San Diego Zoo, be sure and drop by the gorill-yas.

## Books by Ruth Jean Dale

**HARLEQUIN LOVE & LAUGHTER**
6—THE SEVEN-YEAR ITCH
15—A ROYAL PAIN

**HARLEQUIN TEMPTATION**
679—THE CUPID CONSPIRACY
809—A PRIVATE EYEFUL

For Susan Sheppard, who "discovered" me—not at a soda fountain in Hollywood but at a pizza parlor in San Diego. Her perspicacity alone would make her One in a Million!

# 1

ONE MINUTE Amber Brannigan and her four-year-old daughter, Sophie, were rushing through Silver and Fine China at Sterling's Department Store and the next minute they were being showered with coins.

Which was not what you'd expect on the third floor of an upscale department store in San Diego—or maybe in any department store, anywhere. This, however, did not deter Sophie, who immediately fell to her hands and knees to scoop together the metal disks littering the marble floor.

The little girl, all bright-eyed and happy, looked up at her mother with a big grin. "Pennies from heaven!" she declared, claiming the copper-colored coins while shoving larger silver ones aside.

Amber felt a pang of regret. Sophie had just quoted what Johnny used to say whenever the little girl had rifled through his pockets for loose change. He'd always let her keep the pennies and she'd become quite the little collector. Now that he was gone, Sophie's stash wasn't growing quite so fast, but she still managed to grab every penny she could lay her hands on.

It was going to be fun trying to pry *this* stack away from her.

Amber didn't join the general scramble of shoppers as they bent to retrieve the coins; she had more important things on her mind. She'd dreaded coming into the store in the first place, but she'd been summoned—again—and all she wanted now was to get out of here.

Glancing around, she located the source of the barrage of money. A tall, attractive man was holding on to the side of a glass display case with one hand, a shallow velvet-lined tray dangling empty from his other as he tried to shake loose a tenacious Pekinese attached to his ankle.

Amber stifled a surprised giggle. She didn't know the man, although there was something familiar about him. The dog, however, she *did* know. He was Octavia Sterling's bad-tempered little Pekinese, Jiggs.

A pleasant-looking middle-aged woman dropped several coins onto the surface of the glass case. The man turned to thank her, making a valiant attempt to plant both feet firmly on the floor and ignore the dog trying to rip off his sock. He smiled, and Amber knew instantly why he looked familiar.

She'd recently seen his photo in a magazine, where he'd been named one of San Diego's "Most Eligible Bachelors." He was Quintin Sterling. She pursed her lips in an effort to recall what had been written beside the photo of this man who, she vividly remembered, had been dressed in tennis whites that showed off a great physique and long, muscular legs. Thirty-three, ascended to the presidency of Sterling's two years ago when his father died, partial to tall blondes and the confirmed bachelor life-style. As she recalled, the magazine had breathlessly concluded that he was, indeed, a "hunk-and-a-half."

Amber had had to agree, but her mild spark of interest had quickly died. Though the magazine had gushed on, she'd tossed it aside. She'd never been interested in high-society business types.

Good thing, too, seeing as how none of them had ever been interested in her.

And though Amber might not know Quintin Sterling, she knew his stubborn and elderly aunt Octavia *too* well. She had just come from her umpteenth meeting with Miss Sterling, a society dowager who was utterly bound and determined to make Sterling's the sole distributor of One in a Million, Amber's craftily eccentric line of handmade clothing.

Amber was equally determined that such a merger would never occur, in spite of the outrageously high numbers Octavia Sterling kept tossing around.

Amber firmly believed that there was more to life than money, and that's how she tried to live. Unfortunately she was beginning to feel like a victim of her own success. She'd been perfectly happy with her little business, but now that it was attracting attention, things had reached the point where some serious decisions would have to be made.

Amber *hated* making decisions. She liked to let things—things like *life*—just happen. She didn't much like temptation, either, mainly because she wasn't very good at resisting it. Just as that thought crossed her mind, her gaze locked with that of the handsome Quintin Sterling. His eyes—she couldn't tell what color they were at this distance—widened with a sudden interest she recognized.

Fortunately, Sophie chose that moment to trill with pleasure and scramble across her mother's sandaled feet in pursuit of more loot. Looking down at her daughter, Amber felt herself melt into a warm puddle of motherly pride and adoration.

If she hadn't given in to temptation, there would be no Sophie Kate Brannigan.

Before turning her full attention to Sophie, she spared a passing thought as to why on earth the rich and attractive head of a major department store was standing in the middle of a mass of spilled coins with an angry little dog gnawing on his ankle.

EVERY YEAR Quint Sterling let his aunt Octavia badger him into personally putting her valuable coin collection on display at the store for a week. Every year he regretted it, but never so much as now.

Trying to shake Jiggs loose while keeping an eye on the people swarming after coins, Quint could only be grateful that there had been no more than a handful of customers in the vicinity when the accident occurred. Or *was* it an accident? Maybe the damn dog had some nefarious motive.

Quint had been minding his own business, carefully and calmly stacking trays of coins to be inserted into the display case, when Jiggs had crept up and flung his hairy little body at Quint's right ankle— Jiggs' favorite target. Completely unprepared or forewarned, Quint had flung up his arms and the coins had flown out of their tray. For a minute there, it had looked as if a swarm of locusts had descended upon innocent shoppers.

This situation had all the makings of a disaster. The fact was, Quintin *had* to get all the coins back. The collection, while worth a lot of money, had an even higher sentimental value to Aunt Octavia. Fortunately everybody *looked* honest—well, everybody with the possible exception of the flashy middle-aged couple with all the shopping bags, huddled behind the silver display.

As he anxiously glanced around, his gaze crossed that of a great-looking redhead and he found himself staring. She wore a simple violet-colored dress made of a soft knit fabric that fell artlessly off one creamy shoulder before flowing all the way down to her ankle—which sported a tattooed bracelet of daisies. Some long-stemmed purple flower—he wasn't big on horticulture—was painted or drawn or sewn or *some* damn thing, up the other side of the dress, across the shoulder and out of sight. The creation clung to her luscious figure without being either tight or suggestive.

Looking away as if dismissing him, the woman turned to kneel beside a little girl. The child's pale blue dress bore a random pattern of little yellow ducks, and Quint noticed that, incongruously, one of her shoes was black, the other red.

They were mother and daughter, he was sure, although the little girl had brown hair rather than red. The woman spoke to the child, her voice too low to carry. He was intrigued. The mother's unusual self-possession seemed to insulate her from the chaos around her.

Jiggs gave a particularly ferocious growl and relaxed his hold on Quint's black silk sock, but only so he could lunge for a better grip. Sharp teeth grazed Quint's ankle and he yelped in surprise.

The little girl looked up abruptly. Seeing Jiggs, she jumped to her feet. "Look, Mama, it's Jiggsy," she cried, heading for the offensive mutt with her arms outstretched.

All Sterling's needed was a lawsuit over a dog bite. "No, wait, don't—" Quint tried to back away, dragging the dog with him, but the little girl would not be denied. Rushing over, she bent and grabbed the dog around the middle.

"Bad Jiggs," she scolded, hauling him into her arms. "No, no, don't bite!"

Jiggs, who had the temperament of a feral cat, didn't lunge for the kid's throat as Quint had fully expected him to do. Instead, he whined and stretched to lick her face.

The furry little hypocrite was pretending to be the wronged party. Quint owed him for that. Damn dog never had liked him and the feeling was mutual.

"Here you are, young man."

Quint turned to find an elderly woman proffering several coins. Others fell into line behind her, including Harvey Wittman. Tall and erect with the bearing of a soldier, the white-maned Harvey had been a persistent suitor of Octavia's for decades, it seemed. Since Aunt Octavia had first insisted that the collection be put on display five years ago, Harvey had attended faithfully out of loyalty to his beloved, who to date had failed to return so much as a shred of his devotion.

Harvey offered the coins with a *tsk-tsk*, then stepped aside as if he'd communicated his feelings perfectly.

"Here y'go." The flashy couple Quint had noticed earlier dropped a thin stream of coins—mostly pennies—into his hand. The man was skinny and leathery, too sharply dressed in easily recognizable labels. His scanty hair was that indefinable shade of brown that comes out of a bottle and fools no one.

The woman, at least three inches taller and forty pounds heavier, glittered with chunky costume jewelry, tight silver lamé pants and a leopard-print blouse. Theatrical makeup and big, blond hair topped it all off like whipped cream on a sundae.

"Thanks." Quint took the coins.

"Y'gotta be more careful," the man advised in a confidential tone. "Not everybody out there's as honest as—"

The woman elbowed him silent. "He knows that, Phil. C'mon, our banker's waiting." She batted mascara-caked eyelashes at Quint. "No matter how busy I am, I can't resist a chance to shop at Sterling's when I'm in town."

Quint smiled obligingly, but from the corner of his eye he was watching the sexy redhead and the little girl sitting on the floor with the dog in her lap.

AMBER KNEW there would be trouble. Sophie wasn't going to give back either dog or pennies without a struggle. The showdown couldn't be put off, unfortunately, for here came the man in charge.

"Hi." He halted beside them and gave Amber a charming smile that crinkled his blue eyes and created attractive creases at the corners of his mouth. "I'm Quintin Sterling."

"How do you do, Mr. Sterling." She saw no reason to introduce herself. "I guess you want your dog and your coins."

He rolled his eyes. "The coins, anyway. As far as I'm concerned, you can keep the dog."

Sophie's head jerked back as if on a string. "Can I, Mama? Please, can I keep this dog?"

"Now, honey, you know—"

Quintin looked horrified. "Oh, damn—I mean darn. I was just joking. I didn't really mean—"

"But you said!" Tears sprang into Sophie's hazel eyes and she appealed to her mother. "He said I can have this dog! He said—"

"He was only teasing, honey." Amber knelt beside the girl, who clutched Jiggs so hard his tongue hung out. She began scooping up the pennies scattered around dog and child.

"No!" Sophie grabbed for the coins with one hand. "Don't take my pennies!"

"They're not your pennies, sweetheart. They belong to this man."

"My daddy gave them to me! He threw them out from heaven."

Amber's stomach knotted and she struggled to keep her voice calm. "No, darling. I explained to you that Daddy—"

Sophie began to scream at the top of her lungs. Quintin Sterling fell back a step, his face blanching. Amber felt sorry for him; the man looked as if he'd never seen a kid up close before. Cocking her head, she looked at her beloved Sophie with disapproval.

The child stopped howling as quickly as she'd begun. "Do I gotta?" she sniffled, wiping at her nose with her forearm.

"I'm afraid so."

Thrusting out a trembling lower lip, Sophie glared at the man towering above her. "This is *my* dog," she whined. "Jiggs likes me."

Quintin, looking relieved, squatted beside the two. "I wish he *was* your dog," he said with what sounded like grim sincerity, "but the lady he belongs to would be very sad if I gave her pet away."

"Mama!" Sophie clouded up again.

Amber held firm. "I'm sorry, but you know the rules. We can't take things that don't belong to us."

Sophie gave a final sniffle and pushed the dog off her lap. When Quintin reached for the animal's collar, Jiggs growled and showed his teeth.

Quintin Sterling swallowed hard, still looking uncomfortable. "I...have to have the pennies, too."

"Mama!"

"Honey, they don't belong to you."

"But—"

"Sophie, please give back the pennies. All of them."

Face sullen, Sophie felt around beneath the flaring edge of her skirt and produced five pennies. Holding Jiggs at arm's length, Quintin accepted the coins.

"Is that all?" He looked entirely prepared to accept her word on the matter. In fact, he looked as if he'd just been mugged.

Sophie nodded emphatically, all the while spreading her skirts even wider on the marble floor.

Amber leaned over, slipped her hands beneath Sophie's arms and lifted. The little girl uttered a cry of protest, but it was too late; another seven or eight pennies fell from the folds of her clothing.

Quintin looked astonished. "Thanks," he said to Amber, his tone admiring. "She's kinda tricky for such a little kid."

"I'm *ten*," Sophie yelled. "How old are you?"

"Thirty-three." Quintin blinked as if he couldn't believe he'd responded so readily to the command in the little girl's voice.

She nodded approvingly. "That's almost grown up," she said.

Amber sighed. "You're not ten, Sophie, you're four."

Sophie gave a so-what shrug.

"And I don't think you've given the man all his pennies."

"I have so, too." She stomped the foot shod in red and another penny fell from the ruffled top of her sock. She didn't look the slightest bit ashamed of herself, just disgusted at being found out.

Amber stared deliberately into the little girl's petulant face. "One last time. Do you have any more pennies?"

Sophie shook her head violently.

"You're sure?"

Sophie nodded, just as violently.

"Cross your heart?"

Sophie did.

Amber straightened. "I guess that's all of them, then," she said apologetically to Quintin Sterling. "What can I say? She just really likes pennies."

"Hey, no problem. Uh…" He stood there, slavering dog in one hand and coins in the other. "I might have some pennies in my pocket. I'd really like to give her a reward for—"

"No, no, please don't." Amber took Sophie's hand in a firm grip. "I don't believe people should be rewarded for doing the right thing."

"That's fine for adults, but she's just a kid."

Sophie nodded, letting out a big, self-pitying snuffle. She pulled on her mother's hand insistently. "I'm just a little kid!"

"No," Amber said, regretting that she had to. "That's not how we do things. Thank you for offering, but Sophie has plenty of pennies at home."

"Mama?"

"We have to go, Sophie."

*"Mama!"* Amber started for the escalator, the little girl holding back while casting many an anguished glance at Quintin, who trailed along after them.

He tried again. "Isn't there *something* I can do to—"

"Not a thing." Amber smiled politely. "Goodbye, Mr. Sterling." She stepped on the escalator and Sophie, who loved escalators, suddenly forgot all about her revolt and hopped on, too.

"That's Quintin," he called after them as the stairs moved lower. "And you are?"

Three chattering teenage girls stepped onto the escalator, breaking contact with the attractive Mr. Sterling and sparing Amber the necessity of an answer.

QUINTIN DUMPED Sophie's coins onto the top of the case with the others. Everyone had wandered away except for Harvey, who looked as if he'd just sucked a lemon. Even his trim white mustache with the sweeping ends quivered with indignation. When Quint thrust Jiggs at the man, Harvey grimaced but accepted the furry bundle.

"That's not all of them," he said with utter conviction.

"Now, Harvey, you don't know that." Quint tried to sound confident, but he had a sneaking suspicion the man was right. There just didn't seem to be enough in the stack. "I thought everyone looked honest enough. I'm sure everything was turned in."

Harvey's bushy white eyebrows soared. "You jest, my boy. What about that couple who looked as though they'd just escaped from a road show production of *Guys 'n' Dolls?*"

"Hey, they turned in a whole handful." Busy sorting pennies into one tray and silver into another, Quint acknowledged to himself that Harvey could be right. You couldn't trust anyone nowadays, not even little old white-haired ladies who looked like someone's grandma.

"Then there's that *child.*"

Quint perked up. "What about her?"

"I'm confident she didn't leave empty-handed."

"You mean literally? Her mother shook her down pretty good."

"Did you notice that her hands were clenched into fists?"

"She was mad," Quint argued. Actually, he could hardly blame her. Losers weepers, finders keepers and all that sort of thing. "I thought she was getting ready to pop me one."

"Perhaps, but it has occurred to me that there may have been other reasons."

"Jeez!" Harvey could be right. Quint took an eager step toward the escalator. "Will you watch this stuff while I try to catch them?"

"Certainly, my boy. Anything for Octavia." His voice drifted after Quintin. "Good luck!"

Quint's luck was all bad; mother and daughter were not to be found. Hauling the trays of jumbled coins to Aunt Octavia's office a few minutes later, Jiggs snarling and snapping on the end of a makeshift leash of twisted plastic shopping bags, he tried to put the duo out of his mind. He needed to concentrate on the looming crisis, not some strange woman, no matter how extraordinary she was.

Opening the door which bore a plaque proclaiming Octavia to be Vice President In Charge Of Ideas, he walked inside.

Octavia sat on a comfortable red leather chair placed in front of a floor-to-ceiling window, knitting needles flying. "Knitting helps me think," she always said as she turned out afghans and socks and hats by the dozens, most destined for donation to homeless shelters.

She looked up with a smile that quickly faded from her carefully made-up face. When she rose, Quint was struck by the sudden realization that her dress was remarkably similar to the beautiful redhead's, although on Octavia the effect was almost Victorian. He stifled a grin, at the thought of the sexy redhead having something in common with his aunt.

One hand, still holding the needle trailing coral yarn, flew to her throat. "What's happened?"

"Just a slight mishap." He placed the heavy trays on the table in front of Octavia's matching red leather sofa. She hardly ever used the big walnut desk at the other end of the room.

"My collection!" She looked on the verge of collapse. "What's happened to my coins? And why are you dragging Jiggs around like that? I thought he was sleeping under my desk."

"Obviously, he snuck out. It's his fault your coins got spread all over Silver and Fine Crystal, by the way. Little bas—little beast attacked me when I wasn't looking."

"Oh, dear." She hurried forward. "Is anything missing?"

"I don't know," Quint said. "I'm afraid there might be."

"Not my special penny!"

"I don't know, Aunt Octavia. I honestly don't." He put his arm around her; she barely came to his shoulder and he suddenly felt warmly protective. Sure, she was a tad eccentric, but at heart—

"Heads will roll!" She straightened her shoulders, her blue eyes flashing. "If my 1943-S cent is missing—"

Quint didn't even want to *think* about that possibility. As did everyone else in the Sterling orbit, he knew the story of how Octavia's Only Love, Loren Bascomb, gave her his collection just before he went into the army in 1944. The last coin he added before sailing away to war was a 1943-S Lincoln copper penny.

Octavia had explained—over and over again—that what made this penny so special was that in 1943, more than a billion cents were made of zinc-plated steel because of wartime conservation of strategic metals. Only four were known to have been struck on 1942 bronze alloy blanks, making them rare and valuable—worth up to fifty thousand dollars. Add to that its *sentimental* value and that penny was worth the moon.

Quint lacked even a passing interest in coin collecting. While trying to assist his aunt, who knew every single piece in the collection by sight and by heart, he listened to her grumblings of despair and swore to himself that if they ever managed to restore the collection it would never, ever, go on display again.

"It's gone!" Octavia's pale blue eyes widened and she caught her breath. "Three pennies are missing and a handful of silver. I can live without everything but my special penny. It truly is one in a million."

Quint groaned. "Are you sure? Maybe we just overlooked it."

"I'm sure." She turned to him on the couch, grabbing the lapels of his jacket with trembling hands. "Quintin, you must find it!"

"I'll try, but—"

"You must succeed! I refuse to contemplate any other outcome." Releasing him, she stared at the coins in the tray as if she couldn't really see them. "Obviously someone has stolen it."

"I doubt anyone would know its value," he argued. "Maybe it was an honest mistake."

"Never! It can't be a coincidence that that particular coin is missing. It was deliberate theft. When we find that penny—and we will because we must—we will prosecute to the fullest extent of the law."

"Not necessarily." Quint remembered the little girl, Sophie, trying desperately to hang on to her stash of hot pennies. "Anyone could have taken it, even a kid. You know kids and pennies."

Octavia sat bolt upright. "Kids? There were children present?"

Quint shrugged. "Well, yes, one at least. A little girl."

"Find her! Grill her! If she has stolen my penny—"

"Octavia, calm down. She isn't even old enough to know what stealing is. Besides, I couldn't find her. I don't know who she is or where she lives. All I know is that her mother called her Sophie." He cocked his head thoughtfully. "Funny name for a kid nowadays."

"Sophie," Octavia repeated softly. "Sophie Brannigan! Quint, I know that child."

"Are you sure? How?"

"Her mother is Amber Brannigan. She owns the One in a Million clothing line I've been trying to get for Sterling's for the past year. Unruly red hair, tattoos—" Octavia shivered delicately.

"That's right." Astounded, Quint stared at his aunt. "This is incredible—that you'd know who she is, I mean."

"Mrs. Brannigan was just in my office with that child, refusing yet again to listen to reason. It's humiliating, Quintin—I have to go to a shop in La Jolla to buy the things she makes."

"We live in La Jolla, Aunt Octavia. It's not that big an imposition."

"Not to *you*, perhaps. For me—for *Sterlings*—it's a bitter humiliation." Octavia began to pace, her small frame quivering with indignation. "All right, now that we know who took the penny, go get it. Then we can discuss charges."

"We don't know for sure Sophie took it," Quint noted, not liking the sound of discussing charges.

"Oh, we do, we do know." Octavia stopped pacing. "I never cared for those two, if you must know the truth. I think the mother is—" She sniffed in disdain. "Some kind of *hippie* or something."

Quint smothered laughter. "Sorry, but hippies have long gone the way of dodo birds and dinosaurs."

"That is your opinion." She lifted her chin to a regal angle and fixed him with a frosty stare. "A few months ago, that delinquent child pilfered a handful of pennies from the silver bowl of change I keep on my desk. Her mother made her give them back, of course, but I've never trusted either of them since that day. As it turns out, the child has some sort of penny *fetish*.''

"She does seem overly fond of them," Quint admitted. "Still, her mother—Amber, did you say?" Amber. The name suited her. "Her mother shook her down pretty good." He grimaced. "On the other hand, Harvey suggested that Sophie might have been clutching something in her fist."

"Quintin, you must go at once to that woman's house and force that child to confess."

It was becoming clear to Quint that Octavia had lived her entire long life with no exposure to children whatsoever. This was not a good thing. Even though his acquaintance with Sophie was short, he didn't take her for a kid who could be "forced" to do much of anything.

On the other hand, he wouldn't mind seeing Amber Brannigan again. In fact, he'd like that just fine.

"I suppose I could try," he conceded, trying to make it sound as if it would be a big sacrifice on his part. "But on the outside chance that we're wrong and in case we have to file an insurance claim—"

Octavia gasped and once again clutched her throat.

"Sorry, Aunt Octavia, but there's always that possibility. As I was saying, I'd better call the police before I do anything else."

"Absolutely not! I forbid it."

"You're kidding." He couldn't imagine why she'd take such a tack when something so valuable was missing. "The police *have* to be notified."

She was looking more stressed by the second. Shaking her silver head emphatically, she repeated, "Absolutely not. The police would only get in the way. No, Quintin, dear, *you* will find my penny."

And then she slipped in the coup de grâce. "After all, you're the one who lost it."

ALONE AT LAST, Quint called the cops. As expected, he received little encouragement about the eventual return of the missing coins, but at least he'd done his duty and cleared the way for an insurance claim.

Sitting there in the middle of ringing telephones, purposeful executives and efficient secretaries, he found it virtually impossible to keep his attention on business. Octavia was right; he was responsible for the lost penny. It was up to him to get it back.

It occurred to him that there was more than one way to skin a cat—or collect a coin. Clearing his office of staff, he reached for the telephone and dialed the number of the local daily newspaper.

# 2

AMBER AND SOPHIE had run several errands after leaving Sterling's, so it was a couple of hours later before Amber inserted her key into the lock of their small bungalow. Normal Heights was one of the older and less affluent suburbs in San Diego—blue-collar solid with small fenced yards and cracked sidewalks. When they'd gone house-shopping three years ago, the neighborhood had appealed to Johnny because it seemed quiet and safe.

Amber had thought it dull and boring. Time had proven them both correct.

Sophie entered the house whining. Once inside, she put her hands on her hips and launched her attack. "I *wish* I had a dog," she said in a tone that was half demand, half plea. "I *wish* that *Jiggs* was mine, Mama."

"If wishes were horses..." Amber said absently, stacking her packages on the kitchen table.

"I don't *want* a *horse*," Sophie insisted, "I want a *dog*."

Amber pulled a loaf of brown bread from a grocery sack. "There's no room in our life for a dog," she reasoned, a futile gesture in dealing with an unreasonable four-year-old. "The fence has holes in it. He'd get out."

"I'd catch him," Sophie replied promptly.

"He might get hurt or lost." Amber crossed the cracked linoleum floor to put the milk away in their small, old-fashioned refrigerator. After a moment's hesitation, she floated her trial balloon. "Besides, we may be moving soon."

"Moving?" The little girl looked startled. But then, she'd been too young to remember living anywhere else. "To where?"

Amber shrugged, deliberately casual. "I don't know. *Somewhere.* Somewhere new, where we can make new friends and do new things."

"I like old stuff," Sophie said. "I don't wanna go." She pursed her lips. "Mama, why did you make me give back them pennies?"

"Those pennies, dear." Amber paused with her hand on a five pound bag of oranges. "And you know why. They belonged to the nice man."

"But—" Again the out thrust lip.

Amber left the oranges on the table and knelt in front of her daughter. "Tell Mama the truth, Sophie. Do you have any more of the man's pennies? This is important, sweetheart."

Sophie drew her pale brows down low over her eyes. "I got pennies of my own."

Amber nodded. "But you keep wanting more."

"I don't want *that* man's pennies!" Sophie stomped the foot with the red shoe.

Amber sighed. "All right, darling. Here, I'll peel

an orange and you can take it out in the backyard to eat.''

''Okay.'' Sophie's instant smile was like sunshine shooting through clouds. Amber could only hope her child didn't grow up to be an actress—or a politician.

Amber's living room was a mess—always. Bolts and folds and scraps of fabric tumbled over sofa and chairs and hung off folding tables shoved against the wall. Her sewing machine was permanently set up, ready for her to make use of any stray moment that came her way.

Fabric was relatively neat compared to what she used for dyeing and stamping and painting. Those supplies she tried to keep in her bedroom, away from curious little hands, but things spilled over into other rooms sometimes.

Like now. She'd spent the past couple of weeks experimenting with new ways to stamp and bleach velvet. Added to the regular living-room mess were several spray bottles, paints and dyes, and numerous boxes corralling hand-carved stamps and brushes.... Long lengths of plastic, mostly former dry-cleaning bags, protected the floors.

Living in chaos was worth it, she thought as she gazed with pleasure and pride at a long velvet gown hanging from a curtain rod. It had started as un-adorned teal blue. Amber had lain a winding trail of Sophie's pennies up one side, then misted bleach over the entire piece of fabric. The bleaching had produced a vibrant lime green color, but where the pennies had lain there was now a cascade of small teal blue circles that resembled bubbles rising from the ocean depths. She'd designed the dress and cut the fabric to showcase the effect.

*Nicole will like this,* Amber thought with satisfaction. Nicole Daniels, owner of Nicole's of La Jolla, was more than a business partner, she was Amber's best friend and biggest booster. If Octavia Sterling thought for one moment that Amber would ever pull Nicole's hottest-selling line of clothing…or that she would succumb to the prestige and money Sterling's offered—

The doorbell rang, its sound rusty from disuse. Thinking it must be Deenie, her sewing assistant, Amber moved to answer. Deenie was overdue to pick up supplies for the linen line that had been such a hot seller all summer.

She threw open the door and the smile on her lips quickly turned to an *O* of surprise. Quintin Sterling stood there, but it was not the same man she'd encountered earlier at the department store. That Quintin Sterling had worn a coat and tie and shiny shoes. This one wore khaki trousers and a yellow polo shirt that set off his lightly tanned skin to perfection. She felt an unexpected shaft of pleasure.

"Sorry to bother you," he said with a charming smile, "but I'm afraid we still haven't located all of the coins from this afternoon."

"I'm sorry to hear that, Mr. Sterling." Amber waited, giving him a questioning look.

"I'd like to try once more with your daughter, Mrs. Brannigan."

Amber's brows soared. "I didn't tell you my name."

"My aunt Octavia told me who you were." He cocked his head. "Mind if I come in?"

"I suppose not." She didn't know why she was so reluctant to have him in her little home, but she was. Nevertheless, she stepped aside and gestured him to enter.

"Is Sophie here?"

"Out back."

"May I talk to her?"

Amber chewed on her lower lip for a moment. "Mr. Sterling—"

"Quint."

"Quint. I know that when it comes to pennies, Sophie is the logical suspect, but I've grilled her ever since we left your store. She's adamant in her denials, and I don't know what else I can do. Besides, there were other people there, too."

He looked definitely uncomfortable. "I don't mean to harass a little girl," he said carefully, "but this isn't a simple, everyday penny I'm after."

*Oh, boy.* A valuable coin missing and Sophie the chief suspect. "Give me the bad news," she said bravely.

"This particular penny was coined during the Second World War. It's worth a great deal of money, but beyond that, it has great sentimental value to my aunt."

Amber sighed. "All right, we'll ask her again. But I don't think we'll get anywhere."

It certainly appeared as if her prediction was correct when Sophie took one look at Quint and started howling at the top of her lungs. Only after he'd emptied his pockets of change and offered her all the pennies—seven of them, over Amber's objections—did she come to a hiccuping conclusion.

Amber realized that Sophie's tears had frazzled him. She didn't like to hear any child cry, but there was a big difference between honest tears and the crocodile type her daughter was so adept at turning on and off.

Sophie gave a final sniff. "You can't have my pennies."

"I'm not after *your* pennies," Quint assured her. "I'm trying to find mine, Sophie. Three are missing. Are you sure you didn't keep any of the ones you picked up today at the store? Accidentally, of course." he added quickly.

Sophie's shoulders slumped dramatically and her lower lip quivered. After a long hesitation she thrust out her clenched hand where she held the pennies he'd just given her. "Here," she said. "You can have these ones back."

Quint shook his head. "No, I gave those to you and you can keep them. But the pennies you picked up at the store—you did bring some home, didn't you?"

Sophie looked torn.

Amber put a hand on her daughter's shoulder. "Why don't you and I go get the nice man his pennies?" she suggested gently.

"I can do it my own self." Sophie declared, and scampered toward the house.

Amber and Quint exchanged amazed glances and

followed. Was it going to be this easy, all of a sudden?

Sophie came running from her bedroom in an instant, offering up a grubby little fist. She opened her hand above Quint's, but nothing fell out. Startled, she turned her hand over to find a penny stuck to her gluey palm. Juice from her orange.

Quint reached for the coin, his expression suddenly tense and hopeful. "Is this the only one you took?"

"Uh-huh. Can I go now, Mama?"

"If you'll just tell us *for sure* that you didn't take two more pennies from the department store today."

Sophie puckered up. "My daddy gives me pennies to keep."

"*Gave* you pennies to keep, honey bunch. Daddy's gone now. I explained that to you."

"I want my daddy! I want my pennies!"

Amber leaned down to give her daughter a hug and a kiss on the top of her head. "I know, sweetie. Look, go wash those hands and then you can play in the backyard. When I get finished in here, we'll go eat Chinese, okay?"

"*Kung hay fat choy!*" Sophie said delightedly, taking off for the back door with grubby hands intact.

"Huh?" Quint did a double take.

"The lady who runs our favorite Chinese restaurant taught her that. I think it means Happy New Year."

"Jeez." Quint sounded awed. "At four, she's speaking Chinese?"

He held the liberated penny up so he could peer

at the date, then groaned. "Nineteen twelve. It's not the Lincoln copper but it might be one of the other two that're missing." He hauled a folded piece of paper from his pocket, checked it and nodded. "Yeah, it's Octavia's, but it's not *the* penny."

"I'm sorry."

"Hey, it's not your fault. She's just a little girl. She sure does have a thing for pennies, though."

"There's a reason, of course."

"There always is. Care to share that with me?"

"Sure, although I don't know why you'd want to hear it."

"I think I'd like to hear anything you're willing to tell me."

That response caught Amber by surprise and she glanced at him sharply. He smiled; she had already learned that his smiles were hard to ignore.

"Every night when Sophie's father would come home from a hard day at the ice rink—"

"Ice rink?"

"He played ice hockey professionally. Anyway, every night he'd let Sophie go through his pockets and keep the pennies. By the time he died last year, she had pennies stashed all over the house. I still find them in the most unexpected places."

"You're a widow?"

"Yes." He'd said it with the proper sympathy, but she had the distinct impression that he was pleased to hear this bit of news. "Look, I don't know what else to do. Would you like to haul away all the pennies we can find around here and check them?"

He looked relieved. "Yeah, I would."

His response to her sarcasm astounded her. "There must be thousands," she warned him.

"I promise not to keep any." He grinned, then turned serious. "I feel like a bum for harassing a little girl, but Aunt Octavia is about to go into cardiac arrest over this."

"I understand. I suppose I should be grateful that you're doing it yourself instead of sending the police, but—"

A fierce pounding on the door startled her and she stared at him, wide-eyed. "Sounds like somebody's about to knock the door down. Do you suppose—" She started for the door.

Behind her, she heard him mutter, "Ah, jeez, talk about timing."

Naturally, it was the police, two men in blue with firm jaws and heavy gun belts. Amber invited them in, then cast a condemning glance at Quint.

The worst part was, they wouldn't go away, even after he identified himself as the caller. They just looked through him and insisted they were only doing a job. That job included calling Sophie in from the backyard.

She walked into the room and her eyes went wide at the sight of the uniformed officers. Quint steeled himself for the tears, but she surprised him.

"Policemen!" she exclaimed delightedly. "Mama says, the policeman is my friend."

The cops looked startled. The tall one muttered, "Nice to meet someone who still realizes that, ma'am."

Sophie went on brightly. "Are you going to put me in jail?"

"A nice little girl like you?" The short cop knelt. "We just want to know if you took anything that doesn't belong to you today. Like, when all that money got spilled?"

Sophie hung her head. "That's stealing," she said. "Mama says stealing is bad."

"It sure is, but sometimes we take things by mistake. Did you do that, Sophie? Sophie's your name, isn't it?"

"Uh-huh, and I did that." Slowly she held out her hand. "What you said."

The cop glanced up at the adults hovering above him, his expression triumphant. "Took something. And now you're gonna give it back, right, Sophie?"

"Do I got to?" She gave her mother a plaintive glance.

"You sure do." The policeman held out his hand.

Sophie dropped a penny on his palm. "I'm nine," she said brightly. "How old are you?"

The policeman laughed. "Don't try to change the subject on me, young lady." He handed the penny to Quint.

Quickly Quint compared it to his list, but didn't find it. He gave his head a sharp shake. Poor kid was so traumatized she was trying to buy them off with her own stash.

Quint, who wasn't accustomed to being the bad guy, felt rotten about the whole thing.

"THAT WAS A DIRTY TRICK," Amber said after the police had departed. "Did you come over to soften us up for interrogation or what?"

"I had to report the missing coins, because if they don't turn up, there's insurance and all that to worry about," Quint explained. "I didn't know they'd actually show up here."

"Why not? My four-year-old daughter is apparently the only suspect."

"She's not a suspect! Well, not exactly." Unwilling to meet her gaze, he glanced around the room. "About Sophie's pennies—"

"Here!" She snatched a canning jar full of the coins off the end table and thrust them at him. "Take them—take them all." Flouncing around the room, she began gathering up containers of pennies: a small flower vase, a jam jar, a plastic bowl.

When the living room was cleared of pennies—or as cleared as she could get it with her sewing supplies complicating the project—Amber disappeared into other rooms. Shortly she reappeared hauling a plastic laundry basket into which she'd tossed everything willy-nilly. She dragged everything back to where he stood.

"I'm really sorry," he said, feeling like a ruthless jerk.

"So am I." She took a deep breath. "How long do you think it will take you to—"

The back door flew open and Sophie bounced in. "Mama, can I have a— *My pennies!*" Rushing forward, she threw her small body across the basket.

"I'm just borrowing them," Quint said desperately. "I'll bring them back very soon, I promise."

"Don't steal my pennies!"

"I'm not! I'm just trying to see if my pennies got mixed up with your pennies—by accident, you know? Sophie, don't cry, *please!*"

She wasn't crying, she was screaming. His plea reminded her to burst into tears, which she did with gusto.

"Look, I'll bring you some new pennies. Bright shiny ones. Would you like that?"

"I want my old pennies!"

"Okay, how about this…. After I return your pennies, I'll take you on a shopping spree at Sterling's. You can have anything you want."

She stopped crying and looked at him with damp hope in her eyes. "Can I have Jiggs?"

He groaned. "Jiggs isn't mine. You can have anything else in the store—" He glanced desperately at Amber, but found no support there. "Or anything money can buy. We've got a real nice kids' department."

"I want my pennies! I want my dog!"

Getting out of there with the pennies was a nightmare. Quint's last sight of Sophie was of her sobbing in her mother's arms.

As he drove away, he knew he'd never felt worse in his life.

THE STERLING FAMILY mansion had been built on a bluff overlooking the beach in La Jolla during the Roaring Twenties and had been inhabited by Sterlings ever since. Quint had grown up there, eventually inheriting the place and the three Sterling's department stores.

He'd invited Octavia, his only living relative, to move in with him a little more than a year ago, thinking she was all alone in the world and they'd be good company for each other. Unfortunately, Jiggs had been part of the package. Quint's life hadn't been the same since.

Jiggs and Octavia both met him in the front hallway. Jiggs went for Quint's right ankle, grabbing his trouser cuff with needlelike teeth.

Octavia's hands fluttered. "Do you have good news for me, Quintin?"

"I recovered one of the pennies from Sophie Brannigan," he said, "but not *the* penny. I'm sorry, Aunt Octavia."

She looked on the verge of tears. "This is terrible."

"I know it is, but at least the missing coins are insured. It might not be the same, but you *can* replace it."

"Don't say that! You've got to find my penny."

"I'm trying." Quint shook his right leg in an attempt to dislodge Jiggs. The dog flopped like a rag mop, but hung on.

Octavia clenched her hands into fists. "You must put aside everything until you get that penny back from that four-year-old felon," she said in a voice quivering with determination. "She's got it. I know she does."

"On the off chance that you're right, I took every

penny in Mrs. Brannigan's house and brought them home with me.''

"Fetch them! We must check each one.''

He recoiled. "*Who* must?''

"Why, you and me. This is too important to trust to strangers.''

"Octavia, there must be *thousands*.''

She looked taken aback, but recovered quickly. "In that case...you bring them in while I round up the servants. Quickly, Quintin! We have no time to lose!''

Everyone pitched in, from the butler to the upstairs maid. Soon pennies were spread from one end of the marble hall to the other. Beneath the glow of a crystal chandelier, coins were sorted and checked and piled into containers brought from the kitchen.

Using a broad-tipped marker Quint had noted the vital statistics of the missing pennies. It took hours, but finally even Octavia admitted it had been an exercise in futility. The missing pennies were not among the multitude.

She turned to him in desperation. "What are we going to do now, Quintin?'' she pleaded. "If I don't get that penny back, my life and reputation will be ruined.''

"Don't you think that's overstating the problem, Aunt Octavia? I know how much that penny means to you but—''

"You just don't understand,'' she interrupted miserably.

"Then make me understand and I'll try to make

*you* understand. Hell, I'll go out and buy you a replacement, if that would make you feel any better.''

"I told you no!" She looked determined. "It's the original or nothing."

"Be reasonable, Aunt Octavia. There's not much more I can do."

"You must. Quintin, for the sake of your favorite aunt, you must."

THE NEXT MORNING at breakfast, Quint picked up the newspaper and turned immediately to Crane Rogers's "Scene About San Diego" column. Impatiently he scanned the print until he found the article he sought.

*Pennies from heaven?*

Talk about a dream come true.

Usually it's the customers who lay out the loot at department stores but the other day at Sterling's, it was the other way around. Surprised shoppers suddenly found themselves pelted by pennies—not to mention doused in dimes, nailed by nickels and quashed by quarters.

Seems Quintin Sterling, Boy Wonder of the Sterling's Department Store chain, screwed up big time—a direct quote from the man himself, by the way—when he fumbled a tray of rare coins he was about to fit into a display case. Coins flew every which way, he reported, and soon shoppers were scrambling around on all fours to scoop up the loot.

Most of it was turned in, according to

Sterling. "People are basically honest, I'm happy to say," he admitted. "But we are still missing a few pieces from the collection."

Funny thing is, the missing silver coins aren't worth much—a few hundred dollars per coin at most. But among the missing pennies is the real jewel of the collection. Sterling describes it as a rare 1943-S Lincoln copper cent worth...oh, in the neighborhood of $50,000. Some neighborhood!

Only four of the 1943-S Lincoln copper cents were known to be struck on 1942 bronze alloy blanks. Sterling is offering a $5,000 reward for the return of the one-in-a-million penny, no questions asked.

But beware of fakes! There's apparently a lot of them out there—plain old 1943 Lincoln pennies copper-plated to resemble their rare brothers. But if you're not a collector, how can you tell the difference?

Easiest way is to haul out a magnet to see if the penny sticks. If it does, it's a fake; real copper isn't attracted to magnets.

Any suspects in this case? Sterling laughs. "Only one, but we're holding off on making an arrest," he says. "She's only four years old, so she doesn't have a record. Seriously, she was just passing by with her mother when it happened—and the kid just happens to love pennies."

So would we, if one worth $50,000 dropped out of the sky.

# 3

IN A CHEAP MOTEL somewhere in the suburb of Imperial Beach, Crane Rogers's column was not on the minds of Phil Tubbs and Vilma Bankhead, a couple of low rollers looking for enough dishonest dough to get them back to Las Vegas. Hunched over lukewarm cups of plastic-flavored coffee, they pursued their individual interests: Phil gobbling stale doughnuts provided by the surly staff of the Bide-a-Wee Motel; Vilma checking out the newspaper in case opportunity was preparing to knock. Her avaricious glance fell upon Crane Rogers's column quite by accident.

Phil fidgeted in his chair. "Uh…you want that last doughnut, Vilma?"

"I might." Little weasel ate doughnuts morning, noon and night, then tipped the scales at a hundred twenty-two soaking wet. A big woman could resent a thing like that. Not big, Vilma corrected herself. Zaftig. Amazonian.

Substantial.

Phil reached for the doughnut and Vilma went back to the paper. That's when her glance fell upon the "Scene About San Diego" column. "Hey!" she exclaimed. "We're in the newspaper."

Phil blanched and dropped the doughnut. It bounced off the table and rolled across the floor, coming to rest against the wastepaper basket. "Nobody's got anything on me, I swear it!"

Vilma, proud owner of what brains the team possessed, rolled her eyes and curled her lip in disdain. "Calm down. We're not mentioned by name. It's about what happened yesterday at Sterling's. Lemme read it...yeah, yeah, yeah, 'pelted by pennies...' Uh-huh...'rare coins...basically honest...' Ha!" She snickered.

"What else does it say?"

She peered back at the paper, did a double take and read out loud. "'Funny thing is, the missing silver coins aren't worth much—'" She glared daggers at Phil as if it were his fault.

"What else?" He looked pale, as if bracing himself for the worst.

Somewhere along the line, she realized, he'd lost his nerve. Well, either he got it back or she was outta here. "What difference does it make, what else? We'll be lucky if that change we took will buy us a cup of coffee."

"Just curious, is all."

She grimaced and resumed her abbreviated recitation. "'...Jewel of the collection...rare 1943-S Lincoln copper cent worth—'" Her eyes went wide and she blinked, looked closer, then announced, "Worth *fifty-thousand bucks!*"

"You're kidding." Phil looked awestruck.

"Do I look like I'm kidding?" She smacked him upside the head with the newspaper. Smoothing out the paper, she quickly skimmed the rest of the column, interrupting herself now and then with a grunt of displeasure. At the conclusion, she looked up grimly. "Do you believe this? They think that kid who was scooping up all those pennies must have taken it."

"Yeah, she did."

Vilma's jaw dropped. "How do *you* know she took it?"

Phil shrugged. "I saw her. Little bandit was palming pennies like a pro. I thought it was kinda funny."

*Whap!* Vilma's newspaper struck again. Jumping up, she grabbed her purse off the rickety bedside table and dumped the contents onto the messy bed. Pawing through the jumble, she scooped up all the loose silver that had been rattling around in the bottom and threw it on the floor, then proceeded to stomp back and forth over it a few times to register her chagrin.

By the time she stopped, she was breathing hard. "We gotta find that kid and get that penny before the cops do," she said tersely. "But how the hell we gonna do that?"

"Uh…" Phil hunkered down for a moment. "Maybe this will help." Sheepishly he pulled a handful of papers from his pocket: grocery receipts, pencil sketches of seagulls made on a napkin, a carbon copy of a bill for car repair paid by a *Samer Rramagim*—as best they could make out the smudges—and a business card that read "One in a Million, Exclusively at Nicole's of La Jolla." A penciled notation on back read 10:00 a.m. Wednesday.

Today was Wednesday. A great smile creased Vilma's pancake makeup. Good old Phil! He'd been groping in the redhead's tote bag for cash and this was all he had to show for it.

It was enough.

EVERY MONDAY, Wednesday and Friday, Neona Jones looked forward to sharing amusing tidbits from Crane Rogers's column with her family. Despite the fact that they seemed indifferent to her efforts to culturize them, it still made her feel as if she were a part of the pulse of the city—in the know, one of the beautiful people.

So where was this morning's edition of the newspaper? For that matter, where was her son, Mizell, whose only job, just about, was to bring in the newspaper each morning?

Neona had to do everything around here and she was getting darn sick and tired of it. Marching to the front door, she threw it open.

There stood Mizell on the bottom step, the paper beneath his arm, his goony seventeen-year-old-in-love expression aimed at the house next door. *That woman* lived there—Amber Brannigan, every decent mother's nightmare.

Just then the redheaded troublemaker appeared on the porch. She actually had the nerve to smile and wave her newspaper at them.

Mizell waved back. Neona did not.

"Get in this house, Mizell!" she yelled, stamping her foot. "I can't read the newspaper if you don't bring it in!"

With a last regretful glance toward the house next door, Mizell trotted up the steps and inside.

Grumpy at having her day start so badly, Neona followed him to the breakfast table. Sitting, she opened the paper and spread it in front of her. Her husband, Maynard, grunted, spooned a soggy corner of the front page out of his cereal bowl, gave her a dirty look, and kept on shoveling down Sweetie De-lights.

Mizell settled into his chair with a pile of cold toast and a jar of peanut butter. Pushing aside his cereal bowl for the moment, he smeared a glob of peanut butter on a corner of the toast, ate it, smeared on more, ate it....

Neona ignored them both, turning quickly to Crane Rogers's column. The first item was about a kitten trapped in a tree and how the firemen wouldn't rescue it and how excited everybody got, running around on the ground trying to figure out what to do until, when they finally looked up, the cat was gone. They were so happy they took up a collection for the humane society. Much ado about nothing, Mr. Rogers concluded.

He had such a wonderful way with words!

The next item was about an incident at Sterling's Department Store—Neona gasped. "Somebody stole a penny worth fifty thousand dollars from Sterling's," she announced.

Maynard looked up from the two-quart mixing bowl from which he always ate his cereal. "Get outta here," he scoffed. "How can a penny be worth that kinda money when it starts out worth one lousy cent?''

Neona sniffed. ''According to Crane Rogers, it was part of a big expensive collection of rare coins that got spilled. I guess people didn't turn everything back in and they come up short.''

Maynard picked up his bowl and drank the last of the milk. He set the bowl down and licked his lips. ''I still don't think any penny is worth—''

''There's a five thousand dollar reward for its return.''

That got his attention. Father and son exchanged impressed glances.

''Any suspects?'' Maynard asked.

''It says here…'' She read quickly. ''They don't give the name, but the suspect is four years old and loves pennies.'' She stared at her husband and he stared back. ''Are you thinking what I'm thinking?'' she exclaimed.

''If I am, it's a first.'' He stood. ''I gotta go to work.''

She turned her gaze on Mizell. ''I'll bet dollars to doughnuts that little pirate next door stole the penny.''

Mizell returned her fevered gaze blankly. ''Say what?''

''That kid took the penny. I'm sure of it.''

''How you figure, Ma?''

''It just stands to reason. Everybody in the neighborhood knows that kid is nuts about pennies.''

''Yeah, but that don't mean—''

''It *means*,'' she interrupted sanctimoniously,

"that when she gets a chance, that kid grabs every penny in sight. Why, I dropped my purse when I was hauling in groceries the other day and change spilled out. That kid was all over my pennies like a duck on a June bug. I practically had to call the cops to get 'em back. But then, she was raised by trash, so what do you expect? Tattoos and Rollerblade skates and up all hours of the day and night—"

Mizell popped the last wad of peanut-buttered toast into his mouth. "Ah, Amber's all right," he said around a series of vigorous chews.

"Any woman with *tattoos* is nothing but trash, and trash begets trash."

"Aw, Ma—"

"I mean it, Mizell. Now they've added thievery to their sins." She shook her head in condemnation. "You stay away from that pair, you hear me? They're a bad influence on an impressionable boy."

Mizell perked right up. After his mother rose to carry the dirty dishes to the sink, he remained at the table, thinking.

A penny worth five thousand dollars honest or fifty thousand *dis*honest. Just made a boy's head reel with thoughts of sand and surf—in Hawaii.

BEFORE OPENING her dress shop that morning, Nicole Phillips glanced at Crane Rogers's column. When she got to the part about the coins, she started smiling. When she got to the part about the four-year-old suspect, she laughed out loud.

Nicole knew that Amber had had an appointment with Octavia Sterling yesterday, and where Amber went, Sophie went. Poor Amber! It wouldn't be fun to have your child suspected of stealing a fifty-thousand-dollar penny.

Nicole put the newspaper down on the glass display counter and glanced around to make sure everything was in perfect order. Her salesclerk would be a couple of hours late due to a dental emergency, so Nicole was filling in. She'd have been here anyway, though; Amber was dropping by to discuss her new fall line.

Thoughts of One in a Million brought a smile to Nicole's lips. The label was her biggest seller, despite the fact that the price tags put the line beyond the reach of all but the wealthy. She knew this bothered Amber, who would have liked to design for the masses, but handmade and hand-decorated did not lend itself to economy.

Of course, if Amber decided to go with the exclusive Sterling's deal...

Crossing to unlock the front door, Nicole admitted to herself that her friend and business associate was unlikely to succumb to the blandishments of Octavia Sterling. For one thing, she wanted to maintain the integrity of the line.

But even more important, Amber was loyal. Unless Nicole released her from their handshake agreement to market the clothing here, Amber would never—

A woman burst inside, tearing the door from Nicole's hands. Nicole stepped back in surprise, but the woman plowed past her to the first rack of clothing.

"Good morning," Nicole said tentatively. "May I be of some assistance?"

The woman glanced over one beefy shoulder and Nicole saw she was chewing gum.

"Just looking," she chirped, her hands settling on the shoulders of a delicate voile swimsuit cover-up.

Trying not to flinch, Nicole moved back behind the counter. She wasn't accustomed to seeing women such as this one in her expensive La Jolla shop—not that she was a snob. Everyone was certainly welcome. But she didn't think this particular customer was going to find anything she liked, if what she was wearing indicated her taste in apparel.

Leopard-print pants couldn't be all that easy to find nowadays, especially not in a size that large. The white lace shirt over-embroidered with big bright sunflowers wasn't a common item, either. Her feet were encased in see-through plastic mules with two-inch heels, and on her head she wore a tightly fitting hat covered with floppy poppy-colored flower petals. Oversize sunglasses completely concealed her eyes. Her mouth was a bright fuchsia slash.

After her mad dash into the store, the woman was now going through everything on the rack with precise attention. At the rate she was going, she'd be here all day.

Smiling, Nicole approached her. "Is there something in particular you're looking for?"

"Nah." The woman chomped on her gum, then added, "Well, maybe. You got any stuff here called One in a Million?"

Nicole blinked in surprise. "As a matter of fact, I

do.'' Surely, *surely* this woman was not interested in Amber's witty and eccentric designs. ''They're right over here.''

Leading the way to a rack in the back, Nicole took out the first item and held it up for confirmation. It happened to be a natural-colored cotton knit with several bright block prints of fish, plus pockets tied onto tabs with matching bias tubing strings.

It was one of the most popular styles in the shop.

The big woman stopped short and stared. ''You're kidding. *That's* One in a Million?''

Nicole was starting to enjoy herself. She nodded, suppressing a smile.

The woman reached out and grabbed the tag. *''Two hundred and forty-nine dollars?''* Her jaw dropped. ''It doesn't even have a belt!''

''That's true.'' *Don't laugh, Nicole. This is a customer.* ''Perhaps you'd prefer something a little...'' She bit her lip in an effort at control. ''A little less *out there*. I have some nice—''

''No, I want to check this stuff out.'' The woman's jaw set at a determined angle. ''I had a friend—I mean, I *have* a friend who swears by this stuff.''

''Oh? Who is it? I probably know her.''

''No chance.'' The woman lifted out a pair of wide-legged knit pants, checked the hundred-and-seventy-five-dollar tag and put them back. ''I think she got her stuff in Phoenix.''

''Oh, no, that's impossible. You see—''

''Or maybe L.A.—I forget. Whatever.''

''But you don't understand. One in a Million is exclusive to—''

The front door opened and a small figure dashed inside. "Aunt Nicole, where are you? I'm visiting!"

Sophie. Although Nicole wasn't actually related to the little girl by blood, she was definitely related by affection.

"Please excuse me," she said to her large and misinformed customer. "If you need any assistance, just—"

"Yeah, sure, you run along."

So Nicole did.

AMBER KNEW it was coming, and she was right. Nicole stopped short at the sight of her and gasped.

"Amber! Your hair!"

Amber couldn't help touching her hair with one defensive hand. "It's windy outside," she said lamely, although she knew that wasn't what elicited the attention.

"I'm talking about the *color!*"

"Oh, that." Amber glanced across the room and caught a glimpse of her own reflection in a mirrored wall. The short golden-blond curls were startling, sure, but everyone would get used to them.

Eventually.

"Aren't you the cool one," Nicole said, laughing. "You may fool most of the people most of the time, but I happen to know what a sudden change of hair color means."

"That I got tired of being a redhead?"

"Very funny. It means you're wrestling with some big decision that you don't want to make. Don't forget, I *know* you, my girl."

Amber smiled ruefully. "I guess you do. It's just—"

"Auntie Nicole, can I color?"

"Sure, sweetie. Your crayons are in my office where you left them and I got you some new coloring books. Run get them and you can sit over there in the window seat and color to your heart's content."

"Goodie!" Sophie darted through the door that led to the office and the dressing rooms just beyond, her small drawstring purse bouncing on its string wrapped around her wrist. The purse matched her dress, which was a baby-blue knit with butterfly stamping, made by Amber, of course.

Nicole smiled fondly. "I read about our Sophie in this morning's newspaper."

Amber groaned. "Wasn't that awful? Now everyone will know."

"No one will know!" Nicole put a hand on Amber's shoulder and pulled her toward the small sofa set into a flowery bower on one side of the store. "I only knew because you told me you were going to talk to Octavia Sterling again yesterday."

"Oh, that's right." Amber sighed. "I guess it's okay, then. But Quintin Sterling seemed so nice, and I thought he'd forgotten the crazy idea that Sophie—"

"*The* Quintin Sterling?" Nicole's eyes widened.

"I think there's only one." How could there be any more as incredibly good-looking and charming?

Suddenly the laughter went out of Nicole's expression. "So how did one of San Diego's most eligible bachelors get mixed up in this? Is he joining with his aunt to try to get One in a Million for Sterling's?''

''Goodness, no. He's the one who dropped the pennies and I guess he's the one who's supposed to get them back for his aunt. See, Sophie and I had just come out of Miss Sterling's office when...''

As they spoke in low voices, Sophie reappeared to take her place on the window seat nearby, where she spread out her crayons and coloring books. There was only one customer in the store and she was browsing, not buying.

When Amber finished explaining, Nicole nodded. ''So you turned Miss Sterling down again.''

''Of course.'' Amber cocked her head questioningly. ''As long as there is a One in a Million, it'll be sold here, Nicole. I told you that at the very beginning.''

Nicole looked torn. ''I know you did, but this could be an enormous opportunity for you. Are you sure—'' She stopped speaking and her eyes widened again. ''Is that the decision you don't want to make? Is *that* why you bleached your hair?''

Amber shifted uneasily. ''That was no decision at all. The question is, how long will there even *be* a One in a Million?''

''What are you talking about? The line's doing great. I'm selling your stuff as fast as I can get it on the rack—''

The large woman shopper called from across the room. ''Are the dressing rooms back there, just in case I find something I want to try on?''

''Through that door to the left.'' Nicole responded

automatically. She turned back to Amber. "Honestly, I could sell twice as much if I could get it."

"That's the problem."

Nicole laughed incredulously. "Success is a problem?"

Amber nodded. "If you're not prepared to deal with it. My dinky little business has reached the point where I can't handle it anymore with three woman sewing for me. I'm either going to have to commit totally—worry about expansion, take out loans." She shuddered at the thought. "Or walk away."

"Walk away?" It was an incredulous cry. "Why on earth would you walk away from all you've accomplished?"

Amber had dreaded that question because she didn't like the answer. Yet, she had to be honest. "I don't need any more money or stress or problems," she said. "As it is now I can make my clothing exactly the way I want to, and I love that part. It's the business side that terrifies me. It's only bearable because I'm dealing with a friend."

"I *am* a friend, honey, which is why I have to point out that if you went with Sterling's—"

"No. Never." Amber shook her head furiously. "Besides, there's something else...."

Nicole waited patiently. After a few moments Sophie jumped up.

"I lost my green," she announced. "Can I go look in your office, Aunt Nicole?"

"Sure, honey."

The little girl ran out. Amber sighed. "Nicole, I want my life back—the carefree life I had before One in a Million took off. I want to be able to just pack up Sophie and move on whenever I feel like it. I—I guess I'm a little frightened of success because it ties me down so. I've been in San Diego for almost six years. Too long.''

"Oh, Amber!" Nicole looked stricken. "It's not your business tying you down, honey, it's your daughter.''

Amber recoiled. "What are you talking about? Sophie doesn't tie me down. We go everywhere together and do everything together. How can you say such a thing?''

"Because it's true. Sophie starts school next year and then it won't matter if you have a business or not because you'll *have* to stay in one place, for her.''

"But—" Amber stumbled around for a response, feeling a flicker of panic. Of course she'd have to stay put *somewhere;* what was she thinking about?

"And if you have to stay," Nicole went on anxiously, "why not develop your business? Honey, the things you design for women and children could take the fashion world by storm, especially if they could be produced in quantity.''

"But then I'd be in a worse bind than I am now." Amber refused to meet Nicole's impassioned gaze. Instead she watched the lone shopper head toward the dressing rooms with an armful of garments. "I can barely handle what I'm doing now. I sure couldn't handle any more.''

Nicole's sudden grin lightened the atmosphere. "No. You'll run out of hair colors soon.''

Amber laughed ruefully. "You always make me feel better. Of course, you're the one who got me involved in this in the first place. If you hadn't—"

A furious shriek split the air and both women froze for just an instant before leaping up and plunging toward the hallway that led to office and dressing rooms.

Sophie was in trouble!

QUINT, poised with his hand on the doorknob of Nicole's of La Jolla, heard a scream. He knew instantly that the screamer was Sophie Brannigan, and chills shot down his spine.

What could possibly elicit such a sound? Ripping open the door, he plunged inside.

And saw nothing and nobody. The shop appeared to be deserted. His frantic gaze found a curtained door at the back and he started forward, ready to do battle.

The curtain burst inward and Sophie dashed into the room, her eyes wild and her breathing labored. Spotting Quint, she sprinted straight up to him and threw her arms around his knees.

"She tried to rob my pennies," the little girl shrieked at the top of her lungs. Hugging him tighter, she threw back her head. "She tried to rob my pennies!"

A blonde dashed through the door, closely followed by a slender dark-haired woman. But where was Amber— Quint stared. The *blonde* was Amber?

"Sophie, are you all right?" She grabbed the child

into her arms and buried her face in the dark hair. "Oh, honey, you scared me to death!"

Quint looked from one woman to the other. "What's going on? I heard Sophie scream."

Amber looked around anxiously. "Oh, my gosh, that woman! Sophie, was it the lady who was shopping when we came in? Tall?"

Sophie nodded emphatically. "She said, 'Come here little girl.'" Sophie sounded like the wicked witch. "'I'd like to see your pennies!'" she hissed.

"Is there a back door?" Quint demanded. "Because nobody came out this way." It was probably already too late to catch the perpetrator, but he intended to try.

"I'm afraid so." The brunette pointed. "It's at the end of the hall—"

He didn't wait to hear the rest, just plunged through the curtained door. To the right he saw an office; to the left a sign that said Dressing Rooms, and directly ahead, a door leading outside.

He tried the outside door first, but found only an empty service parking area. Next he went through each dressing room with care, pausing to pick up the stack of clothing on the floor of the first one. Then he stuck his head into the office, but it was too small for someone to be hiding in there.

Reemerging, he found Sophie reclining on a small sofa looking like Cleopatra with her subjects hovering around to do her bidding. When she saw him, she gave a pitiful sniff and clutched her small drawstring bag to her chest.

"*My* pennies," she said, and he knew she still resented him carrying away those bottles and jars and bags of pennies yesterday.

"I'll bring them back soon," he promised. "Uh…could I just look inside that bag and—"

"No! No! Mama, save me!" Sophie flung her arms around her mother's neck and began to weep piteously.

The brunette turned on him with a condemning gaze. "I see you take pennies from babies. Do you also kick dogs?"

"Give me a break, here." He glanced around the room. "I take it nobody came through here while I was gone."

"That's correct."

"Well, the office and back were clear. I checked out the dressing rooms and this is all I found." He held out the tumbled pile of clothing and the brunette took it.

She glanced down and made a face. "Size ten. As if." She gave him a reluctant smile. "By the way, I'm Nicole Phillips. This is my store."

"I'm—"

"I know, Mr. Sterling. Your fame precedes you." She turned to carry the clothing to the counter.

Quint looked at Amber, who hadn't said a word. He couldn't get over how different she looked with that blond hair. Not sexier—that probably wouldn't be possible. Just different, like an entirely new person.

He forced himself to concentrate on Sophie. "Can you tell me what the woman looked like?" he asked as gently as he could.

Sophie swallowed hard. "Like…" She concentrated hard. "Like a *monster*. Like a great big monster." She curved her fingers into talons.

"Not too helpful. There are so many monsters around these days." He met Amber's solemn gaze. "Did you see her?"

"Nicole and I both did."

"What did she look like?"

"Well…" They exchanged frowning glances. "She was big," Amber said finally. "I mean tall and…not slender, but not fat or anything. Just big."

"Okay. I got that. Big. What else? Like…what color was her hair?"

"I don't know. She wore this kind of floppy hat that covered it."

"How about her eyes, then?"

"Big dark glasses. I'm sorry."

"Anything you *could* see?"

"Now that I think of it—no." She appealed to him with the same golden-brown eyes he remembered. "Do you think she was some kind of a—" She glanced protectively at Sophie. "A *pervert?*"

Nicole gasped. "Oh, Amber, no! Surely not!"

"No," Quint agreed. "I don't think she was a pervert at all."

"Then what?"

She looked at him with such *need* that he felt himself drawn to her more strongly than ever.

"I think Sophie knows," he said. "Sophie, what did you say the woman wanted?"

"My pennies," the girl responded promptly. She

hugged the bag closer to her chest. "But she didn't get 'em! They're mine!"

"But...but—" Amber frowned. "Why? She couldn't possibly know that Sophie was the suspect so kindly pointed out in the newspaper article—could she?"

Everyone looked at Quint, who felt rotten. He had no more idea than they did how the item in the paper could be traced to Sophie, but somehow he knew that it had been.

And it was his fault for planting the item in the first place. Not only that; if some strange woman had figured it out, others might, too. And somebody might decide to get rough in the search for the one-in-a-million penny.

That meant Quintin Sterling was responsible for the well-being of Sophie Brannigan and her mother.

Under any other circumstances, he could enjoy that.

# 4

NORMAL HEIGHTS was clear across San Diego from La Jolla, and Amber drove with only half a mind until she had to slam on her brakes to avoid running a red light. A half dozen angry drivers responded, hands heavy on their car horns.

Sophie took it personally. "Don't you honk at my mama!" she cried, her tone quivering with outrage. "Don't you guys do that!"

"Now, now." Amber tried to soothe her irate daughter. "It was my fault, sugar. I have to start paying attention."

Sophie frowned. "Are you sad, Mama?"

"Sad?" Amber shot a quick glance at her perceptive daughter. "Maybe a little. Mostly I'm worried because that lady tried to steal your pennies."

Sophie nodded wisely. "Quin says that's no lady!"

Amber smiled at the shortening of Quint's name. "He's right about that. Ladies don't steal pennies from little girls—or anyone else. But because she *did* try, I think we have to be careful now."

"I'm careful." Sophie sounded supremely confident.

"I know you are." Amber turned onto their street.

"But just for a little while, let's be *especially* careful. You mustn't wander off, ever. Always stay where you can see me. That kind of thing."

"Okay, Mama," Sophie agreed blithely.

Amber pulled into the carport beside her house. Helping Sophie from the car, she thought about the decisions she must make and wondered how she'd do it. Maybe she and Sophie should just—

She stopped short, frowning. What was that sound coming from the backyard? "Sophie," she whispered, "I want you to sit down on the front porch and wait for me, okay?"

"Why, Mama?"

"I just want to check on something." Leading the little girl to the small front porch, she pressed her down to sit on the first step. "Wait there and count the flowers on that hibiscus bush. I'll be right back."

"Okay," Sophie agreed. "One, two, three, four, nine, eleben…"

Leaving the child engrossed in her counting exercise, Amber slipped around the corner of the house. A tall wooden fence concealed the yard itself, but Amber knew where all the cracks and chinks were. The easiest way to see, however, was to just rise up on tiptoe and peek over carefully.

A tall skinny figure swung a pick over his head with more enthusiasm than finesse. His back was toward her, but it could only be one person. Throwing open the gate, she strode through.

"Mizell Jones, what are you doing in my backyard when I'm not home?"

Mizell jumped a foot. Whirling around, he

dropped the pick and hunched his shoulders. He stood in the middle of an area of fresh dirt, surrounded by the fruits of his labor: broken bottles, tin can lids, a couple of mangy fashion dolls and a can opener.

She knew, of course, that these were not the things he sought.

The gangly kid swallowed hard. "I, uh…hi, Amber."

"Hi yourself, Mizell. Now, tell me what you're doing here."

"Oh, yeah, that. I, uh, that is…Ma read in the paper about Sophie stealing that penny—"

"Mizell Jones, Sophie didn't steal *anything!*"

"Oh, sorry. I mean, she didn't steal it, she took it. And I thought it stood to reason—I mean, she's always digging around out here. If I had a hot penny, I'd probably bury it in the backyard, right?"

"A hot penny!" Her voice rose at hearing her beloved daughter characterized as a thief. "Sophie doesn't have a hot—"

*"Out of the way! I'll handle this!"*

Amber shrieked in surprise as a new presence hurtled past to strike the skinny Mizell like a battering ram hitting a wall of matchsticks. With a howl of fear, Mizell toppled over backward with Quintin Sterling on top of him.

"I'll hold him," he yelled over his shoulder to Amber, "while you call the cops!"

"Don't be ridiculous." She wrung her hands anxiously. "Mizell's my neighbor."

"But Sophie said there was a burglar—actually, she said 'burg-laher'—but I knew what she meant."

Sophie herself strolled up. She peered down at the kid flat on his belly with his cheek grinding into the fresh dirt he'd just turned over.

"Hi, Mizell," she said cheerfully. "Can I play?"

"Go away, grommet," he groaned, not making the slightest effort to escape the iron grasp of the man on his back. "Or better yet, go tell my ma I'm being *mugged.*"

"You are not being mugged," Amber protested. "Quint, please let him up."

"But he's been digging up your backyard. Are you sure you don't want me to—"

"Quint, *please.*"

"Well, hell." Quint shoved to his feet, his jaw thrust out at a belligerent angle. Mizell followed more slowly, dirt clinging to his grungy denim cut-offs and his Shredders Rule T-shirt.

"Are you all right?" Amber asked anxiously. She could just imagine a lawsuit over this.

"He coulda killed me," Mizell whined. "That's what I get for bein' a nice guy. Next time, I'm putting up my dukes!" He raised his fists in a pitiful approximation of a fighter's stance.

Quint's lip curled. "Did you find any pennies?" he demanded in a nasty tone.

"No, but if I'd had a little more time—" Mizell ducked his head. "Guess I better be going, Amber."

"Good idea, Mizell."

"I still say we should call the police," Quint said. Mizell didn't wait for Amber's reply before taking off for the gate. Without looking back, he slipped through and was gone.

When Mizell was safely away, Amber tried to calm Quint with an explanation. "Mizell lives next door. He's a good boy."

Quint scowled. "Sophie, do you like him?"

The little girl shook her head furiously. "He calls me grommet. I'm not a grommet, I'm a *girl*." She looked very solemn and serious when she said it.

A grin played around Quint's attractive mouth. "You sure are." He gave Amber a triumphant glance. "I rest my case. He figured out Sophie was the kid mentioned in the newspaper and he was looking for the penny."

"I'm not a kid, either," Sophie, clearly annoyed, reminded him.

"Sorry. I lost my head there for a minute." He turned to Amber. "Look, I feel responsible for this whole thing. Why don't you just let me—"

"No, thank you."

"But you don't know what I was about to say."

"It doesn't matter. My answer is no, and thank you."

"But—"

"Quint, I'm busy!" Feeling a little desperate, Amber caught Sophie's hand and turned back toward the gate. She should go inside and get to work; she had a large order to fill for Nicole. But she couldn't do it, not now with everything closing in on her.

"Busy doing what?"

"Sophie and I are going to the park where I can—"

"Which park?"

"Balboa Park, not that it matters. We want to be alone."

"I'll come with you."

"If you do, we won't be alone, will we?"

He tagged along behind. "Why do you want to be alone? What can you do alone you can't do with me?"

"Think!" she said more emphatically than she'd intended. "Think straight, anyway. I've got a lot to think *about.*"

"Such as?"

"Good*bye,* Quint."

"Sophie—"

"Good*bye,* Quin," the little girl called, sounding exactly like her mother.

Quint stood at the curb next to his silver BMW and watched them drive off in Amber's rattletrap of a car. For some reason, seeing her in that old junker made him feel even more protective toward her.

Hell, the woman was a danger to herself. That neighbor kid was definitely up to no good. And the woman who'd accosted Sophie earlier in the dress shop—

Jumping into his car, he turned on the engine. He wouldn't be able to get anything done, knowing she was wandering around that park with blinders on. Besides, he'd gone to Nicole's to talk to Amber and he hadn't gotten the chance to do that yet. So he had an excuse: he wanted to make arrangements to return Sophie's pennies.

Yeah, to return the pennies.

Amber's old car chug-chugged around a far corner just as he pulled away from the curb. This would work out fine, he assured himself. She had a one-track mind; she'd never even think to look around to see if anyone was following. And once they reached the park, if he just happened to bump into her—

It *was* a big park, after all. It would hardly be his fault if they happened to run into each other.

PHIL TUBBS WATCHED the silver BMW pull away from the curb. A cell phone lay beside him on the seat of his rental car. For a moment he considered calling Vilma, who was getting her hair done, but then decided against it.

Hell, he'd got along without her before he'd met her and he could damn well get along without her now. Now that he knew where the kid lived, he could come back anytime to check out the inside of the house. For now, he was going to follow the rich guy following the mother of the kid with the penny.

When he got where he was going, then he might decide to call Vilma.

Hell, he didn't need her telling him every move to make!

MIZELL, still smarting over being attacked in Amber's backyard, saw her come out and get into her car with the grommet. Squirting water from a hose at his mother's car in the driveway outside the carport, he watched them drive past. Man, she was good-looking!

The guy with the heavy hands pulled away from

the curb in his fancy silver BMW and followed her. Mizell perked up. Was that dude after the penny, too? He'd seemed pretty cozy with her, but maybe he was going to mug her first chance he got.

A white car with rental plates suddenly crossed his vision and derailed his train of thought. A weaselly little guy was driving, his gaze pinned on the silver BMW. When the first two cars turned right, so did the rental.

*Ver-rry interesting.* Mizell tossed the sponge into the bucket of soapy water and threw himself behind the wheel of his mother's car. She'd raise hell when she found out what he'd done but no way was he going to let those two dudes get *his* penny.

VILMA HAD THE CABBIE let her out at the zoo. She reasoned that nobody could bring a kid to Balboa Park without visiting the zoo, so all she had to do was wait and the pigeons would fly to her.

Too bad she hadn't been able to get the penny this morning at that dress shop, but the kid had bitten the hand Vilma had clapped over her mouth, then screamed bloody murder. Fortunately, Phil had been waiting outside the back door with the getaway car. No harm done.

He'd let her out at a beauty shop with a Walk-in's Encouraged! sign in the window, then continued to shadow the kid while Vilma went inside to "get beautiful." By the time he'd called her to report, she was both looking and feeling better. They'd agreed to link up later at the park, and she'd called a cab and come right over.

Just in the nick of time, apparently, for there came
the kid and her mother now. The two strolled along
in blissful ignorance, as if they didn't have a care in
the world.

Maybe they didn't, at the price that store charged
for those crazy-looking clothes. Sheesh! Vilma
glanced down at her own ensemble: tight black pants
and a gold Lurex sweater. She'd changed in the car
while Phil followed the blonde-former-redhead out
of La Jolla. No point taking chances.

And now, with her hair teased and sprayed and
piled just the way she liked it, she felt alert and eager
to take up the chase. But where the hell was Phil?

The woman and kid strolled past, bought their
tickets and entered the zoo. Vilma looked around, but
didn't see Phil anywhere. Son of a— Did she have
to do everything herself?

But before she could take up the chase, she saw a
man she recognized hurrying toward the entrance.
That would be the alluring Mr. Quintin Sterling. So
he was also following the kid with the penny—or the
kid's mother. Vilma snickered.

Sterling had no sooner disappeared inside the zoo
than Phil came jogging up. Vilma was just about to
step out from behind her blind of bushes and give
him a piece of her mind when she realized that he,
too, was being followed. A tall, grungy kid who
looked to be about seventeen, but could be much
older, came loping up. Hell, he could be an under-
cover cop or a detective, the way he was dogging
old Phil's trail.

Only when the skinny kid had passed did Vilma

take a tentative step out, look around, then follow the whole damn parade into the San Diego Zoo.

SOPHIE LOVED the "mingos" just inside the entrance to the San Diego Zoo, so of course, they lingered to look at the exotic pink flock, all of which stood around on one skinny leg watching the people watching them. Just being here among the birds and beasts and exotic plants soothed Amber's soul. She glanced at her daughter, who stared entranced at the flamingos. As most children, Sophie adored visiting the zoo.

If they left San Diego, where could they go that had such a wonderful zoo?

"Mama, Mama, I want to see the gorillyas."

"Gorillas, sugar lump. Okay, we'll wander in that direction."

Someplace else. They'd go someplace else.

But wasn't that running *away* from something, instead of running *to* something? When Amber was young and unencumbered, that might have been acceptable. But now she bore sole responsibility for her child and figured she always would because she couldn't imagine ever finding a man who would pass muster with Sophie.

A shiver of apprehension tightened Amber's shoulders. That sole responsibility was awesome. Maybe she *should* consider taking One in a Million to another level. Maybe she should do it for Sophie.

"Mama, look at the teddy bears!"

Sophie slipped her hand free of her mother's grasp and ran forward to lean against the barricade enclosing the koala bear habitat. None of the animals in the San Diego Zoo were kept behind bars, which was one of the things Amber liked most about it. She couldn't have stood seeing them caged. Here, every effort had been made to give the animals the most freedom possible in surroundings close to their natural habitat as humanly possible.

Sophie laughed and pointed at the cuddly koala clinging to a tall eucalyptus tree. Amber followed her daughter, putting a hand on her shoulder.

"Don't go darting off like that," she said. "You could get lost in this crowd."

"Okay, Mama," Sophie promised readily. "Can I see the monkeys? Can I see the g'raffes? Can I see—"

Amber laughed. "One thing at a time," she suggested. "Let's just walk along this trail and see where it takes us."

And while Sophie looked, Amber thought... thought that she wanted her life back, the carefree life she'd had before One in a Million had taken off. Her own success frightened her because it tied her down. She'd never been tied down before, not by anything or anybody...

She'd never considered Sophie an impediment to *anything,* but Nicole had very succinctly pointed out the error in such thinking. The reality was, Amber would always put her daughter's welfare before her own.

"Mama, can I have a lemonade?"

"May I have a lemonade, and yes, you may." Amber paid for the drink, automatically passing the pennies to Sophie, who dropped them into the pocket of her yellow pinafore, which was decorated with abstract seashells. What did she need to do to make Sophie happy and secure? Besides giving her her father, of course, and Amber couldn't bring Johnny back.

They resumed their stroll through shady canyons, along with a multitude of others enjoying the beautiful summer's day. After a while, Sophie's steps began to lag. Amber put her arm around the child. "Are you getting tired, honey? We can head back to the car…"

"No! I want to see gorillyas!" She had that stubborn look on her face.

"All right, but—"

A movement in the crowd streaming past brought Amber's glance around and she did a double take. For some reason the woman hurrying away reminded her of the woman who'd been in Nicole's. Though this woman was dressed completely different, there was something about the way she moved, her mannerisms.

"Gorillas—right!" Amber checked the signs at the intersection of the walking paths and guided Sophie in the proper direction. Her thoughts also turned in a new direction.

Remembering the woman at Nicole's, the woman who was after the missing penny, made Amber uneasy all over again. She darted a quick glance at her daughter, skipping along beside her. Sophie didn't have the two missing pennies, she *couldn't* have them. She'd given back one, so why would she keep the others and lie about it?

Not that it would be a lie to Sophie. She honestly believed that all pennies belonged to her by divine right. If Sophie *did* have it, though, and it was never recovered by the Sterlings, could Amber be held financially responsible? Might she owe restitution to Octavia Sterling?

She shivered. She'd never be able to come up with fifty thousand dollars. Her only option was to pray that someone else had the missing coin and that it would be recovered.

Of course, if that happened, she'd see no more of Quintin Sterling. A faint regretful smile curved her lips. He really was a very kind man, even if he had called the police and told them Sophie was the prime suspect. In his shoes, she might have done the same thing. But his reaction to Sophie's encounter with the would-be penny snatcher was one of remorse, as if he took full responsibility for putting them in some kind of jeopardy.

Jeopardy. Amber didn't like the sound of that word.

In his zeal to protect them, Quint had nearly frightened poor Mizell to death. The kid spent all his time surfing and skateboarding, not robbing banks.

"Mama! Gorillyas!" Sophie took off at a run for the railing that enclosed the gorilla exhibit. Between a steep slope down from the sidewalk and up to the habitat where the animals lounged, lay a moat that prevented either species from getting close enough to seriously annoy the other—not too much, anyway.

Sophie pointed. "See the baby!"

Amber nodded. "And look at that big one over there, Sophie. I think he's mad about something, don't you?"

"Never trust the big ones," murmured a voice right at her ear. "They get by on brawn instead of brains."

Amber whirled around in surprise to find Quint Sterling smiling at her somewhat whimsically.

His smile turned into a full-fledged grin. "Well, fancy meeting you here," he drawled. "Hi, Sophie. How's tricks?"

"I don't do tricks," Sophie said with dignity. "I'm looking at aminals." She glanced quickly at her mother and corrected herself. *"Animals."*

"You followed us," Amber accused him. That realization didn't exactly make her angry, but it did surprise and fluster her. Why would he go to the trouble? Did he think Sophie had the penny with her at all times?

"Yeah," he admitted sheepishly, "I did. I'm concerned about what happened in La Jolla this morning."

"You mean, the woman at Nicole's shop?"

"That's right. There was no harm done, but what if there's a next time? We have no idea what—" He stopped speaking abruptly, glancing at Sophie, who was listening with avid interest.

"Of course there's nothing to worry about," Amber said quickly. "We're not even sure she was after the penny."

Sophie's hand was clenched inside the pocket of her pinafore. "Somebody wants my pennies."

"No, they don't, darling." Amber patted Sophie's tiny shoulder. "We're talking about something else."

"Oh." Satisfied, Sophie turned back to the gorillas.

Quint lowered his voice. "Then there was that kid digging up your backyard. I wish you'd let me call the police."

"There was no need. Really, Mizell is a nice boy."

Frustration swept across his face in an instant. "Amber Brannigan, you're a stubborn woman."

"I'm not stubborn. I just know what I know."

His expression softened. "You *are* stubborn. You're also..."

She waited for him to say "beautiful...charming...adorable."

What he said was, "Different."

She didn't feel different. She felt like any other woman looking up into the eyes of a man she found incredibly attractive. Straitlaced and total establishment he might be, but sexy, so very sexy.

"Thank you," she said with dignity. "I've always strived to be different. It's what every woman longs to hear."

He looked taken aback. "Have I hurt your feelings? I didn't mean—"

Her laugher interrupted his apology. "I'm just putting you on," she said. "I don't mind being different.

I don't pursue it, but I don't mind it. I am what I am.''

"I like what you am." He leaned closer. "I like that you didn't yell at me for bringing the cops to your door."

"You did what you thought was right. Why should I yell at you?"

"And I like that you've been so patient, letting me try to talk Sophie out of that penny."

Sophie cast an incensed glance over her shoulder. "I want my pennies, Quin!"

"I'll return them soon, honey. I promise."

She turned back to the gorillas, grumbling under her breath. Quint watched her for a moment, smiling. It brought a lump to Amber's throat to see the expression on his face. It was obvious that he really liked Sophie, and Amber really liked people who liked her daughter.

Amber said softly, "You still think she's got it, don't you?"

He sighed. "Yes. If an adult took it, I think it would have been turned in for the reward. I mean, that penny's hot now, and an honest five thousand dollars would be the smart way to go."

"Are crooks usually smart?"

"I don't know enough of them to draw a conclusion. Amber..."

"What?" She was suddenly mesmerized by the way he was staring into her eyes.

"You could be in danger."

"Don't be ridiculous. We don't *have* the penny, so no one's going to hurt us."

"We don't know that. Maybe people won't believe you, and people have done terrible things for less than what that penny's worth. Whatever happens, I can't help feeling responsible."

"Then I hereby release you from that responsibility," she said promptly. "Sophie and I don't need anyone to take care of us, you know. We get along quite well on our own."

"I wasn't insulting you, I was just saying that—"

"I understand, and I appreciate your concern. But the police are on the case now, and since Sophie doesn't have the penny anyway..." She shrugged.

"If you believe that, you may be the only person in the civilized world who does. What about that woman at Nicole's? What about that geeky kid digging up your backyard?"

"What about *you?*"

"Hell," he said roughly, "I'd give that penny to Sophie if it was mine. Unfortunately, it isn't. But I can think of worse things than following you, her beautiful—"

"Different!"

"Mother around. Amber—"

*"No, you can't have my pennies!"*

Sophie's scream streaked between them like a runaway train. Whirling in panic, Amber spotted her daughter. Sophie stood ten or twelve feet away facing a slender middle-aged man with an outstretched hand.

And before she could do anything to influence the situation, Amber saw Sophie fling a handful of *some-*

*thing* into the open gorilla habitat. The noise of that "something" striking the man-made floor of the enclosure suggested that the child had just showered a tribe of astonished gorillas with pennies.

# 5

MIZELL SAW IT ALL.

He saw the skinny guy in the Bermuda shorts sidle up to the grommet and say something in a voice too low to be overheard, and he wasn't smiling when he said it. Mizell didn't need to hear the words because the kid's reaction said it all. She stepped back and glared up at the guy. Shoving her hand into her pocket, she pulled out a clenched fist. "No, you can't have my pennies!" she screamed at the top of her lungs.

Then she tossed whatever she was holding at those damn gorillas just sitting there scratching as if there was nothing going on, while the grommet threw away a fortune. She'd just tossed that penny away, had to be. Mizell couldn't stand it. With a howl of alarm, he rushed for the fence. Maybe the coin had landed on the slope leading down to the water. Maybe he could reach it without actually jumping into the gorilla den. Maybe—

"Where the hell do you think *you're* going?"

A savage grip stopped Mizell in midstride, but he wasn't scared. Big tough dude was a good four inches shorter than Mizell, who took a wild swing.

"Turn loose'a me, grandpa!"

"Don't you 'grandpa' me, you young asshole!"

Mizell took a pop on the jaw and staggered back. Grandpa was tougher than he looked, but Mizell was no Sister Mary himself. Throwing wide his arms, he grabbed the guy and squeezed. He'd choke the little weasel, that's what he'd do. He'd—

Mizell lost his footing, staggered back against the rail and tumbled right on over it, down the damn slope into that damn ditchful of water that surrounded that damn gorilla island. And he did it hanging on to the dude who'd started the whole thing, screaming every inch of the way until water closed over his head.

AMBER GRABBED Sophie's hand and ran.

She knew she should stay and support Mizell—he was, after all, fighting on Sophie's behalf. Why, he was a hero! And Quint thought Mizell had ulterior motives.

"Amber, *wait!*"

She heard Quint's voice, but she didn't slacken her pace. Sophie's feet barely hit the ground as they skimmed along, knifing through the crowd gathering to watch the goings-on. All Amber had on her mind was Sophie's safety.

She was beginning to believe Quint was right about at least one thing: Sophie was apparently in some kind of peril. First the woman at the dress shop, then this man...

Sophie lagged. Amber snatched the little girl up into her arms, barely breaking stride to do it, and rushed on.

QUINT WAS TORN.

He wanted to follow Amber and Sophie, but he also wanted to hang around to see the tussling two-some versus the gorillas. Damn, he'd pay big money to watch that!

Now Amber had been swallowed up by the crowd and there was no telling where she was headed or what she would do when she got there. With a last longing glance at King Kong and a mentally trans-mitted command to *Sic 'em, big fellow,* he turned his back on the spectacle and took off in the direction Amber had dragged Sophie.

He caught up with them outside the Polar Bear Plunge. When he called her name, Amber didn't even look around. Running up alongside her, he touched her arm.

She screamed, saw who it was and flung herself and Sophie against his chest. His arms closed around her as if they had a will of their own. He felt Amber tremble, even with Sophie squashed between them. Burrowing her face into his shoulder, she moaned.

Protectiveness welled up in his chest. Damn, he wanted to just stand here holding them safe. He would protect her from everything that threatened her, and when the threat had passed, he would—

"Oh-hh! Ouch! You're crunching me, Quin!"

He took a step back and looked down at the little girl curled between his body and that of her mother. "Sorry about that, honey."

Amber kissed her daughter's temple. She was still breathing hard, but in control again. "Are you all right, baby? Did that bad man hurt you?"

Sophie looked surprised. "That man wanted my penny."

Amber and Quint exchanged guarded glances. "Uh...was that my aunt Octavia's special penny you threw into the gorilla enclosure?" Quint asked, afraid to breathe until she answered.

Sophie grinned. "That was old candy." She burst into delighted laughter.

Quint sagged with relief. His brain was clearing. For now everything was all right. "Listen, I think we'd better get back to see if anybody's rescued those two guys from the gorillas."

"Are you sure it's safe?" Amber glanced pointedly at Sophie.

"Sweetheart, there must have been a hundred people crowded around and more coming. There's safety in numbers." He waited for her to reprimand him for calling her "sweetheart."

She didn't. All she said was, "If you're sure." Taking Sophie's hand, she turned her trusting gaze upon him.

Quint felt himself grow another three inches taller. Everything she said or did affected him so much more than he expected. There was something about her that spoke to him, called to him.

Unsettled by the strength of his feelings, he reached down to swing Sophie up onto his shoulders. She squealed with delight and grabbed his hair with both hands.

They set off, walking fast. After a few minutes Quint took Amber's hand, ostensibly to guide her onto the proper fork of the path. She didn't pull away, nor did she acknowledge his touch. He felt *her* touch all the way up his arm.

Back at the gorilla habitat, they found excited on-lookers milling around. Several security guards were also on hand, but the combatants were nowhere to be seen.

Quint, with Sophie still clutching his hair, turned to his nearest neighbor, who happened to be a sailor. "Did you see what happened?" he inquired, trying to make it sound like idle curiosity. "I heard some-body climbed in with the gorillas."

The sailor laughed. "More like fell in. Two of 'em, actually. They were fighting about something and just toppled over the fence. Craziest thing I ever saw. It looked for a while like that big bull gorilla over there was gonna have himself a high old time, but the guards came and broke it up."

"Did they arrest the two men?"

"I think they would have if they could'a caught 'em. Those two guys climbed back out and one took off that way—" he pointed "—and the other took off *that* way." He pointed in the opposite direction.

"I don't suppose anybody knows what they were fighting about?"

"I don't." The sailor shrugged. "Guess the show's over." He touched the brim of his white cap and turned to leave.

"Look, Mama," Sophie said clearly, "a swab jockey."

The sailor whirled, gave Quint a challenging glare, got an embarrassed shrug in return. Tipping his hat to a jauntier angle, the sailor swaggered away.

"Thanks, Sophie." Quint rolled his eyes back in a vain attempt to see the kid clinging to his shoulders. "You trying to get me in trouble with the navy?"

"My daddy was a swab jockey," she said, and began to cry. "My daddy gave me pennies to keep."

Feeling like a jerk all over again, Quint swung her down onto her feet. Wanting to comfort her but feeling awkward, he knelt and cautiously put his arms around her. His gaze met Amber's and he was surprised to see tears in her eyes.

Damn. He'd screwed up again.

QUINT LED THEM to the nearest vendor, bought lemonades all around, then found a shady bench where they could conference. While he stood over them, Amber and Sophie settled down side by side.

Amber still felt dazed by all that had happened, but especially by the comfort she'd taken from the feel of Quint's hand closing over hers. She'd needed that comfort just then, and was astounded that he'd seemed to know it.

Quint cleared his throat. "About that swab jockey remark…"

Amber patted Sophie's hand. "Sophie's father was in the navy before she was born. He always called sailors 'swab jockeys,' and I guess he could because he was one. She didn't mean anything by it."

His struggle to remain stern showed on his face. "Okay, but I don't think it's a good idea to call sailors names. Next time there could be more than one of them. Okay, Sophie?"

She nodded. "Okay, Quin." She cocked her head. "How 'bout jar heads? How 'bout doggies? How 'bout—"

"Stop!" Amber stifled laughter. "Don't say any of those things, honey. It was just Daddy's joke."

"Oh." Sophie looked confused. "Okay."

Quint folded his long legs to kneel in front of her, which meant he was also kneeling in front of Amber. Overcome by a sudden, inexplicable desire to run her fingers through his dark hair, she nervously thrust her hands into the big patch pockets of her skirt.

"Sophie, you know what the bad man wanted, right?"

"Oh, yes," she said in a piping voice. "My pennies."

"That's right. And the lady this morning—"

"You said that's no lady, Quin."

"I stand corrected. That *woman* also wanted the special penny, the one you picked up the other day at Sterling's. Remember? That's the department store where some clumsy oaf dropped a whole tray of money."

Amber stifled a giggle. "I wouldn't call him a clumsy *oaf*...exactly."

"Generally speaking, then." He returned her smile before resuming his conversation with the child. "Sophie, you're a bright girl. I'm sure you've figured out that that there are a lot of people who want that special penny."

She thought about that for a moment, her rosebud lips pursed. Then she nodded. "You, too," she announced. "Huh, Quin?"

He groaned. "Yes, me, too. But I don't want it for myself, I want it for my aunt Octavia. It belongs to her. Those bad people only want it because it's worth a lot of money."

"Worth a whole penny," Sophie agreed. She glanced at her mother. "Is Mizell a bad people?"

"Oh, no, honey, Mizell is our friend."

"But he wants my penny?"

She was obviously getting confused—and so was Amber. "He didn't want your penny, he wanted to help you. He was trying to make the bad man leave you alone."

Quint let out an exasperated grunt. "Amber, you live in la-la land. That Mizell kid was fighting the other guy for the *penny,* not for Sophie."

"He was not!"

"He was, too!"

"Hey!" Sophie looked anxious. "Don't fight."

Amber shot Quint an accusing glance. "We're not, Sophie. We just want you to be especially careful about strangers."

"That's right," Quint agreed. "And Sophie, one more time— *do* you have Aunt Octavia's missing penny? Tell the truth, okay? This is really important."

Sophie caught her lower lip between tiny white teeth. She looked at her mother, then at the ground, then at her hands twisting in her lap. When she finally met Quint's steady gaze, her own was earnest and open.

She was going to own up to it, Amber thought, shocked but eager to have this whole thing over with.

"Tell the truth," Quint repeated gently. "Do you have Aunt Octavia's special penny?"

"No, Quin," Sophie said serenely. "I only got *my* pennies." Tears slipped down her round cheeks. "But you took them and now my daddy will never come back. You took them away!"

She began to weep. He gathered her into his arms, looking completely miserable. He obviously didn't know what Amber knew; that to Sophie, any penny she touched instantly became *her* penny.

She wouldn't know Aunt Octavia's ownership rights from the Man in the Moon's.

So it wasn't quite over, after all.

QUINT FOLLOWED THEM HOME in his car. When he'd suggested it, Amber hadn't objected, which was an indication to him of how worried she was about the day's events.

Once safely inside her little house, she seemed almost embarrassed.

"Thank you for everything you've done," she said.

"Glad to." He really was, and not just because he wanted the penny back. "Hell, it was my fault anyway. If I hadn't put that item in the newspaper—"

"I don't blame you for that," she said quickly. "You couldn't know that anyone would be able to figure out who Sophie was just from that."

"Yeah, that is strange. Well, I guess I should be going."

"I suppose." She hesitated, looking through the window into the backyard. Sophie was happily sailing up into the sky on a homemade swing suspended from a bar hung between two palm trees. "Unless…you'd like to stay for dinner."

*Would he!* "Yeah," he said coolly, "that'd be nice."

Her sudden smile sparkled. "Maybe I should tell you I'm not much of a cook before you commit yourself."

As if that mattered. "I'm willing to take a chance." Hell, he thought indulgently, she was probably just being modest.

She wasn't being modest. She burned the grilled cheese sandwiches, although she did trim off the black parts. The salad had everything but the kitchen sink tossed into the bowl, including a wide variety of raw vegetables and bits of leftover peas and corn. The vinaigrette she'd "whipped up" practically shriveled his taste buds, but he smiled and said, "Mmm, good," and gamely kept eating.

Sophie ate her salad without dressing. Now Quint knew why.

Dessert was a slice of angel cake, thankfully from a grocery store shelf. Quint didn't want to think about what she'd do to a pie.

After supper, he supposed he should go, but he couldn't bring himself to make the move. He'd just wait until she threw him out, he decided, settling into a worn overstuffed chair in the living room while she bathed Sophie.

He burned with curiosity about this woman and her life. She was unlike anyone he'd ever known, really. He even liked her precocious daughter.

But they seemed so...alone. Amber and Sophie against the world. What had their lives been like when Sophie's father had been alive? Had he sat in this chair, looked around this crowded living room with its tables and sewing machines and piles of fabric and wondered how he'd gotten so lucky?

Sophie ran out of the hall, laughing and shaking wet hair until droplets flew in all directions. She wore a long blue nightgown with silvery stars painted on it.

"Mama said tell you good-night." Without even slowing down, she threw herself onto his lap and wrapped her arms around his neck. Planting a firm kiss on his cheek, she giggled and slid off again.

Quint just sat there, stunned, still smelling the warm little kid scent of bath bubbles and toothpaste. For the first time in his thirty-odd years, he understood at least a little of what it must feel like to be a father.

And also for the first time, he realized that the something missing from his life was all tied up with the feelings this little girl and her mother brought surging to the fore.

They were making him want things he'd sworn never to consider seriously. Maybe he should get while the getting was good....

WHEN AMBER REEMERGED from tucking Sophie into bed, she found Quint sitting in Johnny's favorite chair. He was leaning forward with his forearms braced on his knees, his hands clasped and a thoughtful, faraway look in his blue eyes.

She stopped to gaze at him, her hands on her hips. "Are you all right?"

He jerked upright. "Yeah, sure. I guess I was...thinking."

"About the penny?"

He hesitated. "Yeah, that, too. Is Sophie in bed?"

"Yes." Now it was Amber's turn to hesitate. She should thank him for everything he'd done and send him on his way. But she couldn't bring herself to do it. She'd underestimated how much she'd enjoy a man's presence in this house again, even for a few hours. "Would you like a glass of wine?" she asked spontaneously.

He looked pleased. "That sounds great. Want me to open it?"

"It's already open," she said, heading for the kitchen. "It's in the refrigerator—supermarket special, as a matter of fact." She returned moments later with two water tumblers full of white wine. She offered him one with a smile and an explanation. "I don't have any wineglasses. Hope you don't mind."

"Not at all." He took his glass and raised it. "What shall we drink to?"

She considered. "How about to the return of that blasted penny—pronto!"

They drank. *Now what?* she wondered. It had been a long time since she'd spent time with an eligible man when she herself was also eligible.

He gestured toward the piles of fabric. "Tell me about your business."

"That's not a simple thing to do."

"I don't need simple."

"The story of my business is also kind of like the story of my life." She was hedging—why? She wasn't ashamed of anything she'd done. "It's long and doesn't always make sense."

"I'd still like to hear it." He sipped his wine. "Were you born in San Diego?"

"No." Sinking onto the sagging couch, she watched him carefully. She saw nothing but genuine interest. "I'm from the Bay area originally—San Francisco," she said finally. "I was put into foster care when I was just a kid—younger than Sophie is now. That's where I grew up, in a series of foster homes. I've been on my own since I was sixteen and decided to head south. I stopped off in Bakersfield and Los Angeles and ended up here five or six years ago."

"Sixteen." He shook his head as if he could hardly believe it.

She shrugged. "I've always been self-reliant." What she'd also been was wild. "Which is a good thing because I don't have a lot of education and what little I did get wasn't all that great. I'm very lucky in one sense, though."

"And that is?" He leaned back in his chair, his probing gaze upon her.

"All it took was a few art classes early on for me to discover what I like to do and what I'm good at."

"And that is?" he said again.

"Wearable art. I learned to sew in high school and I've always made my own clothes, but I never thought of it as a business until…" Oh, why was she telling him all this?

Because she always made snap judgments about people, that's why. And her judgment about Quintin Sterling was that he was a decent guy who could be trusted.

"Until what?" he asked softly. "Go on, Amber. I'm really interested, in case you can't tell."

She could tell. "I never thought of getting into business until I went to work for Nicole and got to know her. We became friends. I worked there while I was pregnant. When I started to show, she let me wear my own clothes—the stuff I made, because it was so comfortable. Before that, she'd insisted I wear clothing from her store, and she gave me a fantastic discount to do it."

To this day, Amber could hardly believe what had happened next. "I honestly liked the clothes I made better than the hot designer stuff, and so did the customers. Half the people who came in wanted to buy what I was wearing, so when I had to stop working, Nicole commissioned me to make up a few things for special customers."

"And that was the beginning of One in a Million," he concluded.

"Yes. Every piece that went out with my label was unique, made and embellished by me. They sold faster than Nicole could get them on the racks."

"What happened after Sophie was born?"

Amber chewed on her lower lip. "I just couldn't leave her in day care and go back to work. Besides, I was much more valuable to Nicole doing what I'd been doing—designing and sewing and embellishing. When she said she'd like to carry my line and would take everything I could turn out, I jumped at the opportunity.''

"And that's what you've been doing." He toyed with his glass, took another sip. "When did Octavia get into the act?''

"About a year ago. She seemed really shocked when I told her I had no interest in Sterling's having an exclusive on my line.''

"I can understand loyalty." His blue eyes were warmly approving.

She lifted her chin stubbornly. "Nicole helped me out when I needed it. Now my line is her biggest seller.''

"And that's your only reason for refusing Octavia—because she wants exclusivity?''

"Well, since I'm being painfully honest...''

"Please do.''

"I don't much care for the way your aunt talks to me, like I'm just some—like I'm just some tarty bimbo who got lucky." She felt her cheeks grow warm with resentment.

Quint groaned. "That's the way she talks to everyone, I'm sorry to say. She doesn't mean anything by it—I hope.''

Amber shrugged. "It doesn't matter, because I'm not going to do it." She stood suddenly. "Do you think it's getting a little warm in here?''

He looked surprised. "Not really.''

"Well, I do.''

Without another word, she crossed to the double sliding-glass doors and stepped out onto the patio.

Stars twinkled in a black sky and the night air carried the fragrance of flowers.

It was all very romantic. And scary, when he followed her.

His low voice came from out of the shadows behind her. "How did you meet your husband?"

*Why not? Why not tell him everything?* She was already committed. "Rollerblading in Balboa Park. He was with friends, I was with friends, somebody knew somebody—"

"Was it love at first sight?" he asked lightly.

"Actually, it was lust at first sight." She turned away restlessly. "Look, Johnny was a sweet guy and a wonderful father, but I don't want to talk about him."

"Because you're not over him."

"No," she said sharply, "because he wanted to marry me and I didn't want to be tied down. But then I got pregnant with Sophie and I was scared to death to go through all that alone."

"So you married him, after all."

"That's right. At the time I thought being pregnant was the worst thing that had ever happened to me. If a husband would tie me down, how do you think I felt about a helpless *baby?* But the minute I held Sophie in my arms, it was love at first hug."

"She's a great kid."

He moved closer, so close she could feel the essence of him as if it were a physical touch. Breathlessly she said, "So, tell me about you."

"Me." He sounded almost rueful. "I guess you could say I was born with a silver spoon in my mouth. I've never had to struggle very hard for anything.''

"Fine family, fine education, fine prospects."

"Does that...annoy you?"

She considered. "No," she said at last. "You just happen to be one of life's golden boys. Enjoy it. I would."

She felt his hands settle on her shoulders, felt the light brush of his breath against her ear when he spoke.

"Enjoy it. That sounds like good advice."

He turned her around to face him. She stood in front of him, paralyzed, thinking that she hadn't been kissed since Johnny died and this man was surely going to kiss her. She fought to keep her eyes from drifting shut, her body from swaying toward his.

He pressed his lips to the spot where her shoulder curved into her neck. She sighed, feeling all the starch flow out of her, leaving her limp and needy. She had never felt quite this way before, not even back in the beginning with Johnny.

"Quint?"

She whispered his name and he responded by kissing his way up her throat to the corner of her mouth. Lightly he explored with tiny, get-acquainted kisses while his hands began an exploration of their own.

He stared down at her. "Amber," he said in a deep, intense voice before lowering his head. When his lips touched hers—

A car door slammed, the sound echoing through the still night air.

They both froze, holding their pose, waiting.

And what they were waiting for came: the sound of running feet followed by the roar of an engine and the squeal of peeling tires.

# 6

IN THE UNCERTAIN illumination of the dome light, Amber stared at the interior of her old car—or at what *used* to be the interior of her old car. Now it looked like the interior of a junkyard. Stuffing spilled from seats slashed and laid open. A gaping glove compartment revealed an empty cavern; even the contents of the box of drawing tools she always carried in the back seat had been tossed on the ground outside. Several of Sophie's toys and Amber's old tan shawl added to the mess.

"Trashed." Quint sounded incredulous. "They completely trashed your car."

"I feel sick." She grabbed the car door for support. "Do you think they were after the penny or simply looking for anything worth stealing?"

"Vandals or crooks... That's a great choice." He put his arm around her shoulders and pulled her close to his side. "Looks like the cops will have to decide when we report this."

"What's the point? The police are after bigger fish."

"It's their job, Amber." He slammed the car door, cloaking the pitiful sight in darkness. Turning her toward the gate so they could go in through the back door as they'd come out, he added, "We've got to call this in, you know."

She sighed. "All right." She let him lead her a few steps, taking comfort from his arm still around her shoulders. She couldn't resist adding, "But after the last police visit, I think you're wasting your time."

"I WASTED MY TIME."

Amber looked around at the sound of his voice and saw him standing in the kitchen door. She gave him a tired smile. "Hate to say I told you so, but I told you so."

"You were right. Pennies and old cars are not on the average policeman's list of pressing concerns."

"Why am I not surprised?"

He crossed to where she stood in front of an open window, breathing in the soft night air and trying to calm down. The invasion of her car had shaken her more than she cared to admit. The car wasn't worth much, but it had been *hers*.

He put his arms around her and she stiffened. "Please don't do that."

He withdrew his touch. "Why not? When we were so rudely interrupted, we were just about to—"

"I know what we were just about to do, but we didn't. It's too late to get back into that now."

"It's never too late," he said, his blue eyes gleaming.

"The moment's passed," she insisted, "and so has this evening. You'd better go, Quint."

He looked shocked. "I can't go off and leave you here alone when somebody just broke into your car."

"They didn't break into it, actually, since it wasn't locked. All they did was trash it."

"Do you lock your house?" he inquired sharply.

"Of course. I didn't just fall off a turnip truck." She straightened her shoulders. "I know how to take care of myself, and Sophie, too."

"Don't need any help from a *man,* is that it?"

Their gazes met and held. Then she said, very softly, "I haven't so far. Go home, Quint. Thank you for everything, but go home."

His face tightened. "I'm leaving under duress."

"Duress duly noted."

"If anything happens to you, it won't be my fault."

"Like I'd blame you! Like anyone would blame you. You're not responsible for me."

"So why do I feel as if I am?" He turned toward the front door, eyes bleak. "What if they come back?"

"Do vandals often return to the scene of the crime?" She opened the door and tried to wave him through.

"I don't think that was the work of vandals. I think it was somebody looking for the penny. Since they didn't find it in your car—they didn't, did they?"

She took a long, exasperated breath. "I have no idea what they found, since I hadn't held an inventory recently, but I sincerely doubt it was the penny."

"Then the next place they'll want to look is inside your house. And if you're inside when that happens—"

"Good night, Quint."

"But—"

"Good *night*, Quint."

After he was gone, she stood there for a few moments, trying to breathe slowly and calmly. He could be right, couldn't he? And if he was...

A RAPPING ON THE WINDOW of his BMW awakened Quint the following morning. He'd spent a miserable night twisted like a pretzel on the front seat of his car before finally falling into an equally miserable sleep.

He opened bleary eyes to find Amber bending to peer at him. He'd left his car window open to the pleasant night air, so she was very close. He could see every detail of her face: the smooth skin and tender lips curved in a disbelieving smile. The dimple flashed in her left cheek.

"I can't believe this," she exclaimed. "Were you here all night?"

He yawned and stretched. "I didn't feel right about leaving you alone."

"But nothing happened."

"How do you know it wasn't my very presence that prevented something from happening?"

"I guess I don't, but that's a real long shot."

"Long shots are my specialty." He looked at her expectantly.

"All right," she mumbled, but the dimple betrayed her. "You're invited for breakfast. It's the least I can do."

"It certainly is."

Following her inside, he tried not to feel *too* smug.

AMBER BRANNIGAN was a truly rotten cook.

She'd warned him about that but he hadn't completely believed her, not even after his first meal in this house.

Now he *knew* she couldn't boil water without burning it, but it didn't matter. He was so entranced with her that he could be eating charcoal and probably wouldn't notice. Which was a very good thing, because the pancakes she set in front of him were charred around the edges.

Sophie was already digging into her stack, which didn't look a lot better than his. Reluctantly, he picked up his fork.

"Don't wait for me," Amber said cheerfully. She tossed the dish towel she'd been using in the general direction of the cabinet. "I'm going to squeeze some oranges for juice."

He followed the flight of the towel to its unintended destination: the electric stove. It settled unerringly on a burner and promptly burst into flame.

"Fire!"

She blinked, turned, saw the blazing towel, picked it up by a corner and dropped it into the pan of dishwater in the sink. She performed this ritual with such calm efficiency that he could only believe it was a frequent occurrence.

"You do like orange juice?" She reached for a

basket of oranges on the counter. "I only like fresh-squeezed myself."

"I don't think they let people live in California if they don't like orange juice."

She smiled. Then her glance shifted to his plate and she frowned. "Something wrong with the pancakes?"

"No, nothing." Maybe if he used a lot of syrup...

By the time she placed a big tumbler of orange juice—and pith and seeds—in front of him, he'd managed to consume most of what was on his plate. Charcoal, he vaguely remembered hearing somewhere, was actually good for the human body. Or at least, it wasn't poisonous.

"Orange juice, Sophie?"

The little girl pushed her plate back. "I wanna go play now."

"What do you say, then?"

"Can I be excused, *please?*"

"You may."

Sophie scampered away and Amber sat down. The small round table was *so* small that her knee nudged his.

"Sorry," she said.

"Don't be." Hell, he liked it. Footsies would be all right, too.

*Anything* would be all right with this woman, he realized, for he was, as Aunt Octavia would say, smitten.

She set her glass of juice on the table and picked up her fork. "I'm sure you have a lot to do today, since you lost most of yesterday following me around," she said kindly. "If you need to go now, don't let me keep you. As you can see, we're perfectly all right."

"Trying to get rid of me?"

"Sort of."

He groaned. "You're either the most honest woman I've ever met or—" *The shiftiest*, but he didn't want to say that. Her apparent lack of personal interest in him would be crushing to a less secure ego.

Her golden-brown eyes remained perfectly cool and self-possessed. "I try to be honest," she said. "I don't always succeed."

He frowned. "Why do you want to get rid of me? I can be very handy to have around."

"Can you? I rather thought you'd be a distraction."

He liked that.

"Besides," she went on, "I'm sure you have a million things to do. Did your aunt expect you home last night?"

"I called her on my cell phone." Besides which, she was used to him keeping peculiar hours. He had an extremely active social life and a large circle of friends—women friends, mostly.

"That's good." She looked puzzled. "I have the feeling you're…waiting for something."

He was; for a good idea that would either keep him here or give him some reason to see her again. Soon.

"I can't go until we work something out about your car," he said.

"What about it?"

"It's trashed. How will you get around?"

"I've already figured that out," she said calmly. "It'll still run, so all I have to do is put a few old pillows on the seats."

He groaned. "I can't let you—"

"It's not up to you, Quint."

"But—"

"Don't start telling me how responsible you feel," she said, the corners of her mouth curving down. "We've been there. It's time for you to go." When he made no move to do so, she frowned. "What are you waiting for?"

Inspiration struck with blinding intensity. "I'm waiting for the nerve to ask you something."

Her eyes widened. "You, lacking nerve? You're joking."

He licked his lips; he wasn't joking at all. Nor did he have reason to be nervous about this. No woman in her right mind would turn down an invitation to the social event of the season: the annual Seagull Charity Ball. He'd finally hit upon the ploy to gain what he was after. Of course, he'd have to figure out what to do with the date he already had, but good old Trudy Ebersoll would understand.

"Amber," he said, anticipating her delight, "I'd like to take you to the Seagull Charity Ball on Saturday night. Maybe you've read about it in the newspaper."

"I don't think so."

He blinked in surprise. "But… Everybody will be there. Lots of good food, good music, good booze."

"Sounds like the social event of the season."

Ah, he had her! What woman could resist the social event of the season? "So you'll go with me?"

"No."

"You're kidding!"

"No, thank you?"

His jaw dropped and he stared.

She shrugged. "It's nothing personal. I've never liked big formal affairs."

Past the initial shock, he found his voice. "Have you ever gone to a party like this?"

"Well, no, but I wouldn't like it."

"What *do* you like, Amber?"

"Now I've hurt your feelings." Picking up his plate and her own, she carried them to the sink. Turning to face him, she looked contrite. "You've been very kind to me and I'm sorry, but I just don't want to get all dressed up and go to a party where I know I'll feel out of place."

"You wouldn't be out of place. I'd be there."

"It's a kind thought. Goodbye, Quint."

"Amber—"

"Goodbye, Quint. And thank you for looking out for us, but we'll be just fine."

She'd not only turned down one of the most sought-after invitations of the year, but she was throwing him out again, to boot. Why was he wasting his time with this woman?

Over and above the search for the missing penny, of course.

HE FOUND OCTAVIA in the solarium, enjoying coffee and scones and properly squeezed and strained orange juice. When he entered, she looked up with a disapproving frown.

Jiggs darted forward to attach himself to Quint's right sock. Quint tried to shake the animal loose with the usual lack of success.

Octavia's smile was pained. "Have a nice evening?" she asked with a touch of sarcasm.

"Nice enough." Dragging Jiggs along, Quint crossed to the sideboard to pour coffee and juice. "How about you?"

"I had a miserable evening, and night, too." Her eyes were moist. "Quint, do you think we'll ever get my penny back?"

He sat stiffly across the glass table from her, the effects of an uncomfortable night kicking in big time. "Aunt Octavia, I honestly believe we'll get your penny back." Or another one just like it if he could find one.

"But what if we don't?" She was now on the verge of full-blown tears. "If that miserable child took it, and I'm convinced she did, there's no telling where it is now."

"Hey, Sophie's a nice little kid."

"That nice little kid could have spent my precious penny on bubble gum!"

"You haven't priced bubble gum lately."

"Don't joke, Quintin." She dabbed at her eyes with the corner of a snowy linen napkin.

"Sorry." He covered a yawn with his hand. "I've got to get dressed and go into the office now. But I want you to know I'm doing everything humanly possible to get that penny back, including double checking the batch I brought here from the Brannigan house.''

Octavia's face became set in stern lines. ''I may have to take a hand in this myself.''

''Now, Aunt Octavia.'' He didn't want her upsetting Amber, or herself, if he could help it.

''No, no.'' She waved his protest aside. ''I'll be subtle.''

''How subtle?'' He gave her a dubious glance.

''I'm going to speak to *that woman* again about her line of clothing. It will give me an excuse to subtly inquire about the penny.''

''Subtle, huh.'' He wasn't sure she knew the meaning of that word, but if he just happened to be around, he'd have a built-in excuse to see Amber again. ''I suppose if you insist...''

''Besides, I want One in a Million exclusively in Sterling's,'' she said, lifting her chin to a regal angle. ''Not as much as I want my penny back, of course, but quite a lot.''

There was something Quint wanted quite a lot, too, he admitted to himself as he took the stairs two at a time, Jiggs scrabbling after him.

He wanted Amber Brannigan.

QUINT HAD BEEN ATTENDING big formal parties all his life. First he'd been invited as his parents' son, then as an eligible man who moved in the right circles. As a result, he was perfectly at ease at the annual Seagull Charity Ball.

So was his date.

Trudy Ebersoll's family blood was at least as blue as Quintin's, and they'd known each other practically since childhood. Their parents had moved in the same social circles.

Quint had watched Trudy grow into the kind of woman he'd always found devastatingly attractive: tall, blond, cool and sophisticated.

Amber was a blonde at the moment.

He gritted his teeth, sorry he'd thought about her. She wasn't *actually* a blonde, although she looked damn good as one. He thought she was probably a redhead, as she'd been the first time he'd seen her, but he couldn't be sure.

He knew everything there was to know about Trudy.

He hardly knew anything about Amber.

"More champagne, Quintin, darling?"

Trudy held out a flute filled with bubbly golden wine and he took it with a polite nod. She moved with a kind of elegant grace that bespoke years of dance lessons, tennis lessons, swimming lessons. Whatever could be taught, Trudy had been sent to learn. In later years she'd studied in London and Paris and could converse fluently in French. She held the title of vice president in her father's land development company.

She regarded him with tilted brows. "You look as if you're here, but I don't think you really are," she said.

"Sorry." He sipped the wine, which wasn't his favorite, but good enough.

"Is it the penny?" she asked.

Quint leaned back against the stone balustrade overlooking formal gardens. From beyond the open French doors he heard the orchestra strike up another tune.

"The penny?" Trudy nudged his arm.

He nodded belatedly. "Aunt Octavia's really upset about that."

"I thought the reward might bring some action," she mused. "But if a child took it—"

"We're not sure of that," Quint cut in. He was getting tired of hearing Sophie maligned.

"Whatever." She set her glass on the stone balustrade.

In the moonlight she looked elegant though painfully thin. Funny, he'd never noticed that about Trudy before. Amber, on the other hand, was a fully rounded armful...

"Okay," Trudy said shortly, "who is she?"

"Who's who?" But he felt guilty acting innocent.

"The woman who's on your mind. Don't play cute with me, Quintin Sterling."

"It's nothing, Trudy, really." Embarrassed, he cast about for a change of subject. "Would you like to dance?"

"No, I'd like to know who has you all tied up in knots. I've waited a long time for this to happen, Quintin. I'd like to savor this victory for women everywhere."

He glared at her. "That's cold, Trudy."

"Maybe. Why didn't you bring her to this party instead of me?"

"Hey, what kind of a louse do you think I am? I'd already invited you before I ever met her."

"I think you're the nicest kind of louse. But I would have understood."

She cupped his chin with one hand and gave him a quick sisterly kiss on the lips.

Which made him feel he owed her at least minimal honesty. "Actually," he said, "I did invite her. "

"And?" Trudy glanced around as if she expected to find another woman skulking behind the potted palms.

"She turned me down."

"She turned you—" Trudy burst into laughter, well-bred to be sure, but still stinging. "Whyever for?"

"She said she doesn't like getting all dressed up for big parties."

"Who does?"

"Now that you mention it..." He frowned. "I thought *you* did."

She made a face. "I used to, I suppose, but things are...well, they're changing. Which is why I'm glad you've found someone to replace old faithful." She tapped herself on the low V-neckline of her slinky black gown.

"I said she turned me down," he reminded her.

"Charm will win out in the end," she predicted. "Quint, I'm trying to tell you something here."

"Such as?"

"I've found someone."

"Someone for what?"

She caught her breath. "To love me, I hope."

"My God!" He stared at her, aghast. He'd always been able to count on Trudy; she'd always been there to take up the slack between liaisons. Somewhere in the back of his mind he might even have harbored the belief that someday the two of them might— "Who is it? Reg? David?"

She shook her head. "No one you know, actually."

"We know the same people."

She smiled. "Except for your girl and my guy."

His girl? He wished. "So who's the lucky man?"

"He's a policeman."

Quint gaped. "A *policeman?* Did your father have a heart attack when he found out?"

"No, but he will when I tell him we're moving in together." She raised one brow. "Only until I can talk Jim into marrying me, of course."

"Trudy, I don't know what to say." He didn't, either. Nothing could have surprised him more. Ritzy Trudy Ebersoll marrying a working stiff? Would wonders never cease.

"Just say you're happy for me," she suggested. "And I'll say, 'Go forth and do likewise.'"

"Sounds like a plan."

"Then why are you standing here?" She made graceful shooing gestures. "You don't want to be here any more than I do. Why don't you go see what your mystery woman is up to?"

Energy shot through his body at the suggestion. "Wouldn't you like me to drive you home?"

"There are plenty of people here to do that. You

run along." He started moving and she called after him, "I'll invite you to the wedding!"

"I'll be there," he called back, but he was thinking forward.

It was after ten when he left the ball and after ten-thirty before he neared Amber's little house in Normal Heights. She was probably already in bed, he warned himself, trying to prepare for disappointment. And if she was awake, what was he going to say to her? "I was just in the neighborhood—in my tuxedo..." She'd go for that one, sure.

He turned onto her street and sure enough, her house was dark. Shutting off the engine, he coasted to a stop at the curb and stared at the dark silhouette of the house. There were no streetlights nearby and clouds covered the moon. The entire neighborhood was eerily quiet.

Which was probably why he heard the faint *click-click* coming from somewhere in the shadow of the house. He tensed. Was someone trying to break in? He hesitated, unsure how best to proceed. Then he heard it again: *click-click*. Shifting for a different view, he saw a faint ray of illumination that might have come from a penlight blinking on, then off.

Quint turned off the interior light before, very slowly and carefully, easing open the car door. Stepping onto the street, he paused to close the door as quietly as he'd opened it. Crouching, he circled to the back of the car and squatted.

He caught movement out of the corner of his eye and shifted in that direction. For a moment his gaze couldn't penetrate the shadows near Amber's carport, but suddenly the clouds shifted and a nearly full moon burst forth in all its glory.

He saw a tall, skinny form hunker down and start around the back of Amber's car, heading toward the house next door.

Son of a bitch! It was Mizell, sure as anything, skulking around where he had no business being. Infuriated, Quint stood abruptly.

"Hey!" He roared it, wanting to scare the kid bad enough that he'd think twice about messing with Amber again. "You! Come out with your hands up!"

The head atop the string bean of a body jerked around. The kid let out a frightened yelp and started running. So much for an easy surrender. Quint took off after him, righteous indignation lending wings to his heels.

He caught up with Mizell halfway between his house and Amber's, and stopped him with a low tackle. They went down heavily, Quint on top, and he knew he'd knocked the air out of the little bastard. He scrambled to his knees, grabbed the front of the sagging T-shirt and yanked.

"What the hell do you think you're doing at Amber's house?" he demanded, shaking the kid like a rag doll. "I ought to—"

"Lemme go!" the kid howled, raising his arms to protect his face and head from blows that had not been struck. "You got no right!"

"We'll see what right I have." Quint got to his feet without releasing his captive, then hauled him up, as well. "C'mon." He hustled the kid toward Amber's dark house.

"Hey, I wanna go home. You can't make me—"

"Watch me." Quint growled with gut deep sincerity. He gave the kid a shove that took him right up to the step in front of Amber's door. "We'll see what the police have to say about you skulking around your neighbor's house in the pitch dark. Ring the doorbell."

"It's too late," Mizell whined. "Amber's asleep. She'll be mad."

"Not when she realizes what you were up to." Reaching past the narrow shoulders, Quint jabbed at the doorbell.

They waited, the only sound Quint's harsh breathing and Mizell's wheezing gasps. Suddenly the porch light came on, temporarily blinding them. When the door swung in Amber was standing there in her red shorty nightgown, all warm and womanly and sweet with sleep.

"Sheesh!" The exclamation seemed yanked from Mizell.

Quint swatted the kid on the side of his pointy head. "Quit staring, you little creep."

Amber's sleepy eyes blinked wide and she seemed to see the scene in front of her for the first time. "Why, Quint," she said, "what are you doing here—and in a tuxedo, yet."

"Never mind me. I caught this clown coming out of your carport. When I yelled at him, he ran."

"Oh, Quint!" She shook her head in what looked

like disbelief. "Turn Mizell loose. He's here to help me, aren't you, Mizell?"

"I sure am." Mizell pulled loose from Quint's suddenly relaxed grip. "This dude's way outta line. I could—why, I could sue him! He beat the sh—beat the hell outta me. I'd be within my rights if I—"

"You're sure?" Quint demanded grimly of Amber. "You're absolutely one hundred percent sure you want me to turn this idiot loose?"

"I'm sure."

"Okay, but he better get the hell out of here before I lose my head. Then you better tell me what's going on because I'm getting real damn tired of making a fool out of myself on your behalf."

Mizell scurried off the porch into the darkness. For a minute Amber just looked at Quint, her eyes shadowed. Then she opened the screen door, stepped out onto the small porch, put her arms around his neck and kissed him.

# 7

AMBER KISSED HIM because he looked so bewildered, so frustrated...so handsome in his tuxedo with the shirt askew and his hair tousled. And she kissed him because she knew he'd thought he was protecting her, but he wasn't because she didn't need protection.

His bewilderment did not extend to his kissing reflex. No sooner had she slipped her arms around his neck and touched her lips to his than he clamped an arm around her waist and bent her back with enthusiasm. She'd intended a friendly don't-feel-bad-you-made-a-fool-out-of-yourself kiss but that sure wasn't what *he* had in mind. Swept away by his fervor, she hung on tight and kissed him back.

After a long time he lifted his head and looked down at her. "Don't you think we ought to take this inside? Your neighbors are getting an eyeful."

"Oh!" Now she was the one befuddled. Glancing around, she realized she was standing on her doorstep beneath the unforgiving beam of the bare porch light, wearing a red shorty nightgown and kissing a man in a tuxedo. "Yes, of course," she agreed hastily, aware that her neighbor, Neona Jones, would not be amused. "Come inside."

He followed her into the house. When he reached for her again, she jumped back.

"No more of that," she said primly.

He glowered. "Okay, fine. Then tell me why you made me turn that little twerp loose."

"Because he was doing me a favor," she said, wondering why Quint hadn't figured that out already.

"In pitch dark at ten-thirty at night, sneaking around in your carport? Yeah, right, he was *about* to do you a favor."

"Oh, Quintin!" Exasperated, she planted her hands on her hips and frowned. "He was fixing a lock."

"What lock?"

"I'll show you."

She led the way to the back door, which opened into the carport. Swinging the door wide, she pointed to the lock. "The keyhole was jammed. He got most of whatever it was out earlier, but he said he needed a different tool and would come back when he got the chance. I guess he got the chance tonight."

"Gimme a break." Quint knelt to examine the lock and the metal plate surrounding it. "Someone's been messing with this lock," he announced.

"Sophie probably just stuck something in the keyhole. Who else would be messing with—"

"Amber, *look!*"

Grabbing her arm, he dragged her down until she couldn't miss the scratches and gouges on the metal plate.

"So?" she said, confused. "It's an old lock."

"And those are new scratches."

She managed an uncertain laugh. "You don't know that!" He was trying to scare her.

"I *do* know that. See how much brighter the scratches are than the rest of the plate? Someone tried to get in here. The question is, who and when."

"Well, it wasn't Mizell," she said, heatedly defending her young neighbor. He'd been very nice about helping her out lately and she wasn't going to let Quint bad-mouth him.

"Amber Brannigan," he said, "you're going to be the death of me."

He pulled her into his arms and kissed her again, so thoroughly that when he let her go she had to grab the open door for support. Whirling around, he stomped through the carport toward the curb where his car was parked.

"Quint, wait! Why are you wearing a tuxedo?"

He halted at the end of the carport and turned around, arms spread wide. "Because I was at the Seagull Ball and had the sudden insane urge to see you," he said. "Good thing, too. I don't care what spin you put on it, that kid is trouble."

"Let's don't talk about him," she suggested breathlessly, taking a step forward. "I know you're trying to help me and I appreciate everything you've done. It's just…"

He eyed her suspiciously. "Just what, Amber?"

"Just that…Sophie sure would like her pennies back."

For a moment he simply stared at her. Then he grinned, and the tension seemed to flow from his

body. "Okay, I'll see what I can do. Is there anything
Sophie's mother wants that's within my power?"

Oh, my, such a leading question. She lifted her
chin, striving for haughty dignity. This was a stretch
for a woman wearing a short red nightgown. "Not a
thing," she said, "except maybe—except maybe for
you to stop persecuting poor Mizell."

Quint laughed. "Don't worry about poor Mizell.
He's slick enough to take care of himself."

Turning, he sauntered out of the carport. After another yearning moment, Amber went back inside her
house and shut the door.

QUINT SPENT most of Monday hanging around Aunt
Octavia's office and waiting for Amber to show up
for the meeting. She had—reluctantly, Octavia
said—agreed to drop by sometime in the early afternoon.

He didn't intend to miss her. He'd spent all day
Sunday worrying about her and that dippy kid next
door. A dozen times he'd picked up the phone to call
her, then put it down again. He wasn't accustomed
to being at a woman's beck and call. If anything, it
had been the other way around.

Then Amber stepped off the escalator, Sophie in
tow, and Quint nearly went into shock. If it hadn't
been for the little girl, he might not even have recognized her.

Amber's hair was black, jet black, and she wore
oversize sunglasses that further disguised her face.
Of course, both mother and daughter were wearing
One in a Million dresses—he'd come to recognize

her designs by now. Amber's dress was fire engine red with dark ivy vines twining around it and Sophie's was sandy beige, decorated with colorful painted fish.

He forced himself to wait for them to approach, which they had to do because he stood between them and Octavia's door. He greeted them with a smile.

"Fancy meeting you here," he said.

"I have an appointment with your aunt." Amber took off her dark glasses and dropped them into a matching drawstring bag.

She looked tired, and he thought he saw dark circles beneath her eyes. Had anything else happened?

He wouldn't ask. He refused to keep coming back after she'd made it abundantly clear that she didn't welcome his involvement. He could hardly believe it when he heard himself say, "You look tired. Has anything else happened?"

"I guess I am tired. I worked all weekend on a big order for Nicole." She stifled a yawn. "And no, nothing else has happened."

"That's good." He smiled and changed the subject. "It's nice of you to keep humoring my aunt. I know that's what you're doing."

She shrugged. "I don't know a polite way to refuse when she issues one of her summonses." She tightened her grip on Sophie's hand in preparation to move on.

The little girl held back. "Do I have to? Miss Octavie doesn't like me."

"Yes, you have to. And don't get Jiggs all worked

up this time, okay? You know how that upsets Miss Sterling.''

''But—''

''Hey, I've got an idea,'' Quint interjected.

They both looked at him.

''Why don't I baby-sit while you're with Octavia.''

Sophie thrust out her lower lip in a pout. ''I'm no baby!''

''Kid sit, then—girl sit. What do you say, Amber? We've got some special displays in the children's department I think Sophie would like.''

''Please, Mama? Can I please?'' Sophie turned beseeching eyes on her mother.

Amber sighed. ''I suppose you can, if Quint is sure—''

''I'm sure.'' He snatched Sophie's hand from Amber's. ''If we're not back by the time you finish, you can find us in the kids department.''

And he hustled Sophie away. Hell, he thought as they stepped onto the escalator, he owed the kid something for impounding her pennies. This was his chance to pay off, make a few brownie points and maybe even get her to confess.

SAYING NO to Octavia was never easy, although there was no doubt in Amber's mind that yes and no were the only answers the old lady understood. And the answer was never going to be yes when it came to One in a Million. So Amber drank tea and listened respectfully to all the familiar arguments and then said the necessary word as gently as she could. Then she said it a few more times.

Octavia glared across her impressive desk. "Young woman, you are passing up the opportunity of a lifetime," she declared.

Amber sighed. "Probably." She started to rise.

"Not so fast! We have one other little item to discuss."

Amber sat back down. *Now what?*

"There's the little matter of my penny."

Amber groaned. "Miss Sterling, I don't know anything about your penny."

"Quintin is certain that your child stole it."

That was a bit of a shock, to think that Quint hadn't changed his mind. Amber wondered if he would actually consider this a theft if Sophie turned out to be the guilty party. "I've spoken to Sophie about it at least a dozen times. She says she's given back all the pennies she took." Amber stood all the way up this time. "I'm terribly sorry about all this, but I'm getting a little tired of seeing my child persecuted."

"Persecuted!" Octavia huffed. "That is a very valuable penny."

"I know it is, but Sophie is only four years old. I absolutely refuse to let you use thumbscrews on her." Amber turned toward the door.

"You come right back here! I'm not finished talking to—"

For once, Amber wasn't concerned about offending anyone. What did these people expect from her? She'd tried every way she knew to get Sophie to relinquish that penny—if she even had it, which Amber was beginning to doubt.

To heck with it. She opened the office door and stepped through, then stopped short to stare at the apparition in front of her.

QUINT WAITED EXPECTANTLY for Amber's reaction to the fairy creature at his side. He'd turned Sophie loose and she'd chosen a long-sleeved pink silk dress with a sheer overskirt decorated with a big silk chrysanthemum at her waist and smaller flowers around the hem. A fancy zircon tiara anchored her brown hair on top of her head; he'd had to go to Sterling's Beauty Spa to find someone who could attach the thing properly. Pink tights and white patent leather shoes completed the ensemble, though she still carried the little beige drawstring bag over her wrist that had been part of her One in a Million ensemble.

To his confusion, Amber look shocked, rather than charmed.

"My God," she said faintly, "what have you done to my child?"

Quint threw his shoulders back proudly. "I took her to the children's department and told her to pick out anything she wanted."

"But that…that—" she gestured to the mass of pink "—is so *little girl traditional.*"

Quint frowned. This wasn't going the way he'd expected. "She picked it herself," he stated.

Amber looked wounded. "Maybe so, but she's too young to know a bribe when she hears one."

"A bribe!" Quint took a disbelieving step back.

"You think this is a bribe?" It was, of course, but he hadn't expected Amber to state that fact so categorically.

Sophie looked puzzled. "A bride?"

"No, sweetie, a *bribe*. That's when someone gives you something because they want you to give them something back, or do something for them."

The little girl got that familiar stubborn look on her face. "This is *my* dress!" She balled the fluffy sheer layer between small fists.

Amber shook her head. "No, dear, we have to give it back. We can't take something we didn't pay for."

"I'll pay!" Sophie ripped the bag from her wrist and fumbled at the strings.

"You don't understand—" Amber began, but Quint cut her off.

"No, *you* don't understand. I gave that stuff to Sophie. It would be cruel to make her give it back. I don't expect anything in return."

"Here!" Sophie held out her hand and on her palm lay a penny.

Without thinking, Quint snatched it from her. She let out a shriek that rattled off the walls.

"What the hell?" a passing shopper exclaimed.

"Sounds like somebody's hurting that child!" another chimed in. "What's going on? Here, you people, you can't—"

Quint made a quick examination of the penny, saw immediately that it was not Octavia's, and dropped it back onto Sophie's palm as if it were a hot potato. Her cries ceased as abruptly as they'd begun, punctuated by a couple of hiccuppy sobs.

Amber glared at him. "That's as bad as taking candy from babies."

"But I thought she was giving it to me! I got a little carried away, but I wasn't going to *rob* her." Sophie tugged at his sleeve but he was too busy concentrating on Amber to pay any attention.

"And you don't call that horrible outfit a bribe?"

"Horrible! I want you to know that 'horrible outfit' would cost five hundred and thirty-seven dollars, plus loose change, if someone came in to buy it." Sophie continued to tug at his sleeve, but he was too worked up to respond.

"Which no one has, or would, if they were in their right minds and above the age of five." Amber's golden brown eyes snapped. With that short curly black hair, she looked like an entirely different person. "Come, Sophie, you've got to put on your own clothes so we can go home."

"Mama!" Sophie stomped a shiny white shoe. "Quin!"

She had their attention at last. "I want to do it my own self," she said. Taking one of Quin's hands in hers, she deposited the disputed penny in it. "Now this beautiful dress is all mine." She sighed with satisfaction.

Quint looked blankly at Amber, whose shoulders slumped.

"I guess," she said, "the moral to this story is, Don't grab. Wait for it to be offered."

"Some things are never offered," he shot back. "What am I supposed to do then?"

"Do without," she countered. "Come, Sophie, let's go get your old clothes—"

"They're here." Quint offered a shopping bag.

"Thank you. Now we're going home."

"But—"

The door to Octavia's office opened. "What is going on out here?" the old lady demanded. "It sounds like a riot."

Jiggs shot past her and launched himself at Quint's ankle. Sophie squealed and clapped her hands.

"Hi, Jiggs. Wanna go play at my house?"

Octavia bristled. "Don't touch my dog, child."

"Sophie, it's time to go."

The little girl turned on the waterworks again. "I gave Quin my penny," she sobbed. "Why can't I have Jiggs?"

Quint tried to shake off the growling dog while Amber tried to reason with Sophie, who continued to cry. Amber herself looked distraught, which was quite a contrast to her usual calm self, while Octavia was obviously fit to be tied.

And all Quint wanted was to make everybody happy. Hell, that left him at a total loss.

BY THE TIME she got Sophie home, Amber was a nervous wreck. For one thing, her old car was in such a sorry state that even with the aid of several cushions, she could hardly get herself up high enough to see to drive. For another, Sophie wept the whole way, splashing salty tears all over the beautiful silk sewn into that horrible design.

Or was it so horrible?

Had Amber been missing something, where Sophie was concerned? Did the little girl long for more tradition in her life?

That was a shocking possibility to a mother who'd always believed that consistency was, indeed, the hobgoblin of little minds. But maybe Sophie needed more consistency in her life.

Maybe packing up and moving away at this particular time was not in the child's best interest.

But a woman had to do what a woman had to do, right?

QUINT LUGGED Sophie's pennies up onto the small porch and rang Amber's doorbell. It was just about dinnertime and he was counting on that. If she didn't ask him to eat with them—and in the interest of his stomach, he had to pray she wouldn't, he intended to take them both out to dinner.

The sky was the limit. Anywhere they wanted to go....

The door opened and Amber stood there. This close, without the distractions of screaming kids and biting dogs and dotty old ladies, he could see that she had dark circles beneath her eyes and her mouth drooped at the corners.

"Hi," he said. "I brought Sophie's pennies back."

"Oh." For a moment she just stood there and he thought she was going to close the door in his face. Then she sighed and stepped back, gesturing for him to enter.

He carried the heavy canvas tote bags inside and

set them on the floor. The room was its usual mess with bolts and scraps of fabric everywhere, the worn carpet littered with loose threads, clothing on plastic hangers suspended from every curtain rod.

"I'm sorry I kept the pennies so long," he apologized. "We've been through them three times and Octavia's penny just isn't there."

"Why am I not surprised?"

"I don't know. Maybe because you don't think Sophie took it?"

She shrugged. "At this point, I have no idea who took it and I'm beginning to wonder if we'll ever know. Has there been any response to the reward?"

"No."

"Then there you go." She glanced at the canvas bags. "Thank you for returning everything. She's missed her pennies."

"Thank you for—" He broke off with a growl of frustration. "Why are we standing here talking to each other like strangers? How are you, Amber? You look exhausted."

She rolled her shoulders forward as if to ease aching muscles. "I'm tired, that's all. I've been working almost day and night on the last big order. My schedule may be catching up with me."

"Last big order? Does that mean Octavia has finally made a dent in your resolve?"

"No, and she never will. Forget I said that."

"I will if you and Sophie will come out to dinner with me."

Her eyes widened. "Why?"

"Because I think you could use a good meal."

Even if she'd been cooking, which he doubted, she'd *still* need a good meal. "I also happen to enjoy your company. Sophie's, too, of course."

"I don't know…" She glanced at the sewing machine in the corner on a card table overflowing with fabrics.

"You have to eat," he prompted gently.

"What if someone breaks in while we're gone?"

"Did anyone break in when you went to Sterling's earlier today?"

"No, but—"

"And if someone did break in, what could you do about it? You don't have a black belt in karate or anything, do you?"

That drew a reluctant grin, the first he'd seen since his arrival. "No. But sometimes I wish I did."

"Too late. Call Sophie and let's go eat."

She did, and they did.

SOPHIE WORE her pink outfit from Sterling's, although by now her upswept hairstyle was straggling badly. She also received the honor of choosing the restaurant.

She picked Mama Mia's, a local pizzeria. Gray-haired and rotund Mama herself bustled forward to greet them.

"My, my, what a beautiful dress," she said to Sophie. "And a crown, too."

"I'm a princess," Sophie said serenely.

"I can see that," Mama agreed.

Sophie beamed. "I like you," she declared. "Would you care for a penny?"

''That's very generous of you,'' Mama said, ''but I already have several. Is this table all right?''

It was. Waiting for their pizzas—veggie for Amber, Mama's supreme deluxe with extra cheese for Sophie and Quint—he couldn't resist the temptation to probe Sophie's generosity.

''Do you give away lots of pennies?'' he asked her.

She shrugged.

''Where are you carrying your pennies tonight? I notice you didn't bring that little bag you usually have on your wrist.''

Sophie laughed delightedly. ''In my shoe!'' Leaning down, she pulled off a white patent leather Mary Jane and emptied it onto the table. Several pennies tumbled out.

''Sophie!'' Amber plucked the shoe from the red-checked tablecloth. ''You know we don't carry pennies in our shoes or put our shoes on the table.''

''Quin wants to see,'' the little girl protested.

Quint, who was finally learning, made no move to touch the scattered coins. ''May I look at them?'' he asked Sophie. ''I promise to give them back.''

''Sure, Quin.'' She said it as cheerfully as if she'd never heard of little girls who burst into screams when their pennies were touched.

Quickly he examined the coins, then returned them. ''Thanks, honey.''

Amber leaned her elbows on the table. She was looking a bit perkier since they'd left her house, the scene of her labors. ''Not there, huh?''

''Afraid not.''

"Quint, why is that penny so important? I mean, besides its value, of course. No one wants to lose fifty thousand dollars, but you could easily replace it with the insurance money."

"No, I couldn't, because the sentimental value is even higher than the monetary value. The coin collection was left to Aunt Octavia in the will of the only man she ever loved. The Lincoln copper cent was the last coin he added before he was sent overseas during the Second World War. He never came back. I think she's clung to those coins with such intensity because they're the only link she has to her lost love."

As he spoke, he could see Amber melting before his eyes. She was such a romantic!

"Poor Octavia," she murmured. "In a way, she and Sophie have a lot in common. They're both grieving for lost love."

"What's *greefing*, Mama?"

Amber smiled. "Little pitchers," she said to Quint. "Nothing, Sophie. It's just the way big people talk sometimes."

"Oh. Okay." She returned her attention to coloring the place mat in front of her on the table.

Amber sighed. "Quint, I'll try again to find it. I honestly don't know if she took it, or if she still has it if she did. But I promise I'll try harder to find out."

"That's all I can ask." Her hand lay on the table beside her napkin and he covered it with his own. She didn't pull away, just sat there meeting his steady gaze, her own eyes questioning. "Amber, I—"

''Pizza's here!'' Mama sang out, placing one large and one small round on the table. ''Hope you're all hungry because Mama makes the best pizza this side of Italy.''

*What had he been about to say?* Quint reminded himself to give Mama an extra-large tip.

The meal went so well that Amber wasn't sorry that she'd agreed to come. More importantly, Sophie was having a wonderful time. Quint teased and joked with her while she giggled and devoured several slices of pizza.

Still, Amber maintained that it wouldn't be a good thing to get any closer to him than they already had. She and Sophie would be leaving in a matter of weeks. Nothing could come of a relationship with him.

Not that anything would come of it even if they were staying. She and Quint lived in completely different worlds. If it wasn't for Sophie, they might not find any common ground at all…except they'd already found the common ground of mutual attraction. Maybe once…but Amber had too many responsibilities to act on that now.

With a large cardboard box containing several leftover slices of pizza, they trooped out to Quint's fancy car and headed for home. Amber had to admit she felt in much better shape to tackle another couple of hours' work tonight.

Quint parked at the curb and climbed out to walk them to the door through the darkness. The house blazed with lights, since Amber's theory was that potential evil-doers would be fooled into thinking someone was home.

At the front step, he lingered. "Thanks for coming," he said. "I had a great time."

Amber pulled the key from the pocket of her knit tunic. "We enjoyed it, too, didn't we, Sophie?"

"I like pizza," the little girl agreed. "Quin, want to see my teddy?"

"I'd love to see your teddy." What he'd love, obviously, was to come inside.

Amber patted her daughter's shoulder. "Not tonight, Sophie. It's past your bedtime now. Maybe another—"

Something crashed to the floor inside, interrupting her attempt to dismiss him. Her apprehensive gaze met his surprised one. Without another word, he snatched the key from her hand and thrust it into the lock.

Scuffling sounds came clearer now. "Be careful," she pleaded with him. "Maybe we should just stay outside and call the police."

"*You* stay outside," he ordered in a clipped tone, "and keep Sophie with you."

Throwing open the door, he charged inside.

Before Amber could grab her daughter, Sophie charged in after him.

# 8

QUINT BURST INSIDE to discover two figures locked in mortal combat in the middle of Amber's living room. At his precipitous arrival, both froze. One was tall and young, one was short and not so young, but both were skinny—and fierce.

"Don't anybody move!" Quint roared. "The police are right behind me. Don't even *think* about making a run for it because—"

A small figure darted past with an affronted cry. "My pennies! You spilled my pennies!"

"Sophie, don't—" Quint made a grab but she eluded him, running straight toward the two intruders.

"Sophie!"

Amber tried to claw her way past Quint to get to her child and only succeeded in tripping them both. By the time they got untangled, man and boy had disappeared through the open patio door.

"Mama!" Sophie shrieked. "Somebody messed up my pennies!"

Amber gave a cry of relief and scooped up the little girl in a bear hug. Quint bounded through the back door, colliding with Mizell who was on his way in.

"He got away," the lanky kid grumbled. "You let him get away, man."

"*I* let him!" Quint grabbed the kid by the collar and hustled him inside. "You've got a lot of explaining to do, Mizell."

"Ow!" The boy tried to shrug out of the grip on his collar. "Lemme go! I'm the good guy."

"That's a laugh. What were you doing, fighting over the loot?"

"No!" Mizell finally wriggled loose. "I saw him sneak in here. I was protecting Amber's property."

"Or your own interests. If you didn't have ulterior motives, why not just call the cops?"

"If I didn't have *what?*"

"Inferior," Sophie piped up. "Inferior motions." She frowned. "Only I don't know what that means."

"It means," Amber said firmly, "that Mizell is a hero!"

Quint groaned. "You're kiddin' me, right? If he was on the side of law and order, he'd have called the police."

"Are you for real?" Mizell exploded. "They munched on me once for no good reason."

Quint could just imagine; the kid looked like a potential lawbreaker if ever there was one, his clothing ragged, his hair ragged, his expression cunning.

"We understand," Amber said soothingly. "How can I ever thank you?"

"Aw, that's all right." The kid eyed Quint. "Can I go now?"

She took his arm. "Of course, but why not use the

front door this time? Sophie, you run along and put on your nightgown, please.''

Quint fumed while he waited for Mizell to leave. Then he said, ''Amber, that kid's no good. Why would a doofus like that risk life and limb to protect 'your property,' as he put it.''

She looked at him as if he were pitifully ignorant. ''Because he has a crush on me,'' she said.

Quint brushed that aside. ''I still say that's not a good enough reason to—''

''*Some* men find me attractive,'' she interrupted tartly. ''Of course, lately they've been mostly too young or too old to be interesting but—''

''*I'm* not too young or too old!'' Incensed, he'd blurted what amounted to a confession, then regretted it.

She looked dubious. ''You've just been trying to get your penny back,'' she said in a sad little voice. ''You're not interested in me.''

''I'll show you how interested I am.'' He pulled her into his arms and glared down at her. ''So help me, if it wasn't for Sophie I'd—''

''Quin, are you mad?''

Sophie's little voice shocked aside all extravagant thoughts of sweeping Amber away to romantic adventures hitherto unimagined.

Amber smoothly stepped out of his embrace. ''Why would you ask that, Sophie?''

That lower lip quivered. ''Quin said, no Sophie. I'm Sophie.'' Tears trembled on her lashes.

''Now, honey, he said 'if it wasn't for Sophie,'

which is entirely different." She gave him a warning glance. "Isn't that right, Quint?"

"Absolutely." He had to salvage what he could from this. "I was about to say, if it wasn't for Sophie—" He thought fast. "If it wasn't for Sophie, I'd take everyone to the Wild Animal Park tomorrow, but Sophie doesn't like wild animals so..." He shrugged.

Sophie began to smile before he finished spinning his web. "Sophie does so like wild aminals," she cried. "Let's go, okay, Mama? Let's go to the Wild *Animal* Park!"

And that's how they came to be breezing up the freeway the next day, heading for Escondido and the San Diego Zoological Society's wildlife preserve for the breeding of endangered species. Amber knew she shouldn't be here; she knew she should be working to complete the order for Nicole. But she'd been working so hard that somehow she couldn't be too sorry about spending this glorious summer day with her daughter and a man who had somehow managed to slip beneath her defenses.

He would obviously do anything to retrieve that penny, even make love to the mother of his number one suspect. So why would she let him do it?

"Are we almost there?" Sophie asked for the dozenth time. "I wanna see the elephants!"

Quint directed his voice to the back seat. "You will. Just be patient."

Patient. Sophie didn't know the meaning of the word—literally.

Like the zoo, the park presented animals in re-created habitats as close to natural as was possible for Southern California. Quint, whose family had always supported the zoological society's efforts, was quite conversant with these efforts.

Their first stop was the African village, where Sophie headed straight for the petting kraal. Soon she was surrounded by goats of various hues and sizes. When one of the little animals took a nip at the drawstring bag dangling from her wrist, she laughed and pulled it away.

"He's gonna eat my purse!" she giggled. "No, no, bad goat!"

The goat, a boney little white creature, promptly nudged her with his nose. She threw her arms around his neck and hugged him hard.

Quint spoke in Amber's ear. "I'm surprised she didn't whack him with that purse," he said. "If it's loaded with pennies, she could have knocked him silly."

"She reserves that response for people," Amber said sweetly. "To Sophie, goats are higher up the social ladder."

Grinning, he looked down into her beautiful face. Today she wore bright orange leggings and a lemon yellow tunic painted with stylized parrots. He'd gotten used to her with black hair and actually liked the way it feathered around her face.

He would have liked to stare longer, but the kraal was becoming too crowded. "Think it's time to move on?" he suggested, feeling himself jostled from behind.

She nodded. "Sophie, want to go look at the babies through the nursery window?"

That was all it took.

For the next two hours they visited not only the nursery but the Mombasa Lagoon, where Sophie joined other children scrambling over a giant "spider web" and hid in an equally giant tortoise shell; admired the hummingbirds in the Hidden Jungle; and exclaimed over the inhabitants of the Gorilla Grotto.

After a snack and a cold drink, they headed for the Wgasa Bushline, a fifty-minute, five-mile electronic monorail tour that promised to transport them to the wilds of Africa and Asia. While they waited in line to board the train, Sophie stifled a big yawn and leaned her head against her mother's side.

"Are you tired, honey?" Amber brushed silky brown hair away from the little face.

Sophie popped upright. "I'm not tired," she said. "I wanna see the aminals!"

That they did, starting with the elephants, followed by giraffes and rhinos and antelopes. Sophie spent the tour popping up and down in her seat, pointing and exclaiming.

Quint, who'd already taken the monorail tour several times and long ago figured out that when you'd seen one elephant you'd seen them all, enjoyed the little girl's antics much more than the herds of exotic animals spread out around him. Sophie's enthusiasm was contagious. By the time they pulled back into the station to disembark, he was enjoying himself as much as she was. Amber, too, looked happy and relaxed.

Passengers surged forward. Quint tried to clear the way while Amber sought to maneuver Sophie to safety between the two of them. For some reason, the child seemed to be holding back. Suddenly she let out a scream that went right down his spine.

"No—stop! That's mine!"

Whirling, he snatched Sophie up into his arms. "What is it? What's the matter?"

"That woman stoled my purse!"

"Good God, a purse snatcher in a crowd like this? Who—"

*"Her!"*

Sophie pointed over the heads of the crowd. All Quint could see was a floppy black hat moving rapidly away.

"Are you sure?"

"She stoled my purse!"

"Here." He thrust the child into her mother's arms. "You two wait here. I'll see if I can—"

"That woman in the black hat stole the little girl's purse?" The speaker was a middle-aged man who happened to be passing by.

"Maybe. We're not sure—"

"She stoled my purse!" Sophie screamed. "She stoled my money!"

"Catch that woman! She stole this little girl's money!"

Quint pushed through. "That's all right, I can handle this."

"After her! There she goes, toward the Nairobi Village! Let's get 'er!"

"No, stay out of this—" But nobody was staying

out of it, he realized. He'd just have to beat them to her.

Quint jumped off the platform and took off running, quickly outdistancing all but the most fit of the vigilantes. The woman in the black hat darted out of sight behind a thatched hut, an athletic-looking man in hot pursuit. Maybe they could corner her. Veering left, Quint raced around the other side of the hut—

And ran right into her. They went down on the ground in a tangle. The woman fought and clawed, a wild swing clipping him on the cheekbone and a foot landing firmly on his shin. She was a big woman, and strong. He had his hands full trying to control her without hurting her.

The man who'd been following hauled her up, giving Quint a chance to leap to his feet. "Okay, let's have it," the stranger snarled. "Where's the kid's purse?"

"I don't have it, you idiot!" She lashed out at him with a foot and he jumped aside. Her sunglasses lay on the ground and her big black hat hung precariously over one ear. She straightened it with an impatient push. "What's the meaning of this?"

The strange guy shrugged; he didn't know.

Quint said, "If you didn't heist the kid's purse, why were you running away?"

"I wasn't running away, I'm late to meet my husband and—wait a minute, I should be asking the questions here. Two big strong men, beating up a helpless female! You should be ashamed of yourselves!"

"Hey, lady." The other guy held up his hands in

a placating gesture and backed away. "I *am* ashamed of myself. I was just trying to be a good citizen but..." He glanced around at the gathering crowd. "I'm outta here. Let *him* answer your questions."

Sophie and Amber arrived with the others. Sophie glared at the woman, but didn't release her mother's hand.

"Where's my purse?" she yelled.

The woman sneered and held out her empty hands. "Do you see your purse here, kid?"

Amber turned her stricken glance on Quint. "Oh, dear, it looks like there's been some mistake."

"I'll say there has, girlie." The woman's lip curled. "And that kid made it!"

Everybody looked at Sophie, who was unwavering. *"She stoled my purse!"*

"I'm gonna sue," the woman shouted. "How dare you accost me this way? I demand an apology!"

The crowd edged back, as if afraid of getting caught in the bursting radius of her righteous indignation.

Amber licked her lips. "If we made a mistake—"

"Whadda you mean, *if?*" The woman bent to retrieve her sunglasses.

"All right, I apologize!" Amber blurted.

"That's more like it." The woman sniffed.

"That woman stoled my purse!"

"Oh, Sophie, stop it. You made a mistake, honey."

Quint, who'd been watching the exchange, couldn't shake the feeling that despite the fact that the woman did not have Sophie's purse, there was something definitely wrong here. "Maybe we should call park security and let them sort this out," he suggested.

He thought he saw alarm flare in the woman's eyes just before she clapped on the sunglasses.

"I told you I was late to meet my husband," she barked. "You do anything you want, but I'm getting out of here."

"Don't be so hasty." He stepped into her path. "I still think—"

Amber touched his arm lightly. "Oh, for heaven's sake, Quint, let the poor woman go. We've already caused her enough trouble, don't you think?"

"But—"

"Please?"

Defeated, he stepped aside. The woman gave him a last derisive glance before marching away. When he turned to Amber, she looked less sure of herself than she'd sounded.

"What?" he asked.

"Something just dawned on me."

"What?" he asked again.

"She not only didn't have Sophie's purse, she didn't have a purse of her own."

"So?"

"Quint! Women don't go out without some kind of purse, especially an older woman. And there's something else…"

He didn't even want to hear it. "What?" he said for the third time.

"When she put on her dark glasses, I had a flash of déjà vu, like I should know her from somewhere."

He was getting a sinking feeling in the pit of his stomach. "And that somewhere might be?"

"Nicole's shop. I'm pretty sure she's the woman who tried to take Sophie's purse that day."

As one, they looked at Sophie, standing there with her lower lip thrust out. When she realized she had their attention, she said in a loud voice, "That woman stoled my purse!"

Quint was very much afraid she was telling the truth.

VILMA REACHED the parking lot of the Wild Animal Park in record time. Phil had the rental car idling near the exit, right where he was supposed to be, for once. Throwing open the passenger door, she jumped in. He gunned the engine and peeled rubber out of there.

She was sitting on something. She knew what it was before she even managed to drag out the two purses, one big and one little, from beneath her.

She dropped the larger of the two onto the floor-board and fumbled with the little drawstring bag she'd snatched from the kid. "Is it here?"

"Hell," Phil said, whipping a left to head back to San Diego, "I haven't had time to look."

"Pretty slick, the way I handed this off to you." She ripped open the bag and turned it upside down. The contents tumbled out onto her lap: two un-wrapped and extremely sticky red-and-white-striped peppermints, a shiny pebble, a hair ribbon and two pennies. Snatching up the pennies, she gave them a quick once-over, then let out a howl of disappointment and flung them onto the floor.

Phil glanced at her. "Guess that's not them."

"No kidding, Sherlock. We trail them all the way here from that dump in San Diego, then I'm stuck on some damn train with a bunch of tourists all staring like halfwits at a bunch of stupid animals. Next I take my life in my hands to grab that kid's purse, get chased to hell and gone for my trouble, get tackled and manhandled, and *this* is all I have to show for it?"

"Life stinks," Phil agreed.

"Yeah, well, I'm not licked yet," Vilma promised grimly. "That kid has that penny and I'll by God get it or know the reason why. The gloves are coming off, Phil. Now listen close, because this is what we're gonna do...."

QUINT AND AMBER tried to recapture the mood, but it was gone. Even Sophie was subdued. Finally bowing to the inevitable, they left the Wild Animal Park and headed south toward San Diego.

The loss of Sophie's purse had cast a serious pall over the day. Even a stop for pizza failed to cheer everyone, or even anyone, up. Still, Quint was sorry when he pulled the BMW to the curb in front of Amber's house. Somehow he felt responsible for what had happened.

"I'll walk you in," he said.

"There's no need to bother." Amber unsnapped her seat belt.

"It's no bother."

Before she could protest further, he climbed out, opened the back door to retrieve Sophie, then led her toward the house. Amber fell in beside him.

"It really wasn't your fault," she said gently.

He gave her a quick glance. "How'd you know that's what I was thinking?"

She frowned as if really considering her answer. "I'm not sure. It almost feels as if—well, as if I'm getting to know you."

That pleased him. "I'm getting to know you, too." He stopped short, pointing. "Did you leave the door to the carport unlocked?"

"No, of course not. Why?" She saw the same thing he saw and gasped.

He shoved both of them behind him. "Stay back— and this time I mean it. *Stay back!*"

Moving with quiet stealth, he approached the open door, then slipped inside.

The minutes he was gone seemed like hours to Amber, waiting on the sidewalk in front of her own house holding Sophie's hand and afraid to go inside. By the time the front door swung open, she was trembling with tension.

"It's safe," he said in a flat voice. "You can both come on in."

"If it's safe, why do you look so grim?"

"It's a mess," he said. "Amber, I'm sorry."

Almost holding her breath, she stepped inside the door and gasped. The place was a disaster area. Compared to this, her car had been gently treated. She moaned helplessly; how was she ever going to get this mess cleaned up?

Sophie walked to the middle of the room and looked around, her gaze sliding over slashed couch cushions and shattered glass. She frowned. "Mama, where's my pennies?" she demanded.

The answer to that query, they soon discovered, was "Gone." Gone without a trace, bags and all. Amber, standing in the middle of the kitchen, felt numb. The stove had been toppled, the door smashed off the refrigerator, almost every dish swept from the cabinets to shatter on the floor.

The sound of Sophie's copious weeping entered Amber's consciousness. Well, she felt like crying herself. This was horrible.

Quint approached and put his hands on her shoulders. "Steady," he said. "You're not alone."

"I feel alone," she whispered. "Quint, why would anyone do such a thing?"

"You mean, break in or trash the place?"

"I'd call it wanton destruction."

"My guess is frustration. See, I've worked out this whole scenario in my mind. The man at the zoo and the woman at Nicole's are in cahoots. I'll bet she passed Sophie's purse off to him while she was running through the African village, then met him later. When the penny wasn't there, they got mad and came here to look for it."

"They know where I live?"

"Honey, they'd have to. Mizell surprised the man in here, remember?"

"Oh, God." Trembling, she turned in his loose hold and buried her face against his shoulder.

For a moment he simply held her. Then he said, "We've got to call the police."

"Yes."

"And then you're coming home with me."

"No." She stepped away from him.

"It's the only way. You can't stay here."

That, sadly enough, was true. "I can't move in with you, either."

His grin was sudden and unexpected. "That has a nice ring—move in with me. But that's not what I meant and you know it. I live in this great big house with room for a dozen people."

She shook her head stubbornly. "Impossible. I have work to do. I have to find someplace to put my sewing machine—pray it's not ruined like everything else. You know I have to finish this order and then—"

"Then what?"

"Nothing." But she was thinking, *Then we're leaving town. This is a sign from heaven. I've stayed too long as it is.*

He glanced at the telephone on the floor, then at the ragged wires ripped from the wall. Shrugging, he unhooked his cell phone from a belt loop. "While I call the police, why don't you start gathering up what you want to take—what you can salvage. Then we're getting out of here."

He spoke with such authority that she felt her objections melting away. Besides, she had no place else to go. And with Sophie and Octavia in residence, surely nothing could happen between Amber and

Quint—nothing that could change her determination to leave town, anyway.

"Wow!"

The soft utterance brought her swinging around. Mizell stood in the door, eyes round and jaw hanging. Quint, busy on the telephone, hadn't noticed. Amber silently gestured Mizell outside again and followed.

Watching him closely, she asked, "Do you know what happened here, Mizell?"

"I know what you're thinkin'." The boy looked miserable. "But, Amber, I'd *never* do anything like this to you."

"Are you sure? Because I'm out on a limb here. If it turns out that you had a hand in this—"

"No way!" He clenched his fists. "You can trust me, honest. Sure, I could go for that reward, but I didn't do *this!*"

For a long moment she looked at him. Then she said, "I believe you, Mizell. Don't let me down."

MEANWHILE, back at a certain seedy motel in Imperial Beach, Vilma and Phil were faced with a monumental task they did not relish. Coin books in hand, they began to sort through the mounds of pennies covering the bed and flowing onto the floor.

"Fifty thousand dollars," Vilma muttered. "Just keep reminding yourself, fifty thousand dollars…"

"OCTAVIA? Are you in here?"

Quint stuck his head through the doorway to the solarium. He was eager to get past the initial awkwardness that would inevitably follow his insistence that Amber and Sophie come home with him.

"What is it, Quintin?" Octavia rose from one of the white leather couches.

"I, uh, I—"

Her eyes widened. "Whatever are you trying to say, Quintin? You're scaring me!"

He laughed, realized he sounded nervous and stopped. "I've brought home houseguests."

"You've...*what?*"

"Brought Amber and Sophie Brannigan home with me. They're waiting in the front hall and I want you to go out and greet them as graciously as if they were royalty."

"You've brought *that woman* into this house?"

He loved his aunt Octavia, but no way was he going to let her indulge her class prejudices at this point. He placed his hands on her shoulders and peered into her horrified eyes, willing her to understand—understand and believe—what he was about to say.

"Amber's house has been trashed by someone looking for that damn penny. It isn't safe for her to stay there and she has nowhere else to go. Since this is all my fault anyway—"

"Your fault? How is it your fault? It's her daughter who stole the penny."

"We don't know Sophie took it, but even if she did, I'm the one who dropped the coins and started this chain of events. But now that I think about it, Jiggs is really the one who—aargh!"

Jiggs, who'd crept up on silent paws, flung himself

at Quint's right ankle and clamped his teeth in the sock. It was as if the damn dog had been galvanized by hearing his name. Quint glared down at the snarling mass of hair and fangs; some things never changed.

"Octavia," he said, "you will be gracious. If I can put up with that godawful excuse for a dog, you can put up with two people who have..." Have what? He sucked in a deep breath and plunged on. "Two people who have come to mean a great deal to me."

Octavia's jaw dropped and she sucked in a deep breath. "I can't believe you mean that. Why, that Brannigan woman is nothing but a—"

"A fine woman trying to take care of her daughter." He cut her off harshly. "Until she ran into me, everything was going fine in her life. Now she's had her car vandalized, her daughter's purse snatched and her house trashed. From now on, she's staying here where I can keep an eye on her."

"I—" Octavia sputtered to an indignant halt. Quint just stood there, grim and determined. He would not back down on this issue. His aunt could bow to the inevitable or he would rent her a nice suite at some overpriced hotel.

After a moment she said a strained, "You mean this, I see."

"I mean it with all my heart."

"In that case, I shall do my best to rise to the occasion. But please remember that this is all *your* idea and—"

Sophie burst through the doorway, Amber on her

heels obviously trying to catch her and haul her back. The little girl skidded to a stop, taking in the situation with a glance.

"Jiggs!" she cried, kneeling and holding out her arms. "Here, Jiggs!"

"Jiggs!" Octavia said sternly. "Heel!"

Jiggs looked from one to the other, then raced to Sophie and hurled his furry body into her arms to lick her face enthusiastically.

Sophie looked up, giggling. "Doggy kisses," she explained, hugging the wiggling dog. "He loves me!"

At that moment Quint loved her, too. And his feelings for her mother were also on the warm side.

# 9

MOTHER AND DAUGHTER MOVED into the Sterling mansion lock, stock and sewing machine. Included among their possessions was one raggedy teddy bear, a squishy junior-size beanbag chair, and a pink outfit from Sterling's complete with tiara.

Quint's housekeeper, fortunately a grandmother herself, welcomed Sophie with open arms. "A child is just what this big old house needs," Marie Wolchek declared before leading Sophie off for the ubiquitous cookies and milk. "I was beginning to wonder if we'd ever have one." She gave Quint an oblique glance that spoke volumes.

Octavia harrumphed. "I suppose peace and quiet will be a thing of the past," she said sourly. At that moment Jiggs took off after their pint-size guest and she let out a squeak of alarm. "Jiggs, come back this instant! Jiggs!"

The Pekinese didn't even dignify her command with a backward glance. She glared at her nephew and the mother of her nemesis, but found no sympathy there. "Oh, for heaven's sake," she started after the disappearing pair. "What is that child, a Pied Piper?"

Quint had the good grace to wait until Octavia was

out of earshot before laughing. "Sophie *is* the Pied Piper," he declared.

Amber looked dubious. "Maybe so, but Octavia dislikes her so much that I feel squeamish even being here."

"Give my aunt a week and she'll be eating out of Sophie's hand just like the rest of us," he predicted. "Besides, you have no place else to go."

She rolled her eyes. "Thanks for sharing that. Makes me feel all warm and tingly inside." She turned back toward the west wing, where she and Sophie had been installed.

He fell into step beside her. "Amber, the truth is, you could have had a hundred options and you'd still be here."

She cast him a surprised glance and he shrugged.

"All your troubles are my fault. I dropped the coins, then I somehow managed to put the finger on Sophie with that newspaper item. You've had nothing but trouble since."

"Maybe so, but that doesn't make you responsible for us."

"Yes, it does."

"No, it doesn't." At the foot of the stairs she faced him, her expression determined.

"You're a stubborn woman."

He reached to pull her into his arms but she stepped back quickly. "There'll be none of that," she said firmly.

He didn't much care for her attitude. "Why not?"

"Because we're both victims of circumstance. I've

spoken to my insurance man about the house, and once we're able to move back in there, we will.''

"I won't let you do that until I'm sure it's safe.''

"It's safe *now*, Quint. They—whoever 'they' are—already know there's nothing of value there. They won't be coming back.''

"You don't know that. Until that penny is located—''

"If I hear any more about that penny, I may scream!''

"Okay, okay, don't do that. Just tell me what I can do to help you feel at home here.''

Her smile was welcome. "Quintin Sterling, there is no way on earth I'll ever feel at home in this mansion. But you could help me get my sewing machine and drawing equipment set up somewhere.''

"The pool house,'' he said promptly, for he'd already thought about it. "There's plenty of room, lots of good light, and the pool is rarely used. C'mon, I'll help you.''

SOPHIE WAS RAPIDLY fulfilling Quint's prediction and Octavia's dread: that the child was a miniature Pied Piper. By the end of the first day, all the servants were willingly at her beck and call, Jiggs doted on her, and by the second day even Octavia showed signs of weakening.

Quint, who'd turned over routine management of Sterling's to his assistant so he could act as facilitator at home if need be, walked into the solarium on the third morning to tell Octavia that she had a visitor. He found her there with Sophie. They were talking so earnestly that he hesitated, unsure whether he should disturb them.

Sophie peered intently into Octavia's eyes. "Are you sad, Miss Octavie?"

Octavia, her back to her eavesdropping nephew, sighed audibly. "I'm afraid I am," she said in a long-suffering tone.

Sophie placed her small hand over Octavia's blue-veined one resting on the glass tabletop. "I'm sorry," she said with unquestionable sincerity. "*Why* are you sad? When I get sad, Mama fixes it."

"Your mama can't fix this." Octavia sounded terribly unhappy. After a moment she added, "But you could."

Sophie's eyes widened with surprise. "Me? I'm just a little girl."

Octavia's laugh sounded mirthless. "When it suits you, you're just a little girl. Sophie, I'm sad because two of my very special pennies are still missing. If I don't get them back, I don't think I'll ever be happy again."

"Oh-hh." The word came out long and slow and mournful. "I like pennies, too, but a bad man stole them. I got no plenty." Digging into the pocket of her lemon-yellow shorts, she hauled out a handful of copper disks and dropped them on the table.

Octavia gasped and spread her hands over the coins. "Please let it be there," she murmured, beginning to sort through them.

Quint stepped up to her side. "That was very nice of you," he said to Sophie, who was frowning at the old lady and being ignored for her trouble. "I'm sure my aunt will thank you as soon as she comes to her senses.''

"You're welcome," Sophie said. She looked relieved.

"Oh, God!" Octavia held up a penny with trembling fingers.

Quint's stomach dropped; was it going to end so suddenly, after all they'd been through? "You found it? It's the Lincoln penny?''

Octavia shook her silvery head. "No, but it's the other missing penny. The Lincoln penny isn't here. It isn't here!''

At her wail, Sophie took a quick step backward. "Let's go play, Jiggs," she said.

Octavia leaned forward anxiously. "No, wait, you have to tell me what you did with the other penny!"

"Mama's calling." Sophie whirled and skipped toward the door. "C'mon, Jiggs!''

Jiggs gave Quint's ankle a longing glance, then scampered after the little girl. Quint could hardly believe it. The kid *was* the Pied Piper.

Octavia leaned back in her chair and closed her eyes as if in anguish. "So near! I know that child has my Lincoln penny! Oh, what am I going to do to wrest it from her grasp?''

"You may not have to," Quint said. "Aunt Octavia, Harvey's here and he has something important to show you.''

Harvey Wittman stood in the marble hallway, his thick white hair impeccable and his bearing as erect and crisp as a soldier's. As Quint and Octavia entered from one direction, Amber arrived from the other with Sophie in tow.

Harvey saw Octavia and took a step forward, his formal facade cracking. "Octavia, my dear!"

The woman lifted her chin and held up a hand to halt his mad, impetuous charge. "What are you doing here, Harvey? I thought I told you—"

"Indeed you did, but—" He glanced around at their audience. "If we could perhaps speak alone?"

The idea seemed to incense her. "Absolutely not. Please state your business and be gone."

Harvey sucked in a deep breath that caused his chest to rise beneath his conservative blue suit and white shirt. "As you say, my dear." Digging into his coat pocket, he extracted a small velvet box. "This is for you."

"What is it?" she asked, her question dripping with suspicion.

Harvey seemed to blossom. "It's your missing penny, Octavia. Your 1943-S Lincoln copper cent," he said proudly. "I've brought it back to you."

"WHAT'S WRONG with Miss Octavie?" Sophie asked anxiously, looking at her mother across the supine form of the old lady.

"She fainted, dear." Amber pressed a cool washcloth to Octavia's brow. Quint had caught her aunt as she'd toppled, then carried her into the nearest room where he'd deposited her on a chaise longue before rushing off to summon her doctor. "She'll wake up in a minute or two and be just fine."

Probably. Amber had never fainted herself, or seen

anyone else do so, but that's how it worked in the movies.

Harvey's face was ashen. "The shock was too great for her," he said. "What have I done?"

"Now, Mr. Wittman, I'm sure she'll be just fine."

"Harvey!" Octavia's eyelids snapped open. "You have my penny? How do you know it's mine? Where did you get it? Who took it? What—"

"Calm yourself, my dear." He offered her the box. "I do have a few contacts. I put out the word that I wanted your penny and there'd be no questions asked. I can't tell you who returned it to me but—"

Octavia grabbed the box and flipped open the cover. For a moment she stared at the coin, then snapped the lid closed. "That," she said in an ominous tone, "is not *my* penny."

Her pronouncement stunned Harvey. "How can you say that? How can you take one quick glance and know it's not yours?"

"Because," Octavia said grimly, swinging her legs around to sit up, "I know my own penny!"

"But, Octavia!"

"Get out!" She pointed toward the door, her arm as stiff as her finger.

"But, Octavia!"

She turned her face away, dismissing him.

With a mournful sigh, Harvey took the hint. Amber followed him out to be polite, and because she felt sorry for him. At the front door she sought to comfort him. "I'm sure once she's feeling better she'll reconsider."

"You're quite mistaken."

"But she barely looked at that penny. If you're sure it's hers…"

"It isn't hers." He spoke in a low, shamed voice. "I bought it from a coin dealer to replace hers, thinking she'd never know the difference. All I wanted was to make her happy."

Amber was impressed. "You spent fifty thousand dollars just to make her happy?"

"Fifty-two-fifty, to be exact, but who's counting? For one smile from Octavia, I would move heaven and earth!" His handsome, craggy face betrayed his anguish.

"What a terrible shame," Amber commiserated. "If there's anything I can do—"

"There is," he interrupted quickly. "Do you believe your child still has the penny in question?"

"Mr. Wittman! There isn't a shred of evidence that she ever had it."

"Ah, but there is. I saw her at Sterling's that day, scooping up the pennies. She's the only one who *could* have it."

His certainty shook Amber. "You may be sure but I'm not."

He considered for a moment, his piercing black eyes thoughtful. "All right," he said, "let's put it this way. I *must* be the one to restore that penny to Octavia. If I can do that, she'll be so grateful that perhaps she'll look upon my suit with favor."

"I'm totally sympathetic," Amber said, although she really wasn't; who would want to romance such a crusty old woman? "But if that penny ever comes into my possession, I will immediately return it to its rightful owner. That coin has already caused me untold trouble.''

"If you know what's good for you, young woman, you'll give the penny to *me* to be returned."

Amber shivered. That had sounded very much like a threat to her. Could Mr. Wittman have anything to do with the horrible things that had been happening to her lately?

But before she could question him, he performed a sharp military turn and marched from the house.

"HERE, AUNT OCTAVIA, drink this." Quint offered her a glass of water. "Dr. Shaw should be here in just a few minutes.

"I'll drink your water, but I don't need a doctor." She took the glass and lifted it to her lips.

Quint frowned. "You just fainted."

"From shock." Holding on to his arm, she managed to stand.

"Where's Harvey?" Quint glanced around.

"Gone."

"And the penny? Do you have it?"

"Quint, it wasn't my penny. He tried to bamboozle me." She looked totally outraged at the very idea.

"How can you be so sure? How do you *know* that wasn't your Lincoln penny?"

"I know, that's all." She gave an indelicate snort. "He must take me for a fool!"

Quint looked at her and felt nothing but pity. "No, Aunt Octavia, he must take you for the most wonderful woman in the world to go to so much trouble to try to make you happy."

"Ha! He—" She stopped suddenly, as if a light had just dawned. "Do you really think…"

"What other reason could he possibly have?" Quint asked gently. "He's worshiped you for years. He'd do anything for you."

"He would?" Octavia's eyes were wide with astonishment.

Just then Sophie skipped through the door with Jiggs dancing around her feet, totally ignoring Quint.

"Here, Miss Octavie!" Sophie held out an enormous cookie, showers of crumbs drifting down. "This will make it all-lll better."

Octavia looked doubtful. "Are you sure?"

Sophie nodded solemnly. "Cross my heart and hope to fly."

Octavia burst into laughter and accepted the cookie. Quint watched in astonishment, wondering if his aunt had any idea how much this little girl had softened her up already.

AMBER COULDN'T HELP worrying about Octavia, and later in the day went in search of her hostess. Octavia was in the solarium, drinking ice tea and knitting furiously. When Amber approached, the old lady looked up.

"I hope you're feeling better," Amber began tentatively.

Octavia gave an impatient grunt. "Have you come to rub it in, young woman? I made a fool of myself. Can we just drop it?"

Amber frowned. "You didn't make a fool of yourself at all. What did the doctor say?"

"I didn't see any doctor. I am perfectly fine, as should be apparent."

No place to go with that. "Then I'm glad," Amber said sincerely. "But after it happened…"

"Yes, go on, I don't have all day.'

"Well, I got to thinking about what an imposition Sophie and I have been."

"And still are." Octavia cocked her head. "Do you have a point to make here?"

"Only that I appreciate your patience. Sophie is having a wonderful time."

"As well she should, alienating the affections of my dog."

"She loves dogs, especially Jiggs." Amber plowed ahead with determination. "And I'm getting so much work done, which I couldn't have managed otherwise."

"Yes, well, that's probably true. I understand you've turned the pool house into a factory."

"I'm afraid I have. And I wanted to express my gratitude to you."

"It isn't my house, you know, it's Quint's."

"Yes, but I don't think he'd like what I have to offer."

"Young woman, I have eyes. I think he would like *anything* you might offer."

"Huh?" Thrown off stride, Amber pulled the fall of fabric from behind her back. "Not this!" She shook it out and held it up: a river of midnight-blue velvet, simply cut and shaped into a gown patterned with stamped and gilded stars and moons.

Octavia's eyes widened and her lips parted on a

exclamation of pleasure. "How beautiful!" she said without the slightest touch of venom. "For me?"

Amber nodded. "It's the least I can do." She offered Octavia the garment. "It's from my new fall line."

Octavia ran her hands over the lustrous fabric. "I must have this," she said.

What part of "gift" didn't she understand? "It *is* yours." Amber belabored the obvious.

"No, I mean the line, the label—*everything*." She looked up from the blue velvet in her lap. "I must have One in a Million. Name your price."

"I'm sorry, I thought you understood. I've promised Nicole's of La Jolla the right to sell my clothing exclusively, in perpetuity. I can't go back on my word."

Octavia shook her head impatiently. "I don't want distribution rights, I want the company. I want to buy the entire operation."

"Buy my company?" Amber stared at the woman in astonishment.

"That's right—keeping you on as designer, of course."

"That…that's impossible."

"Nothing's impossible. Think about it. I understand you don't like the business end anyway, so my plan would relieve you of that. All you'd have to do is design, which must be what drew you to dressmaking in the first place. Am I right?"

She was right, but sell One in a Million? Betray Nicole?

Better to simply dissolve the company and find someplace to start anew.

"Think about it," Octavia urged. "Just think about it."

As if she'd be able *not* to. Amber nodded, turning away.

As she walked out of the solarium she heard a mumbled, "And thank you." Such a sudden improvement in Octavia's manners made her wonder if that, too, was Sophie's doing.

IT WAS AFTER ELEVEN that night when Amber heard footsteps outside the pool house. She paused in her work, waiting without so much as a pang of concern. She felt completely safe in Quintin Sterling's mansion. Located above the seaside cliffs of La Jolla, the entire estate was guarded by tall wrought-iron fences and an elaborate lighting system.

She'd never been inside such a place and was astonished at how easily she and Sophie had settled in. They'd been put in connecting rooms that included dressing rooms, sitting rooms and bathrooms, forming a suite larger than their entire house in Normal Heights. The whole space was beautifully decorated in creamy shades of peach and sand.

The only discordant notes were Sophie's tattered teddy and the green vinyl beanbag chair her father had given her, but no one seemed to mind. Certainly Amber didn't. After the trauma of losing all her pennies to burglars, Sophie deserved a break.

She'd already begun to assemble a new collection. Amber found pennies in the water glass in the bathroom, in her slipper on the closet floor, in the small crystal box on the ornate table in the hallway. Sophie needed a bank, and as soon as Amber had time to go shopping she'd buy one.

"Hi." Quint shoved his head through the light curtains over the open sliding-glass doors. "Can I come in?"

Amber's heart leapt and she caught her breath. "Of course. It's your pool house."

He looked displeased. "Don't be like that." Stepping through, he glanced around with approval. "Looks like you've got everything under control here."

"Does it?" The restlessness that had been building in her all day surged up with such force that it surprised her. She didn't know what it was, but if this had been May instead of August she'd have labeled this uneasy yearning Spring Fever.

When she didn't answer, he frowned. "Are you all right? You look a little..."

"A little what?"

"A little ready to jump out of your skin."

Not very poetic, but certainly accurate. She steadied herself and said rather pointedly, "I'm sorry, you must have had a reason for coming here so late at night."

"Oh, yeah." He offered her the large box tucked beneath one arm. "I got this for Sophie."

She raised her brows. "You shouldn't be buying her gifts. You've done enough for us already—more than enough."

"It's nothing, just a piggy bank to keep her pennies in."

"I'm sure she'll love it. Thank you." He must read minds! She set the box on a table and looked away from him. The air in the pool house seemed charged and heavy, although the seventy-plus temperature was absolutely balmy.

He leaned one shoulder against the wall, feet crossed at the ankles, and stared at her. "Are you going to make your deadline on the dresses?"

"If I don't get distracted."

"Is that likely to happen?"

"Yes."

He looked startled. "Is anyone bothering you—getting in your way?"

She wanted to say, *Yes, you!* He bothered her night and day.

He added, "Say the word and I'll have a talk with whoever it is."

She had to laugh at that. "He wouldn't listen." She jumped to her feet and glanced about for something from which to draw strength. Nothing. "I'm tired," she said in a rush. "I've been working almost around the clock and I need some diversion...something to clear my mind."

"I'm at your service." He straightened away from the wall and his blue eyes darkened.

"There's nothing you can do," she said in a tight voice. "I'll be all right. I'll just swim a few laps and get back to work."

"Don't you think you've done enough work for one night?"

"Obviously I don't." She faced him with a stiff smile pasted onto her face. "Thank you for the bank and good night."

"Amber—"

"Thank you for the bank and good night."

For a moment he hesitated. Then he shrugged and turned away. "Whatever you say."

She waited until the curtains closed behind him before letting out her breath. Then she kicked off her sandals and whipped her loose-fitting One in a Million dress over her head, letting it fall to the floor. Beneath it she wore sheer panties and nothing more.

She hadn't even brought a swimsuit with her to the Sterling mansion, but that didn't matter. She'd have the great blue-tiled pool all to herself. Throwing back the curtains, she stepped outside onto the wooden deck.

In front of her the pool lay crystal clear and inviting, its underwater lights glowing against a backdrop of planted and potted greenery. Sucking in a deep breath, she ran lightly to the edge and flung herself forward in a low, flat dive.

Laps. Many laps. Maybe she could swim away her edginess.

Or maybe she couldn't, but she could try.

On the short grassy slope leading up to the house, Quint heard the splash as she entered the water. Turning, he stood for a moment looking back. All he could see was a ghostly blue glow through the landscaping.

She obviously wanted to be alone, but did that mean he had to go skulking off into the night as if he'd done something wrong? Hell, it *was* his pool, after all.

He stared at the blue glow until, in his mind's eye, he could picture her frolicking in the water. He'd bet her swimsuit was red—no, make that a wild flowery print similar to her own designs. She'd look great in it, too, all rounded and womanly.

He wanted to see her in that suit.

Reversing directions, he headed back the way he'd come.

THE IMPACT of a body hitting the water brought Amber swinging around in a panic. Pushing wet hair out of her eyes, she continued to tread water while searching for the source of the disturbance.

Quint came up across the pool from her, and he came up grinning. "Hi." He waved. "I decided to join you."

Amber knew this was the beginning of the end. "Go away," she said in a strangled voice.

That wiped the smile right off his face. "Why should I? This is a big pool. You can always ignore me."

She bit her lip. "I don't think I can do that."

"Why not? Damn it, Amber!" He swam toward her, the only sound that of water lapping around his body as he moved strongly through the pool.

She held up one hand. "Don't come any closer," she warned.

He stopped dead. "Why not? I don't get it. Why are you so skittish?"

She licked cold water off her burning lower lip. "Because…"

"I want to help you, if I can."

She believed him. He'd been nothing but kind and thoughtful and therein lay the problem. "I don't need any help." But she did. She needed help to clear away the image of the two of them locked together in a passionate embrace right here in his swimming pool.

"I don't believe you," he said. "Can't we talk this over?"

"No!" She was all but naked. It would take only an instant for them to join…

"If I can't come to you, then why don't you come to me?" he coaxed. "I promise I'll behave, if that's what's worrying you." As if to prove his sincerity, he raised his hands above the waterline.

"You promise? Really?"

"Yep." He kept his hands high.

She moved her own hands beneath the surface, maneuvering herself toward him. "Do you often swim at night?"

"I don't often swim at all. Too busy." He kept his attention on her face, as if he thought he could figure out what was going on if he tried hard enough.

"That's a terrible shame." Only a few feet separated them now. "To have this lovely pool at your disposal and not use it."

"It needs a beautiful woman in it to keep my interest," he said. "Amber—" His arms dropped until his hands were barely visible.

"Remember your promise!"

The hands shot up again. "Amber, I'm really happy to have you and Sophie here."

"Are you?" She could see his body beneath the surface. He wore blue swim trunks. "Why?"

He closed his eyes and leaned his head back, as if he were looking at the stars. "I've never known anyone like you. You...fascinate me."

"You're stuffy, Quintin."

"Nobody thinks so but you."

"I'll prove it." She put her hands on his shoulders. He snapped his head up and opened his eyes. She smiled.

She didn't often get this way anymore—not since Sophie's birth and all the attendant responsibilities of motherhood. But for some reason, tonight was different. Tonight, the old Amber was taking control.

Still smiling, she touched his legs with her feet, then pulled herself flat against his chest and wrapped her legs around his. She had just a glimpse of his shocked expression before they slipped beneath the surface together, their mouths seeking and clinging beneath the water.

MEANWHILE, in that seedy hotel in Imperial Beach, Phil Tubbs was showing an admiring Vilma the pistol he'd picked up earlier in the day on the black market.

"You done good," she said with uncharacteristic admiration. "Tomorrow we'll open that gate we found on the west side of the Sterling mansion and lure the kid out. We may not get our hands on that damn penny, but snatching the kid could be just as good in the long run...."

# *10*

---

AMBER AND QUINT MADE LOVE in the pool and then they made love in the pool house and then they fell asleep in each other's arms on the sofa bed.

Unfortunately one of them was destined to wake up alone.

Moving on tiptoe in gray morning light, Amber gathered an armload of dresses, then hesitated beside the still sleeping Quintin. He looked so supremely peaceful, all unaware that he was being observed. As she stood there watching him, something seemed to expand and tighten in her chest until she could barely breathe.

To a woman who had never made commitments easily, the way she felt about this man terrified her. The only person to whom she'd ever given her whole heart was Sophie.

So, how to explain the emotions Quint created in her? Even leaving him this morning would be a supreme act of will.

He sighed and flopped over onto his back. Unruly dark hair tumbled over his forehead and she stifled an impulse to brush it away. He'd been so thoughtful and loving last night, but she knew now that that was just his nature. No reason for her to become sappy and sentimental about it.

Relying on willpower alone, she slipped through the drawn curtains and stepped out onto the pool decking. Taking a deep breath, she turned away from the man who made her feel things she'd never truly believed existed.

Feelings she couldn't possibly deal with...

"HOLY COW!" Nicole said. "I don't know what to mention first, the hair or the car."

Amber hunched her shoulders defensively. "I suppose it would be too much to expect you not to mention either?"

"Entirely too much."

"Quint won't let me drive my car. The Porsche is a loaner."

"And the hair?"

Amber touched her newly brown-and-blond-streaked locks self-consciously. "I had a sudden urge for a change." She offered the armload of dresses. "I'm sorry, I didn't have time to put these in a nice neat package. I was lucky just to get them finished."

"No problem." Nicole took the garments and carried them to the counter, where she deposited them. She looked pointedly at Amber's new color. "I've never known anyone who fought the decision-making process the way you do."

Automatically Amber raised a hand to her hair. "Does it look all right?"

Nicole's eyes widened. "I don't believe you've ever asked me that before. I've seen you as a redhead, a brunette, umpteen shades of blond from honey to platinum, plus everything in between, and you've never asked my opinion.''

''I'm asking now.''

''Honey, it looks fine. Every color you've ever tried has looked fine.'' Nicole led Amber to the window seat. ''So, where's my favorite little girl today?''

''Back at Quintin's house.'' Amber sighed. ''She's getting awfully attached to the people there, and who could blame her? They treat her as if she were a princess or something.''

''Every little girl should be treated like a princess,'' Nicole said. ''Want a cup of coffee?''

''No, thanks. But about Sophie—they wait on her hand and foot, and I'm afraid she's getting terribly spoiled. This will make it more difficult when we—'' She sucked in a quick breath and made herself finish. ''Leave.''

''Leave!'' Nicole looked horrified.

''One in a Million is dead,'' Amber said, the words heavy on her tongue. ''This is the last order I'll be taking. Sophie and I are leaving town.''

''To go where?''

Amber shrugged. ''North. Maybe Seattle. I've never been to Seattle.''

''How are schools in Seattle?''

Amber frowned. ''I don't know.''

''Hadn't you better find out? Sophie is growing up and those things count. She'll be starting school soon and then it won't be so easy to just pick up and go.''

"Well, gosh, Nicole, thanks for reminding me of that."

"You've got to quit running some day." Their serious gazes met. "Have you told Quint?"

"No." Amber chewed on her lower lip.

"But he's a big part of the reason you're going, right?"

"Yes." Amber had never been very good at lying. "But I will tell him. I—I don't want him to think badly of me when I'm gone."

Nicole's expression revealed compassion. "I know how hard that's going to be for you. You're the most totally nonconfrontational person I've ever known."

"Yes, well…" Amber sighed. "It has to be done…doesn't it?"

QUINT WAS PACING the front hall of the mansion when Amber returned midafternoon. "Where the hell have you—" He stopped short, staring. "What did you do to your hair?"

The corners of her mouth plunged down. "Take a wild guess."

"Ah, honey, I didn't mean to sound critical. You look great. You'd look great bald." He tried to take her into his arms.

She managed to avoid his embrace. "I have something to tell you, Quint."

"I have something to tell you, too. We can talk in the library."

She led the way and he followed, his heart banging painfully against his ribs. He was about to say words to her that he'd never said to any other woman and he was nervous as an untried boy at the thought.

She walked to the middle of the room and turned to face him. For a moment their gazes met and the tension between them escalated sharply.

She spoke first. "I want to thank you for all you've done for Sophie and me." Her tone was flat and without emotion.

"Forget it," he said impatiently. "It was nothing—nothing compared to what I want to do for the two of you."

"You're too generous," she said, matching his tone, "but that won't be necessary."

"It won't?"

"No, because we're leaving."

For a minute he thought he hadn't heard her correctly. "You mean, moving out? You can't go back to your place for weeks, maybe months. I talked to your insurance agent today and he said—"

"No, no, not back there." She half turned so that she was no longer looking into his face. "I mean, leaving town."

Again he struggled to understand. "For a vacation?"

"For good." She swung back to face him, her expression filled with frustration. "Quint, are you deliberately trying to misunderstand? Sophie and I are moving away."

"But *why?*"

"It's the right thing to do." She started for the door, head down. "I can't deal with any of this anymore. I've got to get away."

He caught her by the arms to halt her flight. "Can't deal with what? What happened between us last night?"

"No!" She stared at him, her eyes wide and haunted. "I mean, all this penny business."

"Amber Brannigan, I do believe you're lying to me."

Her chin snapped up and bright spots of color appeared on her high cheekbones. "I n-never lie," she said in a voice that trembled. "Last night was nothing more than...nothing more than..."

"Can't say it, can you?" He pulled her closer and she came without resistance. "What happened between us last night was nothing more than..." He dragged it out. "...Love."

*"No!"* She twisted her head away.

*"Yes!* I love you and I want to marry you. I know that's kind of conventional but—"

"You *don't* love me and I don't love you. But even if we did, I'll *never* marry again."

"Why the hell not?" He was finally getting annoyed by her attitude.

"Because Sophie would never accept another father."

"How do you know that? Have you ever asked her?"

"Of course not. It's only obvious." She frowned. "Where is Sophie, by the way?"

"Last I saw of her, she was on her way to the kitchen to wrangle a cookie." Remembering his brief conversation with the little girl, he couldn't help smiling. "What if they don't have any more cookies?'' he'd teased. She'd responded very solemnly, ''But a house *must* have cookies!''

Hell, he loved the daughter almost as much as he loved the mother. If Amber thought he was going to let her run out on him—

The big door swung open and Octavia stood there. ''Oh, here you both are,'' she said. ''Have you seen Sophie or Jiggs?''

''Not lately,'' Quint said. ''Amber just got here.''

''Well, if you see them—''

''Wait a minute!'' Amber's distressed gaze swung between the two of them. ''Do you think there's anything wrong?''

Octavia looked affronted. ''Certainly not. I just don't know where they are, that's all.''

Quint could feel Amber's panic almost as if it were his own. ''Everybody calm down,'' he instructed. ''The last time I saw her, she was looking for cookies. We'll find her.''

But not in the kitchen. According to the cook, Sophie had talked her out of a plateful of cookies and carried them away, saying that she and Jiggs were going to have a picnic.

Amber and Octavia looked to Quint for guidance. ''Let's split up,'' he decided. ''We'll go through the house first, then the grounds if we haven't found them. Everybody meet in the front hall in twenty minutes, okay?''

Only it wasn't okay; twenty minutes later Quint and Amber met with nothing to show for their efforts. This time she walked right into his arms and buried her face against his shoulder.

"Oh, Quint," she cried, "I'm so worried! Where can she be?"

He caressed her back, wanting nothing more than to stand there holding her, but knowing he couldn't spare the time even if she was willing. "We haven't looked outside yet," he reminded her gently. "This is a big place—too big at a time like this."

She looked up at him with faith in her eyes that sent shivers down his spine. No one had ever looked at him that way. "All right, let's—" She stopped short. "Where's Octavia?"

Obviously not here, where she was supposed to be. So now Quint and Amber would have to scour the extensive grounds looking for three instead of two. Stepping outside and turning to the right, they started their search by walking alongside the tall brick fence that protected the property from the cliffs above the beach.

Quint could almost see Amber's fear growing with each step. Sophie was her life and he understood that, but it also seemed to him that Amber needed her own life, as well. She loved him, he was sure of it, but about Sophie he was less confident. She seemed to like him all right, but she still clung fiercely to memories of her father.

Quint felt as if he were trying to fight a ghost.

Amber gasped sharply and pointed. "My God, the gate's open!"

"How could that happen?" Quint reached the opening in the fence in a few long strides. "We never leave the gates open around here."

"Somebody did." Amber rushed forward.

Quint, well aware of the rocky cliff on the other side, stepped into her path to slow her down. "It could have been Octavia," he noted. "She could have gone through to look for Sophie and just neglected to close it."

"Well, don't just stand here guessing, let's go see!"

Through the gate, they looked down the rocky cliff to the pounding surf below. The beauty of the scene hardly registered in their rush to descend the wooden stairs leading to the beach.

At the bottom step, they hesitated, unsure which way to turn. Suddenly Quint looked down and, sure enough, immediately spotted disturbances in the occasional patches of sand between boulders.

"This way." He pointed to the left.

Without a word, Amber began scrambling over the rocky beach, silently intent on finding her child. Quint followed, his own alarm growing.

Rounding a bend, they stopped short. Ahead of them, Octavia knelt on the sand, holding Sophie in her arms. Jiggs sat nearby, scowling at both of them. The woman's very posture betrayed her relief at finding girl and dog safe.

Octavia was obviously in no state of mind to notice that Amber's teenage neighbor, Mizell, was advancing upon them from one angle, while a strangely familiar man and woman advanced from another.

"Octavia!" Quint's shout brought the woman's head swinging around. "You're about to have company!" And he took off across the perilous rocks as fast as he could.

Quint to the rescue, Amber thought, starting after him with her heart in her throat. Mizell didn't worry her, but she recognized the woman from the Wild Animal Park, as Quint doubtless did, and the strange man must be the same person who trashed her house and car and stolen Sophie's pennies.

Were they desperate enough to resort to strong-arm tactics? "Sophie!" Amber screamed. "Sophie!"

Quint reached the woman and girl huddled together on the beach, and whirled to plant himself between them and the advancing couple. Amber saw the strange man fumble for something in the waistband of his trousers and— She tripped and sprawled on her belly in the sand, in the process skinning her knee on a rocky outcropping.

The strange man was speaking and she could barely make out his words over the roar of the surf. "Okay, tell the kid to give us the damn penny and no one will get hurt!" He waved a pistol above his head.

He didn't scare Quint, who took a belligerent step forward, his hands clenched into fists. "She doesn't have it, you—"

"*Everybody* hold it right there! We've got you covered!" The sudden blast of sound came from a loudspeaker halfway down the rocky cliff.

Amber scrambled to her feet and ran to Quint. Without taking his attention off the bad guys, he shoved her behind him.

"It's Harvey!" The voice was Octavia's, coming from behind them. "It's *Harvey!*"

And it was. Harvey Wittman, impeccably dressed

as always, was scrambling down the cliff with the agility of a teenager. With him were at least half a dozen men, all of them brandishing pistols and looking as if they were prepared to use them.

The elderly gentleman rushed to Octavia while his men rounded up the three suspects. "My dear!" he exclaimed, taking her hands and helping her to her feet. "Thank heaven, you're all right."

"Certainly I'm all right." She sounded just as snippy as always, but Amber noticed she didn't pull her hand away. With the other she hung on to Sophie, who watched the proceedings with overt interest. "What is the meaning of all this?"

"It's quite simple," Harvey said. "I hired guards to protect you and all those dear to you until this penny business was settled."

Obviously, Sophie had joined the list of those dear to Octavia, judging by the way she'd gone to the little girl's rescue and still clung to her hand. Amber felt tears of gratitude and relief burn her eyes.

One of Harvey's guards approached. "Cops are on the way," he announced. "We'll hold these birds until they get here."

"Excellent." Harvey nodded approval.

"The guy wants to ask a question."

"What guy?"

"That guy." He jerked a thumb toward the skinny man who'd made Amber's life a living hell.

Octavia sniffed. "Absolutely not," she said.

"Please—" Amber touched the old lady's arm. "I'd like to hear what he has to say."

"Me, too," Quint agreed.

The guard shrugged; he obviously didn't care. He gestured for his fellows to bring the man and woman forward. "Phil Tubbs," he said, "meet the folks you've been harassing."

"Ha, ha, very funny." Phil Tubbs gave him a sour look.

"And this," the guard went on, completely unperturbed, "is Miss Vilma Bankhead."

"That's Ms., you ignorant clown."

"We've met Ms. Bankey—"

"That's *Bankhead,* lady!"

"Ms. Bankhead," Amber conceded, "a couple of times. The first time was at Nicole's of La Jolla and the second—"

"Aren't you the smart one." Vilma glared at all of them, but mostly at Phil Tubbs, who leaned forward with an avaricious expression on his thin face.

"I gotta know," he said.

Quint responded for all of them. "Know what?"

"Who's got that *damn* penny?"

For a moment there was utter silence. Then everyone turned to look at Sophie. The little girl had slipped her hand from Octavia's and was kneeling in the sand to hug Jiggs.

The dog, Amber realized, had not shown the slightest interest in Quint's ankle. Would wonders never cease.

Sophie realized everyone was looking at her and smiled. "I have pennies," she said. Stuffing a hand into the pocket on her bright purple shorts, she felt around—frowned, felt around a bit more. Suddenly tears appeared in those big beautiful eyes.

"My pennies are gone!" she shrieked. "Somebody *help!*"

Amber stared at her daughter while a sudden feeling of freedom washed over her. It seemed somehow fitting that *the* penny would be out of their lives at last, the people trying to steal it caught and incarcerated. But if Sophie had lost the penny, did that mean that Amber was financially responsible?

The lovely feeling of freedom evaporated as quickly as it had appeared.

"Here come the cops," one of the guards—the one holding Mizell—called.

Mizell saw Amber look his way and shouted, "I'm innocent! Tell 'em I'm innocent, Amber! I was just floating around on my surfboard when I saw those dudes—"

But then the police were there, and all she could do was call out after him, "It'll be all right, Mizell. I believe you."

After the police carted away the suspects, Amber and Quint, Octavia and Harvey, gathered on the terrace for a post mortem. Sophie had been hugged and kissed and forgiven for taking advantage of a gate deliberately pried open by Tubbs and Bankhead as a temptation for the little girl. Now she sat beside her mother on a padded wrought-iron love seat, her drowsy head in Amber's lap.

A maid served frosty margaritas and withdrew. The silence lengthened as they watched the sun setting over the Pacific. How perfect this scene seemed, Amber thought. How deceptive!

She cleared her throat and everyone looked at her;

even Sophie opened sleepy eyes. "Quint, Octavia, Harvey..."

They waited expectantly.

"I want to thank you all for what you did for Sophie. If anything had happened to her—" She choked and couldn't go on.

"Forget it," Quint said roughly. "Nothing will happen to Sophie as long as there's breath in my body."

Amber believed that. She believed it with all her heart. She nodded.

"Octavia, I'm especially grateful to you. Which makes it all the harder to confess that...that I think Sophie *did* take your penny."

Sophie, her head on her mother's lap, sighed. "I *like* pennies," she said sleepily.

"We know you do, honey."

"There's actually no proof of that," Octavia said suddenly.

"Maybe not, but I feel I'm in your debt." Amber took in a deep breath to steady herself. "If you still want One in a Million, it's yours. Sophie and I are going away, so I can't design for you, but it shouldn't be hard to find someone—"

"Find someone!" Octavia leaned forward in her chair, her eyes flashing. "Amber, without you there is no One in a Million."

Quint let out an exasperated bark of laughter. "I can top that. There's no *Quint* without Amber, and Sophie, too."

Octavia's glance sharpened. "Does that mean what I think it means?"

"I don't know. What do you think it means?" Quint countered.

"That you and Amber love each other."

Amber could feel Quint's stare so intensely that she was forced to look up from Sophie's innocent face. His eyes were so deep with feeling that she was afraid she would lose herself in them.

"I love Amber," he said quietly. "I want to marry her."

Octavia nodded crisply. "And you, Amber, what have you to say for yourself?"

Certainly not a lie; Amber just didn't have it in her to lie. "I love Quint, too, but I can't marry him. I have a child to consider first. If you don't want One in a Million without me, I'll find some other way to repay you for your penny, Octavia, if it takes the rest of my life."

"Damn it, Amber!" Quint sounded exasperated. "You're not responsible for that damn penny. Even if Sophie did take it."

"Yes, even if Sophie took it," Octavia agreed.

There was something in her voice that made them all turn toward her. Amber had never seen the woman look so conflicted; she was practically squirming in her chair and she refused to look at any of them.

"I think it's time you all heard the truth," Octavia said in a strangled voice. "The missing penny isn't genuine. I sold the real one long ago, before I came here to live, because I—I..." She swallowed hard. "I desperately needed the money. But I was too ashamed to let anyone know, so I bought a fake—there are a lot of them out there, you know.''

Amber nodded, although she *didn't* know. She just wanted to give the woman what support she could.

Octavia went on. ''That's why I was so adamant about getting the penny back. If the news of my dishonesty had become public—'' She shuddered. ''Now I just want to get rid of the entire collection and forget all about this unfortunate episode.''

Harvey patted her hand, which rested on the arm of her chair. ''Give the collection to Sophie,'' he suggested. ''Nobody will ever get it away from her and you, my love, will never need money again.''

Amber watched with tears in her eyes. Could she really walk away from all this?

Octavia sandwiched Harvey's hand between hers, but her attention was on Amber. ''And as for you, young lady—''

''I'm sorry, I have to leave. Sophie and I are going away to start a new life.'' Her vision blurred with tears, she added, ''And a new penny collection.''

''Don't do this, Amber.'' Quint's voice was anguished. ''We can find a way to work everything out, I swear to you.''

She shook her head. ''I wish we could, but we can't. Sophie and I are leaving tomorrow morning.''

The tense silence stretched out between the four adults, for there seemed nothing left to say. Finally it was Sophie who, looking up wide-eyed at her mother, spoke in her clear, little girl voice.

''Do we have to go, Mama? I like Mr. Quint and

Miss Octavie. Besides, when Daddy comes back, I want him to know where to find me.''

AMBER, her hair its natural golden brown, wore the first One in a Million wedding dress when she married Quintin Sterling six weeks later.

The flower girl, Sophie, wore her favorite pink dress, which she'd nearly outgrown, complete with tiara; the matron of honor, Octavia Sterling Wittman, wore royal blue stamped velvet. The bridegroom wore white trousers rolled up almost to the knee and a One in a Million shirt from the new men's line, as did the best man, none other than Harvey Wittman himself, who had finally found favor with the woman of his dreams.

The ceremony took place on the rocks below the La Jolla mansion, waves lapping around bare feet and Jiggs scowling and yapping at the lot of them. Two guests looked on: Nicole and Mizell, who, it turned out, *had* been cruising around on his surfboard that fateful day.

Listening to the words that would change her life, but sufficiently in love to risk it, Amber still wondered wistfully if she was doing the right thing for her daughter; she *knew* she was doing the right thing for herself. While Harvey as best man fumbled for the ring, she remembered how shocked they had all been to discover that Sophie had been stashing pennies among the foam pellets in her beanbag chair.

Still, *the* penny wasn't there. Even though it wasn't the valuable coin they'd all believed it to be, the mystery of its fate still managed to drive everyone crazy.

The ceremony ended. Amber turned into the arms of her handsome husband for their first kiss as man and wife. Then Quint lifted Sophie into the circle of their embrace.

"Are you my new daddy now?" Sophie asked shyly.

"I want to be," he said gruffly. "I love you, Sophie, and your mom, too."

Amber held her breath, praying that Sophie's rejection of this concept would not be too painful for this kind and loving man.

Sophie considered. "Okay," she announced. "I guess I love you back." She held out her hand and dropped a penny into Quint's palm. Amber knew instantly that it was the *one-in-a-million* penny.

Suddenly it was raining happiness on Amber Brannigan Sterling, her daughter, Sophie...and the man they both loved.

# KIMBERLY RAYE

## Love,
## Texas
## Style

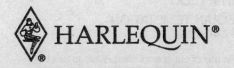

# HARLEQUIN®

TORONTO • NEW YORK • LONDON
AMSTERDAM • PARIS • SYDNEY • HAMBURG
STOCKHOLM • ATHENS • TOKYO • MILAN • MADRID
PRAGUE • WARSAW • BUDAPEST • AUCKLAND

Dear Reader,

What do you get when you cross one marriage-minded
New Yorker desperate to find herself a cowboy with one
commitment-fearing New Yorker desperate to pass
himself off as a cowboy? *Love, Texas Style,* of course!
Throw in a temperamental horse with a hatred for cell
phones, a raccoon named Zorro and a little device I like to
call the Five Finger Fantasy, and you've got the makings
for an evening filled with lots of love and laughter!

I'm thrilled to be a part of the new Harlequin Duets line! I
love writing comedy and I particularly enjoyed this story
because, like my heroine, my heroes have always been
cowboys. Born and bred in the Lone Star state, I live with
my husband and toddler and pray for the day when I'll
have my very own Five Finger Fantasy!

I'd love to hear from you. Please drop me a note and let
me know how I'm doing: P.O. Box 1584, Pasadena,
Texas, 77501-1584.

Hugs and kisses and lots of smiles,

*Kimberly Raye*

**Books by Kimberly Raye**

**HARLEQUIN LOVE & LAUGHTER**
50—GETTIN' LUCKY

**HARLEQUIN TEMPTATION**
828—BREATHLESS

For Heather MacAllister,
for being the first person to make me feel
like a real writer.

You'll always have a special place
in my heart!

# MANHATTAN MAVERICKS

Not quite at home on the range

# Prologue

SUZANNE HILLSBURY picked up the meat cleaver with only one thought in mind. Getting rid of her fiancé.

Make that *ex*-fiancé.

*Whack!* The cleaver hacked into the box of frozen Gourmet To Go veggie burgers sitting on her kitchen counter. Walter loved veggie burgers. *Whack, whack.*

She shoved the mutilated pieces into the garbage disposal, flipped the water on full force and turned to the next Walter item. Rice cakes.

*Whack, whack, whack.* She shoved the bits and pieces into the disposal and ignored a twinge of conscience. Okay, so she was being childish by taking her aggression out on a pile of innocent groceries, but it felt good, and she definitely needed some good to balance the bad. To make her forget Walter and the all-important fact that at thirty-three, and counting, her life totally sucked.

The bean curd met the same fate as the rice cakes. Then the wheat-germ cookies. The bean sprouts. The sesame crackers. The tofu-dipped it-looks-like-chicken-but-it-ain't drummettes.

The cleaver hacked, water sloshed, the disposal grumbled, and Suzanne slapped madly at the tears streaming down her face.

"You've passed the grieving stage," she reminded herself. "You're mad now." She tightened her fingers around the cleaver for emphasis, visualized Walter's face and hacked into a box of Walter's favorite energy bars. Fiber Fabulous.

It figured.

"A prenup," she growled a half-hour later as she killed the last reminders of Walter from her now barren cabinets and flopped down at the kitchen table. She shoved a gargantuan bite of double frosted cornflakes with extra sugar into her mouth and glared at the smiling man in the picture she'd ripped in two.

She slung a spoonful of cereal at Walter's half of the picture and smiled evilly. Walter hated sugar. And processed foods and wrinkled clothes and clutter and straying even two ounces from his ideal body weight.

She purposely splattered milk across her tabletop, wadded up a few napkins for emphasis and shoveled another bite into her mouth. Her deprived tastebuds shouted, "Free at last!" and Suzanne gave herself a great, big mental kick.

Had she really given up sweets for this guy? Not to mention her number-one weakness, Sal's pizza? Had she actually started ironing every morning and dry-cleaning her jeans?

Had she been *deranged* for the past six months?

The phone chose that moment to ring, saving her from having to deal with the answer—a big, fat yes!

The answering machine went beep.

"This is Celia. You can't hide forever."

"I'm not hiding," Suzanne said around a spoonful of frosted flakes. "I'm doing Dr. Ray's Four Step Grieving Process." She glanced at the book open on her coffee table. Shock. Grief. Venting. Healing. She was three for four, and while the book hadn't specifically mentioned comfort food during the healing phase, the buzz in her mouth told her another bowl of cereal would certainly speed the process.

Unfortunately, she'd chucked all the really good stuff out

when Walter had moved his rice cakes in. Upending the cereal box, she watched the last precious few flakes plop into her bowl and disappear into a swirl of milk, the way her future had faded into a blurry white prenuptial agreement.

"A *prenup*. Why, I make two times what Walter makes as a city prosecutor." Which meant a prenup would have been a good idea. Sensible. Practical.

"It's only a piece of paper," he'd told her. "Just in case. You need to protect your assets, and I need to protect mine. This will be a definite time-saver. Who's to say where we'll be in ten years? You, of all people, should know there's nothing certain in life."

Of course she knew. She headed Hillsbury, Vargas and Crawford, one of the top divorce firms in Manhattan. Two marriages failed every minute, according to the latest statistics.

The tears came faster, and Suzanne hurried around the kitchen searching for more comfort food. She was rummaging in the back of her kitchen drawer for the cereal samples she'd gotten in the mail last month when a knock sounded on her door.

"I know you're in there," Celia said. "I could hear you moving around."

"Why couldn't I be friends with someone who lives in a different building?" Suzanne asked as she opened the door to a tall, leggy redhead wearing black hip-hugger shorts, a white tank top that read Hot Babe Alert and thigh-high black boots.

"Because if I didn't live downstairs, we wouldn't be friends." Celia waltzed inside and kicked the door shut behind her. "We hang with different crowds. Actually, I hang with a crowd. You don't hang at all. The only time you socialize is late at night when you're out on that balcony trying to unwind after twenty hours at the office and I'm out on mine winding up.''

Celia danced professionally at one of New York's top gentleman clubs, the only way she could afford to live on the twelfth floor of an uptown Manhattan apartment building.

Her friend plopped down on the couch and paged through Dr. Ray's book. "So where are you right now?"

"Healing."

Celia's gaze shot to the paper-strewn counter, the discarded meat cleaver. "Sorry I missed the venting stage. I could have brought that god-awful peach bridesmaid's dress you picked out for me, a pair of scissors, and we could've had one heck of a time."

"It's blushing coral, not peach, and it's beautiful." She sniffled. "And useless."

"Suzanne." Celia's voice softened. "Tell me honestly, what's the big deal? You've drafted more prenups than Dennis Rodman has changed hair colors."

"But I've never signed one." She shrugged. "It just seems so self-defeating to prepare for a what-if divorce before I've even tied the knot. Whatever happened to till death do us part?"

Celia touched a hand to Suzanne's forehead. "Are you having a sugar rush to your brain? Because you're not talking like the calm, sensible, let's-take-the-sorry-SOB-to-the-cleaners Suzanne Hillsbury that lives above me. *She* would have drafted the prenup herself."

"But this was *my* sorry SOB. My wedding. My life." She shook her head. "I don't want a prenup. I want forever."

With Walter?

She'd certainly thought so. So he hadn't been Mr. Right. He'd been Mr. All Right. They'd had some all-right times.

In fact, they'd been having one heck of an all-right time last night.

Romantic music, candlelight. Walter had even thrown his eat-to-be-fit regime to the wind and brought Fast Fabulous chocolate cake from the deli around the corner. Suzanne had been certain he was going to put some major moves on her and start their family a day early.

She wasn't sure what had excited her the most. The fact that she was going to get another shot at the Big O, which she'd missed out on each and every time they'd slept together—Saturday nights, of course. Same time. Same place. Same position.

Last night had been Friday night. A break from the routine. That should have told her Walter had something up his sleeve.

She'd put on some sexy lingerie and was about to unbutton her blouse when he'd asked her to close her eyes. She did so willingly, anticipating a dozen surprises. Walter spraying her with whipped cream. Walter declaring his undying love and eating an entire pizza to prove it. Walter so sexually excited that he tossed his clothes to the floor without folding them into a neat little pile or setting the timer on his watch so they didn't exceed the scheduled time.

She'd opened her eyes to a nice, fat prenuptial agreement and Walter wearing his black-rimmed lawyer-nerd glasses.

"You did the right thing," Celia said firmly. "You'll find someone else."

"Will I? I'm going to be forty."

"When?"

"Someday."

"Try seven years."

"The blink of an eye. One minute I'm thirty-three, young and successful and single, and the next, I'm creaking when

I walk, turning the TV up extra loud because my hearing's going, buying Geritol by the case and still single.''

''Don't you think you're overreacting?''

''No. Okay, yes, but my poor, pathetic life is flashing before my eyes. Geez, what if Walter was it? My only shot at marriage? What if Walter *was* my soul mate and I pushed him away?'' She turned desperate eyes on Celia. ''Maybe he was it and I just didn't realize it.''

''A girl definitely recognizes her soul mate.''

''Maybe not. I mean, there's the reality factor, you know. You spend your adolescence envisioning life in the real world and when you get there, it isn't so great. Maybe soul mates are like that, too.''

''Soul mates definitely are not like that. They look more like Mel Gibson, and they smell like the men's fragrance department at Sak's, and you deserve a better guy than Walter.''

''There are no guys better than Walter. He's a successful attorney, heterosexual, still in the pre-Geritol phase—the cream of the Manhattan crop.''

Celia gave her a serious look. ''How do you know?''

''What do you mean?''

''I mean, how do you know he's the one for you? The numero-uno stud of your life? He may be all that, but did he pass your test?''

''What test?''

''The *test*. Sue, a girl's got to have a test so she'll know when the right man comes along. Maxine, this girl I work with, has the earring test. She doesn't get serious with guys who wear earrings.''

''But what if he's a great guy?''

''If he has an earring, he isn't so great, at least in Maxine's book. For me, it's the seat test. Out of the forty-eight guys I've dated over the past six years—''

"Forty-eight?"

"Forty-nine if you count Mike, but I never do since we never had an official date. Just torrid sex in the linen closet at work. Anyhow, out of all those guys, not one of them ever put the toilet seat down. Can you imagine that? I mean, I moved to New York to get away from guys who picked their teeth with straw and pissed out in the field, and here I am meeting nothing but prehistoric jerks who act like they were raised next door to my daddy's farm."

"Come to think of it, Walter didn't put the seat down either."

"See? Of course, you really should get your own test. It has to be something near and dear to your heart, something important to you. When you think about the ultimate guy, what's the one quality you imagine him having?"

"His own teeth."

"What?"

"At the rate I'm going, I'll be so old by the time I find the ultimate guy that I'll be content if he has his own teeth." A tear slid free. "Great," she muttered disgustedly. "I'm reverting to the grieving stage."

"You work too hard," Celia announced. "You need some down time to relax."

"I relax."

"With these?" Celia fingered Dr. Ray's book.

"Reading is relaxing."

"Reading something fun is relaxing. A romance novel. An adventure story. You've got an entire wall of nonfiction, most of which require a dictionary to get through the first page. It's no wonder you meet guys who are just like you."

"Like me? Are you saying Walter's like me?"

"Nose to the grindstone, can't-take-five-seconds-to-breathe, nonfiction-loving, anal retentive *you*."

Suzanne's gaze strayed to her den, to the wall-high book-cases overflowing with law volumes and self-help books, the stack of files covering her desk, waiting for her to finish Dr. Ray's Four Step Grieving Process and get back to work. Her attention riveted on her daily planner sitting on the coffee table. The word "wedding" penciled in during the two-to-five slot glared at her, and a sinking feeling spread through her. "Oh, my God. You're right. *I'm* a Manhattan Special."

A workaholic who scheduled her personal life the way she did her professional. Court at nine, depositions at ten, foreplay at six, sex at six-fifteen, quality time at six-thirty, tomorrow's schedule planning at seven...

A chip off the old block.

While her parents, both attorneys, had been good people, they'd spent more time nurturing their firm than their only child. It had taken her father's stress-induced heart attack to wake and shake them up. They'd given up law to move to Fort Lauderdale a few years ago, leaving their only daughter to carry on the family legacy.

Suzanne had followed in her parents' footsteps with no-ble intentions to help victimized women triumph over op-pressive, domineering men, but somewhere along the way, the rules of the game had changed. Fighting for women's rights had become a battle for the Rolls-Royce or the house in the Hamptons—a money game, and she was tired of playing. Tired of watching marriage after marriage end in bitter divorce. Tired of scheduling every minute of her day and feeling at the very end that she had nothing to show for her work. No husband and kids waiting at home.

Nothing but a goldfish named Mitzi who'd been replaced five times because Suzanne kept forgetting to change the water. Her gaze shot to the fish tank and the tiny gold oval floating at the top. Make that six.

Fresh tears stung her eyes.

Not that she didn't think a good career could be enough. For some women it could, but she wanted more, starting with a man willing to violate his tight schedule to get frisky on a Friday night rather than the planned Saturday love hour. Or in Walter's case, the love half-hour. A man who called her himself to ask her out instead of having his secretary do it. A man who didn't ask her to sign a prenuptial agreement the night before she was scheduled to marry him in front of the entire New York legal community, including her parents, who'd flown in this morning and out the minute she'd told them the news. They'd offered their sympathy, then hopped a plane back to Florida in time for the senior's beach bunny fest, of which her mother was reigning bunny.

Suzanne wanted a man who appreciated life, who worked to live rather than lived to work.

A saint.

Or a cowboy, she realized an hour later as she stared at the television set and watched a commercial for Handy Andy's Cattle Ranch and Wild West Getaway.

The camera panned in on a sea of swiveling Wranglers and spangled western shirts at a rocking honky-tonk, then shifted to a mechanical bull-riding scene straight out of *Urban Cowboy*. But it wasn't the promise of round-the-clock two-stepping or thrilling rides that caught her attention. It was the shot of a wide open prairie filled with men.

The salt of the earth types who lived in jeans and dusty boots, tipped their hats when a woman passed by and looked more at home in the saddle than a high-powered executive chair.

*Real* men.

A figment of her imagination as long as she was in Manhattan. But Texas... Now there was a different herd of cows altogether.

# 1

COWBOYS WERE a dying breed, and Brett Maxwell knew why.

He forced himself from the cot, bit back a groan and stepped into his jeans. Even after a week at Handy Andy's Cattle Ranch and Wild West Getaway, deep in the heart of central Texas, he could barely walk. Everything that fit into his now saddle-worn Levi's hurt, from his ankles clear up to his...

He winced, slid the button into place and sucked in a breath as the zipper hissed to a close.

A noise drew him to the window, and he spotted Creme Puff in the dawn's light, snorting her way around the corral not more than ten yards from the cabin Brett had called home the past week.

Forget the Terminator. Brett had faced off with the Emasculator. And from the feel of things—he shifted and bit back another groan—he'd sure as hell lost. He doubted if he would ever be able to have sex again. His nine-month, eighteen-day dry spell—not that the last time had been that memorable, but a guy had to keep track of these things— was this close to turning permanent.

Ugh, permanent. Just thinking about the word gave him the willies.

Temporary. Ah, that was better. Temporary, as in free, as in no ties or commitments, as in relax, it'll be over soon. He'd spent the better part of his life tied down, bound by duty, by love. At seventeen, he'd been the oldest of four boys when his parents were killed in a car accident. He'd taken charge, traded high school football for cooking and cleaning and caring for his brothers. While he didn't regret a minute of it, he'd had his fill of living for everyone else. It was his turn. His youngest brother was off at college, and Brett was here, building up his fledgling ad agency by putting a little drawl into his voice, a little bow into his walk. When he could manage to walk, that is.

A warmth brushed his arm and his gaze shifted to the greedy female who'd waddled into his cabin the first night, and every night since, to do some major begging.

"Where's your pride, honey? I told you, I can't do it anymore. You're going to have to find someone else to give you some goodies." He folded his arms and put on his sternest expression. "From here on out, my nuts are off-limits."

The female in question, a fat racoon with soulful black eyes, scratched at the windowsill and waited.

"And my cookies," Brett added. "And my chips and my cupcakes and my moon pies. No more junk food, Zorro. Your teeth are going to fall out."

Zorro scratched at the windowsill again and eyed him.

"You're going to clog your arteries. Then there's the added calories."

Another scratch, and the black eyes blinked.

"Forget it. I'm not falling for the whisker twitch again." Whiskers twitched, and Brett sighed. "Okay, one cookie. Then you're out of here."

He opened his nightstand drawer and rummaged inside, bypassing a jar of half-eaten chocolate-covered peanuts and two boxes of Twinkies for a bag of Chips Ahoy. He'd made the mistake of leaving the peanuts out his first night while he'd dozed off at his computer. He'd awakened to find half the jar spilled on the floor and Zorro right in the middle of it.

He gave the greedy animal a cookie. Then another and another before closing the bag.

"That's it, babe. Soup wagon's closed."

Zorro, cookie crumbs on her whiskers, stared at him.

"Come on, now, don't look at me like that. You know we can't go on this way. It's better to call it quits now, before either of us gets too attached. I'm out of here in seven days."

Seven more days. Seven long days. Seven.

Forget that. Think *one*. One measly week, and then it would all be over. Brett would know how to sit a saddle and rope a steer, and the Cowboy International boot campaign would be his.

Zorro scurried off the porch, and Brett's gaze strayed to the desk where he'd set up a survivalist camp with life's basic essentials—fax machine, laptop computer, printer and cellular phone. The computer screen was in sleep mode, but the printer still hummed because he'd forgotten to kill the power before he'd gone to bed. Or rather, passed out.

Even though he was dog tired and in desperate need of a real cup of coffee, he was managing to get some work done, thanks to his stash of sugar. He'd come up with several good ideas for the Cowboy International presentation, and he was still thinking. When he wasn't fighting for his life atop the Emasculator. Or pitching bales of hay. Or trying to rope that wooden steer. Or doing his damnedest not to singe off his eyebrows while wielding a branding iron.

"I could FedEx you some goggles," Nancy had offered when she'd phoned him right in the middle of morning branding and he'd nearly poked an eye out trying to retrieve the cell phone from his jeans pocket.

Nancy was his secretary. Efficient, resourceful and the

person responsible for booking him these two weeks of hell.

He could still see her when she'd walked into his fading office on the outskirts of Manhattan and announced the news in her overly dramatic, doom-and-gloom way.

"The most awful thing has happened," she'd told him, her navy support hose squeaking with every step. Navy was Nancy's signature color. Navy shoes, navy hose, navy dress, all reflecting her bluer than blue personality. She even had a navy tinge to her silver hair. "We're one of the four firms asked to make a presentation to Cowboy International for their twenty-million-dollar boot campaign."

Not that a twenty-million-dollar ad budget was all that big to the three other big-gun agencies. But Maxwell Advertising was still a pop shooter. Potential, that's what the boot campaign represented. The chance for him to get his foot in the door of a major company that spent big bucks on promotion. If he handled this campaign and it proved successful, he would be in a prime position to land the rest of their advertising business.

"And the terrible news is?"

"Cowboy International is a Texas-based company. Truman Schneider, the CEO, is one of those good-ole-boy, stuff it, mount it or marry it types, with an aversion to New Yorkers and an affection for horses."

"So?"

"So—" she drew the word out for emphasis "—you're a New Yorker."

"A small technicality." He'd gone to work then, his brain cells spinning, his adrenaline pumping at the thought of moving his agency into the top ten—the most successful ad agencies in New York, number two of which he'd left to strike out on his own nine months and eighteen days ago. "One he'll never even notice if I take a few riding lessons at a nearby stable and wow him with my equestrian skills.''

''You don't understand. Truman doesn't just ride. He's a weekend cowboy. He does amateur rodeos. Riding and roping, the whole bowl of pasta. You're from the Bronx. The closest you've ever come to a cowboy is watching *Bonanza* reruns.''

He shrugged. ''So I'll learn. Remember last month when I took sailing lessons before the presentation to MacGregor Boats? Mac MacGregor loved to sail and he wanted someone who knew the hobby as well as he did. I learned and we were in. I can learn this cowboy stuff. Easy.''

''You're serious?''

''I'll walk the walk and talk the talk, and Truman Schneider will be jumping to turn over his account to a fellow good ole boy.'' He gave her a big smile and a kiss on the cheek. ''They don't call me the Bull for nothing.''

''Determination isn't going to turn you into a cowboy.''

''No, I'll need you to find a good school for that.''

Thirty minutes on the computer with her grapevine of ad secretaries, and she'd found him Handy Andy's Cattle Ranch and Wild West Getaway.

''A dude ranch?'' he'd asked her.

''An authentic working ranch, and it's run by none other than Handy Andy Jessup, an ex–bronc buster. They call him Handy because he's got an iron grip. Myrtle from Peabody and North—'' number three from the coveted top ten ''—had a cousin whose son went there to find himself last year. Said it was a real spiritual experience, and it puts those hoity-toity dude ranches to shame. It's got real outhouses.''

''Now I'm impressed.''

Myrtle's cousin's son had failed to mention a few other amenities the place offered. Such as guest cabins minus air conditioners or king-size beds or room service. One hundred and fifty degree heat. Black tar for coffee. And a deranged horse with a personal vendetta against New Yorkers.

As if the deranged horse in question sensed his thoughts, she snorted and stomped. Black eyes collided with his.

*Come on, city boy. Make my day.*

It was going to be the seven longest days of Brett's life.

"DON'T EVEN think about it." The warning echoed through the cab of the battered Ford truck that had picked up Suzanne and Celia at the small airport outside of Ulysses, Texas, a half hour ago. "You promised you'd give up your reading dependency while we're here," Celia added.

Temporary insanity, Suzanne thought as her fingers flexed on the glossy paper. It was just a brochure, for heaven's sake. Something to help pass the time during the drive out to the ranch.

*And I've got some beachfront property in Colorado, sister.*

"I, um, was just cleaning out my purse." She wadded up the brochure and popped it into a nearby ashtray.

"Right," Celia said, disbelief in her voice. She stared at Suzanne a few seconds more before turning her attention to the thirtyish-looking cowboy named Clem who'd picked them up at the airport. "So, are we the only two people on the face of the earth crazy enough to be vacationing here?"

"Nope, but y'all were the only ones crazy enough to fly in at Stoney's airstrip. Feds declared the runway unsafe last year."

"But our pilot said Stoney's had the best strip in the county," Suzanne said.

"Best strip of chicken fried steak, cooked up piping hot at Stoney's café right next to the airport. You were on a private flight. Those boys fly in anywhere they want to, and

Stoney's offers free lunch to any pilot brave enough to make the landing.''

"We were supposed to fly into Austin, but *someone*—'' Suzanne's gaze shifted to Celia "—messed up on our flight arrangements and booked us into Amarillo. We took the private flight from there.''

Celia shrugged. "Amarillo, Austin, they both start with A.''

"If I didn't know better, I'd say you did it on purpose. To sabotage the trip.''

"I resent that. I would never do such a thing.'' At Suzanne's raised brow, she added, "Okay, so I would, but it doesn't matter anyhow. It didn't work—'' Her words stumbled into one another as the truck hit a pothole.

"Sorry,'' he murmured. "Department of Highways ain't got around to paving the roads back this way.''

"Maybe if you'd use both hands, Slim.'' Celia stared pointedly at his elbow, which rested on the window rim. His fingers tapped the side mirror in tune to the country song blaring from the radio.

He grinned. "The name's Clem, and whatever you say, ma'am.'' Large hands closed over the steering wheel.

"Ma'am.'' Suzanne elbowed Celia and whispered, "Did you hear that? Do you know the last thing a cabdriver back in New York called me? Baby doll, that's what. Then there was the time before that when a driver called me a crazy broad. Before that, I had a driver who didn't speak English. I can't even pronounce what he called me, but I know it wasn't nice.''

"Maybe he was declaring his undying love,'' Celia said.

"While flipping me a universal goodwill gesture?''

"And your point is?''

"The people here are nice.''

"There are nice people in New York.''

"Of course there are, but it's different. The pace in New York is go, go, go. People are busy, life is hectic. No one takes the time to smile." For emphasis, she glanced at Clem. He grinned in response. "See? No hand gestures. No obscene language. Just a smile. This is going to be great."

"Says you." Celia fanned herself. "Can't you turn on the air conditioner?" she asked the driver.

"No air, little lady. Just nature." He rolled his window the last two inches down, and more wind whipped through the cab.

"I hate this." Celia shoved a strand of frizzy red hair from her mouth. "José is going to freak when he sees my perm. It took major chemicals to get the curl to look this natural."

"You didn't have to come," Suzanne reminded her. "I was ready, willing and able to do this by myself."

"And stay in Manhattan, twiddling my thumbs while my best friend makes the biggest mistake of her life by propositioning the first two-bit cowboy she meets?"

The truck lurched. "I object to that on behalf of all two-bit cowboys," the driver said.

"Loosen up, Celia. We've got fresh air, a scenic route."

"That leads straight to hell." Celia spared a glance at the grinning cowboy. "Forget that. We're already there."

"I think it's great." Hot, Suzanne conceded, slapping at a drop of sweat that slid from her temple, but still great.

"That's exactly the reason I'm here. Your thinking is off, and there's no telling what sort of man you'll end up with."

"I know what I'm doing." She'd spent the past two weeks packing and reading Dr. Regina Ray's *The Surefire S.I.G.N.S. To Recognizing Your Soul Mate*. Celia had searched her luggage and removed all books, pamphlets and even a wordy shampoo bottle, but it didn't matter. Suzanne had memorized the five S.I.G.N.S.

That's where she'd gone wrong with Walter. She hadn't studied up on meeting Mr. Right. Instead, she'd simply latched onto the first man who'd asked her out on more than one date. If there was one thing Suzanne had learned in the ten years she'd been practicing law, it was to always be prepared.

No plan, no man.

But she had a plan now. She would simply open her eyes and look around for the one who met all five of Dr. Ray's criteria. With any luck, she'd find the cowboy of her dreams.

And if she didn't?

She would. Eventually. In the meantime, she'd be breathing fresh air and getting back to a more simplistic style of life. And this was no fly-by-night fancy. Suzanne had made up her mind during the long flight from New York that she needed a permanent change. It was bye-bye, Manhattan, and hello, Texas, for good.

"Believe me, cowboys are not all that great," Celia went on. "They smell, and pay more attention to their horses than their women, and don't know the first thing about an Armani suit."

"What do you have against cowboys?"

"Yeah," the driver asked. "What?"

She glared, then put her back to him. "You'll see, Sue. A few days here, and you'll give up this ridiculous notion, go home and find yourself a nice, decent guy who knows how to dress and makes regular visits to the cologne department at Sak's…. Oh, God, my makeup." She grabbed the rearview mirror. "Oh, no! My Elizabeth Arden is melting." She whipped out a tissue. "It's *melting*."

"You'll live," Suzanne said, making a quick swipe at

her own perspiration-dotted brow. Geez, it was really hot. Hotter than she'd expected, even for Texas.

"You're melting, too."

Suzanne ignored the urge to fight for the mirror and managed a disinterested shrug. "Well, I wanted to get back to basics. Might as well start now."

"I'll be damned if I'm starting now." Celia rummaged in her purse and pulled out a cosmetics bag the size of a small third-world country.

Suzanne ignored the urge to grab for some powder and forced her attention to the passing landscape, the endless stretches of green, sun-drenched grass. No roads. No traffic. No people. Just nature. Space. Breathing room.

She drank in a deep draft of oxygen as they passed a pasture full of livestock and tried not to wrinkle her nose at the faint odor. Her nostrils flared.

"Cow," the driver told her.

"*Post* cow," Celia corrected. "What comes after the grazing and the chewing."

"I don't smell a thing." Suzanne drank in another deep breath for emphasis and managed not to grimace. "This is great."

Clem grinned, Celia snorted, and Suzanne prayed diligently that wherever they were going, she could get her hands on some heavy-duty air freshener.

"OH, I'VE GOT ACHES in low places," Brett sang to the tune of Garth Brooks's "Friends in Low Places," "where the skin burns and the pain chases my thoughts away...." He pitched a bale of hay and leaned over to cut the binding on another. He doubted Truman Schneider would be wowed by his hay-pitching technique, but honest work gave a man calluses and backbone, according to Andy, and real cowboys had both.

"But it'll be okay," he crooned "'Cause I've got a

handy tube of Ben-Gay, think I'll slip on back to my my room and rub my blues away, then it'll be okay—'' His singing was drowned by the shrill ring of his cell phone.

In the adjoining corral Creme Puff shook her head and snorted.

"So if it's for you, you're not in, right?" Brett asked the horse. Creme Puff gave an answering snort. "Okay, I'll cover for you, but you owe me, honey. That means no more pitching a fit when I take a ride." He pulled the phone from his pocket and punched the button. "What's up, Miss Nancy?"

"My blood pressure, my cholesterol and my weight. I've inhaled three doughnuts so far and I'm working on number four."

Nancy had been Brett's secretary when he'd been an exec for Freeman and Whithers, the number-two firm in the top ten. She'd kept him organized, and he'd kept her just this side of Prozac for over eight years, and he'd learned early on about her doughnut dependency. He'd watched her scarf down three when her prizewinning Siamese ran off with the tomcat next door. Half a dozen when her only daughter eloped with a punk-rock musician named Snot. And ten when the Knicks lost the NBA Championship to the Houston Rockets back in '94. Hell, he'd eaten a couple himself over that one.

"Mac MacGregor of MacGregor Boats wants a meeting with you. Today. He wants to talk over some ideas for his ad campaign."

"Set up a conference call. If he wants to talk, we'll talk. And stay away from the doughnuts."

"Easy for you to say. You're a thousand miles away while I've got a doughnut shop downstairs."

"My first million, I'm moving us to a Manhattan high-rise. One with a view of the Empire State Building. You can kiss Danny's Doughnuts goodbye.''

"Promises, promises.''

But that was one promise Brett intended to keep. He *was* making a million and moving his firm uptown and into the top ten.

He stuffed the phone into his pocket and wiped his sweaty brow. *If* he didn't die of heatstroke first. He peeled off his sweat-soaked T-shirt and tossed it on a nearby fence post, then tied a red bandanna around his forehead to keep the perspiration from his eyes. He pulled a piece of hay from the heap and shoved it between his teeth for good measure. Might as well go for the complete perspiring ranch hand look—

The thought died a quick death when his gaze snagged on Clem's pickup, which had grumbled to a halt a few yards from the corral. Or rather, on the grade-A pair of legs unfolding from the passenger seat.

"Wowee.'' James Haskell, an IRS auditor and a Getaway guest who'd arrived at the same time as Brett, gave a low whistle and tipped his hat back. "Would you look at that?''

*That* started with a pair of calf-high red cowboy boots and spread upward, showcasing shapely knees and firm thighs before disappearing beneath the hem of a blue-jean miniskirt.

He didn't think things could get much better. After all, Brett was a leg man. No matter how good the rest, he'd seen the main attraction.

His gaze slid upward anyway, just for good measure, and drank in curve after curve enhanced by the tiny skirt and matching blue-jean vest fringed in red leather, and nothing else. Standard first-day wear for female guests. The closest most of them had ever come to a working ranch was watching Country Music Television. That usually changed by day two, when they realized short skirts and sleeveless tops did little to protect them from chiggers or mosquitoes or sunburn.

He'd had a healthy dose of all three after walking around in a muscle shirt to beat the heat while every cowboy on the spread had watched the heat beat him. He still had the sunburn, except the burning agony had tapered off to a nagging sting that only really bothered him when he sweated. Like now.

Only he didn't feel much of anything at the moment except the pounding in his chest as his gaze feasted on the generous display of skin, from her bare arms to the V where the vest parted at her throat. She breathed, the vest hitched upward, he glimpsed her belly button and nearly swallowed his tongue.

Over a belly button?

Nah. He was a leg man. Now if she'd slid on some black stockings and a pair of high heels, he would have been a goner, but just flashing him a belly button...

She took another deep breath, her lips parted just so, and his gaze riveted on her mouth. She had full, pink lips that made him think of hot kisses and long nights and...

*Legs, buddy.* Not lips. Long limbs rated the highest on his lust-o-meter. Always had, always would—

The thought stalled as her deep, rich brown gaze locked with his and held on. And on. Through several frantic heartbeats and a complete mental reevaluation of his preferences when it came to the female body. Maybe he wasn't a leg man. Maybe he was really into belly buttons and lips and eyes. Especially eyes.

"Have you ever seen anything that looks that good?" James, the IRS guy, asked.

"Not in this lifetime."

"I've always liked redheads, but *damn*."

Redhead? "I think the sun's in your eyes, buddy. She's a brunette."

"Not *that* one. She's all right, man, but I'm talking the leggy redhead with her."

Leggy? Oh, yeah, *leggy*. Right.

He wanted to look. Hell, he meant to, but his eyeballs seemed to have a mind of their own. They were happy right where they were. Almost. They wanted a better view. Up close and personal, and damned if the rest of him didn't seem in complete agreement.

Brett stepped forward.

# 2

ARGH... The sound grumbled from Creme Puff's throat, followed by a loud splat.

A glop of white foam plopped over the toe of Brett's left boot, stopping him dead in his tracks before he'd managed two steps.

"That horse really doesn't like you," James said.

"Nah, you think?" Brett shot a murderous glare at Creme Puff who leaned over the fence from the adjoining corral, lather creeping out of the corners of her mouth from chewing at her bit.

By the time his gaze shifted to the pickup truck, the woman had turned to follow her companion around to the rear where Clem unloaded their luggage.

"You really know how to cramp a guy's style," he told the horse. "I was about to make my move."

James chuckled and turned to his hay-pitching, while Creme Puff slung another shot of foam Brett's way as if to say, *No woman in her right mind would be attracted to a dirty, sweaty, half-naked cowboy like you.*

The infuriating part was, even more than getting a face full of horse spit, the animal was right.

Brett needed a shower, a change of clothes and most importantly a lobotomy, because the last thing he should be thinking about was what he was going to say to the woman when they finally met.

*You've got really great legs.*

*And great lips.*

*And spectacular eyes.*

*And it's been so long.*

*Nine months and eighteen days and counting...*

What the hell was he doing?

He had his mid-morning ride with Creme Puff to worry over, followed by a lunch hour spent hunched over his computer, the conference call to MacGregor, then an afternoon helping Clem move some of the herd to new pasture. He didn't have time to think about pickup lines or deep brown eyes or ending his dry spell with a woman he hadn't even met. *Yet.*

Work, buddy. Just *work.*

"LOOK, CLARK," Celia snapped. "I'm paying for this little adventure, and the last thing I intend to do is carry that suitcase. That's your job."

Suzanne stood by the truck and watched her friend stage a showdown with their driver, and it wasn't even high noon.

"It's Clem, darlin', and I'm the ranch foreman here. It's not my job. The only reason I picked you up is because I had to pick up some feed in town and y'all didn't fly into Austin like the other guests. Leave the bags and Andy will send someone after them once you've registered and gotten your cabin assignment."

"Look, Jim—"

"Clem," he said, giving her a wink. "C as in cute. L as in lovable. E as in exciting. M as in—"

"—moron."

"I was going to say macho."

"I hate you."

"The feeling's mutual, darlin'."

"I'm touched."

"Not yet," he said, "but I'll get around to it."

"You really mean to tell me you want one of those?" Celia asked Suzanne as Clem walked away, leaving them to handle their luggage.

"Actually—" Suzanne peered around the truck and eyed the sweaty, half-naked cowboy framed in the barn doorway "—I want one of those." He'd turned to the hay, giving her a perfect view of a muscular back. Damp tendrils of dark blond hair curled at the base of his neck. He wore jeans, dusty boots, a pair of brown work gloves and lots of glistening muscle. Her mouth went dry.

*Sensual awareness.*

The first of Dr. Ray's S.I.G.N.S. popped into her mind and made her heart pound harder. She was totally aware of him as a man, and if the look in his eyes had been any indication, he'd been totally aware of her. She trembled as she remembered the slow sweep of his gaze, the heat in his blue eyes....

Definitely sensual awareness.

"Suzanne Hillsbury?" The voice interrupted her thoughts, and Suzanne turned to see a young boy standing on the front porch of the main house.

"That's me." She raised her hand.

"You've got a phone call."

Minutes later, Suzanne stood in the air-conditioned main house. Ah...

"This is Suzanne Hillsbury."

"Suzanne? Thank God it's you." It was the voice of Suzanne's frantic legal assistant. "We've got trouble. Blaire Covington Smythe Warren needs legal representation."

"Again?" Suzanne let out an exasperated breath.

"She caught husband number four with the dog groomer.

Went ballistic, too. Grabbed the dog clippers and threatened to shave *it* off."

"She didn't!" Suzanne thought of Blaire's other three marriages, all short and sweet and vicious. "She did."

"She's in jail for assault. She couldn't figure out how to turn the clippers on, so she ended up bopping him over the head with them."

"Call a bondsman and post bail immediately. Then hand over the case to John."

"She won't like that. She's screaming for you."

"Tell her I'm on vacation." A *permanent* vacation, Suzanne reminded herself. "John is capable."

"Blaire's in her antiman phase. The two arresting officers were men."

"And?"

"Now they're bald men."

"I thought she couldn't figure out how to turn on the clippers?"

"By the time the squad car arrived, she'd figured it out. She practiced on the groomer."

"You're kidding."

"And then her cheating ex."

"She's lucky her father's a retired judge."

"Yes, thank God. By the time the second squad car arrived, the scene looked like a Telly Savalas convention."

"Hand over the case to Marilyn. The prenup spells everything out. Cheating will leave him with absolutely zero."

"Not quite. He did get a free haircut."

"TELL ME that call was a dire emergency and we have to fly home immediately," Celia said when Suzanne walked out to the truck.

"One of my clients is filing for divorce."

"I bet she married a cowboy."

"A Manhattan Special. Four of them, to be exact." A mistake Suzanne had no intention of making.

Her gaze shifted back to *him,* to tanned flesh and glistening muscles that rippled with each sweep of the pitchfork.

"Forget it," Celia said when she noticed the direction of Suzanne's gaze. "I can smell him over here."

"How do you know it's him and not all that post cow we passed?"

"Experience, Sue. Come on." She hefted a bag, then another and another and waddled toward the main house. "Let's check in. I want a cabin as far away from the hustle and bustle of this place as possible."

"WE'RE STILL in Texas, aren't we?" Suzanne stood on the porch of their cabin and stared at the dirt path that led through a grove of trees, around an enormous stretch of pasture, past a gigantic water well to cowboy central—three working corrals, a monstrous barn, a bunkhouse and the main cluster of guests cabins.

Clem had said that at any given time, depending on season—spring or fall—there were around thirty guests who stayed anywhere from two weeks to two months. Every Friday, the Getaway guest van took departing guests to the airport in Austin and picked up new arrivals. Not that Suzanne had to worry over meeting any of the new guests. Not way out here.

"Because as far as the walk was, I thought we might have crossed the state line or something."

"I'm not that lucky," Celia muttered.

"We're too far away."

"We've got a great view of the lake." Celia motioned

to the panorama of sparkling water visible through a part
in the trees.

"That's because this is a fishing cabin."

"*Was* a fishing cabin. The bellboy said no one's cleaned
any fish here for at least a year. It's been redone and san-
itized."

"With what? *Eau de bass.*" Suzanne put her back to the
water and stared at the fortress of trees surrounding them.
"We must be at least half a mile from the main house."

"Three quarters of a mile, and you wanted to get back
to basics."

*Basics.*

Central air. A whirlpool bath. A king-size bed. A big,
hunky slave named Duke who could sweep her off her
pinched feet and carry her all the way to the main house.
Make that a cowboy slave who pitched hay and looked
really great half-naked and sweaty and—

"You aren't having second thoughts, are you?" Celia's
voice cut in. "Because I'll totally understand. We can forget about orientation, cut our losses and get the hell out of
Dodge before nightfall."

"I'm fine. Everything's fine." The ceiling fan stirring a
minimal amount of air through the cabin would do just fine.
The bathroom had running water. As for the bed, she could
think of the small bunk as a good way to train herself in
mattress etiquette. What husband wanted to share the sheets
with someone who tossed and turned and slept sideways
like she did? As for the slave...

She had a few minutes to kill before orientation. She
would use them to mentally review the S.I.G.N.S. *Look out,
half-naked cowboy. Here I come!*

The prospect made her smile despite the two-hundred-
dollar boots she'd bought at Bloomingdale's that were rub-

bing blisters the size of moon craters on her heels. And her toes. And everywhere in between.

"Great." Suzanne started down the path. "This is great."

"YO, NANCY," Brett said as he headed around the barn on his way to the corral, the cell phone cradled between his head and shoulder, Creme Puff's saddle in his arms. "What's shaking?"

"About twenty pounds on each hip, and I sat down a half hour ago. Did you finish the radio spot for Sally's Sub Shop?"

"Almost."

"Almost isn't done. I need it by tonight."

Even though Nancy was a twenty-year veteran ad secretary, she still had no appreciation for how long it took to condense forty deli subs into thirty seconds of airtime. She was a stickler for detail, and she'd taken him under her wing when he'd been a mere copy boy. Then she'd given up her full dental plan and 401K to follow him when he'd started his own agency. He owed her, and she never let him forget it.

"You'll have it," he promised. "As soon as I finish the ride from hell, I'm headed to the cabin."

"Make sure you wear a helmet," she said as he reached the arena of death.

Brett hoisted the saddle onto one hip, killed the phone and slid it into his pocket.

A helmet. Now there was an idea. The only problem was, it wasn't his head Creme Puff kept dumping him on. He rubbed his sore hind end, prayed for divine intervention and opened the gate.

"I just don't get it." Handy Andy Jessup stood in the

center of the corral and held Creme Puff's harness as Brett approached. "She's as gentle as a puppy."

"Until I climb on. Then she turns into Cujo."

"Wouldn't have believed it if I hadn't seen it with my own eyes. She ain't like this with any of the other guests."

"Must be my charm." Brett hoisted the saddle onto Creme Puff's back while Andy held her steady and shook his head.

"Maybe it's your smell." He took a whiff and squinted at Brett. "You ain't wearing any of that fancy cologne, are ya?"

"Just sweat." He wiped at a trickle near his brow. "Maybe she doesn't like blondes."

"Half the guests here got yella hair. Had a head full of it myself way back when." He pulled off his cowboy hat, scratched his bald head, then set the hat in place. "'Sides, she'd get to kickin' at first glance if that was the case. As it is, she don't catch her mean streak until you climb on her back. Say, you ain't got anything that might be a-pokin' her, do you?"

"Once upon a time." Brett shifted. His thigh muscles screamed, while another vital part of him did some major whimpering. "But after five rides and five near deaths, I'm poke-free."

Andy chuckled. "Why don't you give this up, boy, and ride Lamb Chop over yonder? She's a sight gentler. 'Course, she is old and slow—the arthritis'll do that to you—and near blind. I usually give her to the kiddies that come out here with their folks."

Hmm. An arthritic horse could be good. Slow, but good.

Forget it, buddy. While he'd taken to riding Darlin' Daisy, who was a sight gentler, for his daily work, he wasn't about to give in to the Emasculator. What sort of a cowboy couldn't handle a horse named Creme Puff?

He gathered his courage. "Let's just get this over with. Sooner or later she'll realize I'm not giving up, and maybe she'll behave herself."

"Normally, I'd say no. Last thing I need's a lawsuit and all, but you signed the release. You're on your own, and I've got guests to tend to."

"I'll take over," Clem said as he walked up.

Andy gave Creme Puff a last, soothing stroke, then headed for the main house, where a new batch of guests were gathering.

"Good luck, Bull," Clem told him. "You'll need it."

"Your confidence is overwhelming."

"It ain't confidence. It's admiration. A guy's gotta respect balls as big as yours." Clem had been working for Andy nearly ten years. He was a few years older than Brett, with brown hair streaked from too much time outdoors and a tan every New Yorker who'd ever laid down good money for a tanning bed would envy. Born and raised in Texas, Clem was one hundred percent cowboy, from his walk to his talk.

Truman would have loved Clem.

*He'll love you,* Brett told himself. *All six feet plus of bronc-busting, riding and roping you.*

He fixed his concentration on Cowboy International. To the first of many multimillion-dollar accounts and a surefire ticket to the number-one slot of the top ten. Move over, Ernst and Woodridge.

Creme Puff didn't move as he gripped the saddle horn. He hooked his foot in the stirrup. She blinked. He swung himself up. She sniffed. He seated himself in the saddle. She grunted.

So far, so goo—

The thought stalled as he glanced at the fence and saw

the brunette. The brunette with the legs and the belly button and the lips and the eyes.

"Ready?" Clem asked.

Brett had been ready since he'd first seen her. Of course, his dry spell accounted for most of his enthusiasm, because no way did he pant at just the sight of a woman. She climbed onto the fence, a smile on her face as she watched the activity in the corral. Namely him.

"Can you handle her?"

In a heartbeat. His hands itched just thinking about it, and the rest of him blazed hotter than the Texas sun.

"Bull?"

Yeah, he felt like a bull, smack dab in the middle of breeding season.

"Are you listening to me?" Clem's voice finally penetrated the lust clouding his thinking.

"Uh, what?"

"I asked if you were ready for me to let go?"

"Um, yeah."

Clem's hand fell away. The horse stood still for two heartbeats. Then Brett said "Giddyup." Mistake. Big mistake. The horse snorted and reared, and Brett did what he always did where Creme Puff was concerned. He hung on for dear life.

The ride was fast and furious, the horse bucking around the corral while Brett fought to keep his hands on the reins and his butt in the seat.

A shrill scream broke his concentration, and he saw the brunette's terrified face as Creme Puff reared. She lost her balance and tumbled into the corral, right in Creme Puff's line of fire. Brett jerked on the reins and managed to divert the horse.

Creme Puff swung around, the motion throwing Brett off

balance. He tumbled from the saddle and slammed into the ground, and the air bolted from his lungs.

The minute he managed to catch his breath, two all-important things registered. First, the ground, at least the part cushioning his upper body, was really soft, and second, it smelled really sweet.

He lifted his head and quickly realized that while part of him had slammed into the dirt, the rest of him had sprawled across the brunette with brown eyes that were even more mesmerizing up close.

Then there were her lips, parted just so. Kissable lips, and he really wanted a kiss.

"You," she said, and his gaze shifted to hers.

*You, me, us,* her eyes seemed to say, and he waited for verbal confirmation.

"Y-you don't smell," she half-whispered, half-groaned, and he realized he was crushing her.

He struggled onto his elbows while his brain searched for something brilliant to say.

"Uh, neither do you." Great, Maxwell. You're next in line for the Smooth Talker of the Year Award.

She took a deep breath, a grin curving her lips. "It's Chanel."

"No," he said, his gaze riveted to hers. "It's just you." One hundred percent sweet-smelling female.

"Um—" her tongue darted out to wet her bottom lip "—thanks."

"It's true. I'm not smelling any perfume. It's just you."

"I mean, thanks for saving me."

"Saving you?"

"That horse would have trampled me if you hadn't put yourself in harm's—"

"Suzanne!" a shrill female voice called, then it seemed as if the world intruded. Her gaze shifted to the crowd that had gathered around them, and Brett's sanity returned long enough for him to leave all those soft curves completely to climb to his feet.

A dozen hands reached to help her up, but Brett made sure his was there first. His fingers entwined with hers, palm to palm, heat to heat, as he pulled her to her feet. He never would have dreamed just a simple touch could be so jarring, but he felt an echoing heat roll through his body.

A few intense moments of eye contact, and he knew she felt it, too. Heat. Lots of heat that had nothing to do with the temperature and everything to do with the fact that she was a woman and he was a man.

"Oh, my God!" The redhead pushed between them, and the moment was lost.

But not the response. He still felt that as he stepped back and tried to catch his breath.

"Are you all right?" the redhead demanded. "I knew coming here was a mistake. I tried to tell you, didn't I? I tried to tell her," she declared to the crowd.

"You all right, little lady?" Andy asked.

"I'm fine." She shifted those rich brown eyes to Brett. "Thanks to... I don't know your name."

"My name?" What was his name?

"Bull, you okay?" Clem slapped him on the shoulder. "Creme Puff sure gave you a toss."

"Your name's Bull?" She seemed tremendously pleased when he nodded.

"It's a nickname. My real name's—"

"Brett Maxwell," Clem supplied. "But we call him Bull on account of he's really hung—"

"—gry," Brett interrupted. "I eat as much as any bull." She grinned. "I'm Suzanne. Suzanne Hillsbury."

"And I'm Celia," the redhead interrupted. "And we're

late.'' Celia slid a protective arm around Suzanne and glared at Clem. "Come on, Sue. We've got orientation.''

"I love your accent,'' Suzanne said as Celia steered her along.

"Thanks.'' It was nice to know his hard work was paying off. *Talk the talk and walk the walk.*

"Maybe we'll run into each other again,'' she added.

He touched his chest where her breasts had pressed against him. A guy could only hope.

# 3

A FEW MINUTES LATER, Suzanne stood on the front porch of the main house with a dozen other newly arrived guests and tried to slow her pounding heart.

Having a major coronary on her first day in Texas was not part of her plan.

*You were almost trampled. Of course you're this close to losing it.*

The trouble was, her shaken state had nothing to do with the stomping horse and everything to do with one very real, very warm, very muscular cowboy pinning her to the ground, his heart thundering against hers, his breath mingling with hers, his scent—the musky aroma of sweet-smelling straw and worn leather and sweaty male—filling her nostrils and making her think crazy thoughts like maybe she'd just give up her search for the perfect cowboy because she'd already found him.

Her senses were still overloaded. Testimony to sign number one—*S* for sensual awareness. Then there was sign number two—*I* for instinctual response, aka the call of the wild, meaning she was attracted to him at a very basic level. She wanted to rip his clothes off and make mad, passionate love, and without penciling him into her day planner first.

She smiled despite the sweat trickling from her temples. Her life was definitely taking a turn for the better.

"Howdy, folks." A large man in full cowboy regalia held up his gloved hands to quiet the buzz. "I'm Handy

Andy Jessup and I want to welcome you all to Handy Andy's Cattle Ranch and Wild West Getaway. You folks just got your first glimpse of a real buckin' bronc. That's what this place is all about, and why you all signed those releases when you booked your stay. You did sign your release, little lady, didn't you?'' His gaze singled out Suzanne, and a dozen pairs of eyes turned on her.

"Signed and notarized, just like the instructions said."

"Good." He rubbed his hands together. "'Cause you're about to find out what life's all about. Real folks and real work and real living, and it can be real tough as y'all just witnessed. Ain't no weight rooms or personal trainers here. We get our exercise working the stock. No fancy-schmancy food you cain't pronounce. We eat real beef with all the fixins. And we don't got no pools or game rooms for fun. We crank up George Strait on the stereo and kick up our heels on a dusty barn floor with the moon shining through the windows. So if there's any one of y'all came expectin' a dude ranch, I'll refund your money right now." He stopped and looked uncertain. "Did anybody come expectin' a dude ranch?"

A few hands shot into the air, and Andy shook his head. "Dad blast it."

"Where's the mechanical bull from the commercial?" one of the group called out.

"And what about the western wear shop located on the premises?"

"And I really need to fax overnight to my office. You have an office center for that, right?"

Andy shook his head. "Folks, I'm afraid there's been a little bit of a mix-up. That there commercial you saw was filmed in Austin, not on location here, and I'm afraid the advertising people got our spread mixed up with the Hadley Ranch Western Retreat over in Old Springs. Put the wrong name to the wrong tape, but by the time we figured out the problem, the thing had already been distributed and run on a few stations. We've pulled it, but it's still part of some reruns. Those of you who want to head over to Hadley's, I'll be glad to make the arrangements and have somebody drive you."

"Let's go," Celia said.

"Forget it. I had no intention of riding a mechanical bull, anyway." Or sending or receiving any midnight faxes, no matter how tempted she was to check on Blaire. All she wanted was a cowboy. Her thoughts went to one in particular, and she smiled. "We're here and we're staying."

After a third of the group retreated for fear of no twenty-four-hour copying services, Andy drew everyone's attention again.

"Sorry about that, folks, but that's what happens when you make your first commercial. Anyhow, I take it the rest of you came here for a good dose of country living, and that's what you're gonna get. We're smack dab in the middle of spring roundup. Country looks good, horses look good, and every cowboy is full of vinegar."

"I read about this on the plane," Suzanne said. "Spring roundup is when they brand, vaccinate—" The words died as Celia flashed her a glare. "Sorry. Weak moment."

"We've also got the Lonestar Cowboy Classic coming up nigh on two weeks, and I hope to see some of you city slickers entering the amateur categories. It's always a good time for everybody." He clapped his hands together. "Speaking of good times, we like to start our guests off with a small dose of Texas fun, starting with a welcome barbecue tonight and then the weekly hoedown tomorrow night. You all can rest up on Sunday, and then Monday we'll start turning you folks into real cowboys. I've got work to do, so I'll hand you over to my wife," Andy went on. "She'll get you settled in. See y'all at the barbecue tonight."

Candy Jessup was a walking testimony to the old saying that everything is bigger in Texas. Big fat red ringlets of hair were piled at least four inches high atop her head. High heels, at least three inches and then some, big chunky earrings shaped like armadillos and the longest eyelashes Suzanne had ever seen. Like black tarantulas anchored to her blue eye-shadowed lids. Everything on Candy was big— except her clothing. She wore skintight black Lycra leggings topped with a tight leopard-print top that showed a generous amount of cleavage and a white button that read Shop Till You Drop at Candy's. The Best Little Gift Shop in Texas.

"Whew," Candy murmured, fanning herself with the clipboard she carried in one jeweled hand. "I don't know about you all, but my makeup's about to go into major meltdown—the gift shop has skin cleansers on for half price today. Let's get on inside. You all can meet Mama Jessup, and then we'll have our first of seven Getaway get-to-know-you sessions. We do this every day for the first week. It makes the ranch experience more fun if folks know each other."

Candy herded them into the main house, through the foyer set up similar to a hotel lobby complete with a front desk, into an air-conditioned room with a red velvet couch and gold lamé armchair. A giant poster glorifying a younger, more glamorous Candy decked out in a complete feather headdress and feather bikini hung above the fireplace.

"You're not from around here, are you, Candy?" Suzanne asked.

"Heavens, no. Vegas, that's my hometown." She motioned to the display of pictures along the fireplace mantel, all featuring Candy in various showgirl outfits. "Spent twenty years as the lead dancer in the Dolly Roundtree Review at Caesar's Palace, until I met Andy. I thought he smelled, at first, but then he kissed me, and here I am."

Suzanne shot Celia a *see?* look.

"This is the red room, the main room of the house and a general meeting area open to guests. Then there's the green room, the pink room and the black suede room, all indicated with coordinating dots on your Getaway guest booklet." She held up the glossy book, and Suzanne nearly salivated. "And remember, all travel literature is on special today. A third off."

"Don't get any ideas," Celia whispered.

"Who? Me?" Suzanne tried to look innocent.

"The gift shop is run by yours truly," Candy went on, "and located at the west end of the house, behind the pink room."

"And the pink room is?"

"A fancy-schmancy name for the bathroom," an elderly woman, barely five feet tall and not more than eighty pounds, announced as she walked into the room.

"Bathroom just sounds so blah. I like something with a little pizzazz." Candy took the old woman's arm. "Everybody, this is Andy's mama, Mama Jessup. Say hello, Mama."

"How do."

"Mama helps with the cooking around here. Red-eye gravy's her specialty. Mama's also the pride and joy of the county. Oldest living citizen. How old are you now, Mama?"

"Old enough to know how long you been covering them gray roots of yours."

"Mama!" Candy flashed the old woman a warning look before settling herself on the arm of an overstuffed sofa.

"I like everybody to get to know each other, since you'll be working side by side. Let's go around the group, introduce ourselves and tell everyone why we're here. I'll start."

She breathed, her chest bobbing with the effort. "I'm Candy Jessup, as you well know, ex-showgirl and hardworking wife of Andy. This is Mama Jessup, my mother-in-law—"

"And the best damned shot in this whole county," the old woman interrupted. "I could get my gun and give a little demonstration."

"Maybe later, Mama. Right now the guests need to get to know each other. Now." Candy motioned to the first woman seated at the end of a row, a buxom blonde with long hair, vivid blue eyes and a body that made Suzanne feel like a Vienna sausage next to a platter of caviar. "What about you, honey? What's your name and what brought you here?"

"My name is Fawn Calypso," the woman said in a breathy, nine-hundred-number voice, "and this is my sister—" she pointed to an identical-looking woman next to her "—Dawn Calypso and—"

"—we're twins," Dawn finished for her with a smile, "and also—"

"—married to brothers," Fawn went on.

"Hal and Merle. Hal's mine," Dawn said.

"And Merle's mine."

"Hal and Merle Calypso? The champion team ropers?" A man dressed in a pair of newly starched Wranglers, a stiff colorful shirt and shiny cowboy boots asked, awe in his voice. "They're legends. I follow the rodeo circuit, and they broke last year's record."

"That's what Hal said," Fawn agreed.

"We were on a photo shoot for *Car and Driver*. We're models—"

"You ever do any of them nudie magazines?" Mama Jessup interrupted. "'Cause I subscribe to a few and I might have seen you—"

"Mama!"

"I'm just asking a question."

"That's not really appropriate. It's none of our business how the girls model."

"It's no big deal," Fawn said. "We do swimsuits, but that's as far as we take it off. We're mostly—"

"—calendar models, but we do a few muscle magazines. Anyhow, we missed it." Dawn looked as if she were ready to cry. "Not that we would have understood anything they were doing even if we'd been there. We're not real outdoorsy."

"Except for that Sports Mania calendar we did in Madrid, but that was a beach."

"And we had our very own cabana boy."

"Was he nude?" Mama Jessup asked, her eyes dancing with excitement.

"Mama!"

"Just asking."

"And a fully air-conditioned suite," Fawn continued, "so the Madrid thing wasn't really outdoorsy-outdoorsy."

"And that's what we want. Outdoorsy."

"As in chickens and cows—"

"—and horses. We've never been on a horse before."

"Which is why we're here. To learn more about what Hal and Merle do. They're so sweet and supportive of our careers—"

"—so it's the least we can do for them." Dawn turned to the urban cowboy. "Your turn."

"Gerald Farrington. I'm an accountant from Pittsburgh,

and this is my first vacation since I started my CPA firm. I wasn't going to come, but Shelly, that's my wife, thinks people should indulge their inner child. She's visiting Ireland—she's into castles and all that—and here I am. I've always loved *Bonanza*. I always wanted to be Little Joe, though sometimes I liked Hoss more, especially when I went through my chubby seventh-grade phase...." He rubbed his hands together. "This is going to be great!"

Suzanne thought again of her recent encounter with six feet plus of hunky Texas pride and smiled. This was definitely going to be great.

A well-dressed woman who looked like an older version of Barbie went next. "My name is Buffy Ridgeway. This is my husband, Skip—" she motioned to the Ken-looking man beside her "—and our son, Skippy." She indicated the teenage boy on her left. He seemed oblivious to the group, headphones in his studded ears, his shaved head bobbing with the music buzzing from his portable CD player.

"We're from Beverly Hills," Buffy went on. "Our therapist said we needed to bond as a family."

"Two weeks in a one-room cabin should do it," Celia said. "You either bond or you start duking it out. If the latter happens, my money's on Skippy."

"And you are?" Candy asked.

"Celia Donnelly, exotic dancer from Manhattan."

"Oh, goody." Mama clapped her hands together. "A stripper. I've got a few moves of my own, and I could use a professional opinion, if you don't mind."

"Mama!"

"Just asking."

"So, Celia. What brings you here?"

"For the record, I'd rather be in Jamaica, but my friend

here is on a mission to rope herself a cowboy, so I thought I'd come along and make sure she doesn't drag in a dud.''

"I have no intention of landing a dud," Suzanne interjected, "and I can take care of myself."

"Normally, she can, but she's on the rebound from Walter the tight ass. It wasn't a pretty breakup."

"How terrible." Candy sighed.

"Our hearts bleed for you," Dawn and Fawn said in unison.

"My wife says that tight-ass people were extremely repressed as children," Gerald added. "I, um, speak from personal experience."

"How did you know his ass was tight?" Mama Jessup asked.

"Mama!" Candy cautioned.

"Just asking."

"I am not on the rebound," Suzanne said. "I wasn't in love with Walter. He's not even my type. I just didn't realize it at the time."

"We think cowboys are great," the twins said in unison.

So did Suzanne. One cowboy in particular. Her cowboy.

*Her* cowboy? When had Brett Maxwell become her cowboy? He was a cowboy who could possibly be hers, but she couldn't make such an important decision until she'd seen every shred of evidence. She was down two of the S.I.G.N.S. and going for five.

Until then, the jury was still deliberating. No matter how much her heart pounded at the thought of him or how much her stomach did flip-flops or how much her knees trembled or how much his drawl sent shivers up and down her spine.

She forced herself to take a calming breath and tried to focus as Candy went around the rest of the group—a dentist, a computer programmer, a fourth-grade teacher and her engineering husband, before ending the introductions with a huge smile, a deep breath and a dramatic bob of her enormous chest.

"Since we've all had this nice time to share, let's hold hands and have a moment of positive energy."

"I'm hating this," Celia said.

"Now, now. This is quiet time." Candy breathed. "Feel the energy bubbling and flowing.... There now." She sighed. "Total harmony."

"I'd be in total harmony if I had a pool and room service."

"We can't offer that," Candy said, "but there is a large hot tub in the gazebo behind the main house. The hours are listed in your booklets. Now, are there any questions?"

"Were those real outhouses outside?"

Candy smiled. "You bet, but they're mainly just for local color. We don't actually use them, but I'll snap a picture of you out front for five bucks."

"I want my picture taken," Gerald decided.

"Us, too," said the twins.

"How about postcards?" Buffy asked. "I promised our therapist I'd send updates, and she loves visuals."

"And I'd like to get some T-shirts for my golf buddies back home," Skip added.

Candy smiled. "Come on, city slickers. I think a personal tour of the gift shop is definitely in order. I'm also offering a ten-percent-first timer's discount, so everybody shop till you drop!"

"And remember," Mama Jessup added, "we don't allow no peeing in our hot tub."

"Mama!"

IT WAS NEAR SUNSET when Brett walked into the gift shop and spotted the last lonely tube of Ben-Gay. His muscles wept in relief. After the fall he'd taken that morning, he'd never make it through an evening hunched over his computer without help.

The tube sat on the top shelf behind the counter above a row of gleaming silver belt buckles ranging in size from the Little Joe model to the ultra-deluxe Big Ben. It seemed as if New York wasn't the only place that picked up *Bonanza* reruns.

The tube sat a good two feet beyond his reach, and just thinking about the effort to retrieve it sent a shudder through him. He glanced around the empty store. Where the hell was Candy? He could use her and her five-inch stilettos right about now.

The barbecue had already started, and the shop was empty. A row of stuffed and mounted deer heads stared at him from the opposite wall.

"If it makes you feel any better, I don't even own a shotgun, fellas." Apparently it wasn't much consolation because they continued to stare.

He shook his head. He was losing it. First he'd taken up company with a raccoon named Zorro, then he'd started talking to Creme Puff and now stuffed animals. He needed physical contact. A good conversation that didn't involve riding and roping or how far he could spit a wad of chewing tobacco.

"Is anybody here?" He peered behind the counter and finally spotted the sign taped to the register.

Gotta Tinkle, Be Back in a Twinkle. C.

A twinkle? How the hell long was a twinkle?

Longer than five minutes, he decided after he'd read every pamphlet sitting in the counter display. For a desperately small town, Ulysses, a whopping fifteen miles from Andy's, was quite the tourist mecca. They had an annual pecan festival, not to mention five rodeos, the biggest of which, the Lonestar Cowboy Classic, was scheduled in two weeks.

He started to put the pamphlet in the rack when he spotted the sponsors listed on the back. Cowboy International. He wasn't sure how the knowledge would help him, but more knowledge meant more ammunition in his line of work. Stuffing the pamphlet into his pocket, he turned a desperate gaze to the top shelf. Salvation.

He took a deep breath, forced his arm to move. If he could reach up and grab it, he could leave the money on the counter and—

"I was wondering when I'd see you again."

The voice stalled his arm in midair. His muscles protested, desperate to give up, but Brett gritted his teeth and forced himself to make a less obvious retreat. Slow. Easy. Ah. There. Now he could breathe.

On second thought—instead of dull, flat oxygen, the scent of her—ripe apples with just a hint of cinnamon—filled his nostrils, spiraled through his head and torpedoed straight to his groin.

Get a grip. She's just a woman, and you've been close to women before. A lot of women. Better-looking women. Prime, grade-A deluxe females.

None of whom had smelled half as good as she did.

He drank in another deep breath. And another.

A frown worried her forehead. "Are you all right?"

"Never better." What was he saying? He was in desperate pain, he had tons of work and a sleepless night ahead and he hadn't had a good pasta in nearly two weeks.

But with her smiling at him, her lips parted just so, her soft brown eyes crinkled at the corners, he felt good. Great. Invincible. As if he could climb the tallest mountain, soar over the highest building. Endure another twenty-four hours of cowboy hell.

"I really like the way you smile," he told her.

"Me?" Her smile widened, and his heart gave an answering shudder.

She looked so surprised that it tugged at something deep inside him. "Hasn't anybody ever paid you a compliment before?"

"Sure. I mean, if you count stuff like 'Killer lips, baby!' and 'Come on over here and plant one on me, hot stuff.'"

He grinned. "You just shot down my best pickup lines."

She smiled again. "Does that mean you're trying to pick me up?"

"Not that the idea hasn't crossed my mind." In fact, it was causing a major traffic jam at the corner of brain central. "But I was simply stating a fact."

"Thanks—for the compliment, and for saving me today. That was a pretty brave thing you did."

Brave?

"You could've really hurt yourself," she added, her gaze full of concern.

Well, he *had* jerked awfully hard on the reins to steer Creme Puff away from her before he'd nearly plunged to his death. "It was nothing."

"Yeah." She reached out, and her fingertip grazed the scar at the corner of his eye. Electricity bolted through him at the simple contact. "I guess you do stuff like that all the time."

Get thrown from a horse? He shrugged. "Every day." The past six, to be exact, thanks to Creme Puff. "It's getting to be old hat. Not that this scar has anything to do with a temperamental horse."

"A nasty bull?"

"A nasty water gun."

"Come again?"

"I was playing cops with my youngest brother about ten

years ago. He couldn't get his gun to squirt, so he jabbed me with it. Unfortunately, it had a sharp edge, and he put just enough force behind it. Took six stitches to close it up."

"That's terrible."

"Comes with the territory when you've got brothers."

"How many do you have?"

"Three. All younger than me."

"That's nice. I'm an only child, but I always wondered what it would be like to have brothers and sisters around." The hint of vulnerability in her voice touched something inside him, and he had the sudden urge to reach out, to comfort.

"Just imagine...you'll never have the pleasure of knowing what it's like to wait in line for thirty minutes to use the bathroom. Or look for your favorite shirt in the closet only to turn and find your younger brother wearing it. Or spend an hour fighting over the remote control when the show you wanted to watch lasted only a half hour."

His spiel brought a smile to her face. "Brothers do all that?"

"And a few things I can't mention in female company. So what brings you into the gift shop on this fine Texas evening?"

She rubbed her hind end, and his palm itched to join in. "My bottom's so sore from falling in the corral today, I can barely sit."

"Then you need my ultra-deluxe Tush Cush," Candy called out as she walked from the rear of the store. "Only five ninety-five with the coupon from your Getaway guest packet."

"I guess a twinkle is something like fifteen minutes," Brett remarked.

"Give or take a few." Candy scooted behind the counter.

"Actually, it's twelve and a half minutes, the long-playing version of Wayne doing 'Twinkle, Twinkle, Little Star.'" Wayne referred to Wayne Newton, obviously Candy's favorite, according to the shrine set up in the corner of the gift shop, complete with an autographed poster, an array of CDs and a gold lamé jacket tagged Authentic. "So what can I do for you two? I'm running a special on belt buckles. Buy one, get the second for half price."

"First off," Suzanne asked, "do you have a phone I could use?"

"Got one up at the main house, but there's usually a line about now since it's the only one. Wait a second." Candy leaned behind the register. "I set my blasted cordless back here somewhere. You can borrow that and take it in the back room...." Her voice faded as she started rummaging around.

"Checking in at home?" Brett asked.

"Something like that."

"Your folks?"

"No, my parents are retired and living in Fort Lauderdale. Yours?"

"They died a while back. It's been just me and my brothers since then. So, are you checking in with a husband, then?"

She grinned as if she knew what he was up to. "I'm not married. You?"

He shook his head, and pleasure swept through him when he saw the relief that lit her eyes. "Significant other?"

"Not unless you count goldfish number six, but she's floating at the bottom of the New York sewer right about now."

"You're from New York?"

"Manhattan, born and raised, but please don't hold it

against me, or the fact that I need to check in with my office. Make that ex-office—''

''Ta-da!'' Candy's voice rang out, cutting Suzanne off. ''Here's the damned thing,'' the woman announced, crawling from behind the counter. She handed the phone to Suzanne. ''You can go out back for some privacy. Oh, and by the way…'' She leaned down and grabbed a manila envelope. ''Delivered just an hour ago with your name on it. So, is the phone all you need today?''

''I could really use some muscle cream, too.''

''This is definitely your lucky day, honey.'' Candy whipped the tube off the shelf. ''My last one. And you?'' She turned to Brett. ''What can I do you for, sugar?''

Brett considered tackling Suzanne for the precious tube. While the idea definitely had merit, not only because of the prize but the physical contact, he couldn't bring himself to make a move. She looked so pleased cradling the Ben-Gay.

He knew the feeling. He took a deep breath, and his muscles groaned in response. It was going to be a long night.

In more ways than one, he realized when his gaze locked with Suzanne's. He saw his own hunger mirrored in the dark brown depths. Hunger. Fire.

He'd had his share of women, and he'd seen the look many times before. But there was something different now. A fierceness that made him want to hoist her over his shoulder, cart her to his cabin and love her fast and furious, then slow and sweet, despite that he had a presentation to finish tonight.

The realization shook him. No matter how intense the attraction, no woman had ever taken priority over a project.

Until now.

*Only because it's this close to shriveling up and falling*

*off due to lack of use. You're coming off a major dry spell,
buddy.*

"Sugar? You still with us?" Candy's voice disrupted his
thoughts.

"Uh, yeah." He forced his attention from Suzanne, from
the strange awareness sizzling between them.

His attention shot to the lonely shelf where the Ben-Gay
had been and his muscles whined a version of poor, poor,
pitiful me. His gaze dropped to the gleaming belt buckles.

"Did you say half price?"

So much for an evening of relief. Not that even the Ben-
Gay could help him now. Not when Brett Maxwell was
suffering from a major case of lust, and the cure had just
smiled and waltzed into Candy's back room.

"HILLSBURY, Vargas and Crawford."

"Thank goodness I caught you before you left for the
day," Suzanne said to Marilyn the minute the fellow attorney answered the phone. "How's Blaire?"

"The client from hell."

"I mean, how is she holding up?"

"She's fluctuating between a vengeful bitch and Mary's
lost little lamb."

"Nothing unusual then." Suzanne opened the envelope
Candy had given her and pulled out the local real estate
listings. "Just listen when she wants you to listen and help
her man-bash, and you'll be fine." She flipped through several pictures the realtor had included. Her gaze snagged on
one in particular, a two-story white frame house with a
redwood fence and a porch swing. *Home.*

"She's been asking for you again."

"I told you to tell her I'm on vacation." A permanent
vacation, because Suzanne Hillsbury had no intention of
going back to her old life. She was starting fresh. A change

of pace, a change of scenery. A real home rather than her cluttered apartment on Manhattan's East Side. She slid the picture of the white frame house into her pocket, then shoved everything else back into the packet.

"I already told her," Marilyn said. "It didn't work."

"What do you mean?"

The attorney's voice took on a desperate note. "Please, please, *please* don't be mad. She forced it out of me."

"What?"

"Your whereabouts."

"You told a client where I was?"

"The client from hell," Marilyn corrected. "And I gave her the phone number. I had no choice. She was holding the clippers in her hand, and I've spent five years growing out that awful Dorothy Hamil cut I got on a dare back in college, and she was in vengeful-bitch mode. If it's any consolation, I don't think she'll call you tonight. After she left the jail today, she went straight to her therapist. She's on some heavy-duty tranquilizers right now."

"How comforting."

"You're not upset, are you?"

"No." Furious was a more accurate description for what she was feeling. Furious and anxious and worried, the way she always felt during a crisis at work.

But she wasn't at work. Not anymore.

She forced a deep breath. "I'm fine."

"So you're having a good time?"

Let's see... No air conditioner, no cappuccino maker, no local pizza parlor, no air freshener.

Just one hunky cowboy with a sexy drawl and an easy grin. Her stress faded away, and she smiled. "A great time," she told Marilyn. "I'm having a great time."

"YOU ARE NOT in love with this guy." Celia stalked after

Suzanne, who headed into the barn before daybreak the next morning.

The smell of hay and horse engulfed them, and Suzanne did her best not to wrinkle her nose. "Not yet, but there's definitely love potential."

"This is exactly why I came. You can't go falling for the first cowboy who tackles you, Sue."

"Why not, if he's the one, which is highly likely if things keep going as planned? I fell for Walter, and he wasn't even close. What's wrong with falling for someone who meets the criteria?" Brett was everything Walter wasn't. Everything she was searching for in a man.

"Look—" Celia gave her a pointed stare "—what do you really know about this guy?"

That her stomach fluttered every time he looked at her, that her nerves went into overload, that her knees trembled.

As if Celia read her mind, she smiled. "That's just lust, girlfriend. You've been around those stuffed shirts at your office so long, you've forgotten what crazy animal attraction feels like."

Forgotten? She'd never felt it before. Not like this. Until now. Until him.

"He's got three younger brothers, and his parents died a while ago." At Celia's skeptical look, she added, "Okay, so it's not much, but a girl's got to start somewhere. Besides, I may not know his favorite food or what sort of music he listens to, or whether or not he likes animals or kids or old people, or what football team he roots for, but I intend to find out." Growing Attraction was number three on Dr. Ray's list, and Suzanne's next order of business. "Starting today."

"That explains why you dragged me out of bed before sunrise on a Saturday morning."

"He spends most of his time in the saddle, so the sooner

I get on a horse, the better. Besides, I didn't drag you out. You followed me.''

''Only to keep an eye on you—''

''Mornin', ladies.'' Clem's voice echoed through the barn as he walked in wearing jeans and a western shirt, his hat tipped back.

''What's he doing here?'' Celia demanded.

''Giving us riding lessons.''

''I already know how to ride.''

Clem winked. ''I bet you do, little lady.''

Celia glared. ''I hate you. I *really* hate you.''

''He's teaching *me* how to ride,'' Suzanne explained before turning her attention to Clem. ''So do you think I can learn to do this by lunchtime?''

''Depends. You ever ride a horse before?''

''No.''

''Ever saddle a horse?''

''No.''

''Ever pet a horse?''

''No.''

''Ever seen a horse?''

''I used to watch *Mr. Ed* when I was a kid. So what about lunch? You think I can do this by then?''

''If it's a late lunch.''

''How late?''

He tipped his hat back and scratched his head. ''The end of next week.''

# 4

OVER THE PAST WEEK, Creme Puff had stirred a good many emotions inside Brett. Fear. Anger. Frustration. Even a thirst for vengeance. But never envy. Until now.

Brett gripped the reins of the nice, cooperative Darlin' Daisy and stared across the moving herd at the woman who'd given him the longest, most restless night of his life.

With a white-knuckled grip, Suzanne Hillsbury maneuvered the Emasculator around a nearby corral. She kneed the horse to a trot, her bottom doing an enticing jiggle and bounce that forced Brett to reevaluate his initial opinion that all this cowboy stuff was for the buzzards. That, and the smile that crossed her face when she tugged on the reins and the animal actually stopped. She rewarded the horse with a lingering stroke.

Creme Puff had all the rotten luck.

"Keep 'em movin'!"

Andy's voice jerked Brett to reality, to the sweat pouring down his back, the sizable animal beneath him and the branding pen brimming with cows and calves ready for separating.

Brett pushed the last calf inside, and the gate slammed shut behind him.

"Yo, Bull!" Andy called. "Get a loop around that one's head, and the ground crew will do the rest." The ground crew consisted of three cowboys, two that heeled and tailed the calves while another manned the branding irons.

"You want me to *rope* something?" Brett asked, wheeling Daisy around. "Now?"

"It's just like the dummy."

"The dummy didn't move."

Andy grinned and urged the huge paint he rode after his next target.

Brett gripped Darlin' Daisy's reins and sighted the calf. So the calf could move, but so could he, and he *had* roped the dummy. Not once but a dozen times.

Beginner's luck, one of the other cowboys had said, but Clem had said it had more to do with balance, strength and determination.

Determination. Brett had that in spades when it came to something he wanted.

He reached for his rope, started the loop twirling beside him and did his damnedest to relax, to take the rhythm of the rope. He moved up on the calf from behind, leaned over the horn and tossed his loop. Bingo! He snapped up the slack while the ground men flanked the animal.

Andy tipped his hat back and grinned. "Not bad."

In cowboy lingo, that meant damned good, and that's exactly how Brett felt. Good. Damned good.

Then he turned and caught Suzanne's smile.

The sight of those luscious lips curved just for him sent a spurt of confidence through him. He sat a little easier and held the rope with a steady grip. For the next few moments he forgot how much his thighs hurt and how much he despised Creme Puff and how anxious he was to go back to Manhattan. He felt hot and sweaty and achy and alive, and he liked it.

"Take another down," Andy called.

Brett took a deep breath, set his sights on the next calf and went to work, all the while conscious that Suzanne Hillsbury was watching him. And smiling at him. A full hundred-watt show of teeth and lips that warmed him even more than the blazing Texas sun.

Yep. Maybe this cowboy stuff wasn't half bad, after all.

"I TOLD YOU this cowboy stuff isn't all it's cracked up to be," Celia said when she found Suzanne in the cabin later that day.

Suzanne summoned her best smile despite her throbbing thighs. "It's great."

"Admit it. You were too sore to get out of bed."

"I'm out of bed. I've been sitting in this chair for a half hour."

"Lucky for you I don't want you to miss a moment of this place." She held up a plate draped with a napkin. "I brought you my leftover vittles from the authentic chuck wagon dinner courtesy of Mama Jessup and some grizzly old cook named Chuckie."

Suzanne pulled the napkin off. "Left over? The plate's overflowing." With something very hot and brown and lumpy.

"I only eat stuff I can recognize."

Suzanne sniffed. "It smells kind of like chili." She eyed the plate. "Or maybe it's stew."

"You can tell me later. Gotta go."

"I thought you didn't like hoedowns."

"I don't, but one of the cowboys was headed into town for supplies. He said I could ride along if I promised him a dance after we got back. While I'd rather stuff bamboo shoots beneath my fingernails than two-step, a girl's gotta eat. There's a burger with my name on it sitting over at the Tasty Freeze."

"You're leaving me alone? Aren't you afraid I might pick up some cowboy and marry him while you're gone?"

"You spent two hours on a horse. You're not going anywhere except maybe into a hot shower. So much for this trip being great, huh? See ya.''

The door closed just as Suzanne muttered, "It is great, and I intend to dance up a storm tonight.'' Her legs wept at the thought, but she summoned her courage. So she was a little sore. This was all new to her. Her body had to adjust.

Her thoughts went to the hot tub Candy had mentioned, then she remembered Mama's parting comment about no peeing allowed. Maybe the hot tub wasn't such a great idea.

No, she had to work the kinks out. That meant moving. Dancing. Besides, it was for a good cause. Her future.

SHE WASN'T HERE.

Brett scanned the dancers sliding across the makeshift dance floor, the people holding court along the sidelines, watching and drinking and enjoying the crying country sound of Ulysses' own Cactus Jack and the Prickly Heat.

Cactus wailed about his cheating ex-wife and expert fisherman—or maybe the PC term was fisherwoman, Brett wasn't sure—who'd run off with a guy who had a bigger rod and reel while the Prickly Heat kept the tempo with a country swing.

A fiddle solo finished the number, the guys took a bow, and Candy took the stage.

"For those of you who'd like to sit the next one out, there's karaoke set up in the brown room—that's the tack area for those of you who didn't bring your Getaway guest booklet. Everybody join in and enjoy!''

The music started again, keeping time with the steady throbbing in Brett's temples. He took a gulp of punch, wiped the sweat on his brow and prayed the extra-strength Tylenol would kick in. He had a headache, and he was sore and this close to heading to his bunk. He needed to work on his Cowboy International presentation, not to mention a dozen other accounts, and he needed to sleep.

He didn't need to waste time at a hokey hoedown.

"Hey, Maxwell."

Brett turned to find Andy approaching him.

"You got a minute?" Before Brett could reply, Andy went on, "See, I got this problem. There was a mix-up with my commercial, and I've got all sorts of people coming here expecting something they ain't gonna get. I hired this group of slicks out of Austin to shoot it, and they made us look like a bunch of polished cowboys who ain't got nothing better to do than twirl our women around a dance floor and ride some fancy mechanical bull. Seeing as you're into advertising and all, I'd be mighty obliged if you could make a few suggestions. I need an idea that gives more of a feel for the place."

"I'll give it some thought."

They talked for a few minutes before Andy tipped his hat and went to the tack room to sing a duet with Candy, who was warming up the karaoke microphone with a very loud rendition of "Viva Las Vegas."

Five more minutes, Brett told himself as he stood and drank his sixth cup of punch. He'd give her five more minutes. If she didn't show, he was out of here—

"How do."

The voice startled him, and he nearly spit out a mouthful of punch. Particularly since the voice was followed by a squeeze to his left buttock.

At least he thought it was a squeeze. Surely he'd just imagined it. After all, this was Mama Jessup.

"Come on, hot stuff. Take an old lady for a spin around the dance floor."

Hot stuff? His gaze went to the cup in her hands.

"What are you drinking there, Mama Jessup?"

"Apple cider, sweet cakes. Want a little sip?"

Brett sniffed at the offered glass. "Hundred proof?"

"What kind of a girl do you think I am? It's not a drop over eighty. Come on."

For a barely-five-foot, ninety-pound, eighty-something-year-old woman, she had one hell of a grip.

"You been working out, Mama Jessup?" Brett asked as she slung him around and plastered herself against his chest, her bony arms locked around his waist.

"And bulk up all these feminine curves with nasty old muscles?" She winked at him. "Give me a bowl of Special K, two glasses of prune juice and my Geritol, and I'm as fit as a prizewinning heiffer. I'll leave the bulking to you, studly."

Studly? Okay, so maybe he hadn't imagined the butt squeeze—

Nope. Definitely not.

"Mama Jessup?"

"Yeah, sweet cheeks?"

"This is a fast song."

"Yeah, sugar lips?"

"And we're slow dancing."

"And the problem is?"

"Shouldn't I twirl you or something?" What was he saying? He didn't know how to two-step, much less twirl.

"I'm fine as I am." Another squeeze. Brett started and Mama chuckled. "A feisty one. I like that."

Feisty? Hey, he wasn't that kind of a guy.

He stared at the woman, her arms locked around his chest, her toes riding his as she hummed the tune that blared. He couldn't hurt her feelings.

Brett spent another half hour getting his butt squeezed and his toes squashed before Mama Jessup finally cut him some slack and excused herself to go to the little girl's room. Blessed freedom!

She pointed a bony finger in his direction and winked. "I'm coming back, stud muffin, so don't you move!"

At least for the next five minutes.

"Stud muffin? And here I thought they called you Bull." The familiar voice slid into his ears and jolted him to full awareness.

He turned and drank in every incredible inch of Suzanne Hillsbury, from her shining brown hair pulled into a ponytail to the sweet curve of her jaw and the sexy slope of her neck that led to a silky red blouse tucked into black jeans. Red cowboy boots completed the outfit. She looked out of place amid the loud western shirts and starched denim Wranglers. Like a prizewinning rose amid a sea of wildflowers.

Geez, he was waxing poetic. He was definitely losing it. Seven days and six nights without CNN or the *Wall Street Journal* or *The New York Times* did that to a man. And of course there was the small matter of nine months and nineteen days of celibacy.

A matter which wasn't so small anymore. Not with her standing so close and smelling so sweetly of apples and cinnamon.

"I didn't think you were coming," he said as they stood by the refreshment table.

"Getting dressed took a little longer than I expected."

"Great boots."

"Really?" She glanced down, and a smile played at her lips. "Because I thought they were gorgeous when I spotted them back home, but now that I'm here—" her gaze swiveled to the crowd and the endless pairs of dusty boots sliding across the dance floor "—I'm thinking they might be a bit much."

"They suit you."

"You think?" He nodded, and she smiled again before her gaze shifted to their surroundings. "This place is great."

"Yeah. It's sort of hot, though." Especially since she'd walked into the room. His attention hooked on a trickle of perspiration that slid down her creamy neck.

"A little sweat never hurt anybody."

"Speak for yourself," he said as the drop disappeared into her generous cleavage.

"What did you say?"

"I, uh, said that the speakers," he blurted, "are a little loud."

"You can't miss a beat."

"Does that mean you like to dance?"

"Sure." But she didn't look so sure.

When he took her in his arms, he realized why. She was stiff, her muscles tight.

"Relax," he said, sliding his arms around her waist and pulling her close.

"Easier said than done. I started riding lessons today. My legs feel like they were used as a wishbone."

"Don't worry. The feeling will fade in a week or so."

"You really know how to comfort a girl—"

"Turn him loose!" Mama Jessup's voice rose above the wail of a guitar a split second before she yanked Suzanne out of Brett's grasp. She shoved up the sleeves on her flower print dress and held up her fists. "Come on, missy. Let's see what you got."

"W-we were just dancing," Suzanne said.

"Likely story. I saw you making those cow eyes at him, and I'm here to tell you, he's off-limits."

"Cow eyes?" Brett's gaze shot to Suzanne. "You were making cow eyes at me?" Not that he knew what cow eyes were, but from the fierceness of Mama Jessup's expression and the way Suzanne blushed, cow eyes definitely qualified as the non-contact version of a butt squeeze. Both meant "I want you."

"Come on, girly. Put 'em up."

"Mama Jessup!" Clem's voice rose above a crying fiddle. "Just the woman I'm lookin' for."

"Not now, Clem. I got a score to settle."

"Suzanne was making cow eyes at me," Brett explained.

"I saw her," Clem said, and Suzanne's face flushed brighter.

"*And* she was dancing," Mama Jessup declared, "swaying all sexy-like in them red boots and rubbing herself up against him like some juke-joint loosey-goosey—"

"I did not rub."

"Not yet," Brett said. Suzanne shot him a look that said, *I thought you were on my side?* "But I was hoping."

Before Mama Jessup could get in another word, much less a punch, Clem slid an arm around her thin shoulders. "I know you're busy here and all, but I sure could use you, darlin'."

"If you're lookin' to cuddle up to me to escape those church busybodies your mama's always trying to fix you up with—" she motioned to two very homely, very eager-looking women making a beeline for them "—just forget it."

"Actually—" Clem maneuvered his way around Mama Jessup so he was partially hidden from the two women frantically searching the crowd "—one of the guests is making a run for town."

Excitement leaped to Mama Jessup's eyes. "The Tasty Freeze?"

He nodded. "Left in Zeke's pickup about fifteen minutes ago. I'm going to check it out. Thought you could ride shotgun with me in case things get ugly, but if you're too busy—''

"I'll get my gun."

"Scamming burgers isn't exactly a shooting offense."

"You're right. We'll hang 'em, by dammit!" She clung to Clem's arm and let him lead her to the door. "I ain't seen a really good hangin' goin' nigh on fifty years now...."

"That old woman's scary," Suzanne said once Clem and Mama had disappeared, the church women hot on their trail.

"You're not kidding." And he had the fingerprints on his butt cheeks to prove it.

"Do you think she was really going to fight me?"

"I doubt it would have been much of a fight. One punch. End of fight."

"I don't know." Suzanne rubbed her arm where Mama had grabbed her. "She may be small, but she's really strong. I don't think she'd go down that easy."

"I was talking about you."

She eyed him before a smile tugged at the corner of her full lips. "What makes you think I'd take a punch for you?"

"You were making cow eyes at me."

"Standard reaction to good-looking men. Besides, you can't prove it."

"Witnesses."

"A deranged old woman? Mentally unstable."

"There's Clem."

"An overworked ranch foreman on the run from his mother's matchmaking prospects? Unreliable. The eyes can play terrible tricks once fatigue sets in. Not to mention the influence of outside factors. A smoke-filled room. Poor lighting."

"You're a lawyer."

A sheepish grin spread across her face. "That obvious, huh?"

"You just argued a case over cow eyes. One hell of a case."

"Old habits are hard to break." A determined light burned in her eyes. "But I'm trying. So let's just forget about me being a lawyer. Right now, I'm just a country girl."

"If you say so." The truth was, she was about as far from country as a woman could get in her silk blouse, her designer jeans and her fire-engine red boots. But if she wanted to play it country, he could go along. Anything to keep her smiling.

"So, just for the record, you *were* making cow eyes at me, weren't you?"

A grin curved her full lips. "Now why would I do something like that? I hardly know you."

"I can fix that. Come on." He reached for her hand.

"Where to?" she asked as he led her outside. "Because after the long walk here, just the thought of going a few more feet makes me want to tear up—"

Her voice died as he scooped her into his arms. His sore muscles protested the added weight, but then he felt all those curves pressed against him, her scent filled his nostrils, and all was right with the world.

"So, um, where exactly are we going?"

"Someplace where we can get to know each other."

"I NEVER REALIZED riding used so many muscles," she said after he'd carried her a few feet. Her choice was either to make mundane conversation or wait silently for a heart attack from all this close contact. With each step, each shift of his body against hers, her heart pounded. Thundered.

"It really tones the inner thighs." His lips seemed to linger around the words. The inner thighs in question tingled.

She fought for a calming breath.

*Think growing attraction. Questions. Where were you born? What's your favorite food? Do you squeeze the toothpaste from the middle or the end? Are you an outie or an innie?*

"We're here." His words shattered her thoughts, and she realized he'd stopped.

"Already?" Heat fired her cheeks. "I mean, already, as in, it's about time."

Because she was definitely just this side of a heart attack.

Forget that. She was having the heart attack, right here, right now, she realized when his grip shifted and she found herself sliding down his hard length onto trembling legs. *Hard* being the operative word.

Oh. Ah. *Oh.*

*Questions.* She forced herself away from the mesmerizing glint of his eyes. She needed to breathe, to think, to...

"Wow." Moonlight twinkled off the serene lake surrounded by a fortress of trees, the area peaceful and secluded and so romantic. Her breath caught. "This is really beautiful."

"Yeah."

She turned to find him looking at her, his gaze dark and mesmerizing.

"I was talking about the water."

"Yeah."

"You're not looking at the water. You're looking at me."

"Yeah."

The words hung between them for several heart-pounding moments before she finally found her voice.

"I—I guess we should sit down and talk or something—"

"I really want to kiss you."

"Okay." Okay? No, it wasn't okay. He couldn't kiss her yet. She had at least a few dozen things to ask him first, starting with—

Hungry lips closed over hers and scattered her mental list of questions. He tasted like plums laced with rum. Sweet. Intoxicating. Potent.

S.I.G.N.S., she told herself, even as her arms slid around his neck.

*Bad arms.* But no matter how her brain protested, the rest of her didn't seem to want to cooperate.

It had been so long since a man had really held her. Really kissed her. Forever, it seemed, and maybe it had been, because no kiss, no embrace had packed as much punch as this. Her nerves hummed. Her heart revved. Her skin tingled where he touched her and ached where he didn't.

"Growing attraction is supposed to come next," she murmured.

"My attraction's growing." He pulled her closer. "As we speak."

Her hand brushed the tight stretch of denim at his crotch, and he groaned into her mouth as he devoured her, his lips eating at hers, desperate yet gentle at the same time.

She struggled for her waning control. "Then there's negotiation. We're supposed to share our thoughts," she murmured against his lips, "to discuss issues and see if we can respect each other's ideals." His palm skimmed the tip of her breast, and sensation jolted her. "But this is good, too," she managed to say.

Super sex was a definite sign, and Dr. Ray hadn't mentioned anything about going in order—

Her thoughts disintegrated as he rolled her sensitive nipple between his thumb and forefinger, and heat spiraled through her body to set off an echoing throb deep inside.

"I need to see you."

"Yes," she gasped. Yes? No, no, *no*, she told herself as his fingers worked at the buttons of her blouse. She had to slow down, to be sure....

"Do you have your own teeth?" she gasped, remembering Celia's words about the test.

"What?" The question was a soft rush of breath against her lips as his movements stilled.

"Your own teeth." It was a stupid thing to say, but standing there in the darkness, her heart racing like a speeding New York subway, her body burning so hot, it was the only thing that popped into her head. "You don't wear dentures, do you? Or even a partial? Please say you don't."

He pulled away to stare at her in the shimmering moonlight. His brilliant smile warmed her face. "I don't."

His hands slid inside her shirt, her bra clasp snapped, and the lace fell away. Strong hands cupped her aching breasts, and her doubts disappeared in a wave of uncontrollable heat.

She tugged at his shirt, popped the buttons and pulled it down his arms until she had free access to the powerful male beneath. She trailed her hands over his muscular chest sprinkled with silky hair while strong fingers worried her nipples, stroking and teasing until they sat up and begged for more.

"I don't know what it is about you, but you drive me absolutely crazy." His voice, raw and husky, rumbled in her ears, and a wild thought flashed through her head. He sounded different. His tone deeper, his words more pronounced...

The thought faded as his fingertips abandoned her aching

breasts to slide down until he touched her there...and there...and, oh, my God, right *there*...

"Where have you been all my life, cowboy?"

*Cowboy.*

The word pierced Brett's passion-fogged brain, and a warning went off. Did she think... Aw, hell, she couldn't really think... He opened his mouth to set Suzanne straight before things got out of hand. "I'm not—"

She kissed him, her tongue darting inside to stroke his. Every rational thought flew south for the winter as she unbuttoned him and urged his jeans and boxers down. Things were already out of hand. Then silky fingers stroked his throbbing attraction, and everything was in hand, her hand, and there was no turning back.

No turning, but they did need a detour. If she kept this up he was liable to crash and burn before he made it to the finish line or even managed a pit stop for preventive maintenance.

He urged her down on the sweet grass, shed what was left of his clothes, then turned to her. He pulled her boots off. Buttons popped, a zipper hissed and he peeled her panties and jeans down her legs to land in a growing pile next to his own clothes.

And then he did what he'd been fantasizing about since he'd first set eyes on Suzanne Hillsbury. He kissed her belly button. She gasped and moaned and wiggled, and he slid his lips lower.

He drove her crazy with his mouth, lapping at her, kissing her, tasting her until she bucked and trembled and came apart right there in his arms and he was so hard he thought he might burst at the sight of her flushed, smiling face.

"I hear bells," she gasped.

"Me, too," And he hadn't even had an orgasm, testimony to the powerful attraction between them.

"No," she breathed as he nibbled his way up her body and settled between her open thighs. "I really hear bells."

The shrill ringing grew louder, pushing past the pounding of his heart and pulling him to reality.

"It's just my phone."

"Your phone?" She stiffened, and his gaze snapped to hers.

"Cell phone. Over there in my jeans pocket."

"Which you use when you're out on the range, right? To call in reports on the cows or the weather—"

"Advertising," he interrupted.

Shock gripped her features as if he'd just declared himself an IRS auditor.

"I'm hearing things. I—I could have sworn you just said—"

"Advertising. I'm in advertising."

"I—I have to get out of here." She shook her head and scrambled from beneath him.

"What's wrong?"

"This can't be happening to me." Trembling hands reached for her panties.

"What did I do?"

"Nothing. Everything." She turned accusing eyes, still bright with desire, on him. "You're supposed to be a cowboy." She tugged the edges of her blouse together as if it were the hardest thing she'd ever had to do. "A *cowboy*."

"I'm a guest. I've been here a week."

"But you were riding and roping like you were born in the saddle."

"I'm a fast learner, and it's been a long week."

"You were taming a bucking bronc, for Pete's sake!"

"A bucking bronc?"

"Creme Puff." She struggled to right her jeans, which were inside out.

"Creme Puff is a quarter horse with a mean streak when it comes to me."

Her hands stalled, and her gaze collided with his. "Are you saying you weren't breaking her when I was watching you yesterday?"

"She was breaking me."

She shook her head, her eyes bright and shiny as she gave up on the jeans, scooped everything into her arms and struggled to her feet.

"Don't go." He followed, reaching for her, but her skin was slick from their recent activity and she slid out of his grasp and started down the path.

"Suzanne, wait—"

But it was too late. She was gone.

And so were his pants.

# 5

THE LANDSCAPE PASSED in a red blur as Suzanne hightailed it down the trail before she started crying. Or worse, before she gave in to her trembling body and raced back to the river, straight into Brett Maxwell's arms.

She hardened herself against the notion and concentrated on the ugly truth. A *cell* phone. Of all the rotten, low-down, dirty, sleezy things—

*Bleep!*

Suzanne glanced down and realized that she had not only her jeans in her arms, but Brett's, as well. And his T-shirt. And his boxers.

She smiled until she pictured him standing on the riverbank, naked and sexy and hard in the shimmering moonlight, muscles gleaming, his lips hinting at a wicked smile that made her heart do that funny little flip thing—

*Bleep!*

Forget the funny little flip thing. It was probably from eating all that barbecue last night. Then tonight she'd had chili. Indigestion. That was it, because no way was her heart still flipping now that she knew the truth.

He hadn't just been glad to see her. He'd been packing a cell phone and red silk boxers with polka dots and a smiley face right over his—

Another bleep and she took a deep breath, ignored the dread in her stomach and stabbed the on button. "Hello?"

"Who is this?" A woman's voice carried over the line.

*Hang up,* she told herself. *You don't need it rubbed in your face. He's not the man you thought, end of story.* "This is Suzanne Hillsbury. Who are you calling?"

"Brett Maxwell, but I must have the wrong number."

"The Brett Maxwell who ropes and rides and looks really great in a pair of Wranglers?" She cringed at the hope in her voice. But old lawyers' habits were hard to break. Innocent until proven guilty.

"The Brett Maxwell who worries and works seven-twenty-four and wears three-piece suits."

*We the jury—*

"Armani?" She held her breath.

*—find the defendant—*

"Ralph Lauren."

*—guilty.*

Suddenly the past few days rushed at her, and she remembered the flash of fear in his eyes when he'd been riding Creme Puff, the desperation when she'd bought the last tube of Ben-Gay, the way his slow country drawl had picked up the pace down by the river until he sounded like any of the men in her office. Of course, his voice had been deeper, more seductive.

She forced the notion aside. The clues had all been there, but she'd been too desperately in lust to see them. "Stupid, stupid, *stupid.*"

"I know. I told him, Armani says, 'I'm important, I mean business.' But do you think he listens to me? Of course not. I'm just his secretary. What do I know? Says he likes the way the Ralph Lauren slacks fit. I say, have the Armani tailored, but trying to tell the Bull anything is like beating your head against the wall."

"That's why they call him the Bull? Because he's *stubborn?*"

"And determined. And, apparently, catching on pretty

well down there if he's riding and roping and actually wearing Wranglers."

"Oh, yeah." She wiped the tears creeping from her eyes. "He's got the cowboy thing down pat."

"Good, then he'll be home soon."

"And home would be?"

"New York."

"*The* New York? As in the Empire State Building? Central Park? Wall Street? *That* New York?" They had a Paris, Texas. Why not a New York, Texas?

"Times Square, Rockefeller Center, yada, yada, that would be the one. Look, dear, I'd love to play travelogue with you, but I really need to talk to Brett. Could you get him for me?"

She'd like to *get* him, all right. She could think of a dozen very vicious, very painful ways to get him, especially on a ranch that roped and branded and castrated on a regular basis.

Not that he really deserved it. He hadn't lied to her. He'd simply sinned by omission. Or possibly he hadn't even realized she'd thought he was a cowboy. She'd never actually said it, so she really should give him the benefit of the doubt.

Nah. She wiped at the tears streaming down her face. Not when he'd touched her and everything had felt so right and then he'd turned out to be an advertising executive from *New York,* of all places...

"Dear, are you crying?"

"No, no. I'm fine. Brett's, um, unavailable."

"Then give him this message for me—I'm Nancy, his secretary. Tell him today's conference call and all those late night faxes paid off. Mac has agreed to up his media budget by four hundred thousand to cover the sponsorship of the Gulf Shores Regatta. He's now our biggest client, and we've just knocked Wallaby and Tucker out of the number-eleven spot!''

*Secretary. Conference calls. Faxes. Sponsorships. Accounts. Media budgets. Clients.* The Seven Deadly, as far as Suzanne was concerned.

She dashed away more tears. ''Th-that's great.''

''You're not all right. What's going on? Where is Brett?''

''Probably still back at the river.''

''The river?''

''And still naked.''

*''Naked?''*

''It's a long story.''

''I've got all the time in the world.''

She sniffled. ''And depressing.''

''I could use a good cry.''

''I don't think I can talk about it right now.''

''I've got one word, honey. Doughnuts. Whatever your problem, one bite and all is right with the world.''

''I don't think a doughnut will do it right now.'' She wiped away another tear and sniffled. ''Unbelievable. Thousands of miles away, and I end up with a Manhattan Special.''

''The Bronx, honey. Brett's from the Bronx. It's just his office that's in Manhattan.''

''Psst!'' Brett leaned from behind a tree and hissed at Clem, who'd just climbed out of his pickup several feet away near the main house.

''What's that noise?'' Mama Jessup asked as Clem helped her from the passenger's side.

''I don't know. I think it's coming from over there. It sounds like...'' His gaze snagged on Brett before he cupped Mama's elbow and steered her toward the house.

"Like what?" She tried to glance behind her.

"A mosquito."

"An awful loud mosquito."

"It's really big."

"How big?"

"Big enough to drain you dry in one bite, so you should hurry inside. I'll get a can of bug spray."

"I could get my gun."

"I think the bug spray will work better."

"I don't get to have any fun," she grumbled as she walked inside. "What's the use of having a sawed-off shotgun with a forty millimeter scope if I never get the chance to use it?"

"You've been subscribing to *Militias-R-Us,* haven't you?"

"Maybe."

"I'm telling Andy."

"See if I ride shotgun with you again, buster...." Her voice faded as she disappeared inside the house. The screen door rocked shut behind her.

"Bull?" Clem rounded the truck and peered at the cluster of trees where Brett had been hiding for the past two hours.

His cabin sat at least a hundred feet away, in clear view of God and everybody. While he might be miserable, he wasn't about to go flashing every guest at Andy's. Especially since it had taken him nearly that long to get rid of a monster erection, courtesy of one infuriating lawyer.

"What are you doing out here?" Clem stepped toward him.

"I think you'd better stop there."

"What's going on?" Clem took another step, then another.

"Don't come any closer—"

"Whoa." Clem held out his hands and turned around. "I don't know what you're into and all, but around here we don't usually take our nature walks quite so literally."

"Someone stole my pants down by the river."

"Male or female?"

"What difference does it make?" Clem chuckled, and Brett growled, "Female."

"Musta been some night."

"One I'll never forget." In more ways than one. He'd come this close to breaking his dry spell. Then Suzanne had left, his pants had followed, and he'd spent two hours as the main course for a swarm of Texas-size mosquitoes.

*Slap.*

Pain splintered through him, and he shook his head. "I can't believe it. One minute everything's fine." More than fine. Great. Greater than great, because never had he felt so hot for a woman. So desperate. "Then the next thing I know, she's ranting about cell phones." *Slap. Slap.*

"Women," Clem said. "Go figure."

"As if I lied to her or something." *Slap.* "How was I to know she thought I was a cowboy? What am I? A mind reader? Okay, so maybe I can kind of see it now. Like when she thanked me for saving her from Creme Puff. I thought she was talking about me yanking on the reins. I mean, I *did* try to save her. That ought to count for something." *Slap. Slap.* "I didn't mislead her on purpose—"

"Bull?"

"—and when I did figure out that she might think I was the real thing—" *slap*, "—I tried to tell her, but there's this chemistry between us—"

"Maxwell?"

"—she looks at me and I forget what I'm going to say. Hell, I can't even think." *Slap, slap, slap.* "I've been attracted to women before, but never like this—"

"Bull!"

"What?"

"You want to play True Confessions all night and feed the local insect life, or you want me to go fetch some clothes?"

"Sorry, man. I'm just a little stressed right now." *Slap, slap.* "And the blood loss isn't helping."

"Just stay put, and I'll be right back."

"I'm really not tired." Mama Jessup's voice carried from an open window. "I think I'll go out and get some fresh air."

"Speed it up," Brett whispered as the woman opened the door. He shrank back behind the tree.

"Relax." Clem chuckled. "If you get lonely, Mama Jessup can keep you company. I'm sure she'd be more than happy to whip out her shotgun and go after a few mosquitoes for you. Let's just hope she's got good aim."

"*Hurry!*"

BRETT WAS in the barn saddling Darlin' Daisy the next morning when Suzanne found him.

"I accidentally picked up your stuff last night."

The stuff landed in a heap at his feet, and he paused, his hands lingering on the saddle. While Darlin' Daisy raised her head at the new presence in her stall, Brett wouldn't allow himself to glance up.

His nostrils flared. Suzanne smelled even better than he remembered, a cross between warm female, cinnamon apples and the faintest hint of soap. He barely resisted the urge to close his eyes and simply breathe.

*Don't let her do it to you, buddy. Where's your pride? Your anger? She walked out on you.*

His fingers tightened on the girth. "When did you figure out you *accidentally* swiped my clothes?"

"About twenty feet from the river."

He snapped his head around and glared. "Twenty feet?"

"Maybe twenty-five."

"Thanks a lot for coming back."

She had the decency to look regretful despite her words. "Well, you deserved it. You..." Her voice faded as she seemed to notice his face. She stepped closer, one fingertip going to a vicious mosquito bite on his cheek. "What happened?"

"About one hundred and thirty pounds or so of mean, clothes-stealing female, followed by a swarm of Texas mosquitoes with an appetite."

A smile tugged at her lips. "I'm sorry."

"No, you're not."

"I really am, but I shouldn't be. You lied to me." Hurt flashed in her eyes, and his anger cooled considerably.

"Not on purpose. I didn't even realize you thought what you did until you said it at the river, and then you kissed me and... Hell, you *really* thought I was a cowboy?"

She nodded. "I guess part of it was wishful thinking. I mean, we clicked, and you passed Celia's stupid test, and so I wanted it to be you, but then you turned out to be a Manhattan Special, with a cell phone and a secretary and a firm that's this close to breaking into the Manhattan Ten."

"How close?"

"Nancy said MacGregor upped the budget to include the Regatta sponsorship. You're number eleven."

"Yes!" He clapped his hands. Finally, he was starting to get somewhere.... The thought faded as his gaze locked with hers. "Why are you looking at me like that?"

"Like what?"

"Like I just shot Bambi."

"I most certainly am not looking at you like that."

"You are."

"I'm not. You wouldn't shoot Bambi because you probably don't own a gun, much less know how to shoot one. I doubt you've ever been on a hunting trip, except when searching Manhattan for the perfect Gucci loafers to go with your Armani slacks."

"Ralph Lauren."

"Same thing."

"No, the lines on the Lauren are much smoother—"

"You're missing the point," she said, the Bambi look haunting her brown eyes. "You're not my type. If I hadn't skipped a sign, I would have realized that last night."

"A sign?"

"Dr. Regina Ray. She outlined the five signs for a compatible husband. *S* for sensual awareness, *I* for instinctive response, *G* for growing attraction, *N* for nurturing respect and *S* for super sex. You were down two, and then I got caught up in number five and forgot all about numbers three and four."

He grinned. "If I'm not mistaken, we definitely did number three last night."

She came close to smiling, then seemed to catch herself. "Not that kind of growing attraction. An emotional attraction that develops as we get to know each other's likes and dislikes." She shook her head. "It doesn't matter now. What does is that we have different expectations. I'm making a change in my life. I'm trading my career for lots of sunshine, fresh air and a cowboy. Why are you here?"

"I'm after a boot campaign for Cowboy International. This is research—" he patted Daisy's rump "—and a competitive edge, and guaranteed to push me into the top ten."

"Which illustrates my point exactly. Worlds apart."

He faced her, several feet of hay-strewn floor separating

them. "We weren't so far apart last night. You, me, the two of us. We almost—you *did*—"

"Under false pretenses."

False pretenses? There'd been nothing false about their kisses, about the way she'd gone wild at his touch, come apart in his arms. That had been fierce, not false.

"You're attracted to me." He stepped toward her.

"I was attracted to the man I thought you were." She inched backward.

"But you're not attracted to me now?" Another step forward.

"Why would I be?" She took another step back. "I mean, you're good-looking and you've got a great smile, and that little scar near your right eye is sort of sexy, but…" she seemed to shake away the admission. "But you're still not the kind of man I'm looking for." Her back came up flat against the wooden divider separating Darlin' Daisy's stall from the next.

"Really?" He stopped inches shy of touching her.

She licked her lips and cleared her throat, her gaze hooked on his. "Really."

"You know what I think?" He moved until he blocked the entrance and she had no place to go but against the wooden railing that separated the stalls.

"That we should part friends and forget the past three days?" She looked so hopeful, he couldn't help but smile.

"I think you're lying."

"I am not."

"I think you want me."

"In your dreams."

"There, too." That was part of the problem. She'd haunted him all night long. A particular vision of her stretched out on the riverbank wearing nothing but a smile and her red cowboy boots—

"Where did you get those?" He stared at the simple brown leather boots she wore.

"I told you. I'm making a change."

"I liked those red ones...." His voice faded as he noticed the simple white cotton T-shirt and faded denim jeans she wore. "What happened to your clothes?"

"I went shopping at Candy's. I needed something more appropriate."

"Your clothes suit you better."

"My stuff screams city gal."

"You *are* a city gal."

"Not anymore." She ground the words out. "Now, if you'll excuse me—" she tried to duck past him "—all I want right now is to get to my riding lesson."

He anchored an arm on either side of her, blocking any escape. "We've got great chemistry, Suzanne. What's so wrong with that?"

"We do not have chemistry."

"Really?"

"Really."

He reached out and trailed a fingertip down her arm. "You're trembling, and it's ninety plus out here, which proves, either you're extremely cold-natured or have a raging fever or a nervous twitch. Or there's some major chemistry at work."

"Cold-natured." His fingertips skimmed her collarbone, and a sigh parted her lips.

"Raging fever," she mumbled.

He traced her bottom lip, and she squeaked.

"Nervous twitch."

He kissed her, a soft feathering of his lips against hers that hit him as hard as a lightning bolt. She felt it, too, because fear flashed in her eyes.

"That doesn't prove anything," she blurted, scooting

past him with a quick duck and a brush against his thigh that sent a hum through his body. "I—I really have to go."

"Cowboys to hunt?" He followed her out of the stall.

She stopped in the barn doorway. "Exactly."

Her reply wiped the smile from his face.

Not because Brett Maxwell was the jealous, possessive type. It just seemed a damned shame to waste such an intense attraction. The kind that rearranged a person's priorities, made him forget all about huge western wear accounts and filled his head with thoughts of deep brown eyes and full lips and the sweetest belly button he'd ever had the pleasure of tasting. Last night had been a preview of what things could be like between them, and he couldn't get it out of his mind.

"We're not finished," he called after her. "Not by a long shot." Because he knew she felt the pull between them as much as he did. She just wouldn't admit it.

Yet.

SHE WASN'T going to look.

Suzanne stood in the gift shop and tried to concentrate on the display of cosmetics. She'd come in to spend some money, to shop it out instead of the old-fashioned, useless crying.

She'd done that last night, and she didn't feel any better.

Her gaze shifted to the magazine rack filled with countless offerings, from *Texas Ranch Country* to *Horses and Hay,* and there behind *Lonestar Ladies* was one last copy of *Cosmo.* Last month's issue, but who cared?

She was desperate. She needed a quick fix. An article, an advertisement. She'd even settle for the shopping credits on the back page—

"There you are!" Celia's voice rang out, and Suzanne's fingers snapped together an inch shy of the magazine. "I've been looking everywhere for you! I came in so late, and you were already asleep, and when I woke up, you were already gone. I have to tell you about last night. There I was having a burger in town when Clem shows up—oh, my God. You did it!''

Suzanne's gaze swiveled to the magazine display, and guilt shot through her. ''I swear, I didn't even touch.''

''Not it.'' She waved off the magazine. *''It.''*

''What?'' Fawn asked as she walked in and pulled off her sunglasses. She stared at Suzanne. ''Oh, that.''

''Yep,'' Dawn said as she walked up behind her twin. ''Definitely *that* look.''

''What look?''

''Like you've just had great sex. There's a glow to the skin—''

''—and a softness to the mouth,'' Dawn finished for her twin.

''That's ridiculous,'' Suzanne said. ''I did not have sex.'' Sort-of sex, but that didn't count. Did it?

''You came close,'' Celia said. ''Close enough to hear bells.''

''Okay, maybe I did—''

''I don't believe this. I leave you unchaperoned for one night, and you go out and hear bells, and now you think you're in love and you're going to throw everything away for some country stud named Eli or Zeke or Sam—''

''His name is Brett, and I'm not in love.''

The pronouncement stopped Celia cold. She simply stared, then shook her head. ''Let me get this straight. You almost had sex with someone you have no romantic interest in? A hunky *cowboy* and a few hours of mindless pleasure with no strings attached?'' At Suzanne's nod, Celia beamed. ''That's my girl.''

''But he isn't a cowboy. He's a guest. An ad exec from

New York, which means I'm not about to fall in love with him.''

"An ad exec?" The revelation seemed to please Celia. "Now don't be too hasty. What's the name of his agency? Does he live in the city? Does he drive a BMW or one of those sporty numbers?"

"What difference does it make?"

"You almost had sex with him. We're talking a major connection. You, him, *together.*''

"What happened to a few hours of mindless pleasure?"

"You're not the mindless pleasure type."

She wasn't. And she wasn't about to change. No more mindless pleasure, and most of all, no more Brett Maxwell.

"Last night was a…" *Mistake* was there on the tip of her tongue, but for some reason, she couldn't say it. He'd felt too wonderful. She'd felt too wonderful. *It* had felt too wonderful. "Last night shouldn't have happened. Brett Maxwell isn't my type. I want a cowboy." Which was exactly what she intended to find. If at first you don't succeed, as the saying went. "A *real* cowboy." Minus the cell phone. And the laptop. And the Ralph Lauren suit. And the silk boxers.

On second thought, she kind of liked the boxers.

*Get a grip, girl!* No way did she want silk boxers. She wanted cotton boxers or briefs or whatever it was that real cowboys wore. That's what she wanted.

Forget silk boxers. Red silk boxers. With black polka dots and that little smiley face right over his—

*Forget.*

Yeah, right.

# 6

"NOW YOU TWIRL your loop just like this, then let her rip." The rope sailed through the air and caught the wooden horse set up in the east corral. Enthusiastic murmurs floated through the half dozen guests gathered for the Monday morning roping lesson. "There are different styles of roping once you're on horseback, but for now, the important part is to get you folks comfortable with a lariat. Jack, here, is going to pass some out, and y'all can give it a try for yourselves."

Hmm. Jack.

Suzanne took a rope from the cowboy, who smiled and tipped his hat. He definitely had S.I.G.N.S. potential. Of course his hair was a little too long, too brown, too—wait a second. She *liked* brunettes. Tall, dark and handsome, and he fit all three, not that his looks were the primary lure. He was a real cowboy, from the calluses on his hands to his mud-caked boots. He spent his days surrounded by fresh air and green pastures. He worked to live, not lived to work. *And* he was single.

*Meet candidate number one.*

Her gaze shifted to several cowboys busy mounting their horses in an adjoining corral. One was old enough to be her father, but the man with him, Pete she'd heard Clem call him, was in his thirties. While he wasn't *GQ* handsome with his craggy face and his thin lips, he had a quiet strength, and he was single. *Hello, number two.*

A handful of cowboys worked the nearby branding pen. Suzanne gave each the once-over, mentally retrieving all the information she'd managed to accumulate yesterday after she'd raided the gift-shop snack counter. Unfortunately, the selection had been limited. No soul-soothing chocolate or anything that promised an instant sugar coma. She'd spent the morning crying and eating Texas peanuts, crying and eating Lone Star pork rinds, crying and eating armadillo-shaped crackers, then just plain crying over Brett Maxwell and the thousands of fat calories she'd consumed.

That was then, and this was now. The first moment of the first day of the rest of her life. She was through feeling sorry for herself and hiding in the cabin for fear of running into him. She was taking action, starting with a low-fat breakfast, followed by a morning spent accumulating a list of candidates. Later she'd seek a little one-on-one attention with each man, scope them out for the S.I.G.N.S.—in order, of course. She wasn't making the same mistake twice. And if she happened to see Brett, she would play it calm and composed, the way she did in the courtroom during opening arguments. If there was one thing Suzanne Hillsbury knew how to do, it was play it cool. It was her trademark, an act she'd spent her entire career perfecting.

She studied the other men around her. Too old. Too young. Guest. Guest. Divorced. *Number three, come on down!* Guest. Female guest. *Number four.*

Surely out of four, she could find one man. *The* man. If not, she'd move on to five and six and so forth, but four was a good number to start with.

She turned her attention to the thirty feet or so of stiff nylon in her hands. Cutting a sideways glance, she watched as Clem demonstrated another throw for Gerald Farrington, the Pittsburgh accountant, who wore fringed chaps, matching fringed vest, a bandanna around his neck and a ten-gallon hat at least a size too big.

"He looks like one of the Village People." Celia picked up her rope and started twirling the nylon. She flipped and caught her target with practiced ease, and Suzanne's mouth dropped open.

"Where did you learn to do that?"

Celia grinned. "I was roping before you were playing Perry Mason, Counselor. Pretty good, huh?"

A loud clap sounded as Clem walked up. "I'm impressed. They teach you that back in the big city?"

The grin faded, and she glared at the man. "You know what you can kiss."

He winked, which made her frown harder. "The thought kept me up all night."

"Ugh, I really hate that man," she muttered as he walked over to help the twins, who'd managed to rope each other and were trying to get untangled.

"I think you like him."

"I think this heat's frying your brain."

That was a possibility, too. "You don't know him well enough to hate him. You're probably attracted to him but fighting that attraction. It's a classic case of denial."

"You're supposed to be a lawyer, not a psychologist."

"A good lawyer is a psychologist. You've got to read people. The opposing counsel, the judge, the jury."

"Is that a wistful note I detect in your voice? Missing life back in the real world?"

Well, an air-conditioned office or a freezing courtroom sounded pretty good right about now—

Objection!

She was glad to be away from the office, out of the courtroom, free of the constant stress. Okay, so maybe she wasn't *glad,* but a woman had to do what a woman had to do. She was breaking the cycle of five generations of work-aholic lawyers. Her father had always said being a lawyer meant being a psychologist, a police officer, a social worker, a mother and a father—all rolled into one. He'd been so busy being everything to his clients, he'd had little time left for bedtime stories and father-daughter picnics and just being there. It had taken a heart attack to make him realize what he'd been doing to himself.

Suzanne wasn't waiting for the heart attack to wake her up. She was making a change now. She wiped at a trickle of sweat. If the heat didn't kill her first.

"Admit it, Sue. You're as hot and miserable as I am."

"I am not." She'd been miserable yesterday. Today she was perky. Granted, her thighs still hurt, but she was chipper, all things considered. As for hot…

"You're sweating," Celia pointed out.

"The Comanche called it purification. It was a religious experience for them." She took a deep breath and exhaled. "I'm feeling cleansed as we speak."

Celia's gaze narrowed. "You bought some of those pamphlets in the gift shop, didn't you?"

"I did not."

"You did."

"I didn't. I said I wouldn't and I didn't." Suzanne fixed her attention on trying to get the rope to twirl. "I accidentally elbowed the stand when I walked by to get another tube of Ben-Gay—Candy finally restocked—and the pamphlet sort of fell. I had to pick it up." She couldn't help that her eyes, the poor, deprived things, had gone straight to the printed text on the Comanche who used to inhabit Texas.

"You broke your promise."

"It's not my fault that Candy's display is flimsy. Don't you have some cowboys to terrorize?"

"Actually, that idea isn't half bad. I threaten them, they stay away from you, we hop a plane out of here."

"Celia, wait." But the woman had already walked off, headed for her first victim. Oh, well. Suzanne wasn't really into brunettes anyway.

Since when?

*Since one moonlit Saturday night and one very hot blonde with sculpted muscles and a voice like deep, dark chocolate and hands that did the most incredible things....*

"Miss me?"

The familiar voice sizzled down her spine, and her heart jumped.

She half-turned, and there he stood, wearing faded jeans that clung to his muscled thighs and a black T-shirt. His hair was damp, curling around his neck. Deep blue eyes crinkled against the bright morning sun. Sensuous lips curved into a slow, lazy grin, and for a brief moment, Suzanne forgot the all-important fact that Brett was exactly the type of man she didn't want.

"Miss who?" she finally managed to say in a squeaky voice.

"Me."

"Now why would I miss you?"

"Because you can't stop thinking about the other night."

"Was that you?"

"Why are you so determined to ignore the fact that I light your fire?"

"Why are you so determined to keep me from ignoring it?"

"Aha, so you're admitting you're trying to ignore it." He grinned, and she frowned.

"I've got a rope to twirl, if you don't mind."

"Be my guest, sweetheart." His gaze held hers for five furious heartbeats, before he moved past her to Clem, who'd moved on to help Buffy and Skip with their ropes. A few feet away, Skippy Jr. practiced fastening a noose around his own neck and nodding his head to the music blaring over his headphones.

The sight struck her, reminding her even more of her purpose. She didn't want a dissociated family, absentee parents and kids used to being alone. The way she'd been.

She wanted a real family.

"Clem makes it look so easy," Brett said, drawing her attention.

He had such strong features. Not *GQ* handsome, but strong. High brow, a sculpted nose, strong jaw, sensuous lips. Her gaze lingered at the scar at the corner of his eye. A sudden image of him, tall and wet and delicious, flashed in her mind.

*Stop that.*

"You made it look pretty easy yourself the other day." She forced her attention away from his bluer-than-blue eyes to the matter at hand. The fact that he wasn't a cowboy, but a career-driven, cell-phone-packing Manhattan Special who probably had a fax machine hidden under his bunk.

"It's on the desk."

"What?" She shook her head, saw his smile widen and realized she'd spoken her thoughts out loud.

"I've got a laptop, too, and a printer, if you need to write up a few memos for the office."

"The thought hasn't even occurred to me today." Actually, it had occurred to her yesterday as she'd replayed her decision to hand over Blaire's newest divorce to Marilyn. No one knew the case as well as Suzanne did, and while she might be selling out and leaving Manhattan for good, until she made the official announcement, Blaire was still her client.

Old habits…

She shook away all thoughts of work and stared at her rope. "The only thing I need to do is twirl this blasted thing." Which she managed to do for a split second before it landed in a heap on the ground. She tried again. Two eighths of a second, and she managed to get the revolving circle over her head. *So far, so good.* The thought faded as the nylon collapsed around her. She couldn't practice like this. Brett was too close, his stare too intent, that damned smile too unnerving.

*Tell him to get lost. Or better yet, you get lost.*

"So how long did it take you to learn how to do this?" she asked. *Coward.*

"I practiced a full week until I thought my arms would fall off." He retrieved a lariat from Jack and started twirling a loop, a slow, leisurely motion that made his biceps flex and made her mouth water.

*Shoulda told him to get lost.*

He shifted his arms. The rope lifted overhead. A few more twirls, and the loop flew through the air, snagging the wooden steer.

His smile was contagious this time. She motioned to his lariat. "Where can I buy one of those? I think mine's broken."

"It's not the rope. It's what you do with it. I practiced and practiced and still couldn't get it, then Clem tipped me off to a little secret. Here." He stepped behind her. A wall of solid muscle pressed against her back, strong arms came around her, and his hands settled over hers. "Try holding it like this." He guided her hands and twirled the loop. "Keep your wrist loose."

"That's the secret?"

"In time. Now there's a rhythm to the rope. Just let yourself feel it." He moved closer, the muscles in his chest rippling, tightening, sending goose bumps down her spine. Her grip faltered, and the rope collapsed.

"It's okay," he said, helping her get the rope started again. "Just relax."

Yeah, right.

No matter that she managed to push aside the fact Brett Maxwell was not a cowboy. He had been the giver of her very first Big O, and her hormones refused to forget. They scrambled in anticipation, making her blood rush, her heart pound, her palms sweat.

An exasperated breath rushed past her lips. She could do this. She would do this, and without dropping to her knees and begging him to rock her world one more sweet, memorable time.

She managed to get the loop twirling again, his wrist motion guiding hers.

"Do you feel the rhythm?"

Oh, yeah. She felt it, all right. A symphony of muscles cradling her back—

"Have you got it?"

No, but she'd certainly like to get it—

"The rope? Have you got the rhythm?"

She fought for a calm breath. "Just call me Aretha. So is this the secret? Feeling the rhythm?"

"No. Now set your sights on the steer, and don't think about everybody around you."

"You mean like mental blocking?"

"Bingo."

"That's the secret?"

"Nope. Now don't just block out the visual part, shut out all the external noise, as well. Focus on your heartbeat."

"That's the secret?"

"We're getting there. Now picture the one thing you

want most in the world, count off three wrist movements
and throw.''

"Three wrist movements. That's the secret?"

"The prize, Suzie Q. Roping's one part skill and three
parts mental. You're not thinking about the actual throwing,
about whether or not your aim is straight or your hand is
shaking. You're thinking about what you want the most.''

"What do you picture?"

"The Cowboy International account. The first time I
caught that steer, I pictured the company logo and let her
go. Been snagging Old Bessie ever since.''

*I told you so,* her brain screamed to her traitorous hormones. *He's one-hundred-percent work, work, work.*

Not this girl. She was after blue skies and green grass
and a real cowboy.

"Try it. Hook your gaze on the steer, take a few deep
breaths and block out everything.''

The voices of the other guests faded into a murmur that
quickly drowned in the soft, steady sound of her breathing.

"Now picture what you want most.''

Come on, blue skies... The thought disintegrated as she
saw Brett Maxwell's smiling face. The rope flew from her
hands, and the loop sailed through the air and caught the
horns.

Brett gave a loud whoop, a burst of applause came from
the twins, and Suzanne did the only thing she could think
of. She turned and bolted for the gift shop and blessed air-
conditioning. The heat had obviously fried her brain, because no way in hell, heaven or the in-between did she
want Brett Maxwell.

She wanted a real cowboy. Not a Manhattan Special, no
matter how good he looked in a pair of Wranglers.

Her head knew that, but damned if her body could get
the message.

SHE WANTED Brett Maxwell.

She admitted the truth a few minutes later as she stood in the gift shop and flipped through a rack of western shirts.

Not in a forever kind of way, mind you. He was still a thousand miles and a career shy of real cowboy potential.

She wanted him in an I-have-to-have-you-right-here-right-now sort of way. Lust. That was the culprit behind what she was feeling. Nervous, fearful, excited, anxious. *Lust.*

Understandable. She'd been orgasmless for thirty-three years and counting until Brett Maxwell had walked into her life. He'd made her feel like no other man ever had. It was no wonder she felt the urge to melt at his feet and chuck her well-laid plans every time he touched her. Spoke to her. Smiled at her.

Yeah, all it took was a smile, a crinkle of that tiny little scar and she went from levelheaded Suzanne Hillsbury to wild and wicked Suzie Q.

Suzie Q. She hated that name. Except, of course, when he said it. There was just something about his tone of voice, the way his lips moved around the syllables.

Forget Suzie. Suzie was a live-for-the-moment good-time girl, and while the moment could be pretty incredible, it was the morning after, and the morning after that, that Suzanne was interested in. Long-term.

Which meant Suzanne had to forget him, them, *it,* and stay away from Brett Maxwell. And the sooner she found her cowboy, the better.

"It's your lucky day," she heard Candy saying after she'd answered the cordless phone she kept near the register. "She's right here. It's for you," she said, motioning to Suzanne.

"Me?" She took the phone, mentally running down the

list of possibilities. She could come up with only one really hot prospect. "This is Suzanne Hillsbury."

"Suzanne! Oh, thank God, it's you!" Blaire Covington Smythe Warren's high-pitched voice carried over the line. "The most horrible thing has happened."

"I know. I'm so sorry."

"Forget sorry. Just come home right away. I need you."

"Marilyn is handling things."

"But she's not you. You're the best lawyer in the business, and we have a track record together. You know me, how I think, what I want."

"His head on a platter?"

"More than anything, but I'll settle for snatching that BMW out from under him and putting him into one of those horrible compact cars. The lying, deceitful jerk." Blaire rattled on, telling in much more colorful phrases what had happened while Suzanne sipped a diet soda. "And that's why I'm giving up men for good. I don't want to see a man, talk to a man, hear a man, and I certainly don't want to sleep with one. I'm vowing celibacy from here on out. They're not worth the trouble."

Suzanne could think of one in particular who was worth it.

*Stop that!*

Brett Maxwell was off-limits, period.

"So are you coming back today?"

"I can't."

"Okay, but I expect you here first thing in the morning."

"I can't, Blaire, but I'll check on you, I promise," she said. "And I'll talk to Marilyn. Ex number four will be lucky to be driving anything before all is said and done."

A wave of guilt swamped her as she hung up the phone. Blaire was her client and she was in need. Then again, Suzanne wasn't personally responsible for the love lives of everyone she provided counsel to. Blaire was the very reason Suzanne needed to escape the divorce game. Before she lost hope and declared herself a man-hater, as well.

She needed a change.

She walked outside and took a deep breath. The smell of dirt and animals and sweat made her nostrils flare. *You asked for it, you got it.*

Now all she had to do was get used to it.

She stiffened her resolve, stepped off the porch into a hundred plus heat and went in search of candidate number one. She had fifteen minutes before her riding lesson and she intended to make the most of it. She found Jack in the barn rubbing down Creme Puff.

"There, there, girl." Jack's soothing voice stirred a soft warmth inside her.

*Puppies are warm. And so are thick, furry socks and down comforters, but I wouldn't marry one.*

She frowned. Warm was good. Warmth meant feeling, and feeling involved one of the five senses. Therefore, sensual. Sort of.

"Hi, Jack." She reached for a brush. "Can I help—" She stopped as he snatched the brush from her hands.

He stared at her as if she'd grown two heads. "What are you doing?"

"Well, I've got a brush in my hands. How about brushing the horse?"

His frown deepened. "Don't you think you ought to be taking it easy? I mean, that's why you're here, ain't it?"

"Well, yes." She shrugged. "But I really didn't think of grooming as a stressful chore."

"It's an awful big brush for a little thing like you, and if there's one thing I know, a lady in your condition shouldn't be exerting herself."

"My condition?"

At her blank look, a gentle expression softened his features. He patted her hand. "Don't you worry none. The same thing happened to my cousin Ginny last summer, and everything turned out just fine."

"What happened?"

"Two kicking and screaming baby boys. Carried 'em full to term even though they was fighting to bust out long before then."

Baby? Term? *Bust?* "You think I'm expecting?"

He nodded. "I know twins aren't triplets, but what's one more? The trick is to take it easy and don't exert yourself. I'm sure that's what your husband would want."

Shock beat at her brain. "My husband?"

"The professional wrestler."

"Wrestler?"

He nodded. "Back at home, though he's not actually at home, I understand. He's off on a wrestling tour, and you're here because the doctor said to get some fresh air and relax since you're still in the first trimester, which is why you didn't want to tell everyone. Didn't want to get hopes up until you're out of deep water. Same as my cousin Ginny. She was near to burstin' before she let the news out."

"But I'm not—"

"I got to say," he interrupted, a frown on his face, "you really should have explained the situation to your travel agent, because this is a working ranch." The frown eased into a comforting smile. "But don't worry none, I know once Andy hears about the situation, he'll make sure you have an easy time of it. Soon you'll be bragging everybody's ear off about the coming event! Now—" he swept her into his arms before she could blink "—a lady in your condition has to stay off her feet."

# 7

"PREGNANT?" Suzanne planted her hands on her hips and glared at Celia. "You told him I was *pregnant?*"

"I didn't tell him any such thing. I merely said you had a condition."

"A condition that involved triplets."

"I said more than two. He assumed triplets. It could have been quints."

"And a three-hundred-plus-pound husband named Dark Death who wrestles for the WWF."

"I never said he was your husband. I said you two cohabited."

"Same thing."

"It is not."

"If we're having triplets together, it might as well be the same thing."

"I never said they were Dark's triplets. He assumed it because you two are living together and you've got a condition that involves triplets." She smiled. "I take it he was a bit standoffish."

"Romantically? Yes. But if I need a pack mule, Jack's my man. I had to wrestle my water bottle away from him. He said I shouldn't strain myself. In fact, he even offered to carry me the fifty miles to this fishing hellhole."

"Hark? Did I hear the word hell in association with this wooded, serene escape back to life's basics? Does that mean you're a teensy bit unhappy about our accommodations?"

"No." She gritted her teeth. "I'm a teensy bit unhappy about my roommate."

"That saddens me, Sue, but I'm only doing it for your own good."

"Thanks, Mom, but I'm a grown woman and I can handle myself."

"So what happened to Jack the Pack?"

"I ditched him by the first water tower. I pretended I was nauseous. He jumped at the chance to put me down." Thank God, because the longer Jack had carried her, the more she'd failed to respond to all that cowboy strength. No heart-flipping or knees trembling or any of the other responses she'd felt when Brett Maxwell had swung her into his arms at the hoedown.

"Jack left you?"

"No, he turned his back so I could toss my cookies, and I took off."

"Oh, well. There are other cowboys in the corral."

"There are," Suzanne said. "Plenty." When Celia kept smiling, Suzanne glared. "How many did you feed the cockamamie story to?"

"A few."

A FEW turned out to be Suzanne's four prime prospects and Candy, who happily spread the news for good measure.

But all was not lost. While most of the cowboys at Andy's looked at her like she was just this side of the blessed Mother, the ranch would be filling up for the Lone-star Cowboy Classic in a little over a week.

The ranch would be teeming with cowboys, and Suzanne intended to be right in the thick of things. Between beating her backside in the saddle, trying out her newfound roping skills and doing her best to ignore one infuriatingly sexy ad executive, she volunteered to help with the organizational aspect of the rodeo which included going over entry forms complete with pictures and background information. By the time the men arrived to check in, Suzanne intended to have her favorites picked out and Brett Maxwell completely off her mind.

She headed for the gift shop bright and early Thursday morning and made a quick call to check on her client— make that ex-client—before settling down to help Candy.

"How do you think I'm doing?" Blaire snapped when Suzanne asked how she was. "I'm miserable."

"You don't sound as mad."

"Now I'm depressed." Blaire happily swung the emotion pendulum. "Tomorrow I'll be mad again."

"Try getting out. Get your mind off things. Go shopping."

"There are men out there."

"You don't have to talk to any."

"But I have to see them." The woman groaned. "Maybe some sympathetic female scientist will invent a mysterious virus that will totally annihilate the sex. Wouldn't that be great?"

Thankfully, Suzanne wasn't so totally dejected as to agree.

She hung up the phone and turned to her next order of business. Where there were new cowboys, she thought, staring at the stack of rodeo forms in front of her, there was always fresh hope.

"Make sure there's a photo for everyone and organize them by event," Candy said.

"Yes, ma'am." She settled into her chair behind the counter and started to work on the stack, ice-cold air swirling from the air conditioner.

Ah.

"Are you comfortable, dear?"

"More than you can imagine."

"Because I could get you some club soda and some crackers."

"I already had breakfast." Granted, it wasn't a bagel slathered with cream cheese, but she'd always wanted to try grits.

"Or a pillow for your back."

"My back feels all right." It was her rump that still hadn't gotten used to a saddle.

"Or a stool. You really should put your feet up."

"I'm not pregnant, Candy."

"Of course you're not."

"No, really. I'm not."

"I know you're in the iffy period. It's better to act like nothing, then when the doctor gives you the okay sign, you can rejoice."

"I'm *not*."

"You just keep telling yourself that."

"IF YOU'RE PLANNING on entering any of the events, we need an application from you." Suzanne passed out entry forms that afternoon to a corral full of cowboys. "I know you boys work here, but you still have to go through the motions."

"I'll help you with that, missy."

"Let me tote those pencils for you."

"A little thing like you shouldn't be lifting that stack of papers."

"No, thanks. I can manage." Suzanne hugged the forms and her pencil box and fended off several helpful hands.

"But I'd like to help."

"Me, too."

"And me."

The offers went on and on until Suzanne found herself sitting on a fence post, drinking a glass of milk and munching jelly-slathered biscuits while one of the cowboys passed out the entry forms and another read the list of requirements and yet another offered to whip off her boots and give her aching feet a massage.

Hmm. Maybe there was something to this pregnancy thing, after all.

SUZANNE wasn't the only one interested in cowboy hunting. Brett had the sudden urge to do a little himself. The kind that involved Mama Jessup's sawed-off shotgun and the dozen or so men clustered around Suzanne Hillsbury.

"I'm taking a group of guests up to the north pasture at sunup to move the herd toward the west."

"What?" Brett's gaze snapped to Clem, who was busy trimming Darlin' Daisy's hoofs, a job Brett had been helping with until he'd heard Suzanne's voice in a nearby corral.

"I said, it's too bad you're leaving tomorrow. You haven't been on an overnight roundup, and I'm taking a group of guests out at first light…" The foreman's voice faded as he spared Brett a glance. "You look like hell, Maxwell."

"I didn't sleep much." He couldn't sleep. Every time he closed his eyes, he saw Suzanne Hillsbury bathed in moonlight, her eyes shining, her lips parted, her skin smooth and slick with sweat.

"I know the feeling."

Brett turned and caught Clem, nippers paused, as he stared at Celia. She stood on the front porch of Candy's gift shop talking to Paul, a freelance photographer from

New York who'd arrived a few days ago to do some land-scape shots for his portfolio.

Celia laughed and leaned into Paul, and Clem's gaze hardened. "You finish up here," he muttered before stalking toward the barn. "I got work to do."

So did Brett. Piles of it, to be specific. He was getting absolutely nothing done on the Cowboy International presentation, though he could ride and rope better than he'd anticipated. Still, he had visuals to do, solid ideas to develop, not to mention other accounts to deal with. Last night he'd faxed Nancy his newest logo for thermal-lined fishing pants being marketed by one of his clients.

"We heat your cheeks and promise no leaks? Is that the best you could come up with?"

"They're warm and waterproof. It could work."

"Fax something else before I start bleeding chocolate glaze."

He'd spent all night trying to cultivate a new idea, but the only thing up and coming had been a very anxious part of his anatomy.

His gaze zeroed in on Suzanne. Why did women have to be so damned stubborn?

Things would have been so simple if she really didn't want him. He would never force himself on a woman who had no interest in him whatsover. But Suzanne was interested, all right. He saw it in the flash of desire in her eyes whenever he caught her looking at him. In the nervous way she licked her lips until he wanted to haul her close and do some licking of his own. In the stiff way she held her shoulders, as if she might be inclined to lean toward him if she gave herself half the chance.

Which she obviously didn't intend to do.

Three days and he'd barely managed a handful of words

with her. Forget a decent conversation, much less a kiss or a touch or any serious sex.

Sex. He'd practically forgotten what it felt like until she'd come apart in his arms the other night and he'd come so close.

That's what had him so worked up, so desperate. He'd been sliding into home plate and she'd called him out an inch shy, and now he was itching to get back up to bat and start swinging.

*You're getting rained out, buddy. Give it up and go home.*

He should. In twenty-four hours, he'd be a thousand miles away. Maybe then he could get some work done.

And maybe not.

He couldn't risk it. His agency depended on him, his concentration, his dedication. He had to get Suzanne Hillsbury into his bunk and out of his system, and there was only one way to do that.

"YOU'RE DOING *what?*" Nancy demanded a few minutes later when Brett called her from his cabin.

"I'm staying another two weeks."

"This wouldn't have anything to do with that woman who answered your phone the other night, would it?"

Yes. "No. The Lonestar Cowboy Classic is next week. Cowboy International is a sponsor, and they'll have some reps here for the festivities. It'll be a great chance to meet some of their people and let them see what a down-home country boy I am and why I would be perfect to represent them."

"Do you have any ideas to pitch?"

"I'm working on it."

"So what does she look like?"

"Who?"

"The woman who answered your phone while you were naked at the river."

"Her name's Suzanne, and since when did my personal life warrant twenty questions?"

"Since you got a personal life, and speaking of personal, did you come up with something else for the fish underwear?"

"It's fishing pants, and not yet, but I'll fax something later this afternoon." He stood at the window and stared toward the main corral where Suzanne sat surrounded by cowboys. She munched a cookie, and his mouth watered for her and the cookie. "I need you to send me another care package. The usual."

"What happened to all the stuff I sent last week?"

"Zorro."

"Zorro? Listen, you and this Suzanne person aren't into anything kinky, are you? Because that sort of thing can be very addictive. First it's prancing around naked at rivers, then it's pretending to be Zorro. Next you'll be dressing up like a head of lettuce and she'll be a gravy boat full of Thousand Island dressing."

"Italian."

"Oh, no, you've already done the salad thing."

If only. "No, she's actually Italian. Dark hair, dark eyes." Mesmerizing eyes, like warm fudge. "I've really got to go. Overnight the package. Better yet, same day it." He punched the off button before Nancy could speculate on any more sordid details of his love life. As if he had one.

Soon, he promised himself.

His gaze shifted to the man massaging Suzanne's right foot. If you can't beat 'em, run faster, or so he'd learned in grad school, and that's exactly what Brett intended to do. If Suzie Q wanted a cowboy, then he'd give her one she couldn't resist.

"NOW TAKE a deep breath...feel the positive energy bubbling and flowing...ah...now." Candy clapped her hands, signaling the end of their last Getaway get-to-know-you session. "Congratulations. You've all reached a milestone, seven full days as real cowboys. I'm proud of everyone. Since you're all off for the next forty-eight hours, I'm moving Saturday night's karaoke to Sunday so no one misses out on the fun. If anybody needs any last-minute items, you can use your cattle-drive coupons on your way out. All you cowboys take care, and have a wonderful trip!"

Suzanne gathered her saddlebags and followed the other guests onto the porch.

Riders gathered beside the corral, where saddled mounts lined up along the hitching post. A wagon loaded with supplies sat nearby. The twins, Gerald the accountant, Buffy, Skip, Skippy, and a handful of other guests milled about, waiting for the signal to mount up and move out.

"Why are you smiling?" Celia asked her.

"It's a beautiful day."

"Technically, the sun hasn't come up. That qualifies it as still night."

"Either way, it's beautiful." Suzanne's gaze was riveted on the spot where the Getaway guest van usually sat. The vehicle had rolled out an hour ago headed for Austin with several departing guests.

Her smile widened, and she drank in a deep breath of air. Her nose twitched at the faint smell of sweat and cattle. Oh, well, a girl couldn't have everything. She'd gotten rid of Brett. Life was good.

Or it would be now that she could actually start on the

rest of her life, her cowboy hunt, without fear of running into him and losing the battle with her desperate hormones.

"You're too chipper," Celia grumbled.

"My positive energy is flowing."

"Mine is still asleep."

"A real cattle drive," Gerald said as he walked past them and rubbed his hands together. "This is exciting."

"Overnight from one pasture to the next is not a real cattle drive," Celia muttered.

"Sure it is." Paul waltzed up. "Smile. I'm calling this one Celia at Sunrise."

"Do I detect an ugly peach bridesmaid's dress in my future?" Suzanne asked after Paul had snapped several shots and turned to photograph the cowboys loading their saddlebags and bedrolls.

Celia laughed. "Me and *Paul?*"

"You've spent every minute with him since he got here."

"That's because we have a lot in common."

"You like the same foods? The same music?"

"The same men. He's dated my last two ex-boyfriends, and we were sharing war stories." She turned her gaze to Suzanne. "Speaking of boyfriends, you wouldn't be so chipper because Brett Maxwell got paroled today, would you?"

"First off, he wasn't my boyfriend, and chipper doesn't even begin to describe how I feel." Joyful. Ecstatic. Relieved. Grateful. Slightly disappointed. Hey, how did that last one get in there?

She forced the ridiculous, crazy, insane thought aside. Disappointed? Right.

"I didn't come thousands of miles to end up with a Manhattan Special." She sighed. "Be honest, Celia. Don't you ever get tired of the men back home? The three-piece execs with the beepers and the cell phones and those annoying little alarms on their watches? Don't you ever want someone less...consumed?''

"And cowboys aren't consumed? Excuse me, but most of them are more intimate with their horses than they are with their women. And when they do turn their attention to some unfortunate lady, it's because they want their clothes washed or their stomachs filled.'' She shook her head. "I don't want a man to see a platter of biscuits and gravy when he looks at me.''

"What about a rump roast, darlin'?'' Clem asked as he walked by. Celia glared, and he winked before motioning to everyone. "Let's saddle up, folks. We ride out in five minutes.''

"Scoot over, girlie.'' Mama Jessup pushed past Suzanne and hauled a suitcase down the steps.

"Mama Jessup? You're going with us?'' Suzanne asked.

"'Course I am. It gets awful lonely for these young whippersnappers. They've got to have someone to relieve some of the tension. Give 'em a good workout, if you know what I mean.''

She knew, all right, and it was making her queasy just thinking about it. Then Mama Jessup added a few colorful descriptions, and the picture became even more vivid.

"Could this trip get any worse?'' Celia grumbled as she pulled out her makeup bag, fished for a compact and studied her reflection. "Forget I said that. I've got major pore expansion.''

"Let me get those for you.'' One of the cowboys appeared at Suzanne's side and grabbed her saddlebags.

"I can manage,'' she said, but it was too late. The bags slipped out of her hands a second before she found herself whirled around.

Jack the Pack reached for her. "Let me help you over to the chuck wagon, ma'am."

She dodged him. "I'm riding a horse."

"No, you're not, ma'am. You've got to take it easy."

*"I am not pregnant!"* Her voice rose above the hustle and bustle, and two dozen gazes looked at her. She grabbed the makeup bag out of Celia's hand, held up a container of Elizabeth Arden eye shadow and dangled it over the water trough. "Tell them the truth," she told Celia.

"That's my favorite smoky gray silk— What did you do that for?" she demanded as water splashed and the eye shadow dove to the bottom of the trough.

"Tell them." Suzanne held up a tube of Riveting Red lipstick.

"Give me that—"

*"Tell them."*

"She's not living with a wrestler. He's a kick boxer— Sue!" Her sentence ended in a colorful curse as the lipstick joined the eyeshadow. "Stop that!"

"I'm not living with anyone." She held up a bottle of matching polish. "Tell them."

"She's not living with anyone. I made it up."

"And I'm not pregnant."

"She's not pregnant."

"Say it again."

"She's not pregnant!"

Suzanne smiled triumphantly until a strong arm locked around her shoulders and a slow, familiar, sexy drawl slid into her ears.

"Not yet, but we're working on it."

Her heart stalled, and the air whooshed from her lungs when she looked and found Brett Maxwell smiling down at her.

"You." She managed to say the word, her brain cells

scrambling to maintain law and order in the face of that wicked smile and all that warm male heat. "Wh-what are you doing?"

"Going on a cattle drive. I live to ride and rope, sugar."

"I meant what are you doing right now, with your arm around me?"

"Staking my claim."

"What claim?"

"You, Suzie Q."

Before she could respond, she found herself folded over a broad shoulder, her head hanging upside down, her eyes level with the backside of a very worn, very snug pair of Levi's. She started to protest, but then a warm, possessive hand settled on her rump and... What had she been about to say?

"This traditional me-cowboy-you-cowgirl stuff isn't half bad." He chuckled, the sound vibrating along her nerve endings.

Earth to Suzanne! The protest, remember?

"I—I think you're suffering from a major mental setback," she growled. At least she was going for the growl, but with all that heat so close and the view so enticing and that hand... She swallowed and fought for her sanity. "Put me down."

"We haven't reached the corral yet."

"I can walk."

"And strain yourself? What's a cowboy if he can't give his lady a lift?"

"You're not a cowboy, and I'm not your lady."

"We'll just see about that, Suzie Q."

"Don't call me that."

"It's cute."

"I hate it."

"It sings to me."

"Bite me."

Strong fingers patted her bottom. "You keep sassin' me, darlin', and I just might."

# 8

"I'LL HAVE YOU KNOW that was my favorite lipstick," Celia declared a half hour later as she and Suzanne and two dozen other riders moved toward the north pasture.

"Just be glad you fessed up before I had to get ugly."

"Not my concealer." Suzanne smiled, and Celia held a protective hand over the saddlebag containing what was left of her cherished makeup. "You're evil, Suzanne Hillsbury."

"I'm evil? I'm not the one who's been spreading malicious rumors to sabotage my best friend's happiness."

"I did no such thing." At Suzanne's pointed stare, Celia added, "I mean, I did spread the rumor, but not to sabotage your happiness. I'm trying to save you from making a big mistake."

"I don't need saving." Suzanne tightened her hold on the reins of Anxious Annie, the sorrel mare she'd picked at the hitching post the minute Brett Maxwell had put her on her feet. She'd turned, climbed into the first saddle and started riding without a thought as to what she was getting herself into.

Anxious Annie was…well, *anxious*. And fussy. And jittery.

"All horses are a bit temperamental," Clem had assured her. "Annie's fine as long as you keep a nice grip on the reins and let her know who's boss."

Which Suzanne had managed to do for the past hour,

while keeping up with the other riders and making sure she kept her distance from one infuriating ad exec hell-bent on ruining her plans.

"Why does life have to be so difficult? All I need is one lousy cowboy."

"I think you're about to get your wish."

She turned and discovered Brett drawing alongside her.

"Howdy." His deep drawl sent a tremor dancing down her spine. Tingles of heat spiraled to the most sensitive parts of her body.

*Stop that.*

"Hi, Brett." Celia beamed. "Bye, Brett." Celia pulled back, and her horse fell behind.

Suzanne twisted around. "Where are you going?"

"To take a leak."

"I'll come—"

"Chill, Sue. Brett won't bite, will you, Brett?"

Suzanne remembered his earlier words, and panic shot through her. "I really wouldn't have dumped your concealer," she called after her friend. "I swear!" Dread spread through her as she turned and found Brett watching her, a bemused expression on his face. "Speaking of biting, where's Creme Puff when I need her?"

"Back at the ranch, lucky for me." He grinned. "You know, if I didn't know better, I'd say you're not too happy I'm on this trip."

"Very perceptive."

"You're nervous."

*Ditto.* "Hardly."

"You're afraid."

*Can I have an amen?* "You wish."

"You're mad."

*If only.* "Try furious." She put on her best I'm-the-defender-of-justice-and-you're-pond-scum scowl, which never failed to scare the opposing counsel into a fast plea bargain. "You carried me over your shoulder like a sack of feed."

"You wanted a traditional guy."

"I said traditional, not prehistoric."

"When a cowboy sees something he wants, he goes after it."

"Big news flash—you're not a cowboy."

"If it walks like a cowboy and talks like a cowboy—"

"It's probably a really good imitation, at least in your case. You are not a cowboy," she said, wondering if she didn't say the words more to convince herself than him.

He sure looked the part. Sitting in the saddle, reins held loosely in his powerful hands, his hat tipped back, that bone-melting grin curving his lips, he was every Wild West fantasy she'd ever had. He had the wicked blue eyes of a saloon gambler, the strong hands of a trained horseman, the fast reflexes of the most dangerous gunslinger.

She did her best to picture him in a three-piece suit, a cell phone in hand and an impatient glint in his eyes, but all she saw was one half-naked, very sexy man wearing red silk boxers with black polka dots and that damned smiley face over his—

"You're sweating," he pointed out as a trickle slid down her temple.

"It's hot." *I'm hot.* She wiped the moisture away and tugged at the collar of her T-shirt. "It must be a hundred degrees out here."

"More like eighty."

Another few plucks at her top. "Is that all?"

He nodded, a grin playing at his sensuous lips. "Right now, but the weatherman predicted a record breaker. It'll get hotter before the day's out."

That's what she was afraid of.

SHE'D DIED and gone to hell.

Suzanne crouched beside a winding creek that afternoon. She'd managed to escape the chaos of the cattle drive for a quick break. She splashed water onto her heated face.

Okay, if she'd died, her senses would be useless. She certainly wouldn't be feeling the water. This was a good sign.

She heard the far-off sounds from the cattle drive—irritated moos, a few yee-haws, some loud whistles. Another good sign.

A few more splashes and she straightened. Pain splintered through her stiff muscles. Yep, the verdict was in. She was still alive.

And still in hell.

Because only the devil could be behind the day's events. Brett staking his claim, riding alongside her, giving her riding tips, showing her how to dally her rope, demonstrating the correct way to keep a rowdy calf in line, invading her space, drinking up all her oxygen and just plain driving her crazy. Even when they reached the north pasture and started to push the herd, he'd stayed with her, pushing the cattle from the rear and pushing every one of her buttons.

All the while he was irritating the hell out of her, there was something about the way he did it—the way he smiled, winked, gazed at her with such heat—that was just so damned seductive.

Not mentally, of course. Her mind wanted him to keep his distance.

But her body... Every traitorous inch, from her head to her toes, wanted him closer.

She glanced at her breasts, her attentive nipples chafed from the constant pressure against her lace bra.

"Whose side are you guys on, anyway?"

"Mine, I hope."

She whirled and, at the sight of Brett, tried to mask a sudden spurt of excitement with a fierce glare. "Did I forget the moment we were joined at the hip?"

His gaze made a slow, leisurely trek down her body, pausing at several crucial points before returning to her burning face. "Believe me, honey, the moment we join isn't something you'll ever forget."

"Very funny."

"I'm serious."

That's what had her worried. "I'm not the least bit interested."

Challenge gleamed in his blue eyes. "Is that right?"

"That's right."

He folded his arms and studied her. "Then prove it," he finally said.

"How?"

"Kiss me."

Boy, he was good at this seduction thing. Just the suggestion made her insides quiver. "How is my kissing you going to prove I'm not interested?"

"You pull away first, and I'll know you're immune to the chemistry between us. If you can," he added, his lips hinting at another grin. "Pull away first, that is."

"You don't think I'll be able to stop once I start, do you?"

"I'm counting on it. I'm not a gracious loser."

"So what's in it for me if I win?"

"What do you want?"

"For you to leave me alone and let me find a cowboy in peace."

"If you win, I'll help you find him." At her skeptical glance, he crossed his heart. "Cowboy's honor."

*Don't do it. It's too risky. It's hot, you're hot, he's hot....*

"You're on."

"Ready when you are."

She sighed and shook out her arms as if she were getting ready to lift a few weights.

"I'm waiting," he said.

She rolled her neck and popped her knuckles.

"What are you doing?"

"Loosening up."

"We're not going to wrestle." A twinkle lit his bluer-than-blue eyes. "Unless you want to."

"One kiss," she told him. "And that's it."

"We'll see." He smiled at her, and her heart stalled.

"Stop that," she snapped.

"What?"

"Irritating me."

"I'd like to be doing something else, but that's not going to happen unless you get a little closer."

She leaned in. His eyes drilled into her. Her heart stalled again, and she jerked back.

"Afraid I might be right?" he asked.

"You wish." She wet her lips.

"Then what's the holdup?"

"I can't do this with you looking at me. Close your eyes."

After a knowing grin, he finally did as she asked. She took a deep breath, leaned forward and gave him a quick peck.

At least she thought it was a quick peck, but the moment her lips touched his, it was as if a magnet drew them together. Her mouth softened against his, a slow, lingering touch that made her knees tremble and her body sway forward.

She sighed, and his lips parted, and then their tongues were tangling. The kiss deepened, and the trembling spread up her thighs. Deeper, deeper. Higher, higher.

The kiss went on and on, and by the time it ended, she couldn't remember where she was, much less who'd stopped kissing first. Brett, of course, conveniently reminded her. The jerk.

"I won." He smiled, his triumphant gaze locking with hers for a long moment before he turned and walked away. The perfection of his sexy cowboy swagger made her realize she was facing a far greater challenge than she'd ever imagined.

"ARE YOU all right?" Celia asked as they unloaded their packs and turned their horses out to graze on a lush spot of green grass at the edge of the clearing where Clem had announced they were setting up camp for the night.

"I'm fine." Suzanne gathered her saddlebags and bedroll, her hands trembling, her nerves still buzzing.

"Are you sure?"

"I'm fine."

"Because you don't look fine."

"I'm *fine*."

"You look—"

"Don't even say it." She met Celia's gaze. "Just don't say a word."

Celia grinned, gathered her saddlebags and headed for the small bubbling stream where most of the guests were already washing up while a few wranglers unloaded supplies and one started a fire to cook dinner.

Suzanne felt Brett's gaze as she crossed the campsite, but she refused to let herself look. If she looked, there was no telling what she might do.

Give him a piece of her mind.

Pound his smirking, victorious face.

Fling her arms around him and start kissing.

The last idea made her heart pound that much faster.

*A Manhattan Special,* she reminded herself time and time again. *He's one, you're not. End of story.*

But as he sat across the campfire from her that evening, his sleeves rolled up, his hat tilted back, his eyes reflecting firelight, he looked so much like a cowboy, she found herself smiling at him a time or two.

And when he pulled out an industrial-size can of mosquito repellent while all the other guys were toughing it out, she thought her heart might just melt.

Her heart? Wait a second. No matter how many mosquitoes swarmed around her bedroll, even if they did resemble miniature bats, her heart was definitely not involved. Just her hormones. And maybe a little gratitude, especially when he sprayed the area around her with the repellent, gave her a chocolate cupcake to kill the taste of Mama Jessup's red-eye gravy and retreated the two feet to his sleeping bag.

Too close for comfort, but then it wasn't as if she'd get any sleep, anyway. The ground wasn't near as comfortable as the movies made it out to be. Sure, the stars were pretty, but who could really look with a throbbing rear end and aching thighs?

"You okay?" Celia asked.

"Fine."

"Because you seem restless."

*It's called pain.* "Fine."

"Are you sure—"

"Would you stop fussing over me?"

"Just checking."

"I'm fine."

"Just fine? Because I know this isn't all that comfortable. I mean, I'd much rather be in a king-size bed—"

"I'm fine. The ground is fine."

"I'll understand if you want to call it quits. We could make a run for it while everyone's asleep—"

"I'm great. Would you give it a rest?"

"Fine."

"Fine," Suzanne muttered, putting her back to Celia. Of course, that put Brett directly in her line of vision. He'd shed his shirt in favor of a guest-issue cotton blanket and lay stretched out on his back, hands tucked behind his head, gaze fixed on the sky overhead. He shifted, and the blanket slid to his waist, revealing a hair-dusted chest and a rippled abdomen.

Maybe there was more to this sleeping-outside business than she'd originally thought. The view certainly was something.

SATURDAY DAWNED bright and hot. Another scorcher and a definite sign from above that someone was out to get her. Moving the herd the rest of the way took all morning. She and Brett pushed from the rear by themselves until Clem sent Skippy to help around noon.

The teenager trotted back on Lamb Chop, his head bobbing to the music blaring through his earphones.

As soon as the boy drew within a foot of Brett, Darlin' Daisy started fidgeting. She danced, backing up from the close contact with Skippy and Lamb Chop as if she'd come upon a rattlesnake.

"I think it's Skippy's headset," Suzanne told Brett. "I read something one time about certain horses having an aversion to specific sounds." She motioned toward the boy and tried to signal him. "Would you please turn it down?"

"What?" he asked.

"I asked if you would please turn it down."

"I can't hear you, lady."

Brett held tight to his jittery mount, reached over and yanked the headset from Skippy's ears.

"Turn it down," he said to the startled boy.

With a sullen look on his face, Skippy flipped the volume off and tucked the portable CD player into his pocket.

When Suzanne turned an impressed stare on him, Brett shrugged. "You don't ask a fourteen-year-old boy for his cooperation because you'll never get it. You tell him. Calm, firm." He grinned. "And if that doesn't work, you can always try a headlock."

"How do you know so much about kids?"

"Comes with the territory. My parents died when I was seventeen. John, he's my youngest brother, was five, David was seven, and Richard was nine. When you're on your own raising three boys, you learn pretty quickly how to handle them. Otherwise, they handle you."

"Why didn't the state step in?"

"I wouldn't let them. I was considered an adult, and my parents had named me as guardian in their Will. The boys were mine, and I wasn't about to turn them loose."

"How did you manage?"

"My parents had an insurance policy, which gave us a little money. I went to school at night, got a job during the day to make ends meet, end of story."

"A happy ending."

"Almost. Richard's a producer for a local Manhattan radio station, David's an editor for the *New York Daily,* but John's still in and out of my apartment. He's in college."

"What's his major?"

"Football and fraternity parties. I'm holding off on declaring a happy ending until he picks a major and does something with his life."

"Like following in his oldest brother's footsteps?"

"If he wants. I don't care what he does as long as he's happy."

The admission stirred something inside Suzanne, an admiration. She remembered her childhood, her parents' constant pushing for her to attend law school and go into the family business. They weren't saying that now, but it was too late. She'd spent ten years being a chip off the old workaholic block. While Brett's life revolved around his work, he wasn't pushing his ambition onto someone else.

She could definitely start to like this guy.

Forget that. She already liked him, a truth that troubled her the rest of the afternoon as they worked side by side.

Liking Brett Maxwell was *not* part of her plan.

THE DAY WORE ON as they worked their way through a small valley, then crossed a shallow stream before finally moving into greener pasture. Skippy had gone to help the twins, who, dressed in tight jeans and halter tops, drew the young man's attention like two shiny new CDs.

Suzanne kept a firm hold on Anxious Annie and set her sights on a stubborn calf who lagged behind.

"Come on, baby," she called as the herd kept moving and the animal didn't. "We're getting left behind!"

"Rope him," Brett shouted from several yards away, his voice rising above the sound of pounding hoofs and irritating moos.

"Rope him?" Yeah, right.

"You can do it. Just set your sights, block out everything and let her rip."

She twirled her loop, her gaze fixed on the calf. She ended up roping herself once and Brett twice, much to her mortification, before she finally got the noose over the animal's head.

"I did it!" she squeaked, so excited her hands faltered

on the reins. In a heartbeat, she realized she'd lost her grip on Anxious Annie. True to her name, the horse anxious. The calf went one way, and Annie the other. motion jerked Suzanne to the side, and she toppled off nie. The air bolted from her lungs as she slammed int ground. Pain ripped through her shoulder.

Brett was on her in an instant, gentle hands urging onto her back.

"Don't—" She choked, tears streaming down her f

"It's all right," he crooned. "It's going to be okay

"I—" She gasped. "I—I think I broke something. can't breathe—hurts—"

"Let me see."

"Don't—yow!"

Strong hands gripped her shoulder, her vision blur and everything went black as pain clawed at her. Her sh der was wrenched, and bones popped.

Just when she knew she was going to die, the blin agony lessened.

"What happened?" she gasped, several seconds l: She blinked at the tears until Brett's face, so handsome concerned, came into focus. "My shoulder..."

"You pulled it out of its socket. Better?"

She blinked back more tears and nodded as she ging touched the tender area. The slashing heat had faded t dull ache, and she marveled at the sudden change. "Wl did you learn to do that?"

She expected him to tell her he'd picked up the first-information from Clem or some self-help cowboy vide maybe a book about life on the range. He shrugged wiped her tears with strong but gentle fingers. "My br ers played every major sport there is. I can fix scrapes, s bloody noses and pop every major bone back into its soc if the need arises." He slid strong arms under her hefted her into his arms to carry her to the shade of a nearby tree. "I'm going after the supply wagon . You'll live, but that shoulder will be sore for a few days. I'm afraid your roundup days are over, Suzie Q."

Her sore bottom tingled in anticipation of a nice, normal seat that didn't involve a saddle. She slid her arms around his neck and held on during the short walk to the shade.

For safety's sake, of course. She didn't want to displace the other shoulder.

His arms tightened protectively around her, strong but amazingly gentle.

Brett Maxwell was turning out to be full of surprises. And Suzanne was starting to realize she liked surprises.

"PLEASE DON'T SING another verse from 'Rawhide,'" Suzanne said the next day as they headed to Andy's. Her shoulder, not to mention every other inch of her body, was sore from a second night under the stars, and her frustration level had peaked from sleeping close to Brett Maxwell.

Close, but not close enough. Darn it.

"I'm ready to slit my wrists."

Brett flashed her a grin, her heart—damn the traitorous muscle—skipped a beat, and she marveled at how this trip could have started out so great, with her anticipating a nice cowboy search, and ended up with her actually liking Brett Maxwell.

The fact that he'd doctored her and offered to drive the supply wagon so he could keep an eye on her had made matters worse.

The only saving grace was that Mama Jessup had crawled into the back of the wagon for her mid-morning nap, giving Suzanne extra bench space. Not that it helped. They hit every pothole, every rut, all of which sent her swaying toward Brett or lurching away, which resulted in a strong arm snaking out to pull her against rock-hard muscle—*whoa!*

The wagon rocked again, Suzanne jerked to the side, and Brett caught her, then hauled her back to safety.

Safety?

Muscles rippled, her skin tingled, and the air stalled in her lungs. She was definitely smack dab in the middle of the Danger Zone.

"Don't you like my singing, Suzie Q?" he asked, his hand lingering at her waist, fingers burning through the cotton of her T-shirt.

"What's to like?" She shrugged. "You can't even carry a tune." Funny how the sound of his voice echoed through her head and made her ears tingle, anyway.

"You're missing the point."

"Which is?"

"Cowboys sing when they're out on the trail." He motioned to Jack and the others who were leading a few guests in a loud rendition of "Home on the Range."

"You're not a cowboy."

He chuckled, and they hit another pothole that had her plastered against him for one long moment.

"You're doing that on purpose." She scrambled away and struggled to find her seat.

They hit a rock. She bounced and found herself half turned, her back to him, one breast pushing into the hand he'd slid around her for support.

"You're definitely doing that on purpose."

He tried to look innocent, and all the while his thumb rubbed a small, barely discernible circle an inch below her nipple. The tip sprang to life, a surge of electricity bolted through her, and she fought the incredible urge to turn a fraction and give him better access.

"Stop it," she growled, scooting away.

"Stop what?"

"Copping a feel."

"I'm protecting my woman."

"I am not your woman."

"Still pining for that wrestler you've got stashed away back home?"

"Celia has a warped sense of humor." She lifted her gaze and spied her friend riding point next to Clem, a smile on her face—wait a second. Celia smiling? At *Clem?*

"I don't believe it. She hates cowboys."

"Not from this angle."

"And she really hates Clem."

"Sometimes the chemistry's too powerful to resist."

"There's more to life than chemistry."

"You keep telling yourself that, Suzie, and maybe you'll start to believe it."

"I do believe it." She gripped the opposite side of the seat, determined to hold on no matter how many ruts Brett managed to hit. "Chemistry doesn't see a person through fifty years of happiness. Compatibility does that. If you don't share common interests, forget it. Believe me, I know. I have couples come in all the time who wonder why they ever got married in the first place. She doesn't like him, he doesn't like her. Usually it was a bad case of lust masquerading as love."

"What about lust for lust's sake? If two people are clear on what they're feeling from the word go, what they expect, then what's so wrong with lust?"

"Nothing."

"That's what I keep telling you."

"*If* lust is all you want out of life."

"And what do you want out of life?"

"I already told you—"

"I mean, really *want*. Where do you see yourself in ten years? Twenty years?"

She tried desperately to conjure the picture of the nice house surrounded by trees and the redwood fence with the swing on the porch, with some hunky cowboy named Roy or Jake or Eli busy chopping wood out back, but the image wouldn't come. All she could see was Brett standing there in the moonlight....

She definitely had a bad case of lust and like and...

*Stop that.*

"I know where I *don't* want to be in ten years," she said. "Lying in a hospital bed while some doctor tells me I've just had a massive heart attack brought on by too much stress and not enough rest, or worse, sitting in the emergency room while some doctor tells me my husband just keeled over from too much stress and not enough rest. Been there, done that."

"How so?"

"My father." She meant to let it go at that, to clamp her lips together and stop talking and thinking and feeling the strange heat that crept across the seat and lured her toward Brett.

But then he turned questioning eyes on her, and she found herself blurting out the memory that had sent her running thousands of miles to Texas. "He'd been working extra hard on this case—he worked hard on all his cases, but this one had kept him up practically day and night for several weeks. I went in to say good-night and there he was, unconscious at his desk. I've never been so scared in my life." She shook her head. "I never want to be that scared again. Not for myself, and not for anyone else."

"I'm sorry." His gaze caught hers, and she knew that he really was sorry, and the knowledge made her feel a little less alone.

"My parents are in Fort Lauderdale because of that heart attack. It served as a wake-up call, a warning of things to come if they didn't change their ways. That's what Walter's prenup did for me. Walter was my fiancé, and a first-rate Manhattan Special." She shook her head. "I still can't believe I almost married him."

"Why didn't you?"

"Because he cared more about his job than me."

"Did you love him?"

"I thought so." She shook her head again. "I was just in love with the idea of getting married, settling down, having a family, the family I never had when I was a kid. Don't get me wrong, I love my parents, but they were never really around much. When they moved to Fort Lauderdale, it wasn't near the heartache it should have been because we were never very close. So—" she sighed and cast him a sideways glance "—is there a wife and kids in the Bull's future?"

"The far-off future. I spent a lifetime looking after everyone else. Now it's just yours truly. I'm building my own agency, no one at home to worry over, and I like it that way."

She wasn't sure why the admission disappointed her. He was only telling her what she already knew—his number-one priority was his career. He was a Manhattan Special all the way.

The trouble was, she didn't know any Manhattan Specials who would sacrifice valuable time to stop every half hour to check on Mama Jessup to make sure she was resting comfortably. Or who would forfeit a half hour replacing a fallen bird's nest in a nearby tree while every cowboy on the drive had moseyed on by.

"The animals will eat the eggs if they stay on the ground."

"I eat eggs every day."

"This is different. These aren't chickens bred for the breakfast table. They're robins."

"Did you learn that in your cowboy handbook?"

"I did Scouts with John. We sat in Central Park every afternoon for three weeks straight watching birds for his bird's-eye badge."

Bird-watching. The knowledge brought a smile to her lips, then a frown.

So he bird-watched? Big deal. That didn't erase the fact that he was packing a cell phone and knew how to use it. He was exactly the type of man she didn't want.

She told herself that. She just wasn't so sure she believed it anymore.

# 9

"GUESS WHAT?" Blaire squealed the minute Suzanne picked up the phone in the back room of Candy's gift shop.

"This had better be good because I hauled myself out of a tub of hot water." The cattle drive had ended three hours ago, and she'd just settled into a bubble bath to rest and regroup and torture herself with damning visions of Brett.

"I'm getting married!" Blaire declared.

"Married? I thought you were praying for a man-killing virus."

"That's old news. I lost the urge when I set eyes on George."

"And that was?"

"Three days ago. It was love at first sight. We spent less than an hour together, and he was already proposing."

"But you're not divorced."

"Not yet. Oh, Suzanne, I've met someone, and he's absolutely perfect." Blaire proceeded to describe exactly how perfect, from the dimple in his chin, which reminded her of John Travolta, to his proficiency in the kitchen. "As soon as the divorce papers are final, we're tying the knot. He's the one. I just know it!"

"The way you knew it with Marc and Ryan and Bob and Stan?"

"This is different."

"That's what you said with Marc and Ryan and Bob and Stan."

"Can't you be a little bit happy for me? I've been this close to slitting my wrists for the past two weeks."

"Because of all the other perfect men in your past." Her voice softened. "Blaire, I'm just concerned about you falling for the first guy that makes your favorite sandwich."

"He isn't the first guy I've met who makes a good peanut butter and banana sandwich."

"No, he's the fifth. Things may be wonderful now, but you're bound to get hurt in the end."

"Have you ever been on a roller coaster?"

"What?"

"A roller coaster. Like the Big Kahuna at Coney Island."

She'd never been to Coney Island. As a child, her parents had been too busy working to take her. As an adult, she'd been too busy working to go. "What does a roller coaster have to do with you making another big mistake?"

"Roller coasters make me terribly ill. As soon as I walk off the ramp, there go my cookies into the nearest trash can. I even threw up on Stanley's shoes one time."

"And the point is?"

"I still adore roller coasters."

"Have you been to your therapist lately?"

"Every week, and she adores roller coasters, too."

"And your point is?"

"I always get sick after the ride, but while I'm on it, it's a pure adrenaline rush. There's nothing like it. I'm happy, exhilarated, on top of the world for those fast, furious seconds. Being in love is the same way. It's a great ride, regardless of what happens afterward. You should try it sometime. Live for the moment."

Blaire's words followed Suzanne the long trek back to

her cabin. While she didn't agree with her client's disregard for the sanctity of marriage, she did admire her optimism. And maybe, just maybe, Blaire had the right idea.

Suzanne had no future with Brett. She was newly transplanted to Texas, and he was a die-hard New Yorker. Still, they shared some good chemistry. Okay, great chemistry. Powerful. Consuming.

Why not relax, let it spark and simply live for the moment?

It wasn't as if she had any serious cowboy prospects. Not yet. She was unattached, he was unattached. She had no unrealistic expectations, he had none. She wanted him—boy, did she want him—and he obviously wanted her.

They were both consenting adults.

Why not?

*Because,* her conscience started.

"Oh, shut up," she muttered, as she turned and started toward the other guest cabins. "For the next few hours, just *shut up.*"

"HAVE I EVER told you you're the perfect woman?"

"Every time you want something."

"This isn't sucking up, Nancy. It's gratitude." Brett pulled the handheld massager from the cardboard box Nancy had sent him and leaned against the wall, his tired legs stretched out on the bunk in front of him. He'd slipped off his boots and chucked his shirt the minute he'd reached the comfort of his cabin.

Comfort? Since when had the cabin turned into a comfort zone?

Since he'd spent two days riding and roping and playing cowboy, and now he was paying for it. It was damned hard work making all that cowboy stuff look so easy.

And worth the effort.

He closed his eyes as he remembered the sweet taste of Suzanne's lips, and the dull throbbing of his muscles faded. He'd expected her to kiss him back, he'd known she would by the gleam in her eyes, but no way had he anticipated the intensity behind the simple action. She'd kissed him so deeply, so thoroughly.

"Brett?"

He shook away Suzanne's image. "Uh, yeah?"

"You still there?"

"Just unpacking the box." He stared at the portable massager, and his muscles wept with relief. "So where did you get this thing?"

"The Imagemaker over on Fifth Street, after I picked up the back copies of the *Times*."

"The Five Finger Fantasy," he read on the label. "I bet they're making a killing off these."

"Sex sells, not that I—a twenty-year veteran in the marketing biz—am remotely influenced by the name game. But it was either the Fantasy or a Massage Marvin, and Marvin was more for feet, not to mention, he wouldn't fit in the box I sent you."

He slipped his hand into the glove-looking device, looked around and finally found the on switch, adjusted the speed and held it to his stiff neck. The contraption hummed, vibrated and went to work on the tight tendons and sore flesh, moving his fingers in a soothing motion that wrung a deep groan from his throat.

"How is it?"

"You're the best secretary in Manhattan." *Ooh.* "The hardest working." *Ah.* "Most thoughtful—"

"That's why you pay me the big bucks."

He opened his eyes. "I don't pay you big bucks."

"You will after this trip. Now work out the kinks and get back to your computer. I'll be faxing the proposed ad budget on the MacGregor account in a little while. I need any changes tonight because Mac wants to see this first thing tomorrow.''

"Done."

Brett spent the next few minutes oohing and ahing and thanking the powers that be for Nancy and FedEx and the Imagemaker and whatever genius had designed the Five Finger Fantasy.

He barely heard the knock above a relieved groan.

"Who is it?" he called when the noise sounded again.

"It's me." Her voice pierced the hazy pleasure and brought him up straight on his bunk. "Can I come in?" But she was already opening the door.

Brett bolted to his feet and flung the contents of the care package inside the box, slapped down the cardboard flaps and tried frantically to get the blasted massage machine off his hand before—

"I didn't know if you'd be here."

He whirled and shoved his hand behind his back as he faced her. Rough and tough cowboys shrugged off pain. They didn't get misty at the sight of a handheld massager.

"Well—" he drew the word out in his best drawl despite his pounding heart "—I was thinking about taking a midnight ride or rubbing down Darlin' Daisy." *Good cowboy comeback.* "But I thought I'd give her a little break. She worked awful hard the past few days."

Suzanne smiled, a small tilt to her full sensuous lips, and heat sizzled through his body. "I just wanted to say thank-you for fixing my shoulder. That was pretty resourceful."

"How's it doing?"

"A little sore, but much, much better. And I also wanted to say that I've been thinking about what you said about this chemistry thing—what's that noise?"

"What noise?" The Five Finger Fantasy vibrated and

buzzed. Brett tried to find the switch, but had no luck. Finally, he closed his free hand over it to try to muffle the sound.

"That humming."

"I don't hear anything. So what about the chemistry?"

"That maybe you're right…" She cocked her head as if listening. "Yeah, definitely a humming. And I think—" she tried to peer around him "—it's coming from over there."

He blocked her line of vision, his hands firmly hidden at the small of his back, his fingers still searching for the off button. "You must be hearing things."

"No, there's definitely something there."

"Horse lag."

"What?"

"You're suffering from horse lag. You know, similar to jet lag but it happens to country folk because they ride horses."

"I've never heard of it."

"That's because you're not from around here," he told her. "It happens when you've been in the saddle a few days straight. Your legs feel wobbly and you lose your balance and your hearing. That's the first thing affected. So what am I right about?"

"About chemistry being enough sometimes and…" She tilted her head the other way and circled him. "You know, I'm sure I hear something."

He turned, careful to keep his front facing her. "Maybe it's a cricket."

"It doesn't sound like a cricket."

"A mosquito."

"Too loud."

"An owl?"

"Too soft." She looked thoughtful as she stepped around

him, and he matched her inch for inch. "You know, it sounds just like—"

*Bam.* He bumped into the nightstand. The care package tumbled, and before he could think about what he was doing, he reached for it. Too late, the contents scattered.

A strange expression covered her face as she drank in the sight of packaged cookies and cakes and chips, the tubes of muscle cream, the mini handheld face fan, the back copies of the *New York Times*. Then her gaze settled on the massage machine still attached to his hand, and she smiled.

"I thought I heard a Five Finger Fantasy."

"I've never seen it before—" The words jammed in his throat. Wait a second. A smile? As in, not mad? As in, pleased to find he wasn't one-hundred percent cowboy?

"I'd do just about anything—" the hunger in her gaze stalled the air in his lungs "—for a massage."

"It's mine," he blurted on a loud rush of air. "So—" he drank in a deep breath "—define *anything*."

"Well." She licked her lips and his blood rushed in anticipation. "I'd much rather show you."

*ANYTHING* turned out to be a kiss that made Brett think the sex act itself was highly overrated. Nothing could be better than Suzanne Hillsbury's mouth full on his, her lips parted, her tongue stroking his just…like…that.

Except maybe her body pressed flush against his, her luscious breasts burning through the thin fabric of her T-shirt, her hips cradling his growing erection.

Or the feel of her hands tracing his shoulders, exploring his chest.

Or the sexy little cry she gave when he slid his arms around her and did some exploring of his own.

"You're killing me," she moaned, and he smiled, nibbling a path down her neck, his hands cupping her bottom, rocking her against him.

"I know, baby. It's killing me, too." Another cup, another rock.

"I mean *really* killing me. It's too hard."

"It's been a long time."

"But it hurts."

"I haven't even put it in yet."

"You're going to put it in?"

"That's usually how it's done."

"That's not what my instruction book says."

He paused, his heart pounding. "You've got an instruction book?"

"Don't you?" She trailed her hands over his shoulders.

"Well, no. I mean, I didn't think I needed one." He licked the throb of her pulse, and she moaned again, long and deep in her throat, and heat fired through him. "Some things come naturally."

"Well, yes," she breathed. "But everyone should know the proper way to operate their equipment."

"I've had it forever. Trust me, I know how to operate it."

"Then make it softer."

Softer? "But we can't do anything if it's softer—"

"Ouch!"

His head snapped up. Above the pounding of his heart, he heard the distinct hum and realized the source of her discomfort.

He released her bottom, found the off button on the blasted massager, unfastened the Velcro straps and yanked the thing off his hand.

Then he slid his arms around her again, pulled her against him so she could feel every inch of how much he wanted her and stroked the sweet curve of her bottom. "Better?"

"Much. Mmm. Ah..."

"I knew this cowboy stuff would work," he panted, nibbling at her lips. "So what impressed you the most? My roping technique?"

"Your mosquito repellent."

"Surely my riding display had you salivating."

"Actually, the cupcake did that."

"What about my singing?"

"Now that nearly impressed me right into decking you."

He leaned away from her. "I thought you wanted a cowboy."

"I do." She smiled. "But it looks like I'm settling for you." Then she kissed him, long and slow and deep.

"I should take offense at that," he murmured sometime later as he nibbled the soft flesh of her neck.

"None intended."

"Then maybe I'll cut you some slack." He slid his hands around to tease her breasts. She gasped, a sweet sound he caught with his mouth as he gave her a thorough kiss. "Then again..." He let his hands fall. "I wouldn't want you settling for anything other than what you want."

"You're what I want."

The words sang through his head, and he gripped the edge of her T-shirt to slide his hands beneath it. He snapped open her bra and her lush breasts spilled into his palms. She gasped as he rolled and plucked at nipples that ripened at his touch.

"That's a coincidence, Suzie Q. Because you're what I want. What I've wanted for days." He yanked the shirt over her head and peeled away her bra before his hands went to work on her jeans. Breathless seconds later, after he'd stripped her bare and she stood before him, all lush curves

*Love, Texas Style*

and tempting skin, he leaned back and drank in the view. "God, you're about as close to perfect as anything could get."

"Wanna bet?" She stepped forward. Her hands went to the snap at his waist. The button popped, the zipper hissed and small hands urged his boxers and jeans down. Soft fingers skimmed the hard muscles of his thighs, his calves, and need gripped every inch of his body.

"You're the one who's perfect," she said, her voice full of conviction. Something tightened in his chest, and a small sliver of fear pierced the desire fogging his brain.

But then she touched his erection, a slow glide of her fingertip from root to tip, and the fear faded in a wave of red-hot need.

He urged her onto the bunk, covered his body with hers and kissed her. Then he explored every curve, lingering at her breasts, sliding his hands down her soft belly to slip one into her moist curls.

She was warm and wet, and he couldn't wait any longer. Gently, he untangled himself from her arms and headed for the bathroom and the box of condoms in his shaving kit.

When he walked into the bedroom, the sight of her stretched out on his bunk stopped him for a long second. A wash of moonlight spilled from a nearby window, bathing her naked body. Her skin glistened with sweat. Her nipples puckered, begging for his hands, his mouth. Her lips curved in an inviting smile, and his breath hitched.

"What are you thinking?" she asked as he neared the bed.

"That I might not have enough of these damned things." He tore the foil packet with his teeth and rolled the condom on his throbbing erection.

"How many do you have?" she asked as he positioned himself between her legs.

"A box." He touched her slick folds with the very tip of his aching length.

"How many in a box?" she panted.

"A dozen."

"And we're not going to have enough?"

He slid his hands beneath her bottom and lifted her to meet him as he pushed deep. "Not nearly enough," he groaned.

"Is that a promise?"

A chuckle rumbled up his throat before the humor faded. "It's been a long time for me, Suzanne. A very long time."

"How long?"

But he couldn't remember exactly how long. He couldn't think past the day he'd first set eyes on her. He knew then as she gazed at him, her body pulsing around him, that he could never get enough of this woman.

*Right.*

The deprivation had driven him crazy, because no way would he be thinking such a ridiculous thing. Then she drew her knees up on either side of him, he slid even deeper, and he stopped thinking altogether.

The world faded into intense pleasure as he thrust into her over and over until she came apart in his arms and he quickly followed. Shudders racked his body as he buried himself deep one final time.

From far away, he heard the hum of his fax machine and knew Nancy was sending him the information on the... What account was that again?

Suzanne slid her arms around his neck, and he couldn't help himself. He gathered her close, and the fax machine faded into the whisper-soft sound of her breathing, the steady thud of her heartbeat.

He closed his eyes and let his body relax. For a little

while. Then it would be back to reality, to the pile of work waiting for him.

But not just yet.

NO MAN had ever held her like this, as if he had all the time in the world and wanted to spend every second with her. As if he never wanted to let go.

Her imagination, she knew. Because no way would Brett Maxwell be content with just a woman. He wanted, needed his work. She knew the feeling because she'd seen it drive both her parents. She'd felt it herself for the past few years. The need to do more, achieve more, to keep going and going and going because that's all she knew how to do.

She'd stopped. She was learning how to breathe, to enjoy a sunset and not worry over her schedule.

But Brett was still playing the game, still loving it more than anything else, if the pile of work on his makeshift desk was any indication.

More than her.

Not that he loved her, mind you. She had no illusions. This was just chemistry. Sex.

She snuggled deeper into his arms, enjoying the pure pleasure of all that strength surrounding her.

"What are you thinking?" His deep voice sent goose bumps chasing up and down her arms despite the temperature.

"That I've never slept with a man before."

"You mean you were a—"

"No, no. I've *slept* with men before, three, to be exact, but never like this."

He gathered her close and locked his hands at the small of her back. "I have a similar confession."

She raised an eyebrow. "You've never slept with a man?"

"Very funny." His grin faded as he planted a kiss on her lips. "I've never slept in a bed with a woman. When it's over, it's usually goodbye and to each his own."

"You don't have some terrible nocturnal habits that I should know about, do you?"

A wicked gleam lit his blue eyes. "Now that I've got you here, I'll be damned if I'm going to scare you away."

"Don't tell me you snore?"

"Maybe."

"You hog the covers?"

"Possibly."

"You sing opera or recite the Declaration of Independence?" When he simply smiled, she pulled one of his chest hairs and made him growl. "I keep forgetting. You're a Manhattan Special. You're too busy to have a woman cluttering up your life." When he didn't deny the charge, disappointment flared through her.

Disappointment? No, this was just sex. Physical. No emotions involved. Just a wild, crazy roller coaster ride.

"You've got a schedule to keep," she went on, "and sex has to fit in between the power lunch and the conference call."

"Or between the ironing and the cooking." At her questioning glance, he added, "Up until last year, John was still at home. Before that, it was all three of my brothers. Bringing home women or staying out all night with one didn't exactly scream 'good parent.' It was my responsibility to set a good example. My parents would have wanted that."

The disappointment faded into a wave of admiration.

"Tell me about them," she said.

"My dad was a construction worker. My mom worked at a bakery. She could really cook. That's one thing I didn't have to worry about. She taught me my way around a kitchen, especially the oven."

"You bake?"

He nodded. "I tried doughnuts once, the cake kind that you put in the oven, because Nancy was trying to cut calories, but they didn't turn out so good. Chocolate cake is my specialty. I'm a chocolate nut."

"We're talking real chocolate, right? Not the carob stuff?"

"The real thing. I even add chocolate chips to my icing."

"I think I love you."

He grinned. "You and my three chocoholic brothers."

"I like them already."

"They're pretty good guys, despite the fact that they only had me." The faraway, serious look on his face all of a sudden gave her a glimpse of what his life must have been like. Worrying over three boys when he hadn't been much more than a boy himself.

"You're plenty." Her fingers slid down his chest, skimmed the ridges of his abdomen to wrap around his pulsing length. "More than plenty." A few purposeful strokes, and his troubled look faded into one of pure pleasure.

She watched him for several moments, enjoying that she could make him feel as wonderful as he made her feel, until she caught the movement from the corner of her eye. She turned and found a pair of beady black eyes staring at her, watching.

"Um, Brett?"

"Hmm?"

"Did you know there's a raccoon sitting on your nightstand, eating a chocolate cupcake?"

He cracked an eye open and glanced at the animal. "That's Zorro," he murmured. "She keeps coming back."

"Probably because you keep feeding her."

"I can't let her go hungry." His concern made Suzanne smile, and she had the fleeting thought that maybe, just maybe, she could fall in love with this man if she let herself.

But falling in love with Brett wasn't part of her plan.

No matter that he got this strange glimmer in his eyes when he talked about his brothers. Or kept a pesty raccoon revved with sugar. Or that his smile made her feel like she'd just won the lottery. Or that he cupped her hand and held it over his heart as they drifted off to sleep a long while later, after putting one hell of a dent in the box of condoms.

Just sex, she told herself. If only it didn't feel like so much more.

THE CELL PHONE woke Brett early the next morning.

"What do you want?"

"World peace, a woman president and a fat-free doughnut that actually tastes good. Oh, and it would be nice to have the ad budget for our biggest account to date, which I told you I needed yesterday."

The MacGregor budget. He closed his eyes and damned himself a thousand times. What had he been thinking?

His gaze went to Suzanne, to the soft slope of her breast visible just above the white sheet. He hadn't been thinking at all. He'd been too busy feeling.

"Brett?"

"What?"

"Are you going to get that budget to me sometime before the millennium?"

"Uh, yeah. I'm right on it."

"What about the Cowboy International presentation?"

"What about it?"

"It's in a week, and I haven't seen any ideas."

"I've got ideas." They just weren't about cowboy boots. Not exactly, though he had done some thinking about a certain brunette wearing a pair of red cowboy boots and not much else.

"I hope they're good ideas, because this is the biggie. If you land this, we'll knock Gunther and Simon out of the number-ten spot."

"Consider it done." He tore his gaze away from Suzanne and concentrated on finding his boots. He needed some space. Breathing room that wasn't scented with the smell of cupcakes and sex and one very warm woman...

"Where are you going?" Her voice sent a spurt of panic through him.

"I—I have to go." Brett slipped on his jeans and reached for his boots.

She sat up, the sheet falling to her waist. "Now?"

"I've got work to do." He made quick work of his boots and stood.

"But your computer is here."

"Not that kind of work. Cowboy work." He didn't meet her eyes. Instead, he fixed his gaze anywhere, everywhere, but on her. "You know, hay to be hefted. Herds to be herded. Cows to be roped. Barns to be cleaned."

"You don't have to impress me." She stood up, all sweet curves and enticing woman, and stepped toward him. "I'm already really, *really* impressed."

"Don't do that."

"Which one? The standing? Or the stepping?"

"The looking." He shook his head. "Just don't look at me."

"Why not?"

"Because it makes me want to do this." He reached out, and suddenly they were kissing, tongues tangling, mouths melding, and heat raged into a fire that sucked the oxygen from his lungs, before he managed to pull away. "And this is the last thing I need to be doing after what happened between us."

The trouble was, it was the first thing he wanted to do. The only thing.

He turned, grabbed his hat and left before he dug an even deeper hole for himself and made love to her again.

*Love?* What the hell had happened to sex?

No love. No way. No how.

Love meant sacrifice. Giving up clawing his way to the top to take a nice cushy job with a respectable agency so he could bring home that weekly paycheck. Love meant giving up his dreams, and no way would Brett do that.

He'd put them on hold for so long while he'd raised his brothers. He was free now, and he was staying that way.

# *10*

---

"I'M SORRY I was out all night, not that it's any of your business," Suzanne called the minute she opened her cabin door. "And don't give me any of that stuff about having *that* look, because if I do, it's my concern and…" Her words faded as she realized the cabin was empty.

Barely sunup and Celia wasn't in bed.

No way would she be up before sunup. Maybe she and Paul had pulled an all-night ex-boyfriend-bashing session, which meant she didn't even know Suzanne had been gone. Which meant no third degree about Brett and the future and the all-important fact that there was no future.

She'd done it. Given in to her lust, enjoyed the ride, and now it was time to get off. Brett knew it. That's why he'd hightailed it out of the cabin before she'd had a chance to do more than open her eyes.

He'd already pushed last night aside in favor of today, and that's what she had to do. Registration for the rodeo started this morning, with over one hundred entrants coming from all over the state. Candidates for her cowboy search.

The sooner she found Mr. Cowboy, the sooner she could forget last night. Not that it was all that memorable.

*Lust,* she reminded herself again. Just a night of lust, and now it was over.

With that thought playing in her head, she showered and

changed. When she walked out of the bathroom, she found Celia sitting on her bunk, tears streaming down her face.

"What's wrong?"

"I've done something terrible."

"What?"

"Unforgivable."

"What?"

"Atrocious."

*"What?"*

Her gaze met Suzanne's. "I did it. I slept with Clem." She shook her head. "Last night. I still can't figure it out. One minute I'm telling him where he can shove his stupid jokes and his irritating smile and that damned charm that makes my skin crawl, and the next we're going at it in the barn. And then the front porch of his cabin. And then the bathroom and the bed and sort of on the table, but that was just me so it really doesn't count as a double whammy." She started sobbing. "It was the most exciting night of my life."

"And the problem is?"

"Clem."

"He doesn't feel the same way?"

"No, he loved it. Every minute."

"And?"

She turned stricken eyes on Suzanne. "He's a cowboy."

"Is that all?"

"That's enough. I had my heart broken once by a two-timing cowboy back home. That's why I left Montana. Because Wade Walker up and married Mary Jo Shiloh, and I didn't want to stick around and watch all their wedded bliss." The word ended with a huge sob.

"Come on, Celia." She slid her arm around her friend's shoulder. "Clem doesn't strike me as the two-timing kind. He's a nice guy. And cute."

She smiled. "He is, isn't he? And he's kind of funny, too, in an obnoxious sort of way." A dreamy look crept across her face. "And he's really sexy, and great in bed. And in a hayloft. And on the front porch. And the bathtub. *And* he doesn't leave the lid up."

"He passed the test?"

"With flying colors." She sniffled. "So I guess it's not the end of the world. We had one night. I just won't let it happen again. He's not my type, even if he did pass the test, and I'm certainly not one of those choir girls his mother's always fixing him up with. The ones that fawn all over him. I don't fawn for any man, especially not a cowboy, even if the cowboy in question is Clem."

"You're absolutely right."

Celia's red-rimmed gaze zeroed in on Suzanne. "So did you sleep good last night? You weren't scared without me..." The question faded into a statement. "You weren't here without me."

"Is there a big fat 'I did it!' branded on my forehead?"

Celia smiled. "Brett?"

"Unfortunately."

It was Celia's turn to slide her arm around Suzanne. "You don't sound too happy."

"I'm not."

"Let me guess. You're not his type, he's not yours?" Suzanne nodded and Celia sighed. "Are we a pair or what? What are the odds we'd both wind up a thousand miles from home with the same problem?"

Suzanne blew out an exasperated breath. "Maybe it's something in the water."

CELIA DECIDED sleep was the best distraction from her night of tawdry sex with Clem, while Suzanne opted for work. She hurried to the main house to pick up the morning roster and help Candy with check-in, and not once did she give in to the urge to look around for Brett.

He had his life.

She had hers.

"You look refreshed this morning," Candy said.

Suzanne pulled her hat low on her forehead. While she'd checked for any telltale markings and found none, she wasn't taking any chances. The women here seemed to have a sixth sense when it came to her love—make that *lust* life.

Yeah, lust.

"You look like you might've found that cowboy you've been looking for."

"Hardly."

Candy surveyed her. "Are you sure? Because you look—"

"Look? What look?" Mama Jessup asked, waltzing up to Suzanne and peering over her bifocals. "You got a zit or something?"

"Mama!"

"Just asking." She peered closer. "Say, you been foolin' around?"

"I'll just go and set up the registration desk." Suzanne grabbed the box of forms and fled from Mama Jessup's speculation.

A makeshift desk had been set up on the porch beneath a banner that read Participant Check-in. She pulled out her chair and settled down for a busy morning as the first pickup rolled in. By noon, she'd checked in over two dozen cowboys and even managed to pick out one or two who had possibilities.

But none who jumped out at her. No sign number one— sensual awareness. The most she'd felt was a static electricity when one of the cowboys had rubbed his felt hat too long and reached for her pen. His name had been Slick and he'd been all smiles and cowboy charm.

"Great pair of boots you got there," he'd told her when he'd noticed the blah brown ropers she'd purchased at Candy's. "Nice to see a woman who appreciates the simple styles."

As it turned out, she and Slick were on the same wavelength. He was single and had a weakness for real cowgirls, which she'd become the moment she'd traded in her fancy red boots.

Maybe... But the maybe faded as soon as he walked away. No lingering impression. No trembling knees or pounding heart. No call of the wild.

There was always tomorrow, she decided when five o'clock rolled around. A new day. More cowboys. Fresh hope.

She closed up the registration desk and bent to retrieve the sign that listed the sign-in times. The distinct thud of boots slapping the dusty ground echoed in her head. Her skin prickled with awareness, and her head snapped up. It was about time some man stirred something....

"Hi." Brett stood in front of her, his tall form outlined by the blazing Texas sun, and her pulse leaped.

"H-hi, yourself."

"Pretty hot out today, huh?"

She nodded. "Another record breaker."

"The humidity's pretty bad, too."

"Texas is notorious for it."

"I nearly suffocated. I've been outside most of the day." He wiped the sweat lining his brow. "Practicing for the Class B Bucking Bronc division."

"You're entering the rodeo?"

"There'll be reps from Cowboy International, the account I'm after. I figure if they see me, it'll increase my chances of landing the account.''

''I'm sure.'' So much for him doing it to impress her. He'd already wooed her with his cowboy expertise, roped her into his bed. Now it was bye-bye lust and hello work.

''I'm not too late, am I?'' He handed her his entry form and the fee.

''Uh, no.'' She reached for a registration packet. ''Here's a schedule of events, the release forms you need to sign prior to Friday when you'll compete, and the rules and regulations of Andy's and the State Rodeo Association. Good luck.''

''Thanks.''

An awkward silence settled around them, and she marveled at how two people who'd been so intimate less than twenty-four hours ago could feel like perfect strangers.

''About last night—'' They both started at the same time.

''You go first,'' he said.

''No, you,'' she insisted.

''Last night was really great.'' His gaze locked with hers.

''Yeah,'' she quickly agreed. ''Really great.''

''But now it's over.''

''Over.'' She nodded. ''Right.''

''I just wanted to make sure we were on the same wavelength.''

''Same frequency.''

''Because I didn't want you to be mad that I had to leave this morning. I'd agreed to help Clem with some stuff, and then I'd promised to meet Andy to discuss his commercial.''

''A promise is a promise.''

''And you and I were, um, finished anyway.''

''*Finit*. End of story.''

"Chemistry sparked, ran its course, now we've got it all out of our system, so it's back to business as usual."

"Strictly business."

"I've got less than a week to come up with a presentation for Cowboy International, and I promised Andy I'd help him on those new commercial ideas."

"You've got your hands full."

"And I've got to write copy for two other accounts."

"And I've got cowboys to hunt."

"We're both busy."

She nodded. "Way too busy for a repeat of last night."

"Not that either of us wants one, right?"

"Right."

"So." He clapped his hands. "That's it."

"All she wrote," Suzanne agreed.

"Then I'll see you around sometime."

"Yeah, sometime."

He managed five steps in the opposite direction before he turned, and his hungry gaze founds hers. "So...what are you doing right now?"

She bolted from her seat and nearly knocked the desk over. "Not a thing."

"Now I KNOW why they call it the Five Finger Fantasy," Brett murmured.

"I don't think this is quite what the manufacturer had in mind." Suzanne straddled his waist, the glove on her hand.

"The instructions say it relieves stress. Believe me, this is relieving my stress."

"But it's not made for a scalp massage." She fluffed the sun-streaked hair on his head, working the glove back and forth, and he groaned. "It says specifically, do not use on excessively hairy areas. Your head is definitely hairy."

"Oh, just like that. Yeah, right there near my temple...
It feels so good."

"Good enough to lose a handful of hair if this thing
short-circuits?"

"You worry too much."

"I do not."

"Yes, you do. You can take the New Yorker out of New
York, but you can't take the New York out of the New
Yorker."

She grabbed a handful of hair. "Take that back."

His eyes snapped open. "You're hurting me."

She pulled harder. "Take it back. I'm not a New Yorker.
I stopped being a New Yorker when I stepped off the
plane."

"Sure you did. That's why you've been sneaking glances
at my *Times* whenever you think I can't see you."

"I've done no such thing." He raised an eyebrow, and
she shrugged. "Okay, maybe I have, but it's not because
it's a New York paper. It's just that I have this reading
dependency."

"A what?"

"I like to read nonfiction, but I promised Celia I
wouldn't touch another self-help book. I even picked up a
romance at Candy's. I'm breaking the cycle, and I'm *not* a
New Yorker."

"I bet you've been in every shop in Manhattan."

"I grew up there. A girl has to dress."

"I bet you've got a great apartment with a view of Central Park."

"Celia's is better."

"And I bet you never leave the house without your mace
and a whistle."

"It's pepper spray and a buzzer, buster."

"And I bet you love bagels and you're a cappuccino

hound and you can't pass a pizza parlor without a slice with extra sauce and cheese."

"A fat lot you know. I like croissants not bagels, I never touch coffee unless it's black and... Well," she huffed, "just don't go acting like you know everything."

A knowing grin curved his lips. "You're a pizza nut."

"I'm Italian on my mother's side. I can't help it. It's genetic."

"With extra sauce and cheese," he added.

She sighed. "Okay, okay. Now you know my deep, dark secret. I lust after Sal's pineapple and jalapeño special with extra sauce and cheese. In fact, that new sign hanging out front was courtesy of me and all my late-night business."

He chuckled. "I knew it. A card-carrying, pizza-loving, New Yorker—ouch!" He touched the spot on his scalp where she'd nearly yanked out a handful of hair.

She smiled evilly. "Did that hurt?"

"I screamed, didn't I?"

"You groaned." She pulled off the glove and tossed it onto the nightstand. "I didn't make you scream, but I could have. Just one more crack about my pizza preferences..." She started to climb off him.

He caught her waist, holding her in place atop him. "Now, now, Suzie Q, didn't your mama ever tell you to play nice?"

"My mama didn't tell me much of anything. She was always too busy working." The words came out before she knew what she was saying, and she wanted to snatch them back. But it was too late. "I don't want to be that way for my kids," she added quietly.

"I'm sure you won't." His soft, compassionate words tugged at something inside.

"What about you? Don't you think kids deserve a full-time father?"

"I know they do, which is why I'm not doing the kid thing."

A strange hurt spiraled through her. The more she got to know Brett Maxwell, the more she realized how different their goals in life were and the more hopeless everything seemed. "Well, I think kids are great."

A light gleamed in his eyes. "You'll be a great mother."

The words sent a spurt of warmth through her that erased her earlier disappointment. "I intend to try."

"How many times?"

"Three or four." At his shocked expression, she added, "Maybe five or six."

He grinned. "Six little New Yorkers. Sal will be indebted to you."

"They'll be Texans," she growled. "And I really hate you."

"Yeah," he said, the amusement in his eyes fading into something much more intense. His fingers grazed her hip and skimmed her ribs, and her nipples puckered. "I can see just how much you hate me."

He touched the stiff peak of one breast, and she arched, pleasure spiking through her. He stroked and coaxed until she trembled with need. Strong hands gripped her waist and urged her over his erection. Then he pulled her down with one swift movement and filled her, and she threw her head back, catching her bottom lip against the nearly unbearable pleasure. Seconds later, she lowered her gaze to find him staring at her.

"I really love to watch you. The way your lips part when I'm inside you. The way your eyes go all dark and dangerous and sexy as hell. I bet you're hellfire in a courtroom."

"I've had my moments," she breathed.

"And you're through?"

"With a Manhattan practice and divorce law. I want a change. Ulysses doesn't even have a town lawyer."

"There are less than two thousand people. They don't need one."

"Everybody needs a lawyer sooner or later, especially ranchers, for contract purposes, real-estate and stock acquisitions—you name it. Most of the ranchers around here get their legal counsel in Austin. I'm sure a few would be glad to have someone closer to home, and I've found this really pretty piece of real estate about ten miles outside of town. I haven't taken a look myself, but if the real thing is half as good as the picture the realtor sent me, I'm definitely going to take it."

"You've done your homework."

"Preparing for a case is half the battle, and I intend to win this one. Suzanne Hillsbury versus the Daily Grind."

He smiled and tightened his pelvis, surging into her another fraction. "I love it when you talk lawyer."

"Is that so?" She started a slow rhythm, her breasts bouncing with the delicious motion and snagging his full attention for a long moment. "Your Honor, the defense would like to call Mr. Brett Maxwell to the stand. He has a *vital* piece of information that could free my client, Suzanne Hillsbury, from the terrible need gripping her senses...." She talked on and on, driving him as crazy with her voice as she did with her body until the tension grew unbearable and her breaths came too harsh and quick. He grasped her hips and took the lead.

The ride was fast and furious until she cried out his name and he surged one final time. She collapsed on his chest, and he wrapped his arms around her.

"I'm really not a New Yorker. Not anymore," she murmured against his slick skin, no matter how much she suddenly regretted the fact. She couldn't imagine how in the world she was ever going to let him go.

But she would. And soon. In four days, when the rodeo ended and Brett Maxwell hopped a plane back to Manhattan and the rest of his life.

BRETT CAUGHT SUZANNE on the front steps of his cabin the next morning, just as the sun topped the horizon.

"I thought you were leaving." He leaned against the door frame and ran a hand over his tired face. A good kind of tired, where his bones ached and his muscles cried and he wanted to smile anyway.

Especially when he heard her soft voice, filled with wonder. "I was, but then I saw this." She motioned at the horizon stretched in front of her. "You know, I've watched the sun rise many times in Manhattan, after an all-night work binge or before an early court appointment. For some reason it never looked quite like this. So...breathtaking."

He came up beside her and sat. His hand found hers, and their fingers entwined.

"Doesn't this just do something to you? Fill you with a sort of peace?" she asked him.

"Yes." But it wasn't so much the sunrise that affected him so deeply at that moment. It was her. The sight of her all soft and tousled, her skin reflecting the pink of a Texas sunrise. The feel of her, her arm and hip snug against his, her hand so small and silky in his larger one. There was just something so right....

*Bleep.*

The sound of his cell phone shattered the thought. Thankfully, because Brett had four days left, and he wasn't about to go crazy now when he'd just about finished his jail time.

The phone bleeped again. Suzanne stiffened and pulled

away as if she'd just remembered something important. Like the fact that he wasn't a rough and tough cowboy, which she seemed still to have her heart set on.

The thought bothered him a hell of a lot more than it should have. "I really should get to work," he said abruptly, getting to his feet.

She nodded and stepped off the porch, and Brett had the strangest urge to go after her, to wrap her in his arms and watch the sunrise.

*Keep the faith, buddy. You're out of here in four days.*

He could handle four days filled with cowboy practice and a heavy workload. It was the nights, filled with Suzanne and a loving so fierce he forgot his own name, that had him worried.

ON TUESDAY MORNING, Brett shut the door behind Suzanne and planted himself in front of his laptop. Time was running out. He had three days left, and not one idea for the Cowboy International account. He needed to think. To brainstorm. But then his gaze strayed to the imprint on the sheets.

Suzanne.

Sunlight filtered through the window, spilling across the sheets and bathing them in a yellow glow that reminded him of the small flecks of gold that lit her eyes when she was on the verge of ecstasy. The last thing he could think of were cowboy boots.

Instead, he walked onto the porch and stood there, doing what he'd avoided for the past few days. He watched the sunrise, and it was nice.

Forget nice. It was exciting yet peaceful at the same time. Stirring, yet relaxing. Complex, yet so simple.

*"Don't you ever get the urge to simplify your life?"*

Suzanne's question came back to him and stuck in his brain. *Simplify. Simple. The simple things in life.*

While he'd never felt the urge himself—simple to him meant ordering Chinese take-out and not worrying about doing dishes—the idea wasn't bad. Not bad at all.

He walked inside and sat at his computer. If he couldn't think Cowboy International, he could at least get something done. He'd promised Andy some commercial suggestions before he left, and he intended to deliver.

"HELL OF AN IDEA, Maxwell. Hell of an idea," Andy said as he walked with Brett to the barn that afternoon. "Back to the basics. It's what Andy's is all about."

"The way the commercial runs now, it gives a more glamorous feel, and it's misleading. You're not running a resort."

"Hell, no. I mean, I let Candy put in that damned karaoke machine and the hot tub, but it was give the go-ahead or bunk out with the wranglers, and a man's got to do what a man's got to do." He put a pinch of tobacco between his gum and cheek. "Otherwise, this ranch is about real living."

"About getting back to basics," Brett said. "You play up the nostalgia aspect. Take ten-second clips from six favorite old cowboy movies, and make people yearn for the good old days."

"Like *Red River Valley?*" Andy asked. "Now there's a classic."

"And *The Tall Texan,*" Brett added. "And *El Dorado.*"

"Talk about the good old days. All a man needed back then was his Colt, his horse and a loving woman. Life's necessities."

"People have gotten so caught up in the rat race, they want simple again. Basics." He knew of one, in particular, though he himself couldn't understand it. He couldn't wait to get back to the city, to the noise and the chaos.

"Giddyup!"

"Get her on over to the left!"

"We got a stray!"

The shouts carried from the branding pen. Noise. Chaos. But it was different. Brett wanted car horns and knocking engines, not grunting and mooing. And snorting. And bellowing. And loud cowboys who could whistle high and long enough to curl the ends of his hair. And cuss enough to remind him of the subway during evening rush hour.

Wait a second. There was no comparison. New Yorkers had cursing down to a fine art, and Brett couldn't wait to be back in the hustle and bustle.

Now if Suzanne intended to go back to Manhattan, then they might work something out—

*Work something out?* No way. Suzanne spelled permanent with a capital *P* and Brett had vowed off relationships a long time ago, and that's what would definitely happen if she gave up her crazy cowboy notions and headed to New York. They'd known each other all of eight days, and he couldn't seem to get her off his mind. To forget the way she traced the tiny scar at the corner of his eye and asked all sorts of questions about his brothers and parents. To push away the urge to take her home, wed and bed her properly and give her the house full of children she seemed to have her heart set on.

Children? He'd spent his young adult life raising three. He had no desire to tie himself down with the responsibility of a wife when he'd only recently found his freedom from three demanding brothers.

The trouble was, when Suzanne looked at him, freedom seemed highly overrated. Even downright lonely.

## 11

EARLY SATURDAY MORNING, Brett left Suzanne sound asleep in his bed and went to get a good look at Hades, the bronc he was riding later that day. The meanest critter any amateur could have the misfortune to meet up with, or so Andy had told him. But Brett wanted to see for himself, to prepare mentally the way he'd been doing physically with Creme Puff every afternoon when he risked his neck trying to ride her.

Speaking of the Emasculator...

She stood in the corral. Her ears perked as he made his way to the eastern corral where the rodeo animals were being kept. She snorted.

"Don't get all excited. You're not busting my butt today. Hades is going to do it for you."

She snorted again, as if to say, "But I was looking forward to it," then dipped her head toward the watering trough. A giant pink tongue unfolded to lap at the water.

"What'd I ever do to you, girl?"

She continued to slurp and ignore him.

Maybe he was feeling sentimental all of sudden. After all, it was his last full day at Andy's.

Suzanne's image pushed inside his head, and he forced it away. He needed to focus.

He had the sudden thought that he was avoiding facing the fact on purpose. To think about it being his last day would mean admitting he was leaving her, and he wasn't up to that just yet. Today, he was still here, still a cowboy.

"Can't we call a truce, honey? It's my last day."

*So what?* She raised her head, shook some water his way, then returned to the trough.

"At least I tried." He managed three steps toward the east corral when his cell phone bleeped. He still hadn't faxed Nancy the idea for the fishing pants, and she was hot on his case—

The thought died when he heard the noise, so faint he might have imagined it. But it was just this side of daybreak, and the ranch was quiet.

Except for the bleeping cell phone and the grunting horse.

He turned. Creme Puff eyed him. The phone bleeped again, and she shook her head. Brett stepped closer. Another bleep, and she danced backward a few steps, as if to retreat from him. Or the damned noise.

Brett remembered Darlin' Daisy's sudden start when Skippy had ridden by with his portable CD blaring in his ears. That faint buzz had been nothing compared to the loud bleeps.

Brett's memory traveled back to the very first time he'd ridden Creme Puff. It had been his first solo effort without one of the wranglers beside him. He'd had the phone in his pocket, and he'd just mounted when Nancy had called, and all hell had broken loose.

While he couldn't specifically remember the phone ringing any other time he'd been on top of the animal, apparently Creme Puff wasn't in the mood to forget and forgive. She associated the cell phone with him, so whenever he climbed into the saddle, it was vengeance time.

Guilt washed through him. "I'm sorry, girl. If I had only known, I could have saved us both a world of hurt." He reached out to stroke the nervous animal, but Creme Puff was sly and quick, and she went from poor, poor pitiful me to she devil in the blink of an eye. She gave a vicious snort, butted her head and knocked the phone out of Brett's hand straight into her line of fire.

"Hey! Wait—" Hoof met plastic, and he watched his expensive phone smashed to unrecognizable bits.

"You could have just asked me to leave the damned thing back in my bunk. That cost me two hundred bucks."

*So bill me,* her gaze seemed to say as she scattered the pieces with her hoof and turned to slurp more water.

If this was any indication of what was to come, he was in for the worst day of his life.

HE WAS HAVING the best day of his life.

As it turned out, Handy Andy Jessup served on the State Rodeo Association's board of directors with none other than Truman Schneider, who turned out to be the Cowboy International representative in attendance. Since Brett had been so forthcoming with his advertising advice, Andy repaid the favor by talking Maxwell Advertising up to his old rodeo buddy before Brett even climbed onto the back of one of the meanest buckin' broncs to ever terrorize the amateur division.

Truman caught Brett outside the arena before his scheduled ride and introduced himself.

"Andy and I used to rodeo the circuit together. He's a good man and he speaks mighty highly of you. Says you've got some great ideas."

Actually, he had zero where Cowboy International was concerned, but he was working on it. "Maxwell Advertising is the best firm for the job. We'll give you a presentation like you've never seen."

"I look forward to it. I'll be back in New York on Monday morning, and I'll see you bright and early in my office at nine.'' He clapped Brett on the back. ''Good luck with your ride.''

*Yes!* The aches and pains and heat and horrible food had all paid off—

''Hi.''

He turned and found Suzanne standing behind him, her clipboard in hand and a strange expression on her face.

''They're ready for you. Gate one.''

He nodded but didn't move. He couldn't, not with her so close, looking so…worried?

He didn't blame her. One look at Hades, the bronc dancing in chute one, and he started to worry himself. But that was because he was the one about to risk his neck. She was safe on the sidelines. She had no worries. Unless…

''You wouldn't be getting all misty-eyed on account of me, now would you?''

''Of course not. It smells in here. My eyes are watering.'' She sighed, her luscious breasts heaved, and the air hitched in his chest.

Or maybe it was the sight of those wide, tear-filled eyes that did the hitching.

''Things seem to be working out,'' she went on. ''I, um, heard you talking just now.''

He nodded. ''Truman's anxious for my presentation. I think I may have cinched the deal by coming down here.''

''That's great.''

''Really great.'' So why didn't he feel so great? Why did he feel as if his best day had just turned into the worst?

''So don't get on the horse,'' she said.

''I have to.''

''Why? For some stupid account?''

*For you.* The realization hit him with the full force of one of Creme Puff's head butts, and he finally admitted it to himself. Over the past few weeks, he'd seen her smiling at every man who wore a cowboy hat, and it had gotten to him. She was his woman, and if she had her heart set on a cowboy, that's what he aimed to give her. Because he cared for her. Wanted her. Needed her.

"Suzanne, I—"

"Riders, mount your broncs!" The loudspeaker blared, and cut him off just in time.

*Whew, that was close.*

What the hell kind of fool was he? He couldn't just go blurting out something crazy like that. Not when he wasn't one hundred percent sure. Sure, he had a soft spot for Suzanne, but did that mean he was ready to chuck everything—his agency, his freedom, his future—for a woman who'd made it clear from the start that he wasn't the man of her dreams?

Yes. No. Maybe.

"I've got to go."

"Wait—" She caught his arm, and he turned, his gaze locking with hers. "Be careful."

That's exactly what he was doing, he thought, as he watched her walk away, all the while ignoring the urge to call her back and... And what?

He didn't know. He turned his attention to a much safer matter. A thousand pounds of kicking, rearing horseflesh.

HE WAS LEAVING. She'd heard Truman mention Manhattan, seen the smile on Brett's face, the excitement in his eyes.

Duh. Of course he was leaving. He'd always planned to leave. Never made any promises otherwise.

But she'd sort of hoped...

*Forget him. Just forget him and the fact that he's about to break every bone in his body on account of some stupid advertising account. He deserves what he gets, and you don't need this aggravation. You've got a new life ahead of you.*

"Suzanne!" She turned at the sound of her name and saw the twins coming toward her, both picture-perfect in pink vests and matching miniskirts. Each had a very hunky cowboy by the hand.

"We wanted you to meet—" Fawn began.

"—Hal and Merle." Dawn finished.

"Our husbands," they said in unison, "and best friends."

Suzanne greeted both men then fought back a pang of envy as she watched the twins walk off, hand in hand, with the men they loved.

"They make nice couples, don't they?" Slick asked as he walked beside her. "Though the girls could do with a lesson or two in how to pick the right boots. Pink suede isn't exactly practical."

"They're models. I think they're out to make more of a fashion statement." She turned and met Slick's intense gaze.

Clad in black jeans, black shirt, black vest and black hat tipped back on his head, he looked like an outlaw. A maverick. Full-blooded cowboy. While he wasn't fall-down gorgeous, he had a nice smile, and he knew how to use it, and he smelled good, a cross between tobacco and leather.

A girl could do a lot worse.

Like a bullheaded Manhattan Special who couldn't see that there was more to life than work. Than breaking his neck and risking his life to move his precious agency into the top ten.

"My event's up next."

"I'm rooting for you."

"You could put your money where your mouth is." At

her puzzled expression, he added, "And give me a kiss for good luck."

"I don't think…"

"Just one little kiss."

"I really can't."

"Why not?"

Yes, why not? She wasn't attached to anyone. While she was miserable over Brett, he didn't seem to share her misery. He hadn't so much as said one word about how he felt about her, if he felt anything other than lust, not that it would have mattered.

They were looking for different things in life. They didn't see eye to eye. It took compatibility to make a relationship work. Common goals. Brett may have turned out to be different from the average Manhattan Special—he valued his family, and she'd yet to see him watch the clock when they were together or spend all night hunkered over his computer or fold his clothes into a nice, neat, obsessive-compulsive pile before he climbed into bed the way Walter had always done. But he was still a die-hard New Yorker, and she was a transplanted Texan.

She gazed at Slick. "Okay."

"Well, all right." He smiled, and while her heart didn't do a double flip, it stalled a little. Of course, she had eaten a chili dog for lunch.

*Come on,* she thought as he leaned down. *Rock my world, cowboy. Please.* Because the last thing Suzanne wanted to admit was that Brett and only Brett could make her feel so wonderful, so alive, so vibrant.

Life couldn't be that unfair, could it?

Yes, she admitted the moment Slick's lips touched hers and the only thing that rocked were her eardrums as the buzzer sounded and Brett's event started.

HADES BOLTED FORWARD. Brett held on and tried to remember everything Clem had taught him.

*Remember your form. Grip tight, arm high, now flex, flex, flex, flex—*

His head snapped around, and he caught a glimpse of the sidelines. What the hell?

It couldn't be.

The thought flashed through his mind as the horse jerked and twisted and twisted and jerked, and he held on for dear life. He had to be imagining things, because no way in hell would she be—

Another jerk, a few twists and he saw them again.

Suzanne and Slick.

*No!*

The horse reared, the bell clanged, and Brett tumbled backward. He slammed into the ground. The air bolted from his lungs, and his last conscious thought was that Hades had hand-delivered him straight to hell because the sight of his woman with another man had been as fierce as a pitchfork straight into his heart.

"BRETT?" Suzanne knelt in the arena and leaned over him, her hands clutching his shirt as a crowd gathered. "Can you hear me?" Please, please, please, let him be all right, she prayed. *Please.*

"Can you hear me, Brett, honey? Please! Open your eyes." She blinked back a haze of tears in time to see his eyes flutter open. He looked disoriented for the space of two heartbeats, then his gaze fixed on her.

"You kissed him," he groaned, the sound of his voice music to her ears.

He was alive! The knowledge sang through her head, her heart, and the tears spilled over. "I thought.... Oh, my God, are you all right?"

"You *kissed* him." He struggled to a sitting position, fending off the hands that offered help.

"You didn't break anything, did you? You really shouldn't move until the doctor has a chance to take a look—"

"You kissed him!" His angry voice penetrated the worry consuming her, and she noticed the fire blazing in his eyes.

"You kissed Slick," he went on. "He kissed you. The two of you *kissed.*"

"So?"

"So you don't go around kissing every damned man who wears a hat and a pair of spurs."

Her gaze narrowed. "And why not? I'm single, unattached, completely available, am I not?"

"Well...yeah."

"Which means I can do what I want." She got to her feet.

"Like hell," he growled, following her up.

They faced off, the crowd surrounding them. "I can't do what I want?"

"Exactly."

"And why is that?"

"Because."

"Because why?" she pressed.

"Because..." He ran a hand through his hair, his lips drawn into a grim line. "Because I say so, that's why."

"Oh, really?"

"Yeah."

She planted her hands on her hips. "And just who the hell are you?"

"I'm the man who loves you, dammit."

*He loved her.* The knowledge echoed through her head for a sweet moment before reality set in and his phone beeped.

She fought back a wave of hopelessness and latched onto her anger. "For your information, I can kiss who I want, when I want. I like Slick. He's my type. We're perfect for each other."

"Like hell."

"He doesn't have his stupid cell phone bleeping while he's bronc busting."

"That was a beep, not a bleep. I'm carrying my pager. Creme Puff annihilated my phone."

"Good for her. She knows a real cowboy when she sees one, and you're not one."

"And Slick here wants a cowgirl, and you're not one. Yo, Slick." He motioned to the startled-looking cowboy. "She's a lawyer, did you know that? She wears red boots from Bloomingdale's, she can't rope to save her life and she's got an addiction to the Five Finger Fantasy. She's a fraud."

"A man-stealing, fraud," Mama Jessup added as she walked up to Slick. "Now don't you worry none." She latched onto the cowboy's arm. "If it's a cowgirl you're hot for, I just happen to be available, since Miss Bloomingdale's stole my boy toy...."

Mama's voice faded as Suzanne turned a murderous glare on Brett. "Fraud? Who are you to talk? You've spent the past few weeks playing cowboy just to win an ad account, you got your nickname from being stubborn, you snore and hog the covers *and* you wear silk boxers. What sort of cowboy wears silk boxers?"

A dozen hands raised, but Suzanne wasn't paying any attention. Her heart pounded, her face threatened to explode, and if she hadn't been such a peace-loving woman, she would have murdered Brett Maxwell right on the spot.

There was always the next best thing.

She grabbed the microphone from the startled announcer's hand and flipped the on switch.

"Attention, Truman Schneider. Your bronc-bustin' ad boy, here, just got busted by his bronc, in case you happened to miss it. So much for being one of the good ole boys."

Brett looked ready to do some murdering of his own, and she smiled, thrust the microphone at him and dusted off her hands as a wave of satisfaction swept through her.

Then she turned and walked away before she did anything really stupid.

Like tell the first-class jerk that she loved him, too.

"THEY CALL HIM Bull, but I think you're the one who's stubborn," Celia said Monday afternoon in the cabin. "You love the guy and you let him leave this morning."

"Who said I love him?" At Celia's raised eyebrow, she added, "Please don't start with the look. And it doesn't matter how I feel because it isn't enough."

"Who says?"

"Ten years of experience. I've seen couples who loved each other go through vicious divorce battles because, despite their feelings, they just couldn't see eye to eye on what school to send the kids to, where to go on vacation, who's going to handle the monthly bills."

"All that stuff seems sort of petty, if you ask me. Maybe those couples just didn't love each other enough to make the effort to see eye to eye."

"What are you saying?"

"That love can be enough to overcome quite a bit if you let it."

"Like maybe the fact that you're an exotic dancer from New York and Clem is a ranch foreman from Texas?"

"Exactly."

Suzanne smiled. "I think it's great that you guys are working things out."

"I'm crazy about him, he's crazy about me, and the rest is just sort of working itself out. Clem's mother doesn't even hate me, and she's as old-fashioned as they get around here."

"You met his mother?"

She nodded. "She's helping me plan the wedding." A smile touched her lips. "I'm not going back, Sue."

The knowledge stopped her. "A *wedding?*"

"Who would've thought? I mean, two people can't get more opposite, except maybe Candy and Andy, or the twins and their rodeo hunks. But they're all happily married, which means there's hope for me and Clem." She grabbed Suzanne's hands. "And you and Brett. He loves you, Suzanne."

He did. He'd said as much all day yesterday as he'd stood on the front porch of the cabin, called her all kinds of stubborn and declared his feelings. She'd buried her head beneath a pillow until he'd finally left. And then she'd stood at the window and prayed for him to come back.

*He loved her.*

She did her best to ignore the joy that knowledge brought and focused on the anger and confusion twisting at her. "Where does he get off loving me? It's bad enough that I had to fall for him, a Manhattan Special of all people, but then he has to go and fall in love back, and now I don't know what the hell to do. None of this was part of my plan—" The minute she said the word, it stopped her cold.

Dread churned inside her as Brett's voice whispered in her head. *You can take the New Yorker out of New York, but you can't take New York out of the New Yorker.*

Oh, God. He was right.

It didn't matter how far she went, she couldn't escape

who she was. She didn't have her day planner with her, but here she was still plotting everything, living her life by some prearranged scheme. Still a card-carrying, pizza-loving Manhattan Special.

"I'm so stupid," she murmured. She'd been set on making a change in her life, thinking that if she moved and switched jobs and men, somehow she could escape fate.

But it wasn't about external change. It was about changing who she was on the inside. She'd let the hustle and bustle of the city stifle her. Let her job consume her. Let herself fall into a rut with a boring man who wasn't her soul mate, not because he didn't wear jeans and boots and smell like leather, but because he didn't love her.

No more.

She spied her red cowboy boots in the corner, and a plan took shape in her mind.

"What are you thinking?" Celia asked.

"That it's awful hot here." She retrieved her suitcase from the closet and started packing. "And it smells, and this mattress is too narrow, and if I see one more plate of Mama's red-eye gravy, I'm going to puke."

"That's my girl." Celia smiled. "Go get 'em."

"I intend to."

BRETT CLUTCHED his briefcase in one hand and tried to shove his key into his apartment lock with the other. The slight pressure pushed the door open.

The apartment was dark, with the exception of moonlight spilling through the picture window in the living room and a shaft of light from the kitchen.

"John! If you're here cleaning out my refrigerator again without prior warning, I'm going to tell Emily about Jennie and Jennie about Trudy and Trudy about Melissa—"

"You'd do that to your baby brother?" The soft voice

slid into his ears a split second before he saw the woman's silhouette on his couch. Her feet were propped on his coffee table, red cowboy boots gleaming in the moonlight.

The sight hit him hard and fast in the gut, and he closed his eyes, knowing she would disappear the way she had every night since he'd returned from Texas three days ago.

Slowly, he opened his eyes.

She was still there.

Here.

Real.

"John's the one who let me in. He's really great. We had a nice chat, and believe it or not, I didn't have to stand in line for the bathroom or fight for the remote control, but I'm looking forward to it—"

Her words faded into the *bleep* of his cell phone.

"Go ahead and answer it. I'll wait."

He pulled out the cell phone, stabbed the mute button and tossed it to the floor with his briefcase. "They can wait." *Say something, Maxwell.* "W-what are you doing here?"

"Eating a pizza." She indicated the box on the coffee table. "About to, anyway. Out of all the things in New York, I missed this the second most."

"Second? What was first?"

"You." She stood, and he realized in a heated moment that she was gloriously nude with the exception of the cowboy boots. His wildest fantasy come to life. He blinked again to be sure.

She didn't disappear. Her breasts swayed as she stepped toward him, bringing with her the scent of apples and cinnamon and warm woman.

*His* woman.

Then she opened her beautiful lips and confirmed his thoughts. "I love you, Brett. I don't care if you're not a real cowboy, if you wear three-piece suits and silk boxers. I *like* silk boxers.''

He came so close to pulling her into his arms and living out the fantasy. But this wasn't wishful thinking or desperate longing or simply a bad case of lust. This was reality, the woman he wanted to spend the rest of his life with, the future mother of his children, lots of children, he decided, and they had a few things to settle first.

He clenched his fists and kept his hands at his sides. ''What about simplifying your life? Making a change?''

''I am changing and simplifying, but I'm doing it in here.'' She tapped her temple. ''Where it counts. I'm relaxing and living life. I even read that romance novel from Candy's on the plane home.''

''And?''

''And love can overcome all obstacles.''

''Romance novels are fairy tales, Suzie Q. Fiction.''

''The story, but not the basic values. Honesty, respect, compromise. I know we don't exactly see eye to eye on a lot of things, but we can work it out. I know you don't want a lot of kids, maybe no kids, and your career comes first and you...''

She rushed on and on, laying out all the reasons they shouldn't be together, presenting one hell of a case against them. ''The odds aren't in our favor, but if you love me...'' Her words faded as panic flashed in her brown eyes. ''You do still love me, don't you?''

''You tell me.'' He pulled out the plane ticket he'd picked up on his way home and handed it to her. ''I was going back for you first thing tomorrow. I thought I'd try begging first, and if that didn't work, I was going to throw you over my shoulder and carry you off into the sunset.''

Hope glimmered in her eyes. ''You do still love me.''

''I didn't realize how much until I saw you kissing Slick.

Something snapped, and the feeling hit me harder than one of Creme Puff's kicks. These past few days have been the most miserable of my life—''

A shrill ring cut him off, quickly followed by the click as his machine picked up. ''This is Brett. You know the drill.''

''This is Nancy. We've got major trouble, and after this Cowboy International fiasco, I'm this close to having a heart attack—''

He snatched up the phone, muttered, ''I'll call you later,'' then hung up and stabbed the off button.

''Cowboy International fiasco?'' Suzanne's eyes widened as he turned back to her. ''Oh, no. I ruined things with Cowboy International, didn't I? I declared to an arena full of people that you weren't a real cowboy, and Cowboy took their ad account elsewhere, and now the agency is bust.''

''Actually, Truman Schneider was pretty impressed that I would go to so much trouble just to get his business.''

''He offered you the account?''

When he nodded, she beamed. ''That's great!''

''It didn't feel half as great as I thought it would. The only thing I've ever really wanted was to make a success of my own agency, but I never realized what I'd be missing, who I'd be missing.'' He raked tense fingers through his hair. ''I haven't been able to concentrate. Hell, I haven't wanted to concentrate, which is what Nancy was talking about. I forgot to look over the ad budget for the account.''

''When's it due?''

''In two weeks.''

''That's a fiasco?''

''Nancy's a sweetheart, but she lives for high drama.''

Suzanne smiled. ''When can I meet her?''

''That depends.'' He pulled another envelope from his

pocket and handed it to her. "This was going to be the peace offering after I threw you over my shoulder and rode off into the sunset."

She stared at the picture of the small house with the redwood fence and the porch swing.

"I bought it."

She raised misty eyes to him. "For me?"

"For us." He gazed into her eyes. "I'll give up the agency, my life here, all of it, if that's what you want. Because you're what I want, Suzie Q. *You.*"

She sniffled as her gaze dropped to the photo. "I really love this house. It'll make a great winter retreat."

"And the rest of the year?"

"I think I'd like to stay right here. With your firm and my firm and Sal's pizza and blessed air-conditioning." She turned and retrieved something from the couch. "And a girl's best friend."

He stared at the Five Finger Fantasy and grinned. "I thought I was your best friend."

"You run a close second."

"Second?" He reached for her. "Is that a challenge? Because the Bull can't resist a challenge."

She smiled, melting into his arms as his lips found hers. "That's what I was hoping you'd say."

If you enjoyed what you just read,
then we've got an offer you can't resist!

# Take 2 bestselling love stories FREE!

# Plus get a FREE surprise gift!

# COMING NEXT MONTH

## HARLEQUIN Duets™

## #5

### DOWNHOME DARLIN' by Victoria Pade

When Abby Stanton's fiancé calls off the wedding because he claims she's too boring, Abby sets out to prove him wrong. Abby becomes a "wild woman" for one night and corrals herself a cowboy. Now boot-wearin' Cal Ketchum has to convince darlin' Abby that he has something more permanent in mind....

### THE BEST MAN SWITCH by Liz Ireland

The last thing in the world best man Grant Whiting wants is to be set up with the maid of honor at his friend's wedding. So he blackmails his identical twin brother into performing the *best man switch*. Only after the bridesmaid decks Grant's brother is he forced to take his brother's—that is, *his own*—place and realizes he's found the woman of his dreams...who considers him the man of her nightmares!

## #6

### FOR THIS WEEK I THEE WED by Cheryl St.John

Francie Karr-Taylor needs a husband—but only for a week. So she convinces Parrish McKinley to help. He and his kids come to her reunion—as her happy family. Parrish isn't eager to get involved in such a crazy plan, but one look at Francie told him she was desperate. And after all, it wasn't like she was talking about forever—was it?

### 50 CLUES HE'S MR. RIGHT by Alyssa Dean
*Real Men*

Reporter Tara Butler is thrilled with her assignment from *Real Men* magazine: updating "49 Things You Need to Know about a Real Man." Maybe this is her chance to meet a real man—not the romantic duds she's dated. But when she's paired with sexy Chase Montgomery, who doesn't have a real man quality to him, she begins to wonder if her list is wrong...